Charlotte Grimshaw was born in New Zealand and currently lives in Auckland with her husband and two children. After graduating from Auckland University, she practised as a shipping lawyer and then as a criminal lawyer, working for the defence in criminal trials, before leaving the law to write full time. *Provocation* is her first novel. Her second novel, *Guilt*, is also published by Abacus.

Provocation

Charlotte Grimshaw

ABACUS

An *Abacus* Book

First published in Great Britain
by Abacus 1999
This edition published by Abacus 2000

A CIP catalogue record for this book
is available from the British Library.

ISBN 0 349 11258 4

Typeset in Ehrhardt by M Rules
Printed and bound in Great Britain by
Clays Ltd, St Ives plc

Abacus
A Division of
Little, Brown and Company (UK)
Brettenham House
Lancaster Place
London WC2E 7EN

For Paul

1. CNN

On CNN a debate is raging over genetic engineering. The Jewish community in New York is speaking out for genetic privacy. Throughout history, they say, we've been the victims of genetic theories. You have a one in fourteen million chance of winning the Florida lottery says Flip Spiceland, weatherman, doing his usual graceful weather dance over the map of America. Here it's a grey Auckland morning, the staff are arriving. On CNN a fat woman eats grapes in the September heat. Here it's grey and still, down at the wharf you can see the black pylons rising up out of the cold water, the sea is silver and flat like mercury, the sea looks dangerous and chemical and congealed. On CNN a screaming man is rushed to hospital in the September city heat. The screen street is crowded with screaming people, sweating, howling, shaking their fists. The cat fights with a piece of string. Betty Mary-Lou Plastic reads the news fighting a stray strand of hair, Flip Spiceland fights with gravity and wins, his feet are not attached to the floor of the studio, he swoops over America, detached, joyful, an insane state-side blowup man. They've found a new cure for arthritis, they're rioting somewhere in a place that doesn't matter, there are bodies everywhere, there's a woman breaking the world record for swimming underwater. And the mercury across the Gulf shimmers in a dull way, if the world tipped suddenly the water wouldn't move today, the secretary answers the phone in such a way that she could just as well say 'Good morning, Chicane's office, how dare you call?', Flip Spiceland pauses and looks straight out of the camera for a moment, as if he's staring out at the sullen molten silver I can see, the immovable heavy water, the high grey sky and Rangitoto Island shouldering over the horizon, but it's a momentary blip, Flip flies away again, zooming across to Las Vegas, predicts searing heat.

To switch on here is to be there, watching columns driving through Monrovia, African corpses, fighter planes over the desert, the rest of the world fighting terrible fires while here we battle late-winter chill, mild cold, low wind, a sour taste in the mouth, and a longing for heat.

I often sit here in this morning mood, in a kind of slow, happy melancholy, eating crackers and watching CNN while the house fills up with Stuart's small army of home help: the fat secretary, the 'ex'-drug addict odd-jobs man, the slightly retarded Dutch woman who does the ironing, the tiny Maori girl of indeterminate age who drags the vacuum cleaner around with an air of resigned, gloomy underprivilege. Soon Stuart will bound up the stairs, bristling with energy, crackling with static, cast me a slightly reproachful look and say, 'Shit, darl, what are you doing? What's going on? Look out at the day, beautiful day, hardly grey at all, turn off that box. It's another day in our lives.'

I switch off the world, brush off the crumbs, the clock says 8.30. Time to get on. Another day in our lives.

Downstairs the morning's work has begun. Hinemoa is brushing the fireplace, supervised by the Dutch ironer, who has a deeply racist conviction that the girl will show her true colours and steal everything in the house. The secretary is squatting fatly in the office, threatening Stuart's clients over the phone.

The odd-jobs man moves dreamily past the window, carrying a piece of pipe. He puts it down in the middle of the lawn, pats it thoughtfully and heads off towards the hedge. They are all here this morning, the hard core of Stuart's helpers, minders and personnel. They are all loyal to Stuart. They all seem to feel that they belong to him. And does he feel the same way? They hope so. Sometimes I wake up in the night and stare at Stuart while he sleeps. He lies on his back and snores, with his black hair falling over his eyes. Late at night I entertain my own secret fears and hopes. I stare out at the dark water in the harbour and wonder about the future. Last night I felt lonely and tried to shake him awake. 'What d'you want?' he murmured. 'Go to sleep. Tomorrow is another day in our *lives*.'

It is impossible not to love Stuart. It is impossible to know why. What is this thing that makes us follow people who tell us nothing at all, who give nothing away? Is it just that there is less familiarity, less contempt?

This morning I have a list of errands to run and things to do. Stuart and I are preparing to hold a party to mark the completion of a huge brick barbecue which Wayne, the odd-jobs man, has been building on the veranda. The barbecue is a multi-tiered monstrosity, so large that you could incinerate a whole sheep in its cavernous oven. Its gas pipes, wires and digital control panel are concealed behind clusters of maidenhair fern. Wayne, one of Stuart's favourite clients, has recently completed a twelve-step drug rehabilitation programme and is supposed to have left his old drug days behind.

'I have signed a contract with myself,' he explains solemnly, squinting over the gas canisters in the barbecue's inner core and twiddling with the hissing valves. The barbecue is part of Wayne's occupational therapy, and has grown bigger and more high tech as he has made his way painfully from cold turkey to inner peace. Now completed it is less like the humble sausage griller that Stuart envisaged and more like a gas-powered cremation unit, stolen from a hospital basement or an abattoir.

'Actually it looks like a huge bomb,' Stuart says. 'He's going to take us all with him. Or strap himself to it and make insane demands until he's talked down or explodes.'

I suspect that Wayne has only made it through rehab by fortifying himself with a steady intake of drugs. If he'd had to do it straight he would never have made it. The fact that the barbecue is now finished may signal the end of his stint as a law-abiding member of the community. Now that he has nothing to build on he could fall apart and go back to cooking up homebake heroin in his kitchen, and holding up gas stations. Stuart is aware of this possibility and has already talked to Wayne about reconcreting the drive, digging a swimming pool and landscaping the garden. They have also tentatively discussed adult education courses in car maintenance, house painting and Grade A plumbing. In this way Stuart intends that Wayne will be saved, usefully.

Sitting at the table I work on a long shopping list. Stuart and I have a lot of money to throw around. The house is full of money. Many of Stuart's clients, since they are criminals and therefore unreliable, are asked to pay in cash. Rather than bank it, Stuart stashes it, and so, after I have completed my huge list, I only have to visit a series of cunning hidey holes (in the teapot, under the doormat), to come up with a fist full of notes which add up to a satisfactory thousand-odd dollars.

I balance the shopping list on top of the wad of notes. Even now, after living here for nearly a year, I am sometimes shocked by the amount of money I can rustle up from around the house. It's as if Stuart, having bought this house, ripped out the interior and rebuilt it inside and out, is now lining it with money. There are notes in the curtain linings, wads in the flower vases, even the couch cushions crackle with hastily concealed bundles of hundred-dollar bills. From his cash-lined palace Stuart fobs off the Inland Revenue with the help of his wily accountant, Ron Kabir, and his large and threatening secretary, Vera, who would die for him, and who does the books. I help out in my own way. I live here (unlike Wayne, Vera, Hinemoa and Kabir), and unlike them I get to spend the money, in generous amounts, on whatever I fancy, whenever I like. Right now, I reflect idly, while

doodling on my shopping list, I could pick up that chintz cush-
ion there, carry it out of the house, and spend it (or its contents)
on a Rolex.

Stuart is a barrister and solicitor. Most of his clients are criminal. Crime has made him rich, crime pays and pays. Today he
has a busy schedule, to Mount Eden jail for interviews, to the
District Court for depositions, to the High Court in the afternoon for a bail application, then back to the District Court for
more depositions. He nips around the house before setting off,
handing out instructions: water these, clean this, buy that. He
works from home. The house is huge and painted blue and
stands high on a North Shore cliff road looking over the harbour,
towards Rangitoto Island and the open sea.

Stuart has not always lived in Auckland. Five years ago, he has
told me, he lived in Wellington with his wife Mia and their
daughter. They divorced after a terrible revelation. Stuart found
out that the daughter, aged five, was not really his. The daughter
resembled Stuart, she was black haired and slim with a longish
nose, and her features were similar to his. But an old lover of Mia
turned up in Wellington the year that the child was five, and this
man was also dark haired and slim and long of nose. One night in
a restaurant he made the terrible claim.

It turned out that Mia had been sleeping with them both at the
same time. Once, at the most likely time of conception, with both
of them on the same day.

She was drunk and confessed as the three of them sat there at
the table over their pasta. Something strange came over her, she
seemed to look at them both in the same odd way. She told them
that to this day she had never known which of them was the real
father of the child. She didn't care. As far as she was concerned
they were both the father. Nine months after she had slept with
both of them the child was born, and at the time she had loved
them both. She had loved them almost as if they were the same
man.

After she had made this confession the lover went away. He
never tried to contact her again. He never tried to see the child,

or find out whether she was his. But Stuart in his rage and grief forced Mia to have the girl blood-tested, and when the results came back he was the loser. The test showed that the girl could not possibly be his.

He and Mia separated. He kept running into her and the little girl in the streets and in the supermarket. He decided to move to Auckland and set up a new practice. He never wanted to see Mia again.

Stuart is crisply dressed this morning in his linen suit and silver-rimmed shades. His appearance always arouses suspicion and resentment among his low-key legal colleagues. Down at the court Stuart's contemporaries shuffle about in shiny pinstripes, short socks and round-toed shoes, like ageing and harassed schoolboys, browbeaten by their superiors, their clients, their families and all the paraphernalia of their successful lives. Stuart mingles with them amiably, always different, always set apart. While they trudge and drag and worry, and chew their dusty nails and flick their greasy hair, Stuart glides and smiles and floats, unconcerned by the tyranny of the vicious and petty old judges, the bureaucratic malice of the clerks, the mulish aggression of the police. Stuart is usually polite, occasionally fantastically rude, is also tough, charming, manipulative and sly. Stuart does not allow himself to be burdened. He has no family any more. He has his dog, Howard. He has me.

With my shopping list and my roll of cash I climb into Stuart's Porsche and sound the horn for the dog. The dog ambles down the path and climbs laboriously into the passenger seat panting and stinking and drooling. I back down the drive, slowing to avoid Wayne who is vaguely snipping at the rose bushes, and nose out into the waterfront traffic. The Porsche is another thing that sets Stuart apart from his colleagues. The Porsche looks so indiscreet and flashy and unreliable parked next to the grey station wagons and solid family Volvos in the court carpark.

Like most criminal lawyers Stuart is judged by many of the commercial practitioners to carry the mark of the criminal world he represents. Look at him, they whisper, with his silver shades, his fashionable, spouseless life. He must be up to something. Up to no good! Grudge-ridden detectives dream of catching him with a suitcase full of cocaine. Of his clients Stuart says, 'There but for the grace of God go I.' He is unfailingly kind to his clients. He feels no need himself to break the law, and when his clients try to pay him with stolen goods or favours (any legs you want breaking, Mr Chicane?), he politely but firmly declines.

The dog and I roar towards Foodtown. We pull into the carpark as two Samoans are levering themselves out of their rusting two-tone Chrysler Valiant. They watch, munching drumsticks from a family bucket of Kentucky Fried Chicken as I drag the dog out of the passenger seat. The dog is four years old, an aggressive beast of an Alsatian with short bristly hair. Howard likes to rape, pillage, maim and generally screw up any other dog which strays into his path. With humans he likes to lick, purr, slobber, ingratiate and beg for food. I have become adept at breaking up the most spectacular dogfights. No canine brawl is too bloody for me. When Howard has eluded me on a peaceful beach, or snapped his lead in a cosy shopping mall, and immediately instigated an appalling argument with two Rottweilers, a Dobermann and three bull terriers, while the scene erupts in screams, roars, baying and moaning from dogs and dog owners alike, I don't hang back. I jump in. The trick is to take off all one's jewellery to avoid catching it on a collar or tooth, then get behind Howard's back as he's fastened to the other dog's throat, and yank him out by the collar and tail in one short, sharp heave from behind. It's the yank on the tail that releases his jaws. It's not bravery that makes me jump into the snarling teeth and flying fur, it's not lack of fear. It's just that I like the maul of it. I like the action. I long for a bit of heat.

Leaving the dog to rage and piss his way around the carpark, I head for the aisles. The supermarket is packed with the usual crowd, mostly Pacific Islanders, their trolleys groaning with tins of corned beef, coconut milk and packages of white bread.

Irritated that the place is so crowded I force my way through the sweaty hordes. As I queue, wincing, at the fruit and vegetable stands, I reflect that only Pacific Islanders are huge enough and united enough in their perpetual merriment to be able to inflict ear pain with their laughter. Why are they so big? Why are they so amused? Deafened by the blasts of twenty-eight-stone hilarity at the paw-paw stand I head distractedly towards the delicatessen. Abandoning cultural sensitivity altogether I wonder how an entire section of the community can have let itself get so extraordinarily overweight. I know it's a sign of status in the Islands to be really enormous – at school Pacific Island girls snacked on whole loaves of bread split down the middle and filled with ice-cream, while we looked on faint with dieting – but what about things like fitness, nutritional awareness, full-fibre food?

But then again, those big Island girls found us risible too, with our miserable little bodies, our weird inhibitions. And look at them now, wheeling round the shelves, even fatter and laughing even harder. I had one sad friend in particular who would have caused them great mirth, a recovering anorexic; she was hospitalised once, so the story went, after inhaling the crouton she was having for dinner.

A traffic accident occurs, a huge, aggressive old guy ramming his creaking trolley into my leg. He frowns after me with heavy, ponderous authority as I make my way evilly round the store, small, pallid, my mind full of complaint and abuse, full of all those thoughts you can't articulate if you want to be right on, culturally sensitive, sane. When I emerge with my trolley the dog is crouched by the Porsche mumbling secretively into an ancient and soggy Kentucky Fried Chicken packet, which he tries to smuggle into the car for the journey home.

Disgusting hound, vile dog, I mutter as I dispose of his prize. Most of the time I barely tolerate Howard, with his persistent food foraging and his pungent dogginess. It's the fact that he is a dog which puts me off the most. Stuart does not realise that Howard is a dog. He cooks Howard's dinner every night, usually eye fillet steak, and adds gravy, and questions Howard carefully about his preferences, eager to get it right. Deep down he feels that the dog is his son, which, in the current circumstances, means that I am Howard's stepmother. Cheers! What a beautiful thing.

I speed home with my goods, the happy housewife. I unload the bags in the kitchen, clicking over the tiled floors, one eye on the TV on the bench and the other on the dog that hovers drooling around the bags labelled deli/butch/poultry like a hairy derelict waiting to pounce. The TV weather centre is predicting an easterly after the cloudy still weather, bringing three days of the usual tropical storm from the Islands, strong winds, high humidity, the warm, blind, melancholy rain.

I wrestle Howard out onto the veranda, flinging a bone after him. He ignores the bone and glares through the glass door at the shopping, steaming up the window with his fast, spitty pants. I pull down the blind. He moves off the veranda to the next window and resumes his avid peering.

On the TV an American cop programme is warming up with a series of hot scenes, full of scorched landscapes and desiccated blondes, the blonde now looking out of her dressing-table mirror and saying in her American drawl to a Colombian bad guy, 'Just one thing. Don't shoot him in the *face*.'

The dog and I watch as he winks, loads his gun and strides out of the room. 'OK, baby,' he says. She's so sentimental. The guy gets it right in the heart. Then we watch as the killer drives in his black Ferrari through the badlands and industrial outlands on a concrete road shimmering in the heat. He speeds, his car turns into a black quivering thing, elongated by the mirage. He smokes, adjusts his sunglasses, on his way home to the blonde who paces on her terrace watching the planes flying over the city. The sky is a blue bowl over the scene. She's dressed in silver, he's in an aqua suit. An eighties show. No earth tones. When he roars back into the street she stands on the terrace, her outfit blending into the chrome and blue of the steel and the sky.

Outside, as I sort through the shopping, the first raindrops begin to fall, pattering softly onto the leaves, smacking on the roof of the veranda, causing Howard to snort and sneeze and heave himself back under the shelter of the eaves. Outside in the real world everything is becoming muted as if the world is in tears. The ponga branches droop over, heavy with moisture. All you can hear is the water falling and the lawn is like a green pond. It's that Auckland weather when the suburbs are like a greenhouse and in the humid air everything grows and grows. The guttering blocks and everything in the house seems damp. The sky is white and grey and soon the whole world has shrunk and become only the green, slushy, silent quarter-acre. Stuart has a vague fear that the house could slowly sink into the earth. He is sure that it is built over an underground stream. Water runs under the garden and could be eroding the foundations. Water is already gathering under the house, trickling down from the neighbouring sections. Sometimes, on days like this, I feel like we're already submerged.

Later, when the rain is falling steadily and purple sheet lightning is flashing out at sea I sit at my desk working on one of Stuart's files. He rings, shouting into his mobile phone.

'It's pouring in the city,' he shouts. 'It's hosing down. I'm in the car, just heading for the bridge.'

We agree to go ahead and have the party indoors. Wayne can light up his big bomb on the veranda and pass the food in through the window. Stuart yells a series of questions and instructions above the traffic, then abruptly hangs up.

There is plenty of room in Stuart's huge house with its great expanse of window and views of the sea. The air temperature has risen and all the windows can be left open to allow the noise and smoke to drift out into the night through the beaded curtains of the rain.

Staring out of the bedroom window I watch the rain drift in from the Gulf and the cars queuing under the orange lights on the Harbour Bridge and try to rouse myself from the afternoon torpor of the rain and the white sky and the melancholy of the sodden city.

Stuart suspects that I have a tendency to drift about not getting on with things. Sometimes he tries to catch me doing nothing. He accelerates into the bedroom or swings through the doors of the bathroom to catch me lying on the bed staring at the ceiling, or twiddling with my hair in the silent *en suite*, my face in the mirror as vacant as a fish. Then he'll snort, and nag, about the Protestant work ethic and the dangers of sloth, and chastise me for inefficiency and self-indulgence. Sometimes I jump to, sometimes not. Sometimes I explode and throw things and one of our fights blows up, as sudden and violent as an easterly storm.

I am not actually a housewife. I am not a wife, although I have a fantasy sometimes, of getting married. I see myself in a chic dress, something pale, Stuart takes my hand and smiles his shining smile . . . Such fantasies are secret of course. He stares at me hard when I fall silent. I worry that he can read my mind.

For the last three years I have studied law, and soon I will be fully qualified as a barrister and solicitor, and will look for a job. At the moment, while living here, I work for Stuart on his hundreds of criminal files. We work well together. Stuart is thirty-eight next June. I am twenty-two. Although Howard is four, in dog time he is four years times seven, which means he is an old hand around here, older than me.

At six o'clock fat Vera and I make salads and arrange food on large lettuce leaves and Vera concocts a vulgar keg of poisonous tropical punch decorated with pineapple tops. Vera has forced her bulging self into the type of outfit worn by Country and Western singers, complete with fringes and headband and boots with spurs. Wayne, looking in, stares incredulously at her for a moment, until his mind wanders and he passes through the kitchen looking for something he will never find. 'Where?' he whispers softly to himself. 'Whe-where?'

Vera is flushed under her brown pancake and purple haze blusher, royal blue eye shadow and rose peach gloss. The dog lurks near her, leering up at her straining miniskirt until she shoves him away goodnaturedly with a jingling boot.

Stuart's friends are lawyers, property dealers, stockbrokers, speculators and advertising executives. They are the money people, the champagne-drinking yachties, the pastel-shirted America's Cup good-time set. They are the ones who eat out in fashionable brasseries, drive their speedboats into yachts in the harbour, sing drunkenly in late-night restaurants, drive expensive cars and spend money loudly, insensitively, in front of everybody else. Stuart's friends seem to approve of me. I have been living with him now for seven months. They say we look good together and they compliment him on his find.

I have discovered while living here that a significant number of the women at Stuart's parties have had some sort of intimate interlude with him in the last five years, some of them for a period of a few months, or a few weeks, or as an experiment or out of curiosity, or on a lonely night when they felt down. Now they arrive at the door with someone new and behave as if nothing ever happened. But still, things are different around here now, I'm sure of it. I am the only one who has ever moved in. I'm the only one who hasn't been a blonde.

Recently a fair-haired woman came to the door while I was in the house alone. The dog sat moodily at the back door chewing himself and I happened to be cleaning the fridge with mindless efficiency, throwing out everything I could find that looked crusty or ageing or tired. When the dog began his usual threatening growl and raced to the front door I followed and opened the door to a woman who was in her thirties and wearing a tight fluorescent green dress. She was carrying a bottle of wine and a bunch of dried flowers. Her hair was long and thick and she had tiny, tight wrinkles around her eyes where ultraviolet light and wind and chlorine had dried out her skin. You could picture her standing at the prow of a yacht in the sun in a tiny bikini squinting into the sea wind. She stared at me, licking her dry lips nervously, saying that she had just come back from sailing in South-East Asia and she was looking for Stuart, and she seemed distressed, shifting from foot to foot in her tiny little gold sandals.

'Do you work here?' she asked in her tiny voice, but before I could answer her the dog bounded up to her and danced about while she patted him with a tinkling laugh and called him Howie. Then I said, 'I live here with Stuart and he's out right now. Can I say who called?' She stared, a wounded chipmunk in her golden shoes, as if I had slapped her, and then stammered something about hello and had a good trip and another day and then she turned away and walked down the steps with her hair blowing around her head and the flowers jammed under her arm, all bent and squashed and falling to bits. I went back inside and started again on the fridge, throwing out everything I could find that I hadn't bought the day before. That night I asked Stuart who she was.

'Client,' he said. 'Shoplifter. Don't let her in again.'

And now the guests begin to arrive, shaking off the rain, kissing and hugging, flashing teeth and flowers and bottles of wine. Stuart bustles about with trays of nibbles. 'Gherkin?' he says, beaming at a vampy black dress, clingwrapped round a body in glowing bronze. 'Salami?' he enquires of a toothy Californian, standing six foot two in her organic shoes. 'Pretzel stick?' he offers to a giggling, squirming velvet pair.

Tall and elegant in his marine ensemble and extravagant shoes, Stuart lifts a tray of flutes from the table with its platters of food, the vases, the beautiful art deco jugs. 'Now,' he murmurs into the air, 'more champagne.'

In the glowing house, among the colourful chattering things, clear crystal, rich wood, a soft rainy light, tall hairdos, low bosoms, laughter and clinking, Stuart moves through the crowd dispensing champagne. On nights like this he is a social genius, he excels. He floats through the crowd, brilliant, light on his feet, loving them all. I stand back and watch and admire. He moves with grace, he looks radiant to me. On nights like this, as he shines and beams, it's easy to see why juries want to set his clients free. He homes in. He convinces. He persuades.

Stuart's friends are more fun than my old friends, whom I have abandoned without any regret. I left them still living as poor students, surviving on baked beans, shivering in bleak, shared bungalows under the shadow of Mount Eden, studying in bed on winter Sundays, blind with dust and sadness, grimy pages spread on dull sheets, boots on in bed. I look back on my early student days with none of the nostalgia some people claim to feel. Those days are too recent, too horrible. I was not good at making friends. I was too shy and tended to be solitary. I could not break free of my shell. I knew none of the other students at the start of law school and didn't acquire any companions along the way, except for one repressed parasite called O'Muggins, product of a fearsome Catholic upbringing, who became my 'friend' and who trailed after me through the endless days. He would sit at my table in the stinking caff, counting out enough five-cent pieces for a small cup of coffee, his bony Irish face so stiff and unanimated that it looked like a skull over which the skin had been stretched too thin and too tight. He was as prudish as my Irish grandmother and his soul was as dry as his peeling skin. He was puritanical. He never went to the pub, and he described my frequent visits there as 'cheap nights of fun', with a look on his face that was both insinuating and pious. I would sit across from him smoking and hating him, dying of hate, grateful not to be sitting alone. He stuck with me faithfully, never getting up the nerve to try anything on and be rejected and go off in a huff.

I shared a house with five other students, including one law student who turned out to be a gun fanatic. In the weekends he would roam through the house wearing nothing but a filthy blue bathrobe, Marlboro hanging from his rubbery lower lip, nursing his .303 rifle which was named Colleen after a girl he once loved. Soon after we rented the house it became clear that our gunman had a problem with housework. When any of us got up the nerve to tackle the garbage-strewn kitchen or the noisome bathroom, he would become visibly agitated, and, after much roaming and pacing and fondling of gun, distinctly nasty. While we scraped and rinsed, he would growl and sneer and slam doors, as if he felt that the vile odours we were scrubbing away were important territorial scents which would deter enemies and mark out his turf.

Since cleaning was discouraged in this alarming way, the place quickly went to the pack. Crockery had to be fished out of the greasy sink where it floated brownly, no longer filthy but beyond filthy, by now completely uncleanable. I was desperate to move, but could find nowhere else to go. I believed I would spend the rest of my life in a chilly room in a grimy wooden house, drinking tea out of stained mugs, averting my eyes in the echoing bathroom with its wooden lavatory seat, the moss-covered shower curtain, the grey cobwebs rippling gently in the chill wind which blew constantly through chinks in the worm-eaten walls. Although I managed to keep up my studies I was depressed by my surroundings and even considered moving back in with my parents, but rejected the thought, since to return to the warm claustrophobia of the parental ménage would have been comfortable but suffocating, too much like surrender, or cowardice.

One morning I crawled from my frosty bed, showered in the mildewed cubicle, grabbed a crust from the chaotic hell of the kitchen bench and made it halfway up the suburban street to the bus stop before being crippled by such loneliness, such a sense of *dinge* that I stopped dead, bent double, couldn't go on and felt the street dissolving around me, the frost on muddy lawns, the weeping trees, the stone-grey melancholy of the garden walls, Mount Eden looming over me with its perpetual shadow, its deep green chill, all dissolving and blurring in the brown gloom of the winter day while I leaned on a fence and held my head in my hands and wept for a while into the tussocky mud.

Now Stuart's house is filling with people, the street is lined with expensive cars and I sip wine and chatter with Stuart's friends Bernard Cracker and Alita Kulay.

Bernard Cracker, leaning casually against the fireplace, is describing the features and gimmicks of his latest toy. He owns every type of toy you can imagine: surf skis, jet skis, bungee equipment, fizzy boats, gin palaces, yachts and parachutes. When he is not hanging from a rubber band or spinning through the air or ferrying drinking parties around the harbour, he is raking in a vast income with his advertising partners in Downtown

Auckland. Now Bernard says, 'I hate that dog. Every time I come here it leaps up and fucks up my clothes, and Stuart just lets it. He doesn't know how to train it. I grew up on a farm, I'd show it who's boss.'

'Perhaps he likes the way it fucks up your clothes.'

'He thinks the dog is his son.'

Stuart glides around the room surrounded by his public. Bernard fidgets beside me scanning the room, taking in all immediate data: size of bosoms, length of leg, shape of bum, price of fuck. Howard watches the party from one of the window seats, munching alertly on a sausage.

Sometimes Howard, crossing the veranda or clicking over the kitchen tiles, hears or senses something or catches a scent in the air and goes still, his long nose tilted upwards, his ears slowly revolving, eyes and nostrils wide. And then, if the noise turns out to be Vera lumbering out of the office or Stuart's car turning into the drive he relaxes suddenly and melts, into a head-down, mouth-open, tail-wagging dog. Stuart, too, will stare for a moment, motionless, as if his senses are pricking, his antennae are tuning, and then put his head down, stretch out his arms, shake his head slightly as he welcomes you in, taking your arm, clapping you on the back.

I turn to Bernard but he is up out of his chain, heading for a tall woman whose high-heeled shoe has stuck between the wooden slats of the veranda and who stands lopsidedly, hitching up her skirt and uttering mock screams, her marvellous hair spotlit from above by the green light in the ginkgo tree.

Earlier the same tall woman, one of Stuart's ex-girlfriends, was standing a few feet away from me discussing the economy. 'My darling and I haven't seen much Bollinger since the Crash,' she said as her new husband cruised past in his amiable sharky way, winking and mingling. I smiled politely, privately recalling her wedding which Stuart and I went to a fortnight ago, and the angry scenes that followed. The wedding took place in a tiny and picturesque church in Remuera. The seating arrangements were tiny and picturesque too and I was sandwiched sweatily between

Bernard Cracker and Stuart in a sort of alcove where we couldn't see anything except a bit of the bride's apricot-coloured veil. Throughout the ceremony I could feel Stuart writhing and twisting beside me in a sweat of agitation. By the end of the ceremony he seemed to be in a rage. We drove to the reception at high speed, Stuart hunched over the wheel, muttering and cursing like a vicious drunk, driving at things and swerving away, revving the engine and hauling at the steering wheel. When we pulled up he threw off his seatbelt with violent disgust and sat staring into the rearview mirror. We sat in silence. Finally he said, looking into the mirror, in a voice as cold and flat as the sea, 'She's a nice girl, a good girl. Good luck to her. But she's a hick. She'll always be a *hick* from Whangarei.'

That night Stuart sat on the veranda drinking steadily until 4 a.m. when he finished the bottle and tossed it over his shoulder onto the drive, smashing it to pieces and creating a mess which took Wayne a long time to clear up the following day.

Mingling, pouring wine, kissing cheeks, shouting with laughter, Stuart is all PR. His body has a language all its own. He is tall and when he talks he stands very close, so close to women in particular that they are almost forced to bend themselves backwards. I watch him in action when we are out together. He strides up to women and leans over them so far that they are teetering. Many of them are stirred, I can tell, by so much outrageous height and proximity. Many think he's got a nerve, but he makes them blush and laugh in spite of themselves. They glance to the left and the right, trapped, smoothing their skirts and their hair.

I know all about Stuart's raw powers of communication. I met him in the waiting room of the District Court at Auckland. To my disgust and embarrassment I had been charged with a minor offence, that of telling a police officer to 'fuck off'. I was a law student, and supposed to be incapable of such criminal behaviour.

'Obscene language charge, eh?' Stuart beamed as we were introduced. 'I bet you just turned your nose up at that cop, didn't you,' and he actually touched me on the nose as I leaned back, full of surprise and chagrin, and an odd kind of heat.

It's a mystery, this talent of his. Forget all that stuff about sexual harassment and unwelcome come-ons. He walks like a burglar into your mansion and inexplicably you find yourself offering him a slice of cake and begging him not to leave.

I have to make an effort at Stuart's parties. I am naturally a rather silent person. Stuart does not approve of reticence. Silence is a luxury around here. Stuart believes in *contribution*. He leans over his newly married ex-girlfriend. She is a beautiful woman, a celebrated and important ex. I wonder why they parted. What is it about Stuart? Why does he operate the way he does? I can't tell. He tells me nothing. Everybody loves him and he tells them nothing at all.

Sometimes Stuart has long conversations on the phone in a whisper. When I ask who it was he won't tell me. Perhaps the calls are an assertion of power, a threat. Perhaps he is saying, be warned. I have secrets, I have resources, backers and back-stops you will never see or know.

I am starting to unravel Stuart's codes and patterns and tricks. I am beginning to anticipate his moves. He moves fast in all things. Sometimes he makes me feel that life is a kind of game or race, that he is a greyhound and I am as slow as a snail. And still I am in love with him, and can't do without him, and am completely, frighteningly hooked.

After a struggle Bernard Cracker is pushed out into the rain to help Wayne light up the terrifying barbecue. He shuffles about doubtfully as Wayne twiddles with the controls, jumping back with a bark of fright as Wayne effects ignition and flames shoot out of the grill, torching a pile of paper plates.

Bernard owns an advertising agency (Crackers Ltd) and drives a Rolls-Royce with a personalised number plate (CRACKERS). Under his gelled black hair Bernard glows with a cosmetic sheen. The flames from the barbecue cast orange light on his gleaming skin. He is famous for his flawless smile – these are pearls that are his teeth! He is as shiny and toned as if he goes to a secret clinic to be laminated. Bernard never goes anywhere without at least one hot teenage hopeful selected from his agency's crowded books. The identity of the hopeful changes often but she is usually called Tracey or Shelley or occasionally Darlene, Leanne or Sherrymaree.

While Bernard is beating down the flames with a damp tea towel, I encounter a Deslene in the kitchen. 'My name's Deslene,' she says, 'I'm a hostess with Air New Zealand.'

'My name's Stella,' I say, 'I'm your hostess.'

'Aaauuuwhh,' she breathes with nasal eagerness. 'Who do you fly with?'

'With Stuart' I reply.

'Auwhh wow,' she wheezes. 'Does Stewie own a plane?'

I'm trying to keep it in order, this new life of mine. I'm trying to keep it straight in my head. Things can quickly become unclear. What do we look like, Stuart and I? Do I look like one of Bernard's bimbos? But I'm not. I'm not. Roaring round in the Porsche with my shopping bags, in my shades, I'm full of *deep* and *complicated* thoughts. (So there.) Why does Stuart want me here? Why did he announce one night that his wardrobe was too empty, that he wanted my clothes hanging in there as well? If I asked him one night, do you love me? what would he say? I never ask. If we argue, as we often do, he goes downstairs and sits in the dark with Howard. One night I crept down and watched them as they sat there. Stuart sighed as he patted the dog's head.

'It's just you and me, How,' he whispered darkly. I crept back upstairs, filled with hilarity and dread. 'It's just you and me, How.' And How has had a lot of stepmothers.

I try to keep it in order, all this. I have to. Everything that I love is here. Everything. Including the murders.

2. The murders

Stuart defended my obscene language charge with his usual indestructible style. 'Fuck they *lie*, don't they, these cops,' he remarked to me cheerfully as we waited in the grimy waiting room on the appointed day. Writhing with embarrassment and nerves, I didn't reply. When the arresting constable came bounding into the room, pompous and important, his thick notebook jammed with bookmarks as if he were about to describe a murder or a riot, Stuart didn't ignore him but greeted him with great charm, shaking his hand and smiling warmly. The policeman was not much older than teenage, at odd moments he fell to staring vacantly and playing childishly with one of his ears. By the time Stuart had finished greeting and soothing him he was ready to lie down, wag his tail and push his wet nose into Stuart's hand.

The evidence was duly presented in courtroom three. On a cold night in July, the young policeman had bustled over and ordered me to stop leaning on a car outside a city pub. I might be damaging it, he explained stubbornly, pompously, struggling to cope with the situation that arose when I didn't move obediently as expected, but stayed leaning there, arguing. He was diminutive, tiny-eyed, not much taller than me. He clenched his fists as I and my disreputable flatmates drawled contempt at him, the tiny Nazi, little tool, in his little Crimplene suit. (We were students, we were left-wing, all cops were shit.)

Soon he was not pompous but full of hate, and I was full of something nasty too, the idea of being moved *for nothing* was intolerable. Eventually I gave him a way out.

'Fuck off,' I said, and with relief he bundled me into his car, and presented me grandly at the station counter: 'Arrest. Female. O-ffensive language.'

'Ludicrous,' Stuart murmured as we sat together at the morning tea break in the courthouse. Have you heard the language they use in the police station? It's fuck this and fuck that quite *relentlessly*.'

In court I assumed as instructed a pale, sorrowful expression as the constable took the stand. Stuart leaned towards him and led him through a kindly, loving and completely devastating cross-examination. When it was all over shortly afterwards and the charge was dismissed (the judge curling his lip slightly at the apologetic figure of the little constable), we stood outside for a minute while Stuart talked to another client. The constable came out of the courtroom. As he passed us he turned. 'See ya, mate,' he said to Stuart shyly, and skipped off down the stairs. 'And now,' smiled my lawyer, leaning in my direction, 'can I take you to lunch?'

Stuart rang me often after he had taken me out to lunch, and stayed talking on the phone for hours. If I made noises as if preparing to hang up he would say charmingly, are you going? Why? After each conversation I would come away with the memory of a malapropism or something creaky or quaint. On a dull day he rang from his car and seemed to say, 'The clouds are scudding as I reach the fork . . .'

'What?' I shouted into the static, as he rode into a black spot and the line went dead.

I would try to describe him to my elder sister, my adviser, the fierce and glamorous Una. Una was experienced with men and their ways, their verbal transgressions. She had been pursued since she was twelve by yearning suitors who regularly subjected her to communications of vile and purple corn. Together we would open the lovelorn letters of undesirables and dunces and unfortunates, and while I pored over them with awe and envy Una would writhe with hilarity and disgust and snatch them from me and throw them round the room.

The very first gift was a funereal bundle of sinister carnations ('Carnies!' Una said, with malice) accompanied by a card that read, 'Thinking of you, Maurice.' Una put them on her bedside table. They survived for weeks, slowly fading, smelling faintly of cats' piss. They glowered at Una while she was getting dressed. They turned slightly and peered at us while we talked in her room. She called them the triffids, the surveillance carnies. After that, gifts began to arrive regularly, usually laid tenderly on the hairy doormat at our parents' front door, all crackling cellophane and satin ribbons, cards decorated with kittens and ducklings. Una stacked them in her room and laughed herself sick.

Often things would be going well, Una would be quite flirty and keen, and then the boyfriend would make a wrong move on the verbal front. It would be something like 'I think I'm a kinda sensitive guy,' or 'I think you're a beautiful person, deep down inside,' and suddenly my sister would turn cold. He had exceeded the bounds of taste. He had screwed up. Tragically confused, he would race out to the nearest florist and dash off a really purple card, and Una would bring it into the house and read it out, doubled up with mirth. The more firmly her boyfriends were rejected the more strenuously purple they became. The floral arrangements and cards, phone calls and singing telegrams would rise to a crescendo of purpleness. Our father, opening the front door to retrieve the milk bottles in the morning would find the doorstep festooned with shiny and crackling bouquets, as if someone had been murdered on the steps in the night. Una would fail to respond. After a long time the cards would begin to fade to a plaintive, suicidal mauve as the suitor began to get the message. I stood one afternoon outside her door listening to one of her boyfriends weeping and protesting in her room. After listening in silence to his wretched monologue for some minutes, Una stood up and said briskly, brushing his tears from her shoes, 'Go home, Roger.'

But she is more merciful these days. She has mellowed. Recently her husband announced solemnly that one of his colleagues had 'an aura of spirituality, and awesome karma'. I watched to see how she would go for that, but she just waved a courgette at her husband and smiled with effortless charm.

I was thinking about Stuart. I was thinking about how complicated these things are. This for example: Stuart and I driving in the late afternoon through the countryside, back from a trip to Muriwai Beach. There were long black shadows on the hills and the sun was a red ball dissolving into the sea. Stuart drove for a long time in silence. Then at the top of a hill he stopped the car and we sat watching as the sun flattened along the burning horizon and the curtains of rain moved over the sea. When the sun had melted to a tinfoil strip and the ocean was dark Stuart suddenly leaned over and whispered into my hair, 'All alone, darling heart, amid these sunkissed hills.' In a nearby paddock in the gloom a cow let off a flatulent snort. I sniggered, involuntarily.

But Una and I are different in these things. Stuart's purple moments make me like him all the more. Perhaps it's not the skill that matters it's the will behind the delivery. Through language Una picked out the wankers, the humourless, the incurably insincere. But Stuart's way of talking is one of the things I like most of all about him. Of all his features it is the most wholesome, sincere, the most enduringly, cleanly innocent.

Stuart called the dog Howard 'my boy', and was endlessly fussy and paternal with the worthless animal. One day he rang in an agitated state. 'Shit, dear,' he said, 'I've lost my boy,' and he told me that the dog had not been seen for most of the day. It hadn't turned up for breakfast, its doggo-bites lay untouched. 'You've got to help me,' Stuart moaned. 'I'm in a quandary, I need someone to help me look for him.'

When I got to his house Stuart was wringing his hands. 'He might be lying by the motorway dying, lost and alone.' I had never been to Stuart's house before and was more interested in having a look around it, but he ushered me into the car and we set off armed with torches and dog biscuits. Two hours later the dog was illuminated in the headlights energetically mounting a large hairy bitch. Seriously browned off at being interrupted, Howard barked and howled extravagantly all the way home.

While Stuart was rubbing the dog down and tucking him into bed with a saucer of cocoa, I made a pot of tea. I came in with two cups and Stuart looked up mistily. 'You were a great help, Stella,' he said and launched himself in my direction. As he propelled me towards the bed spraying tea over us and we rolled and fumbled around on the duvet Howard groaned evilly from his dog basket and I thought, older man, strange house, a stranger in an old house. Strange and new. Stuart's face hovered over me, his eyebrows raised, eyes closed, mouth pursed into an O. He clutched me harder. 'Darling,' he said suddenly.

'Darling?'

The tea ran in streams down the duvet and onto the floor, the heater glowed and the warm light shone on the walnut furniture, the bright coloured prints, the Indian rug and the brass bed end. The whispered word (the corn of it, the schmaltz, it was decadent, loose), and the yellowy light on his vases and ornaments made the room seem a cave full of luxury and heat. The duvet underneath me was immeasurably soft. Go ahead, I thought, fuck me to pieces. Fuck me to death.

I didn't get sex before I met Stuart. I got it but I didn't get it. I went out and got it but I never got the idea. Those first times, in the grey morning light of a Grey Lynn bedsit before school, we did it continuously, for hours it seemed, my boyfriend humping and groaning and heaving, subsiding eventually all shagged out and hoarse and tearful over his post-coital cigarette while I joined in with his gentle chuckles and conspiratorial noises and tapped my fingers on his sweat-drenched shoulder, and sighed and smoked and just didn't get it.

With Stuart it was different straight away: he had no unusual positions or tricks, no pornographic props, no fumbling or prodding or doing it standing on our heads. But on the first night he poked his head up from under the covers and asked – quite innocently, quite matter-of-factly – 'So what makes you *come*?'

Thus shocked and prompted, I caught on. I got it right away. And with that he made me want him, and want sex, and think about him with desire when he wasn't around.

One night we were lying on the bed drinking gin and watching *Crimewatch* on television. Stuart got up. 'Wanna see something?' he said. He went out and came back with a little stack of booklets. He gave me one. 'Check this one out,' he said. 'Start at the beginning and go through it.'

I started at the beginning. The first page was a photo of a house. The second was a photo of the front door of the house. The next was a wall covered in a wide spray of blood. Then there was a bed soaked in blood, a pile of clothes and a pair of running shoes, all caked in blood. The photographs progressed through the interior of the house. In the bathroom there was a basin with a bright red streak running into the plug hole. The next scene was a bedroom. The walls were covered in flowery yellow paper. There was a child's finger painting pinned to the wall. The window was open and there was a view of a clothes line and a paddock beyond. On the floor a woman lay on her back naked. Her legs were spread and her arms were stretched above her head. On her upper body and neck were at least thirty long gashes. She was covered from head to foot in blood, and the blood spread in a pool around her. Her face was hugely swollen. The mouth was open in a rigid scream of bloody gums and broken teeth and the eyes were swollen shut. Beside her lay a child of about three. The child's body was slashed. One of his eyes was open and staring towards the window. The grass in the paddock outside was very green and a single little white sock hung on the line.

'You see, darling,' said Stuart, leaning close to me. 'Look closely. That is what I do.'

I think of a man in Auckland whom everyone sees. His name is something like 'Romaniuk' and all he does is walk. He walks everywhere, endlessly, day after day. Driving through Parnell you might see him making his way up the Parnell Rise. Another day on your way through Mission Bay you'll see him striding along the Waterfront Drive. He walks through the suburbs in any weather, all day. He doesn't do anything else. He is always alone. On his head he wears a blue hard hat and he carries a straight walking stick. Mr Romaniuk is a refugee, perhaps a Czech or a Pole. He is a fruitcake, a banana, his lift doesn't go to the top storey. All day he walks off some terrible secret that he carries around inside him. He must cover the whole city every day. He talks to no one and no one has ever seen him sitting down. We all wonder about him as we sit in our cars, watching as he strides across at the lights, pulling his hard hat down over his ears. Where does he think he is going as he walks along going nowhere? What is he walking away from? Some horror or tragedy, some dark Nazi past? I'd like to follow him one day. I like to walk a lot too. Often I walk and walk, from suburb to suburb, when I can, when time allows. At night I work on the files with Stuart. There is no horror that can make Stuart walk away. Horror and tragedy are what he does. And now I help him. Now I do it too.

That night we sat on the bed I turned the pages mechanically, and when I came to the last photo I looked at it and looked at him. He smiled. I panicked, completely. I didn't know him, I had never seen anything so appalling in my life. He smiled, and reached out for the booklet, and at that I ran from the room, out of the house, and along the road.

He caught up with me at the shopping centre and tried to take my arm, apologising and pleading, he was sorry, he looked at this stuff all the time, he forgot it was distressing, he was insensitive, he would never forgive himself. He stood shivering with cold under the neon lights. I'm cold, he said. Can't we go home? He pressed his face against the sleeve of my jacket. I'm just lonely, he said, and he rubbed his hand over his face as if his eyes had filled with tears.

Now, I've seen it all. Photos of shotgun blasts to the head, with rulers poked into the hole to show the depth of the cavity. Stabbing victims, closeups of wounds, post–mortems, strangulations, wet bloated bodies. Stuart and I pore over them as we lie in bed at night. We discuss it with our magnifying glasses, our data, our notebooks close at hand.

New Zealand has about the same murder rate per head of population per year as Australia and Britain. However, business has been better than average in New Zealand this year. Between New Year's Day and 14 January there were at least ten murders. They included the shooting of a policeman, the year's inevitable (it seems) internationally shaming murder of an innocent and beautiful young tourist, and the brutal bludgeoning to death of a friendly old Girl Scout leader.

These crimes naturally provoked an outpouring of outrage and alarm. The media launched into the crime debate with renewed enthusiasm. What is happening to our peaceful society? Do you know the ten steps to keeping your property secure? Is the crime rate due to the decline of the family and Christian values? The items are heavily interspersed with advertisements for deadlocks, security mesh, chains, car alarms and burglar alarms.

There is even a new anti-crime lobby group, Mothers for a Safe Society. The principal goal of the group is the abolition of crime. (Police chiefs nod politely.) Most want to bring back hanging. Some favour more creative retribution, like hand–chopping, whipping, the stocks and castration.

The group is led by an aggressive spokeswoman who advocates capital punishment by lethal injection, also variously castration, hard labour, branding, flaying, tattooing and compulsory religious instruction. She appears on chat shows effortlessly savaging her opposition, all those bearded criminologists, cardiganed sociologists and neuro-foppish wimps who stutter across the table at her while the interviewers struggle to rein her in: 'Mrs Fink-Jensen, Dr Baldwin *is* entitled to give us his side of the argument . . .'

Mrs Fink-Jensen: 'What's wrong with you? Are you sick? Would you *like* your mother to be raped?'

I have been watching the head mother being interviewed on television all week. Watching her talk I wonder if she was beaten as a child. I wonder what she would have got up to if she had been born a man. With her huge muscular hands, her boiling eyes, with her mouth set in a bow of bitter rage, she looks capable of anything.

Her group has begun sitting in on criminal trials. They come in, twenty at a time, and no one knows quite why they are there. They sit silently in the back of the courtroom. Sometimes, weirdly, they all hold hands in a circle and close their eyes, praying. I often wonder what they are concealing under their billowing clothes. I imagine, under their bulletproof vests, that they are armed with their favourite weapons of self-defence: syringes, branding irons, bibles, stun guns and whips.

They have certainly stirred up the atmosphere in the waiting rooms. This week one of the group was heard to say outside the number one court that the man in the dock deserved to be hanged, and was immediately thrown to the floor by the relatives of the man in the dock, who rounded on her, shrieking terrible expletives and abuse.

'We've declared war on people like you,' menaced the mother from the floor as the two groups squared off and the security guards moved in nervously.

The news is full of this strange new group as I go from channel to channel late at night on television. Channels one to three are New Zealand channels, channels four to six are Sky TV and CNN. I flick from Mrs Fink-Jensen to Monrovia, from *Sale of the Century* to famine and war. Channel one says we have a law and order problem of terrible magnitude. Channel two says Tom of Tauranga has won a trip for two to Taupo. Out in the world on channel six, the bodies lie in the sand and flies crawl over wasted faces and tanks ride through the shells of cities and Betty Plastic reads the death tolls in her reassuring drone.

In the evenings I work through Stuart's files. He gives me a lot of money to do this. I have never been so well off in my life. Cash has become almost meaningless. I can afford to buy beautiful clothes and often I reach into my pocket at the dairy and enrage the shopowner by paying for a packet of cigarettes with a hundred-dollar bill.

The defence counsel is entitled to every single piece of material recorded on the case by the police. This means that I wade through a lot of detail, many tiny scraps of information. Some, especially drugs cases, involve electronic surveillance by the police. There are full transcripts in the files, the hardened users and dealers cursing their way through the gruelling sessions of selling or 'pinging' or snorting. Along with the incriminating stuff is the grotesque detail of the sordid ménage under scrutiny, 'What's for chow ya cow? Not now babe I'm off for a crap, I'll smash ya face in ya little shit, what's that on the dog's arse?' and so on, faithfully recorded and politely transcribed. The targets are often vaguely aware that the police might not be far away. 'Imagine if the *pigs* were listening to us now, we'd be for it, man. [Subject A laughs.]' PCs B and C laugh even harder.

But Stuart's speciality is murder. These are the files with the unbearable photos, the autopsy reports, the pathologists' findings, the pages and pages of sadness and squalor and rage. Here the subject weeps, here the subject wails and bangs his head against the wall, here the subject sits with eerie calm, subdued by post-traumatic shock. Most of them make little attempt to deny. Many of them describe in detail what happened. Many of the killings are domestic. Subject describes beating to death his wife. Subject describes stabbing to death her husband. Subject has to pause in the account to vomit, to bang his head, to cry, then goes on to describe how many bottles or gallons of alcohol he has consumed in the last few hours. All of it is relevant to the defence. The level of intoxication, the contents of the statement, the circumstances in which the statement was taken, and so on. The state of mind of the accused. The actions of the victim.

All the files are different. All the circumstances vary. All describe what any of our number might do, unexpectedly, out of rage or fear, insanity or drunkenness, evil intent or hopelessness or despair.

Now Stuart has an important new file. It is a murder charge against a man named Carlos Henry Lehman. Stuart brought me the file before he left this morning. He dumped the two heavy cardboard boxes of papers on the table, saying that he had inherited the case from one of his colleagues, who is giving his files away because he has cancer and has to go into hospital for an operation.

Carlos Henry Lehman has already been committed for trial after a depositions hearing. I have worked my way through the first box of papers.

Carlos Lehman is a thirty-five-year-old married man with four children. At the time of the alleged murder he was living in a small town called Seabrooke, just outside Tauranga. One day he took a shotgun, drove into town and shot a local man, Cyril Leonard, in the head.

The file is large. I have read six interviews with Lehman and many more with the inhabitants of the town. The interviews contain a lot of background information. I have attempted to sort out the relevant facts.

Before he moved to Seabrooke Lehman and his three business partners operated an export business in Mount Maunganui. Two and a half years ago the partners sold the business and went their separate ways. With his share Lehman eventually bought a piece of land near the town of Seabrooke, on which he intended to raise crops, grow an orchard and live off the land.

Lehman went about developing his land in a very driven and

systematic way. But despite his efforts he wasn't able to make his venture a success. It seems that he fell out of favour with the inhabitants of the small Seabrooke community almost as soon as he arrived in the place. He got into a dispute with one of his neighbours, Mr Boyderman Leonard, over the boundary between their adjoining land. The neighbour was a popular member of the community. The disagreement carried on for months and Lehman became extremely unpopular because of it.

He claims in his statements that people in the town began to vandalise his tools and equipment, and that property belonging to him was stolen. After a few months the vandalism and thefts became so frequent that the Lehmans' livelihood was seriously threatened.

As the harassment continued Lehman became withdrawn and depressed. Each time he and his wife went into the town they were more and more dismayed and discouraged by their unfriendly reception. According to his wife's statements Lehman became obsessive about his land, his orchard and his crops. He tried to guard his property day and night but despite all his efforts he was unable to stop the damage being done.

Eventually, his statements say, he lost so many trees and plants and pieces of equipment through vandalism and theft that he was faced with financial ruin. He became so stressed that he began to alienate himself from his wife. According to the wife their relationship, which had been very easy and affectionate, was being placed under such strain that they were hardly communicating, and by this time Lehman was apparently in a state of severe anxiety and depression.

One morning he went into Seabrooke intending to talk to members of the Leonard family about the dispute. He spoke to Cyril Leonard who was the brother of the neighbour with whom Lehman had argued about the boundaries. During the conversation Leonard taunted Lehman, calling him names and saying that Lehman would have to leave Seabrooke since he would never be accepted in the town. Lehman went home. Ten minutes later he came back with his shotgun and shot Cyril Leonard in the head, killing him instantly. After the shooting Lehman dropped the gun and walked away, and was arrested a short time later.

What do you think?' I ask after setting Lehman's story out in notes for Stuart.

The dog groans languidly from his basket. I take out my pen and note, semi-seriously,

> The taunts of the victim went straight into Lehman like knives. They were a confirmation that the people of Seabrooke were aware of his failure to succeed, and that all his attempts to become a hard-working, respected member of the town had come to nothing. It may well be that he had failed because his efforts were actively sabotaged by certain members of the tight-knit rural community in Seabrooke, who were acting out of malice or some other unexplained motive.

I read this note out loud. I am alone with the dog; Stuart has gone to Hamilton to defend a woman client. Charge: assault, with tomahawk. I keep the dog close to me on the nights Stuart isn't around. Even though he only slobbers, begs and ingratiates around humans, his roaring bark of joyful welcome is enough to put off any lurking rapist. At least I hope it is. Thinking of psychoses I add to my notes (improvising further):

> On the other hand Mr Lehman could be completely insane, and could have fabricated all his stories of harassment. They could be figments of his paranoid imagination. However, he appears from his statements to be very lucid and reasonable. He sounds sane, in other words.

Howard looks at me with a slight smile on his chops. 'Think we're a psychiatrist?' I imagine him saying silkily. We leave the file on the desk and go into the office.

There in neat lines on the dark wood shelves Stuart's library is stacked in all its heavy leather, greens, blues and browns, cases, textbooks, statutes. Dragging out a couple of the large textbooks, I find the right section and flick through the defences, past automatism, insanity, intoxication, through duress, necessity, superior orders, over mistake of law, mistake of fact, self-defence, and down to provocation. Provocation in law, I read, is this: an act or series of acts done by the dead person to the accused which would cause in any reasonable person, and actually causes in the accused, a sudden and temporary loss of self-control, rendering the accused so subject to passion as to make him for the moment not a master of his own mind.

Provocation, if successfully raised as a defence, can reduce what would have been a conviction for murder to a conviction for manslaughter.

Provocation, like people destroying everything you set out to do. I know that Stuart is experienced with this defence, he has raised it before. Lehman is in good hands. I am looking forward to meeting Lehman, I know Stuart will want me to. He encourages me to go with him to the prison to sit in on interviews with the capital offenders, as they are still called when they've been charged with murder, a hangover from the days of hanging.

I sit in the office under the green lamp, going through the heavy books, and somewhere in the back of my mind I wonder what Stuart is doing. I wonder whether he is doing it with anyone else. When I came to live with him the thought of jealousy or possessiveness or suspicion never occurred to me. Now, a long time later I find myself straining to hear as he talks behind closed doors, as he goes out of the room after dinner to make a quick phone call. Who is he talking to? I ask silently. 'Who were you talking to?' I ask him. 'What are you doing?' And he waves off my questions with an injured, affronted look. 'Shit, darl,' he says, 'it's my *business*, I don't ask you what you do, who you're talking to, do I?'

I try to keep it straight in my head, all this business. I try not to mess it up. But isn't it true that when he goes away now I look through the cupboards, I go through his things, his ancient relics, his old photos?

Last week, while sifting through the contents of an old ward-robe, I found a photo of a dark-haired, sharp-eyed woman and a little smiling girl sitting on a beach holding buckets and spades. His wife and daughter, or his wife and the little girl he thought was his. He had written on the back of the photo. The inscription read in faded blue pen, *Mia and Marlene, Club Med Noumea. Marlene's b'day (4!)*. Club Med, I thought, feeling faintly sick at the sight of the little girl in her straw hat, her plastic sandals and socks.

Sometimes I creep to the door in *my* socks when he's gone into the office to use the phone. And don't I feel a terrible dull stab in my chest when he says to me for the third time in a week, 'Shit dear, don't hassle me. Some things are private. I don't hassle you, do I?'

Late at night I wake up and look at him while he sleeps. He snores, moves around, looks smooth and handsome and uncom-plicated. But as I stare at him I wonder what I've taken on. Beyond the law, beyond tactics and courtroom technique, Stuart knows what makes people tick. He knows what drives us to do what we do. It is his business to know. I know that the way to win is to ignore his secret calls. But I can't. I haven't got the strength. What battles, what tactical struggles we fight under the surface without a direct word being said. Sometimes I find myself look-ing at Stuart and thinking, I love you but I want to stop losing the game. I want to be able to play it like you. Is that what he wants? I just don't know at all.

I try to forget all this and concentrate on the textbooks, but the dog and I register a new noise, a car approaching at high speed, and we both jump as the hum of the engine becomes a roar and the driveway is lit up with a blaze of light. Howard is already fighting his way out of his dog basket. I put the books to one side. The dog thuds about barking hysterically, and we open the door to Bernard Cracker, drunk and wild-eyed and hanging onto the door for support as he staggers in shouting greetings and aiming kicks at the dog as it leaps around him trying its best to fuck up his clothes.

'Geddoff geddoff,' grunts Bernard. 'It's trying to *rape* me, geddown, y'bastard, y'mutt.' But he is in a good mood. He comes in and settles down with a large gin. 'I'm not expecting Stuart home tonight,' I explain. 'All the better!' Bernard says. 'You can come out with me. We'll go to the Balcony.'

Pleased with the attention and the interruption, the shouting and the commotion, I pour myself a large gin and tonic and banish the dog, and we lounge around for an hour fuelling up. After a couple of gins I begin to beam ruddily at my guest, full of affection for him, the way he fills up the empty house, the way he speaks without barking, the way he doesn't talk death at the table.

'Let's do it,' I say. 'Let's go out!'

We weave our way to the car. There is an owl hooting madly in the garden. 'Watch out,' shouts Bernard, revving the engine, 'I'm on the loose tonight, I'm on form. Get out of my way!'

We roar out of the driveway taking a large piece of the foliage with us. Cracker leans out the window and tears leaves and branches from the windscreen while I cry with laughter in the passenger seat, already drunk enough to die laughing in a blazing auto wreck, every outrageous driving manoeuvre by Bernard sending me into greater merriment as I cling to the headrest of his seat. We head for the Balcony, Auckland's most fashionable all-hours bar. We head there at an indecently fast rate. We are flattened in our seats by the speed. We arrive in the carpark, the car festooned with flora and reeking of burning rubber.

Balcony is a crowded bar with wooden floors and a large balcony shaded partly by the roof of the building and partly by two willow trees which fall over the deck like stage curtains and filter the sunlight. During the day the bar is filled with rainy green light and at night it is lit with small lights hung from the trees. On most nights the place is full of the wealthy and significant people of Auckland, and many rich bachelors, and young hopefuls for Bernard to interview. Many beautiful and famous Auckland relationships have been formed at the bar.

Before I discovered the Balcony, before I met Stuart, my

flatmates and I spent long and fraught evenings in a mean dive called the DB Waitemata in Central Auckland, where the poor and tattooed drinkers would grind their cigarette butts into the carpet, hurl jugs at one another and sometimes give one of us a really good beating in the toilets. One false move, any breach of etiquette and you could find yourself facing a Maori kangaroo court in the Ladies. Or, on lenient evenings you might just find yourself pushed out into the rain with a kick in the pants and a heavy jug whistling past your ears. It was the gun fanatic who insisted on going to the Waitemata instead of one of the more twee pubs, principally because he liked the violence and the filth, the meanness of it all. And he was the one who was never threatened. The headbanging Westies and sweating Samoans, the toothless, scarred, jailbird Maoris never gave him a minute of trouble. They could tell that he wanted it, they could tell that he would never run away.

Bernard and I fight our way to a table near the bar. Then Bernard takes his drink and makes his way around the tables, and I drink wine and scan the room, happily drunk, pleased to be out of the house. The crime files weigh on me sometimes, especially after dark when the house is empty and the rooms are silent. The endless grime, the blood and the guts. I beam over at the people at the next table, admiring their cosmetic tans and their healthy *nouveau* wealth. How far removed they are from the blasted drunks in the DB Waitemata. And how different from all those accuseds in all those files who try to control their trembling hands, who stare with blank seagull eyes and mutter and sob and mumble and shout all their jumbled accounts of violence and misery and loss.

'Let's dance!' roars Bernard, and so we do.

Then we get back into the drinking. Bernard can really put it away, Bernard is a serious drinker, boozer and raver. By this time I am beginning to float and drift, the room has an unreal quality. Things are shifting and blurring. Time has gone slack, colours are pale. In the pastel-coloured Ladies as I am putting on makeup my balance goes and I fall against my own image, the rivers and tributaries of blood in my eyeball, the creases under the lower lids, beads of sweat and hairs and gaps in the makeup, all that terrible detail, up close. Shocked, I lever myself away, into focus. Shaking myself I carry out repairs, rubbing over smudges and filling in holes while behind me a young woman has locked herself into a cubicle and is unable to let herself out. A burly waiter is summoned and tries to talk her through the process of unlocking the door. She replies faintly and tearfully. Every few minutes there is a crash as she falls to the floor of the cubicle. 'I caaan't!' she wails. More waiters arrive and confer. They will have to break down the door. Reeling around at the mirror I notice a greasy imprint of my face on the glass, one kohl eye, one tan cheek, half a mouth, open, gasping.

'There's many a slip twixt cup and lip,' Bernard observes, pouring more all round. 'There's many a PRI to be suffered in such an establishment as we currently frequent. Make no mistake. Make no beg pardons. Drink?'

Bernard carries the scars of many a Piss Related Injury. Once he fell off a table and broke his ankle. Once he drove into a birdbath in the Auckland Domain, knocking himself out and killing a family of ornamental gnomes.

Stuart has developed a clever tactic when it comes to drinking and driving. It's this: Whenever he and I get drunk he makes me drive. 'Shit, darl,' he says patiently, 'I can't drive, I'm a criminal lawyer. You drive and I'll defend!'

At 4 a.m. Bernard volunteers to drive me back to Stuart's. Cheerfully suicidal, I accept. We gather up all the phone numbers he has collected on slips of paper and menus and make for the carpark. We locate Bernard's car, parked lopsidedly, back wheels up on a concrete kerb, a branch of Stuart's pear tree still stuck across its roof. 'Look there are buds on it,' Bernard says. 'It must be spring.'

A few seconds later we are back at the house, clambering out of the steaming, shuddering car. Driving with Bernard is indescribable. It's like being beamed. Strangely all the lights in the house which I'd turned off when I left are now on. Bernard notices this. 'Hey,' he whispers, 'Stuart's home. I'll get out of here.'

Whispering farewells he lurches off down the drive and I go blundering up the path to the back door. Now I can see Stuart through the window standing in the kitchen staring down at the sink. Looking down like that his face is slightly pear-shaped, his cheeks puff out and his long nose seems to curve down over his mouth. His eyes are hooded and his dark hair stands up in fine points. His narrow shoulders are hunched. Standing there under the light he looks graceful and fine, and when I fumble my way in and greet him warmly he looks up and stares at me for a moment, taking me in. 'Where have you been?' he says finally, thinly, looking down at his hands.

'I went to the Balcony with Bernard. Why are you back already? I thought you had a two-day hearing, I thought you had to stay overnight.'

'You were with Bernard?'

'Yes. Did you get through the hearing in one day?'

'It was adjourned,' he says, rubbing his forehead.

'Right at the beginning, in the morning?'

'Yes, actually.'

'Then why didn't you come straight back? Did something else come up?'

'We went and did some shopping, looked around, had lunch, came back to Auckland and went out for a meal.'

'We? I thought you went by yourself.'

'Oh, did I say we? I meant I. I went out to dinner. I decided to have some time off. Are you going to hassle me about it?'

I feel myself struggling, blundering through this conversation. He stands poised at the sink, tall and fine. I circle the kitchen table. 'You said we. Why did you say we? You wanted me to pick that up, you wanted to say it. Why would you do that, what are you trying to do?'

We stand there under the kitchen light and I feel anxiety suddenly, confusion, my head is spinning. I walk right up to him and he steps back as if I am going to hit him. I advance on him.

'Well?' I say, stupidly. He steps behind a kitchen chair.

He says, blinking, 'I've been doing what I always do. I've been achieving. I *achieve*. I can do that without you. You can go off with whoever you want. Why would I care? I don't need you.'

He turns his back. 'You're supposed to help me . . . Who knows what you really get up to.'

'But I've only been out with Bernard. I haven't been up to anything. I work hard, I drive you round, I never stop doing things for you.'

He laughs. 'I don't care what you do.'

And now I am protesting and arguing and saying that I don't understand him and he leaves me in the kitchen and goes upstairs. 'Come on Howard,' he says coldly, 'let's go to bed.'

I walk around downstairs, I walk out into the office and look out the window at the harbour, I can hardly walk with it all. I fall into the chair by the window. Out there the harbour is calm, the orange lights from the harbour bridge shine on the water. I decide to walk out to the point, I want to walk out there in the dark along the marina where the boats are moored, I want to walk off this confusion, this feeling of defeat.

I go to the door and stumble down into the street. All those wet smells of earth and the city steam up out of the damp asphalt. I smell rotten and dead things. I walk past the run-down wooden houses, down to the motorway. I pause and look for a long time at the ugliness of the concrete, piles of rubbish, a smashed street light. I pass a cat lying by the motorway fence, mutilated and decaying. I feel hugely sad, an immense sadness fills me, this decay, this ugliness, this *tragedy*. The concrete structures rise all around, fences sag, the toitoi grows in a ragged line along a bank covered in weeds. I pick my way through the rubbish, past an old car, past the swimming baths where the water is lit with a humming white light and something floats slowly across the pool. I sit down in the park and look out over the city. Slowly, with extravagant tragedy, I make my way home.

Just past the reach of the cold glow from the gas station, near the black mouth of the carpark entrance, I hear footsteps behind me in the street. I turn, there's no one there. Near home I turn again and see a figure walking by the parked cars in the shadow of the trees. I stop. He stops. Nervously I turn and walk again. I look, and he's walking too. Quickly I walk behind a parked car. He's coming out of the shadows, walking slowly, emerging into the light. It's Wayne. The odd-jobs man. Tall, pale, a gritty black woollen hat pulled tightly over his small head, his breath steaming so he looks like a match that's just been struck, and blown out.

'Wayne?'

He smiles secretively.

'You gave me a fright, Wayne.'

I watch him shrug, and walk away.

Back home I squelch up the stairs to the bedroom and Stuart is awake, standing at the window in the dark looking out over the black concrete of the marina.

'Where did you go?' he says. 'Out there? It's so late.' He puts his arms around me in the dark. 'I wanted you to be home,' he whispers.

He presses his face against mine and I feel his eyelid against my cheek.

Later he wakes me up as he often does, elbowing me, levering himself up in bed and muttering in his sleep. 'Me, I'll go,' he mumbles, 'I'll go me . . .' losing the words, sinking back into sleep again.

Before dawn, in the lift and fall of an alcoholic haze, I dream that Stuart has turned into a fiery colourful bird with wide, brilliant wings and bones and talons of the finest, lightest steel.

3. The eelman

Have you ever been into Mount Eden prison in Auckland? The place conjures up descriptive terms like hell-hole, dungeon, toilet. It is largely a remand prison, which seems to mean that the normal rules about hygiene, space and proper facilities can be avoided. After all, many of the prisoners will leave the jail in due course and move into more permanent accommodation. The place has the feel of a building allowed to rot slowly over a long period of time, with no prospect of any improvements. The walls are made of stone. The stone is covered in moss and slime and oozes and leaks in true dungeon fashion. It has been said that the mouldy decay of Mount Eden is preferable to the high-tech sterility of the maximum security prison at Paremoremo. But looking at Mount Eden as I did again today, I'm not so sure about that.

The visiting rooms are an overcrowded, smelly nightmare. Everything is reduced to its barest, most hideous minimum. The walls, the chairs, the grilles, the wives, the kids, the mums and dads are scarred and depressed and wrecked. Everything in there has been wrecked ever since it was born or manufactured. The ceiling is cracked and stained. The lighting is mad. The walls ooze and drip and the air is cold. Take anything in there and it will come out soiled. It will come out closer to being dead. Stuart always wears his oldest suits into Mount Eden. I feel as if I should be wearing gumboots, for the grease and mould, for the slime.

We were shown into a small cell to wait for the new client, Carlos Lehman. There was a battered table and some orange plastic chairs, and a single wire-covered light. A urinal dripped rhythmically and leaked along one edge of the floor.

We stood in the room in silence as he was led in by a warder. We introduced ourselves and he shook hands. Lehman was tall and brown and strong looking. He was nearly as tall as Stuart. He spoke awkwardly as we greeted him, looking away. We sat down on the plastic chairs and he leaned forward, resting one elbow on his knees and pressing his other arm against his stomach. There was a pause. The urinal dripped. And dripped. The light was green.

'Are you all right?' Stuart said. Lehman frowned and straightened up.

'Sorry,' he said. His face was strained. 'Maybe I've got an ulcer.'

'Can we do anything?'

'No, I feel all right now.'

Stuart reached into his bag and took out his notebook and pens. 'OK. This is a preliminary visit, it won't take too long.'

Lehman smiled crookedly. 'I got plenty of time.'

He looked around the room, pushing his hair out of his eyes. He spoke without looking at us. 'I wanted to cut my hair, but they won't let me. They won't let me have sharp instruments. They won't let me shave. I'm not allowed to do the simplest things I want to do.'

'You don't need a haircut, mate. Too short and you wouldn't look normal. You'd look like a skinhead, antisocial. We want you to look average, it's better for you.'

Lehman looked over at me. He said, 'I thought they shaved all your hair off in prison. '

'Well,' Stuart said, 'you might not have to worry about that. I've been thinking about this, and studying your file. I've decided we should try to get you out on bail. I'm going to start working on the application as soon as we leave.'

Bail . . . I was surprised. I gave Stuart a sideways look. He hadn't mentioned this. It's difficult to get bail for any violent crime. And I thought with a murder charge no one got bail, unless they were twelve years old, or ninety, or in a coma. Lehman was charged with shooting a man at point-blank range with a shotgun, and looked pretty able-bodied. I listened with interest.

Lehman seemed agitated. He got up and paced around the room, looking quickly at Stuart and then back down at the floor. 'I wouldn't be eligible,' he said. He wiped his forehead on his sleeve.

'Well, I'm not saying it's a sure thing. It's worth applying for. So I'm going to ask you some questions, and I can use your answers to make up an application for you.'

Lehman stopped pacing. He looked keenly at Stuart. He had an intelligent face. 'They won't let me have it,' he said.

Stuart looked at his fingernails. 'It's worth applying for. You'd get to see your wife and kids.'

Lehman suddenly sat down on the plastic chair and put his head in his hands. 'I'm cursed,' he said.

'You're not cursed, mate,' Stuart said. 'Just up on a murder charge. Worry about one thing at a time.'

They were getting on well, I could see. Stuart's clients always like him. He shakes their hand, he leans over them, he calls them buddy and they feel cheered. They feel as if someone will take care of them at last. They don't want him to leave.

Lehman had strong, brown, scarred arms. No tattoos. His eyes were green. He had a powerful, part-Maori face. Half of his left eyeball was full of blood. He wasn't the usual slumped, broken-toothed, wasted type of shotgun-related client. He wasn't blasted with alcohol or drugs, he had a good healthy physique. But he looked shocked, he looked blank, as if something had happened to wipe all feeling away.

He said suddenly, 'I've been having strange dreams. I asked them for sleeping pills. I had this dream that I was sitting by a fire on a bit of land, somewhere like Central Otago. It was dark. There were other people round the fire too. I just got up and walked away from the fire, further and further away into the dark, until I was completely lost. I wake up in the morning and don't know where I am. These dreams, they freak me out.'

Stuart looked at him for a moment and the urinal dripped. 'It's no good being in here. We'll get you bail, buddy, if we possibly can,' he said.

'I've been charged with murder,' Lehman said, looking at me. It sounded like a question.

'Yes,' I said faintly, uncertain whether to respond.

He stared at me. 'Yes,' he said. 'Yes. Oh Christ.'

Stuart gave me an angry look. 'Can you just keep up with the notes please,' he said.

I took down the details of Lehman's family: names, addresses, dates of birth. He thought his parents would want him to get out on bail. He wanted to talk about the time leading up to the shooting, the vandalism and thefts of his plants and equipment, all his problems in the town of Seabrooke. He took a crumpled roll of A4 pages out of his trouser pocket and gave it to Stuart. 'I've tried to write it all down for you so you can understand what was going on,' he said. I saw that his hands were shaking.

He said nothing about the shooting itself. When Stuart questioned him indirectly about it he said he could remember nothing of it, although he said he might remember it later when it became more clear. He said that he remembered everything up to the moment when Cyril Leonard insulted him and said that he was a failure, and that he would never be accepted in the town. He remembered the insults. Something snapped. Something went wrong in his head.

'I don't want to think,' he said. 'I lie awake at night and try not to think. I have these dreams but they're not nightmares. I just dream about going away.'

Stuart was writing a list of things to do. I could see him writing 'Psychiatrist' on his pad, under 'Affidavits for bail application'. Lehman was pacing again. He had eaten the entire block of chocolate we had brought him. Now he screwed up the paper packaging and looked sick. 'I'll put on weight in here,' he said, drearily. Stuart slammed his pad shut. 'Mate, that won't do you any harm,' he said. 'We'll try to get you out of here. Hold tight. We'll do what we can.'

'You're going,' Lehman said. He looked lost. He said, 'Is it really sunny today?'

We got up. Stuart patted him on the back. 'Work on those notes, buddy, you're doing well. Anything more you remember, put it down.'

He stood, passive, by the green urinal. He stared after us as we left. We were ushered out through the gates and grilles, past the grey, flickering walls of video monitors, through the echoing, scarred corridors, led by a pale, lumpish warder who slammed and opened, jingled and slammed with pointed violence. 'Ssign here,' hissed the warder, thrusting a stained ledger at Stuart. Daintily Stuart fished for his Mont Blanc. 'Just a quick visit this time,' he said brightly. 'Bit stuffy in here today, beautiful day outside, hardly grey at all.' The warder looked on, in disgust.

'Christ. It's a rat hole.' The gate clanged behind us. Stuart wiped his hands with a silken hanky. 'Now, bail. We have to get him bail, and I think I can do it. I want to try.'

I walked out after him into the carpark, interested in the idea of bail, but Kendrick Stain was leaning on the Porsche.

'Hey,' he drawled.

'Stain,' Stuart acknowledged coldly. 'Nice day.'

'Offal day, you ask me, weather like shit. Here for Lehman?'

'Among others. How did I know we'd run into you?' Stuart eyed Stain's greasy waistcoat with distaste.

Stain lit a brown cigarette and leaned back on the car, looking every inch the thing he is famed for being: the rudest and most unscrupulous barrister in the world. A judge-scandalising, rule-breaking, foul-mouthed, no-good rapist and library-book thief. How he got admitted to the Bar in this country nobody knows. How he dares even to show his face . . .

When Ken Stain arrived in Auckland and got his law degree, after he *connived* his way into the legal community, it quickly became apparent that he was not the sort of person who would be invited to play tennis with the judges. With staggering rudeness and insubordination he barged his way through the courts. High Court judges were left stunned by his effrontery. He had slanging matches with them. He made speeches at them. He staged stunts in their courtrooms, he made raucous statements to the media. He behaved, when all was said and done, like some sort of appalling *American*. Everybody rallied, of course, and committees were specially convened to find a way to have him deported immediately to the West Indies, which was where he was supposed to have arrived from. When they were unable to deport him the Law Society began imposing fines. He was fined one hundred times for saying fuck in the High Court precincts. He was fined every week for being egregious, but the more he was fined the more outrageous he became. Since then it has got worse. He has started to become genuinely successful. He is now well established as a barrister and it is apparent that juries mysteriously respond to him. Now it remains to be seen whether he will be imprisoned or deported before he becomes even more successful than he already is. Hanging over his head this week is the latest charge, that he said something obscenely abusive outside the High Court to Mrs Barbara Fink-Jensen.

Stuart was looking sideways at Stain. Stain was garbed in a grubby brown pinstriped suit. He waved his cigarette over the car, showering it with ash. 'Interesting case, Lehman. Good for publicity.'

Stuart glared, at the suit, the fag, the drawl. He remained civil. He straightened his silk tie. With icy tweeness he undid Howard's seatbelt and let him out of the car for a piss. 'I'm going to use the phone,' he said.

I was left in the carpark with Stain, who was stubbing out his cigarette on the bonnet of the Porsche. He looked up in a friendly way, and punched me on the arm. No one is sure what Stain's country of origin really is. Mostly he sounds like a West Indian (although he is European, not West Indian in appearance), but in full flight in court he can suddenly produce pure English vowels in a remarkably powerful voice, and when he is especially drunk his voice becomes so deep that it grinds and growls out of the back of his throat, and something else creeps into the accent that could even be Irish, some flattening of the vowels which comes out after a couple of whiskies and seventy-odd cigarettes. Secretly Stuart and Ken Stain get on well when they are not stealing one another's clients, although Stuart maintains an official snotty distance in recognition of Stain's sensational unpopularity with authority.

'Dog wearing a seatbelt, eh.' I could see a long tear in his grimy waistcoat when he lifted his arm. 'Lucky dog.'

'Nothing but the best for our Howard,' I said, thinking suddenly, privately, that nothing would please me more than to get into the Porsche, run Howard over and leave. It was cold. I wanted to get away from the chill of that hated suburb of Mount Eden. The flat sprawling mass of it laid out cold in the shadow of the mountain. The melancholy of sodden lawns and the lights coming on in the wooden houses, the sun going down over the streets where students walk home through the gritty wind, the distant shouts from the playing field as a game ends in the mud, under the drizzling sky.

'Actually,' I said to Stain, 'it's ridiculous, isn't it. It's ridiculous to have a seatbelt designed for a dog.'

Stain laid a hand on my arm, offering me a cigarette.

'Honey,' he said. 'Oh honey, oh baby. Oh sexy chicken-pie, oh cootchie coo chatanooga poopsie.'

He carried on weirdly. 'Oh baby,' he said, 'I know. Oh baby I know.'

Oh baby I know. Stain rambled on, I stopped listening. I was thinking about Stuart. He makes secret calls, he disappears sometimes. This morning I came into the room and he hung up the phone, quick. Was there someone on the other end, or was he playing games?

Back in the car we roar through the suburban streets away from the jail. I drive, Stuart is taking notes. The streets are empty. Without thinking I take a wrong turn and we're heading west, out through mile after mile of suburban desert, low houses, dead hedges, flat streets, and the dying sun's ahead of us, going down over the Waitakere Ranges. The gardens are empty, the doors are shut, the lights are coming on behind the venetian blinds. The sunset seems to have come very late in the day or maybe it's just carried on later than usual. The light is pouring out of the sky and spreading over the hills. Soon it will be dark. Stopped at the lights I watch a tiny boy capering about on a porch, he's wearing a *Star Trek* headset with earphones and an aerial, he's looking up at the sky through a plastic scope. He levels it down and scopes the Porsche, he tracks us as we kick off with the green light. In front of his porch an incinerator is burning, sending out sparks and flying black paper that rises fast and floats over the road. Down the Peacock Drive, through the low-roofed shopping centre, over the tracks, looping the roundabout, we don't slow down, down the mile to the mental hospital and there's the new motorway on-ramp, the white concrete neon lit and Stuart looks up and says where are we going, where the fuck are we going? It's late in the day, it's late and yet in the trees at the ramp there are hundreds of birds singing and chirping in the neon sunshine. Do they sing and sing day and night and then die young of exhaustion? Or is this the place where they come to stay up late before going off into the dark? Where are we going, where the fuck are we going as we roar unhindered down the fast lane and sparks fly inside the car and out. The sky is orange over the city. Round we go in a curve, finally in the right direction, and drive, so late, into the sprawling city.

'The long way, the bloody long way,' gargles Stuart from the bath. 'You should be a taxi driver.'

Takeaways are strewn around the bathroom. Stuart wants me to get into the bath so he can stand at the edge and scrub my back with the loofah. I refuse. The corn of it, the schmaltz. He's probably thinking of *Last Tango in Paris*. Next he'll be wanting to fuck me up the bum.

'What's so funny?' he calls. 'Where are the chips? Turn up the music, turn down the lights. I don't feel like doing any more work.'

Later Stuart says, lying in the dark, 'I don't know why you get angry with me, Stella. I can't do without you. You're my world.'

Carlos Lehman was a normal man with a wife and four children. He began his new life with high hopes. He was practical and had his project well thought out and planned. He knew what he was doing, and he set about developing his land with care. He worked hard clearing bush and scrub. In the evenings he talked enthusiastically with his wife and children about what he planned and what he'd done that day. The area was beautiful. It was good to be doing something new.

Soon after they moved onto the land Lehman began planting. The thirty-acre block had good soil. In a relatively short space of time Lehman and his wife Leah had planted four thousand fruit and vegetable plants. Lehman planned to expand the plantation to about seventy-five thousand plants. They began to plant shelter belts of elephant grass, bottle-brushes and *Pinus radiata*.

There was a spacious wooden house on the block and Leah painted the inside of it and decorated it, and made it look like home.

One weekend it was very fine and hot and they took the four kids down to the stream for a picnic lunch. Lehman lay in the grass and thought, if I can get the shelter belts done and get the plants in I'll garden it all to the end of my life and die of bloody happiness. They ate hard-boiled eggs and cheese sandwiches and Leah paddled with the baby in the water under the trees.

An hour or so later as he drowsed in the grass he heard his son Leon crying and sobbing some way off and he got up to look. Down by the dirt road a tall, thickset man was standing over Leon and waving something long and thin and black around the little boy's face. Lehman was alarmed. Leon's crying sounded hysterical and he was holding his hands over his face. Lehman hurried down the path to the road. Leon ran to him and hid behind his legs.

'What the hell's going on?' he said. The man was in his fifties, with grey hair, a big, sunburnt face and a boulder of a beer gut. In his hand he dangled a massive dead eel, dried out, with a grey fin and tiny horns on its dead snout.

'I was telling this little shit here, that any little shits I find trespassing on my land, I strangle with my friend here, and throw their body into the fucking sea. I was telling this little shit here to get off my land, and come to think of it I'm telling you the fucking same thing.'

He waved the eel and grinned glassily. Then he spat at Lehman's feet. Lehman jumped back, the aggression was so unexpected. His stomach heaved. Then he was furious. 'But I own this land. It's mine. I've just bought it. You must know . . .'

'I don't want any strangers on my fucking land, mate, now take yourself and your runny-nosed little coon of a kid and get off.'

'This is my land.' Lehman felt as if he'd been hit from behind and was scrabbling, blinded. Leon whimpered into his trouser leg.

'Just stick to your own boundaries. I know where your land is and I know where it ends. Bear it in mind. Round here we don't like trespassers. Trash. Fouling up our land.'

The man slung the huge eel over his shoulder and walked unsteadily off down the dirt road. Leah came down the path with the baby and saw Lehman staring after the man and Leon crying and said, 'What's wrong, Carlos, what's happened?' and she kept asking anxiously as they gathered up the kids and their gear.

'That was our neighbour,' Lehman said.

Two days later, when he went out to check the shelter belt, thirty of the little trees had been destroyed.

'Stuart,' I whisper into the dark. 'St—'
'Fug,' he mumbles. 'Fug. G'fug . . . Fugoff. Fug*off*.'

Carlos and Leah checked and rechecked the certificate of title, the survey plans and the memorandum of transfer. All the land around the stream was theirs. The shelter belts were well inside the boundary, and the land up to the dirt road belonged to them.

'Fuck him,' Carlos said. The planting went well for the next fortnight. Only little Leon remained uneasy, refusing to go over the paddocks without an adult. At night he dreamed that the Eelman was coming and was often found in the morning to have crept into his older brother's bed.

Two weeks after the first lot of trees had been destroyed, Carlos went out in the morning and found that three hundred more were dead. They had been uprooted and mangled, and crushed beyond repair. He put a brave face on it to Leah. He couldn't bear her anxiety. 'Everything's fine,' he said. 'It's an extra expense but we'll handle it, we'll keep going and in the end everything will be all right.' He rejected Leah's suggestion that they go to the police. He said, 'There's no need to let things get out of hand.'

At the interview in the jail Carlos spoke slowly but with precision. He is articulate. He told us today that his favourite leisure activity is reading. Looking at him you would think that the only things he'd read would be tabloids, racing pages and tool catalogues. The A4 pages that he gave to Stuart in the jail contain a lot of detail about the land at Seabrooke, the boundary dispute, the build-up of tensions in the settlement, and the part played in the conflict by the three largest families in the area. The pages are neatly written, and addressed, in some sort of blunt prison-issue crayon, with Stuart's full name: 'To Stuart Rainer Chicane, barrister and solicitor, facts relating to my land at Seabrooke and the problems encountered during development of the land, and details of my dealings with three Seabrooke families, the Garlands, the Seabrookes and the Leonards.'

There are absolutely no details of the shooting. The last hour that Carlos spent as a normal man remains a black hole.

Stuart is suspicious that Kendrick Stain is showing too much interest in Lehman. Stuart has spent hours gossiping on the telephone as usual and heard that certain inmates have said things to certain barristers during visiting times about Stain talking to Lehman. Stuart doesn't want his client to go off with someone else, especially not Stain. He has rung Stain twice and spoken to him jovially about nothing in particular. (Keeping your friends close and your enemies closer.) He came off the phone this evening grinning. 'My God he's a disgrace, that Stain.' Stain has invited Mrs Fink-Jensen to a meeting with one of his former clients. Mrs Fink-Jensen declined, preferring to visit the families of crime victims accompanied by journalists and photographers from various gasping women's magazines. Mrs Fink-Jensen has made another complaint about Stain. Apparently he told her a vile joke while talking to her on the telephone, a joke containing references to bodily functions, dogs and fish.

Stuart is determined that he will get Lehman bailed. He has an instinct about these things, he says. He will prepare a bail application as soon as possible and file it in the High Court at Auckland.

Stuart contacted a psychiatrist this evening. Dr Phyllis du Fresne, author of a textbook, *The Mind in Balance*, has undertaken to examine Lehman and prepare a report giving her opinion of his state of mind.

'She thinks it's an interesting case,' Stuart whispered while Dr du Fresne had put down her phone to go and find a pen. 'She wants me to call her Phyllis. Fine with me, I told her De Freznee's a bugger to get the mouth around. She could be helpful with the bail . . .'

Lehman's wife Leah has moved off the Seabrooke property

and is living in Auckland with the four children in a two-bedroom flat on the North Shore which belongs to her parents. The children are pale and spooked, traumatised. Leah says that she is all right, it's just that she is ill with grief. She is getting extra money from her family and will be able to survive. But she is afraid to surface. Soon she will have to enrol the children in the local school. She doesn't want them to get behind. For the moment the children are doing schoolwork at home. They all use her surname, Levine, and stay at home quietly most of the time.

'Stuart,' I whisper quietly, expecting nothing. In a perfectly normal voice from under the covers he says, 'Another thing, I've decided that we'll have to visit Seabrooke. We need to have a look at the area, map it out in our minds. You and I'll just go quietly down there. If we announce our presence we'll probably get our heads blown off. Know what I mean?'

'Well . . .'

'Shut up. Go to sleep. In a few days we can meet Dr Phyllis du Fresne. She sounds useful . . . She's keen . . . Tomorrow is . . . another day . . . hmmm.'

A few hours later I'm awake. It's daylight. Stuart isn't beside me. I stretch, and kick him in the head. My mind clears, I open an eye. Stuart forms a mound under the duvet. He works his way between my legs. I inhale luxuriously, preparing myself aerobically for whatever athletic morning foreplay he might have in mind. I wait. Instead of beavering away with his usual vigour he remains still. All is silent in the room. My knees twitch nervously. The seconds pass. He clears his throat and delicately lifts the side of the duvet. He moves his head further down, one hand holding up the edge of the duvet to let in the light. I can't stand it any longer. What is he looking at? What has he found? A bump? A growth? A *herpe*?

'Hang on a minute,' he says. 'Don't move.'

Kicking him in the eye I shinny up the bed.

'Well, I've got the idea now,' he says to himself. 'The lie of the land. The perineum . . . It's not far between the two . . . So, screwing or actually raping someone, in the heat of the moment, could you think that you were aiming for the, um, conventional . . . the front bit, but accidentally sort of *skid* along the perineum and end up banging the back by mistake? I wonder if you could argue that? After all, there has to be intent, sodomy and things to do with the *bum* are always such a problem . . . Have to show there was pretty fast and furious consenting sex, of course . . .'

'Of course!' I scream, slamming the bathroom door off its hinges. 'Keep your rape cases to *yourself* !'

Cheerfully Stuart makes some notes, whistles Howard and thumps down the stairs, singing his usual peppy little morning tunes.

Much later in the day we are all at work. Stuart is at his desk, eating wheaten oatie biscuits and Vera is hunched gloomily at the word processor, her back hanging in a fold over the top of the groaning swivel chair. The dog lies regally on the window seat, occasionally emitting a vile stench. I am reading the last of the Lehman letters.

The doorbell rings. Client! We go into a quiet flurry. The dog is shoved out the side door. Vera fans the room with a magazine, Stuart whips out the air freshener. Vera crams the wheaten oaties into her pocket and the client is ushered in and seated and offered coffee or tea. The client is accompanied by a pale little girl, aged about six or seven. Stuart pops his head up from under the desk where he has been scrabbling and heaves a bulging file up onto the desk.

'Now,' he says, leaning over, shaking hands, 'Shaylene, how are you, how is little K'Tel? And what are we working on today, refresh my memory, is it the shoplifting, the agg-rob, the blood-alc?'

'Just the arson,' Shaylene smiles shyly. 'And the other thing . . .' She is tiny and freckled, not much more substantial than her daughter, little K'Tel, who stands against the wall shifting from one foot to the other. They have the same shy, sly look, like little animals.

'The arson, that's it, I've got all the papers here. Christ they lie don't they, these cops. K'Tel dear would you like a bickie? Vera get K'Tel a bickie, will you.' He shuffles through the file, pen in mouth. 'OK. Here we are. Your ex-boyfriend's made the complaint, says you've burnt his clothes, his furniture, his new girlfriend's clothes, her furniture, his hedge, his outdoor washhouse, and set fire to his neighbour's hedge. Any particular beef with the neighbour or was that collateral damage?'

Out in the kitchen Vera and K'Tel have opened another packet of biscuits. (K'Tel has had two, Vera's had nine.) K'Tel is talking happily, blowing a sticky spray of crumbs with each consonant.

'Shaylene's my mum.' Vera and I nod kindly. Poor mite. Vera's eyes bulge as she chews speechlessly. 'My mum's an insect survivor.' Vera's eyes widen. They look like bloody golf balls. She stares at K'Tel, her hand automatically pawing the empty plate. 'My goodness,' she tries to say.

'M'Goonce,' she says. 'I big your parn, dear? Do you know about that? But how dreadful!'

Shaylene has recently become a client of the popular psychotherapist and astrologer, Sunshine Reynolds. After her first few sessions of role-playing, scream therapy and crystal-fondling, the therapist announced that Shaylene had had regular sex with her father, Poppy Marks, from the age of six until the age of about twelve. Puzzled, Shaylene came immediately to consult Stuart. The thing that Shaylene couldn't quite get her mind around was that she had absolutely no memory of this torture occurring. She had tried, with Sunshine's help and pointers, to remember it, but had failed miserably.

'I've let Sunshine down,' she said gloomily in Stuart's office last month. 'She's gone to all this trouble to sort out my head and I can't come up with anything. She says it'll come out in time, it's just very deeply hidden. The mind's way of coping, the horror of the experience, all that.'

Apparently Shaylene's therapist has an excellent reputation

for sniffing out sexual abuse. She has a real *nose* for it. She is never discouraged when the patient has no memory of being abused. In fact, to her the very *lack* of memory is an important clue. According to her theory there is no memory of the abuse because the suffering was so traumatic that the memory of it has been subconsciously suppressed. No memory of it? Must have been an orgy! (You could ask whether people come out of other bad experiences with amnesia. Wars. Famine. Disaster. Ask Sunshine too many questions and she'd prescribe you a herbal poultice and a fiery enema, and send you packing. Unbeliever! Fascist!)

Unfortunately for Poppy Marks, Shaylene has been helped to remember some pretty sordid incidents. She has suddenly become adept at dredging up the colourful and disturbing events that have been lurking in her subconscious. The time when he peered through the . . . the look he gave her as he . . . the brutal agility with which he . . .

'She has opened up a whole new world to me,' Shaylene keeps telling Stuart. Denied access to his grandchild, Poppy Marks also faces a criminal prosecution. He has been ringing Shaylene threatening suicide, which has meant that she has just had to instruct Stuart to take out a non-molestation order on him.

'Sometimes he rings up sobbing,' Shaylene confides. 'It's so *creepy*. I just hang up and ring the police.'

Sunshine Reynolds and Mrs Fink-Jensen seem to come together warily on some issues, the hanger-and-flogger and the caring professional. Sunshine just wants to help Poppy, and Barbara just wants to cut off his balls. But they both want to kill him. And they both need him around.

In the office the conversation has already turned to Poppy.

'I saw him. I know it was him. *Peeping* through the super-market shelves. I *screamed* for help . . .'

I decide at this point to slip out onto the veranda for a furtive cigarette. Stuart is a non-smoker. He frowns on smoking. He spits on smokers. He tells me it is weak and depraved to smoke. But there's always someone around going to make you feel bad when you want to have a cigarette. All that makes cigarettes even more attractive, of course. Forbidden delights!

Out on the veranda I assess wind direction. No point in going out here if the smoke is just going to fly up and billow in through the office window. (This has happened to me before, the shouts of rage, the slamming windows.)

Shaylene is still murmuring in the office. I hear the odd snore or grunt from Stuart. Shaylene will have to go soon so that we can get back to drafting documents for Carlos Lehman.

It is fresh out here looking down at the grey sea. Now it starts to rain on the cold harbour and the wind whips the spray off the waves and the air is full of water and the sound of the rain falling on the leaves. When I go inside Shaylene is getting ready to leave, bundling little K'Tel ahead of her. K'Tel's mouth is covered in jam, she is sad that she has to leave. 'Come again soon, dear,' Vera calls after her. Charming child. So sad. We are like a family waving them off from the veranda. Even the dog comes out to watch them as they climb into their battered white car, K'Tel in the back seat, looking out the rear window, madly waving.

Back in the office we resume our positions. I go back to Carlos Lehman. Back to Cyril Leonard and his brother, the Eelman.

4. Speaking of death

In the morning, before the meeting with Dr Phyllis du Fresne and Carlos Lehman's wife, Stuart went to the Family Court with Shaylene Marks and I took two hours off to visit my sister. It had been raining since early morning and the world was shrouded under the hot blanket of the low cloud. I drove over the bridge, parked, and walked through the fine foggy mist all the way to her house.

Una sat at her kitchen table feeding her son a banana and drinking coffee out of a big blue bowl. Her kitchen is spacious, painted yellow, decorated with finger paintings and pot plants.

In the next room her husband Benedict was lying inert on the floor watching television. Benedict works in orthopaedics, long hours in the bloodbath of the emergency room. His busy time is the middle of the night when the young bro's of South Auckland climb into their Chrysler Valiants and head off down the motorway for some hilarious drunk-driving and pedestrian-maiming. When the bloody and screaming wrecks are brought into the hospital, Benkie springs into action with the latest bone repair techniques. Having smashed his leg to pieces a road warrior would once have had to lie in traction for months. These days, Benkie opens the leg up from the buttock and feeds a metal rod through the bone. The patient can be up and hobbling around after forty-eight hours. Not long after that he can be driving again. Right in the middle of the poorest part of Auckland, the hospital is grim, shabby and besieged. In the waiting room the drunk, tattooed and angry clientele mass together threateningly. Grief-stricken relatives try to bash up the nearest piece of furniture or staff member. Benkie calls his work 'Brorepairs'. It's hard lines out there in South Auckland.

'Someone brings in his wife and she's been beaten up, by her brother, say, with a baseball bat. Just a minor family row, you know. Or they bring in a kid who's been chastised with a piece of metal piping. Some wrangle over homework.'

He treated a guy who'd had his leg broken in a fight and who crawled home and smoked dope for eight days without realising that his leg was rotting. Last week Benkie treated a woman in A&E who had been lying on waste ground for days, unnoticed. She had an open wound which was full of maggots.

In the wards the patients steal everything they can find to steal. Every day the visitors cruise out of the hospital, their clothes clanking and jingling with concealed booty.

'I saw that old Romaniuk today,' Una said. 'In Remuera.'

'I saw him too,' Benkie called from the next room. 'In Mangere, five o'clock in the morning. That old man really gets around. Never in a car. Always walking and walking.'

'Romamuck,' said Harry, mumbling on his banana. 'Moramuck.'

'Mucky pup,' said Una with moist fondness.

Sometimes I think Una's lucky, with her baby and her domestic scene. She hasn't done things the way you're supposed to these days. Career first, then planned parenthood when you're a hurrying, maybe desperate thirty-five or forty-year-old. Then pop the baby into a crèche and hurry back to the office, terrified that you've lost your place on the ladder.

I stared narrowly at Una. She looked cool. She looked happy. She has a degree, in journalism. But when she got pregnant she said, what's the problem? I'll work part-time, I'll work from home. Or do babies first, career second. Una always does what she likes. She never worries or panics, she has a talent for being happy. Once she said to me, 'I don't feel trapped being at home with Harry. I can do what I like whenever I like. You know how I feel really? Free.'

'Tell me what you've been doing then,' she said. We drank coffee. I told her a bit about Carlos Lehman. I have read the rest of the statements in his file, and all of his notes. In fact I have read through the whole lot again three times. The statements and notes are so detailed. It is unusual to read a statement in which the maker is so well able to articulate the facts of the case.

After a while I went outside onto the lawn with Harry. We crouched down under the tree. Harry ignored me. He stared up into the white sky. My nephew is a solemn and intelligent child. Sometimes you'll turn around and Harry will be staring at you steadily from behind a chair or a couch. After a moment he'll turn away with a shrug, as if he finds your behaviour inexplicable and faintly distasteful, or childish. It's unnerving. Even though he is only a baby he is already like Una, slender, deft and inscrutable.

In this sort of weather there is no face to the world. Everything is blurred. There are no hard edges. You lose that raddled look you get after a long spell of dryness. That Australasian old-leather-handbag look of too much UV and wind and chlorine. I commented on the weather to Harry. He was still looking up into the sky. Looking up I could see that the sun was shining faintly through the clouds and there was a ring around it, as there sometimes is when the sky is covered in cloud and there is a fine misty rain.

The ring was huge in circumference, just a single pale band. The sun was dead centre.

'Do you know, Harry,' I said, 'there's an owl in Stuart's garden that I hear hooting every night. It's a morepork. And suddenly it's begun hooting *during the day*. It goes on and on for hours. It seems apocalyptic. It's the sort of thing that happens when darkness is about to descend over the land, when people race in frightened groups to the supermarket and buy all the canned food they can carry. Is something terrible about to happen? Is it linked to the ring around the sun?'

I leaned close to Harry, whispering in his ear. I kissed his warm cheek. Finally he looked around at me. An owl? Just so, an owl. Strange portents and signs. He smiled, and looked away over the vegetable patch, where the weeds had grown to monstrous proportions and Una's vegetables hung fatly in the tangled vines and Harry's tennis balls were lost, somewhere in a hidden place in the uncharted centre.

I gave Una an outline of the things that went on in the town of Seabrooke before Carlos Lehman committed his crime. Stuart remarked drily last night that Lehman certainly chose a very bad time to commit a murder, when every night we are hearing on television of the rising tide of crime and mayhem threatening the very fabric of society.

But there hasn't been any publicity about it. Mrs Fink-Jensen is busy with other things. She plans to set up a project to send child crime victims to Disneyland. This seems to be done frequently in this country, when children become publicly bereaved, or are dying of cancer or AIDS. Charities raise some funds, pack them into balloon-filled jumbo jets crewed by adults in clown suits, and propel them across the world to Disneyland. Perhaps I'm forgetting what things are like when you're a child. Perhaps they enjoy it. Personally I can't think of anything worse, if my world and my body were falling apart. Mrs Fink-Jensen's children stared out of the newspaper photos pallidly, with wild grins. I wonder whether they would really prefer to be left in peace, especially the dying ones.

I guided Harry back into the house. I didn't want to be late for Mrs Lehman and Dr du Fresne.

Inside Una was having an irritable exchange with Benkie; she was refusing to do something or other. Benkie came to the back door. 'My wife been giving *you* any trouble this morning? She's been beating me up all morning. No? Well, call me if she gets violent.'

I could hear the unease in his little laugh. Big Benkie, he's so straightforward and mild. He has no kinks or quirks, no meannesses or angst. He and Una never argue seriously. It would make him unhappy if they did, it would make him nervous. But he doesn't need to worry. Una loves him. She isn't savage with him as she was with her old admirers. She allows him everything. I love him, she says, because he's honest.

Una is always in control in her relations with Benkie, she never falls to bits. Where did she get all that control, I often wonder. Why didn't I get any? Take my life with Stuart. Why do I have this feeling sometimes of confusion, things unexplained? Some days I feel he treats me like one of his employees, and this fills me with a terrible pain. On days like that I spend hours sloping about, worrying about it. I can't disguise it.

'What's the matter with you?' he says. 'Do something useful. Water the plants! What am I living with, a fruitcake?'

'Ah go to hell!' I shout. 'Leave me alone!'

And somehow it changes again, with something small, he takes out a handkerchief, fumbles with it and blows his nose, and for some reason, is it the fumbling fingers or the creased handkerchief or the awkward way he stuffs it back in his pocket? for some reason I love him all over again.

Oh get above it, Una would say. Stop wanting all the time. Let things come to you. But she has been saying those things to me all our lives.

'Goodbye, goodbye!' Una gave me a bag of lemons, Harry kissed me on the cheek. They stood at the door and waved as I set off across the city under the high, pale sky, under the weather, and the ring around the sun.

I feel pent up if I haven't walked at least a few miles a day but Una never walks, only drives around town in her bright little shopping wagon. When Harry was born Una recovered well from all the obvious wounds and scars – episiotomy, stretched stomach muscles, ruined pelvic floor. But it still looks like hard work, motherhood.

I hurried across town towards the bridge. Mrs Fink-Jensen is a mother of ten. To have so many children, it's just out of control. She must have started having them at the age of about twelve. Our mother only managed to have Una and me, she had Una at about thirty-eight and me when she was about forty-two. Our parents tried for years to conceive. They went to clinics and specialists. It's hard to imagine they were ever young and sexually active. They are so vague, so gentle, so old.

Our father, Jacques, is becoming more and more vague. He spends all his time under the house in his workshop, where he grinds things and saws things and hammers and sharpens and screws. When we were children Jacques used to build us toys and gadgets. Una's favourite was the shock machine. Jacques made it for her and encased it in a little wooden travelling box with a handle. When you opened the lid there were two terminals mounted on a wooden base. You would put a finger on each of the terminals and an electric shock would pulse through your whole body. Una carried it around the neighbourhood giving shocks to unsuspecting children and adults: 'Just put your fingers on the knobs Mrs Smith.' The shock was pretty strong.

Our house was a jumble of appliances, gadgets and pets. Jacques liked to take things apart. He took everything to bits, the fridge, the washing machine, the drier, the blender, whether they needed seeing to or not. Now as he has got more aged and vague, his taking apart has become even more recreational and unreliable. Jacques used to be an engineer. These days I wonder, as I come upon him dismembering another household item, whether he's really all there, and whether Phoebe is altogether safe as she wades through the wiring, tripping over electric drills and handsaws, and mumbling in her vague and genial way, 'That one's on the blink too, is it? Good-oh.'

If I ever think about the two of them it's in a helpless way, filled with terrible love and burning pity. They are so old, so kindly, so unhip. The idea of them being killed by an electrical fire or an exploding appliance brings real tears to my eyes. One day last week I went to their house and Jacques was wandering about in sandals and socks and a decaying gardening hat. Phoebe had her hair, her wiggery, done in the usual bizarre, hairsprayed plume . . .

Many people resent their parents, for never understanding them and repressing them and probably marring them for life. Naturally I've raged at mine on many occasions, stormed out into the night full of indignation and claustrophobia at some piece of parental idiocy. But now, when I'm confronted with their kindly bewilderment, their desire for me to do well, their sandals and socks, what can I do? I'd protect them against anything if I could. Anything.

Una didn't need to fight with Phoebe and Jacques. She would ask for nothing and somehow get everything she wanted. She was always self-sufficient, her personality was her fortress. I have an image in my mind, perhaps real, perhaps imagined, of our parents knocking politely on her door and asking her if there was anything they could do . . .

If only *I* was like Una. I began to go over my last conversation with Stuart, my red-faced struggles for control, my ill-disguised discomfort, my anger and my demands. Where does he go when he won't tell me where he's going? What is he doing when he won't tell me anything at all? What will happen if I go on complaining like this? Will we break up, will he . . . will I . . . get *fired*?

I knew it would take me another half an hour to get home. At least. I would be in time, just. I wondered how many miles I walk per week. All this walking cannot be profitable. And what do I think about when I am walking? Am I pondering usefully about the files? Am I bettering myself, helping the common wheel, making money? Am I *achieving*? Occasionally. Once in a while. But what I'm really doing a lot of the time is going nowhere in particular. I remember a quote from somebody famous, who was it, who played patience a lot, all the time. When asked why, he said, I play this game a lot, all the time because it is the closest thing to being dead.

Speaking of death. It is not a pretty sight. Carlos Lehman really made a mess. Stuart had the photos at home for me to look at before the arrival of Mrs Lehman and Dr du Fresne. Quite a gruesome one. A concrete yard, oilstained and cracked. Weeds struggling up through the stones. A red and white oil drum, its shadow bisecting a Jackson Pollock of blood and brains. The small man lying on his stomach with one leg hooked over the other. His head turned sideways, brown hair falling over his face and a hand pressed to the side of the head. The small man trying to hold his head together, trying to get it straight. Imagine the small man spinning into death in a micro-second without any time to . . . without any warning of . . .

'Pathologist's report page four,' said Stuart. 'Usual crap.'

Imagine the small man dying there in the sun beside the old oil drum on the grey stones. Holding his hand over his face. He's wearing a faded blue shirt, old blue corduroy trousers.

Sandals and socks.

5. Shame

Cyril Leonard was not a big man. Nor was he particularly tough, or threatening. How did he come to die so violently that day in front of his house, in front of his wife?

'For this reason,' Stuart said, 'he copped it. He copped it even though he was less to blame than most of the other members of the three families. He got it in the head because he pushed the button right at the time that the bomb was going to go off. And what are we left with? A victim who appears largely blameless, a killing which appears essentially random.'

For months the townspeople of Seabrooke tormented and frustrated the Lehmans. The damage to the shelter belts continued. Despite this, Carlos pressed on with the planting of fruit trees. For a time the crop seemed to be surviving untouched. Carlos and Leah hoped that the trouble might be over. Then, one night, a boundary fence was cut. Fifteen cows strayed through the gap and in the space of a few hours, destroyed almost all of the tiny trees. Carlos heard the cows at 4 a.m. He lay awake for a moment, confused. When he realised what he could hear he leapt out of bed and tore out into the paddock. He picked up a piece of damaged fence post and hit the cows over their heads and legs, he clawed at their hides, in a frenzy he tried to drive them out through the small space in the wire. But they scattered and circled in terror and confusion, and the more he tried to drive them out the worse the damage became. Sobbing with rage he lashed out at the cows with the fence post, trying to smash their bones, pierce their hides. He stopped finally when he heard Leah screaming at him to stop. As he limped back into the house he stared at Leah's pale face, at her misery and distress, and he was overwhelmed with a feeling of shame. He was being beaten; in front of his family, in front of his beloved wife, these bastards were beating him down. From that day on, more than the indignation, more than the sense of injustice and rage, what crippled him most of all was this feeling of *shame*.

Leah took the children to help at the local fair. None of the women there would talk to her. At morning tea time she rounded up the children and left, enraged by the wall of silence, the quiet smirking and childish whispering. How could these women be so blatant, so basic? Rage carried her out to the car. She sat in the driver's seat and felt that she could have cried, except that the children were there asking why they had to leave and shouting and giggling and fighting as usual. She made an excuse to them. They would drive to the beach instead.

As she drove she wondered what on earth was going on. It had to be to do with the neighbour, Boyderman Leonard, and the boundary. The land agent had said something strange to Carlos about the Leonards. 'The Leonards don't really understand about boundaries,' he had said. 'They just think that all the land in the area that doesn't belong to the Garlands or the Seabrookes belongs to them. The families have been here since the missionary days. They're quite tight, that lot. I'd try to get on with them mate, if I were you.' The land agent's secretary said to Carlos one day on the phone, 'You're buying the Tohunga Block. Hope you've asked Boyderman Leonard.'

Leah sat in the office. She sniffed. Stuart handed her a tissue. Dr Phyllis du Fresne scrabbled with her papers.

'He's very intelligent, you know. I was struck with it when I interviewed him. Quite a sensitive guy.'

Leah looked up and gave Phyllis a withering look.

Phyllis coughed nervously. 'I believe he began to be seriously withdrawn when the police threatened to charge him with damaging the fence line. The police seem to have been quite staggeringly unfair about the whole dispute.'

Phyllis was perched neatly on the window seat. 'The thing is, I can't say he *won't* reoffend. I mean I'm not a clairvoyant. But I can talk in terms of likelihoods, based on my professional opinion.'

'With you, Phyllis,' approved Stuart. 'More tea, Phyllis, bickie, er, sausage roll?' He beamed at her.

'No, no thank you, Mr Chicane, Stuart.'

'Just reach for one if you want one, I'll just pop them here on the arm of my chair.'

'The affidavit,' I interjected icily.

'Yes, right, yes. We have Leah here to say that she supports and approves of the idea of bail. We have Carlos's parents who say that they want him to live with them. We have (I hope!) Phyllis's opinion that the public won't be endangered if he is allowed to live in the community. There would have to be strict conditions, of course, restrictions on his movements, virtual house arrest probably, regular reporting. Anything is better than jail, eh?'

'So I might need to swear an affidavit then?' Phyllis asked, handing the plate to the glowering Leah. She was enjoying herself. Leah looked as if she was chewing her way through a particularly disgusting meal. She was trying to be polite. She swallowed. Her eyes watered. She sat listening to Phyllis give a crisp summary of her first interview with Carlos. Phyllis had wiry hair and bulging blue eyes behind chic spectacles, and a special glow about her which told you that she understood *everything*. And what's more, she cared. How she cared. Her sweater was a cashmere of the palest pink and her shirt was white linen. She was all delicate and fluffy. Her handshake was immaculately clean and chilly. She looked at Leah in a special way as she tuned herself in to Leah's life.

'Don't tell me. Let me guess. You sit down in the evening and you haven't thought about yourself all day. Not once. All the children, the problems. Your husband in *prison*, for goodness' sake. What we have to learn to do, Leah, is to put *ourselves* back into the equation. *We* matter too. Talk to yourself. What does Leah want now? Do something only for Leah.'

Leah walked up and down by the window, thin and brown and restless. Phyllis was talking with her eyes closed, being Leah on the couch at the end of the day. She opened her eyes, exhaled and smiled. Leah looked at her angrily and then looked at Stuart with the question clear in her face: Do I have to put up with this hopeless drongo all afternoon?

Phyllis saw. Her glow disappeared. She gave Leah a considerably less caring look.

'Carlos is very concerned about the children,' she said in a light little voice.

'The children are fine,' Leah said, looking dangerously at Phyllis. 'As fine as can be expected, considering what their father is charged with.'

'Children need special *handling* at times like this, times of extreme stress. They react very badly if they are not allowed to *express* themselves. They need loving feedback, not anger and negativity. Above all, a sympathetic ear . . .'

Leah looked as if she would launch herself across the room and attack Phyllis. Phyllis was leaning forward in her chair, also poised, as if she would run Leah through with her Biro. Her glow had turned to steel. Stuart looked dismayed. He said to Phyllis rather roughly, 'You have children yourself, Phyllis?'

The psychiatrist looked away from Leah and sat back in her chair with a coy smile. There was a pause. 'I have a lovely cat,' she said, thinly. 'There's just the two of us actually, now.' She coughed and looked tightly out of the window. Leah gave a snort from the window seat. Stuart looked astonished. Christ! He said in an exasperated voice, 'If we could get to the main matter in hand? Our bail application?' He looked over at Leah. 'Vera, get Leah a cup of coffee, will you.'

Sensing that she had lost his goodwill, Phyllis became efficient. She took out her notes and, arranging them in front of her, began to talk quickly, with just a hint of hurt in her voice.

She had been given as much time with Carlos as she wanted. The authorities had been completely accommodating. Carlos had talked to her freely and cooperatively. He had seemed to enjoy it; in fact, he seemed to gain something from the encounter, a momentary sense of peace, perhaps . . . Phyllis looked up at the stony faces in the room. She hurried on. 'I think you will find that the opinion which I formed is the one which you want to hear. In my view, now that he has been removed from the situation of extreme provocation in which he was living there is nothing to suggest that he will behave violently again. He has no history of violence. He appears to have no psychiatric illness. There is nothing irrational in anything he says. He feels an enormous degree of horror and remorse for what has happened. He is unable or as yet unwilling to talk about the actual shooting. It may well be that he truly does not remember it. He goes as far as to say that he remembers the terrible rage he felt during the argument with Mr Leonard. Then, he says, something just "snapped". The event was clearly utterly traumatic for him. It seems to me that if he comes out and lives quietly with his parents in a country town he won't pose any greater threat to the public than a person bailed on a burglary charge.'

Phyllis enunciated clearly. She emphasised her words with a little click of her nail on the table. Stuart perked up.

'That's the ticket, Phyllis!' He began to map out an affidavit for her. That her middle name turned out to be Marmora brought a series of questions on spelling from Vera, who laboured over the word processor with her tongue stuck out of the corner of her mouth. Phyllis sighed happily. 'My mother chose the name for me when she first laid eyes on me. It means "Radiant".'

Stuart glanced over at Leah. She was sitting on the window seat chewing her nails. 'I'll bring you a cold drink,' he said to her softly.

Phyllis's affidavit was typed up in half an hour. Stuart began to talk to Leah. She told him about her children. About life in the town. She didn't look at Phyllis.

Soon after the fence being cut and the cows trampling the Lehmans' trees their small son, Leon, had become ill.

'He's an asthmatic,' Leah explained. 'He has always been the sickly one. He was very aware of the tension in the house because he was home all the time, off school. He had bronchitis. At one stage we were worried that it was going to turn into pneumonia. He had been frightened by Boyderman Leonard, also he and my other son were being bullied at the school. He came down with a very bad attack of eczema, all over his body. He looked a terrible sight with his skin all inflamed and weeping. I could hardly stand to see him suffering so much. The people in the town saw him and behaved as though we were neglecting him and that it was our fault that he looked so terrible. He was very thin. We took him to the GP in Tauranga regularly, and to the children's clinic at the hospital. They said that they weren't too concerned about him in the long term. He looked a wreck, but he would grow out of the eczema in time, and maybe even the asthma too. They said he would be all right in the end.'

Leah looked up. Stuart made a quick gesture with his hand, telling her to continue. We sat silently, listening.

Leon was in agony with the eczema. Leah had difficulty preventing him from tearing his skin with scratching and scratching. When he had recovered from the bronchitis she took him and her two little girls into Seabrooke to buy groceries. While she gathered up the goods in the shop Leon stood by the drinks refrigerator, pressing his boiling face against the cold door. She watched him as she wheeled the trolley through the aisles. Her daughters looked so healthy, one in the backpack and one in the seat on the front of the trolley. They were compact and tough, sturdy little outdoor girls. But the day before, as Leah waited at the school gate with Leon for the older boy, Mrs Lillian Seabrooke had said loudly to Boyderman Leonard's sister, 'Why doesn't she do something about that boy's skin? It's a scandal.'

And why didn't the old bag and her disgusting family leave them alone? Leah was bitter and sour with anger. She spent so much time worrying about Leon, taking him to the clinic where they tried out all kinds of inhalers and lotions, things to bathe in and rub on, choke down or sniff up. He was five and a half years old and already like a heavily medicated little old man with his rasping breath and his little sticks for legs. Sometimes she kissed him and his breath smelt of chemicals. When he was sick he stared out at her from a mask of flaming swollen skin and wheezed all through the night and broke the skin on his eyelids by constantly rubbing his watering eyes.

She pushed the trolley through the dim shop. Leon was out of sight behind the shelves. Leah hurried. Morven Garland, the shopowner, waited smirkingly at the counter. He punched the prices up on his little digi-till. Leah added it up in her head. He named the right price. Handing him the money, she heard Leon give a yelp. Garland's married daughter Tracey, who helped in the shop, lumbered up behind Leah. 'You should do something about that boy,' she said. 'There's something wrong with him. He needs a doctor.' She leered triumphantly, her freckled chin jutting forward. Leah ran to the back of the shop. There was the little old figure of the small boy bent over by the fridge door. She straightened him up. With horror she realised that he had wet his pants. He hadn't done that since he was a toddler. There must be something terribly wrong with him . . .

Leah bundled him up. She was shaking. Tracey Garland stood behind the counter vibrating with self-righteousness. 'What did you do to him?' Leah shouted, beside herself. 'Don't you *dare* go near him again!' She hurried out of the shop, banging into a shelf and knocking over the newspaper stand. They came out and stood in the doorway as she pushed the children into the car. Garland shook his head in disbelief. His daughter smirked.

'She's mad. Crazy. The whole family is cracked!'

'We're not. We're *not*!' Leah shouted absurdly out of the car window. 'Leave us alone. He's just a *child*.'

Tracey Garland laughed angrily. 'A cracked child!' she called, after the swerving car.

When she got home Leah carried Leon into the house and took off his clothes. She could see at once that he had a high temperature. She calmed down. He had not collapsed, he was just very unwell. She had taken him out of the house too soon and he had relapsed. He threw up on the floor. She washed him down and got him into bed.

When she walked into the sitting room with the girls she stopped in surprise. Carlos was lying on the couch. He should have been working. Was he sick? She went over to him.

'Listen, I think we should leave. We should try and sell and go back to Mount Maunganui because we've been here for months and we're really getting nowhere . . .'

Carlos didn't move.

'It's not us I'm worried about, it's the kids . . .' Her voice rose too high, into a squeak. He didn't move. He lay absolutely still. There was no sound in the room. A blowfly buzzed at the window. She found herself gazing at his bare foot, which dangled limply from the edge of the couch. Beyond, out the window, the washing blew about in the sunshine under the empty blue sky.

Leah drew in a long quavering breath. The blowfly droned across the room, careered against the windows, and bounced back. It flipped, nosedived, righted itself. Spiralling down, it landed gently on Carlos's foot and began crawling busily along the skin. The foot didn't move. In jerky bursts the fly made its way down towards Carlos's big toe. Leah drew in another breath and held it.

'Car,' she said softly. 'Car. Car. Carlos.' Then she was screaming, 'Carlos, for Christ's sake move. What's wrong with you,
there's a fucking fly on your foot, *move*!'

She kneeled over him, shaking him. He looked at her through
red, swollen eyes. He turned his head away.

'Get away,' he said. 'I don't need you. Just fuck off. Fuck off.'

Leah knew that her parents would finally think that they had
been proved right. They had told her years ago that she was
doing the wrong thing, with her university degree and her private
school education, going off and marrying a half-brown man who
wanted to keep her living outside Auckland like some hippie or
peasant bumpkin. They were wrong of course because Carlos
was sharp. He was the most unusual and intelligent person Leah
had ever met, and he knew exactly what he was going to do. With
Leah helping him he set up a successful business exporting
seafood, and for years living in Mount Maunganui they were
affluent. Affluent enough for her parents, who thawed out when
they came to stay in the long, low house near the Mount and
swam at the beach and ate in the evening on the balcony looking
over the sea. Very luxurious, said her acidic mother, who even
rose to kissing her son-in-law on the cheek and talking to him
affectionately, when no one else was listening.

But later, Carlos got bored. He wanted to have an orchard. He
had always wanted to have one. He didn't want to be dealing
with crayfish for ever. Leah didn't want to move, but when they
sold the business she was impressed at the amount of money
they had made, and she entered into the adventure of moving,
thinking that they would always be secure, no matter what they
did.

Now the whole thing was falling apart. She didn't see how
they could afford to lose trees at the rate they were losing them.
And there had been thefts. In the night bundles of wire had been
taken away, and tools and equipment had mysteriously started to
disappear. She had told Carlos that they needed to build themselves some kind of secure lockup. They had a rickety shed but

soon after they had arrived the padlock and chain on the door had simply disappeared.

They needed to get together, like they had always done. They needed to make a plan. But Carlos was becoming more and more silent and withdrawn. He had agreed that they needed a lockup, and had exhausted himself trying to get the materials together and to build it quickly. He was so concerned about the trees that he woke all through the night to listen and often went outside to prowl around in the dark. He never saw anything suspicious on his night-time patrols, and still the damage went on. When she tried to talk to him he looked at her with pain. 'I'll sort it out,' he said. He seemed to regard the situation as his fault. Sometimes she saw him looking so ashamed. He said to her, 'Don't worry. I'll figure out what to do. I'll make everything OK.'

Leah stopped talking. She had to go to pick the children up from the babysitter. Phyllis, having regained her composure, squeezed Leah's shoulder warmly and whispered something that sounded like 'aroha'.

Ignoring her, Leah said to Stuart on the veranda, 'I'm afraid of what will happen to Carlos in jail. He's so depressed. He's in shock. I keep thinking that if he could come out for a while, we could all adjust to the fact that he'll have to go back in, eventually. The children need to see him. I won't take them to the jail . . .'

Her eyes were dark and exhausted with restlessness and stress. Carlos's expression was blank, as if the feeling had been smoothed off it with a large sponge, but Leah's face burnt with tension. The skin under her eyes was dry and dark. Her life had gone spinning away from her; she struggled to drag it back by the few threads left.

'He has to come out,' she said, with a bitter smile. 'He has to be made to go on *living*.'

'You choose, I'll pay, darling,' said Stuart to me as usual, putting his feet up on the seat next to Phyllis. Phyllis looked around the fashionable café and girlishly applied some lipstick.

He smiled at her and said cosily, 'I recommend the smoked salmon, Phyl. Or the Caesar salad. It's just insane.'

When we were all served, and picking through fashionable salads of stalk and weed and stick, trying to find something familiar and friendly, like a bit of lettuce or a slice of tomato, Phyllis brought out the file containing the entire history of Carlos Henry Lehman.

'He is adopted. His background is quite unusual in some respects.' She picked a piece of bark out of her teeth and put it to the side of her plate.

'His biological father was a lawyer in Wellington, Aaron Forman. He was a successful commercial barrister in fact, and the family was well off and very respectable. When he was in his forties, Carlos's father was living apart from his wife. They had separated by mutual agreement. Isobel Forman was very much a socialite in Wellington. They had no children. She kept the house and he moved into a flat in the city.

'Carlos's mother was a Maori, of the Ngati Whatua tribe in Auckland. Carlos doesn't know how they met, or how long their relationship lasted before his mother became pregnant. What he does know is that she was only about sixteen years old at the time. When her family found out that she was pregnant, they approached Carlos's father. Carlos's father told the family that she had lied to him about her age, and that he had not realised she was so young. He freely admitted that he was probably the father of the child.

'It was decided that she would go off and live with members of the extended family in Auckland and have the baby there, and that Carlos's father would pay for the maintenance of her and the child. Apparently he did pay for Carlos quite willingly and even visited him and the mother on and off, but he died of lung cancer when Carlos was about two. When Carlos was three and a half his mother married and went off with her new husband, leaving Carlos with more of the extended family in Northland. Later again, when he was about eight, he was adopted by the pakeha couple, the Lehmans, who sent him to Dilworth School.'

'So where's the mother?' Stuart and I said at the same time, over the shrieking coffee machine.

'He doesn't know. He thinks she might be in Australia.'

'So she doesn't know what's happened.'

'Most probably not.'

'Is he on good terms with the adoptive parents?'

'Oh yes, definitely, they want him to come out of jail and live with them after all, and he's keen to do that. He's very fond of them.'

'We need their affidavit as soon as possible, um, Stella . . .'

Stuart looked at me blankly for a moment, as if trying to remember who I was, what I meant. 'Also we've got to go there and take a look at the place, sooner rather than later. We'll drive down there. Have you got a notebook on you? We need to complete and file this application soon.'

He ran through a long list of things to do. As usual, business was mixed with domestic: Lehman affidavit, Shaylene Marks's papers, letters to Smith, Jones and Bloggs, buy Persil, doggo-bites, flea-vac, smello-fresh, boggo-hoosh. Phone Ken Stain, phone High Court, dinner Balcony tonight, new veranda plant-pots – Stella to arrange.

I perched on my organically grown flax chair, notebook in hand. Coolly, Phyllis du Fresne looked on.

And now the day was over, and we were in the car. Looking over I said sweetly, waving my notebook and pen, are you sure you don't want me to do anything else? Concrete the drive, perhaps, repaint the ceilings, replant the pohutukawas? Honestly it's no trouble, would you like me to re-route any drains, or anything like that? Or anything *fucking* well like that? Stuart looked sideways at me, dead-pan. 'Aren't you happy in your work?' he said and reached over as we stopped at the lights and kissed me on the neck and hair and cheek.

The lights turned green, the car stalled, two ragged squeegee merchants ran out in front of the car waving their tattered wind-screen brushes, their buckets slopping with dead cloths and filthy suds. They peered in avidly, we looked out at them and shook our heads, their expressions changed from fierce concentration to sullen disgust. They drew back, one giving a harsh shout, the other giving the finger. Over the wooden shop verandas the ragged clouds were high, slanting, racing with the sharp wind out of the west.

'Bastard,' I said, sideways, at the leaning sky.

'Aren't they,' Stuart said smiling, waving them on.

'So,' said Benkie politely, 'what's he like?'

'Oh you know,' Stuart said, 'just the usual.'

'So you're going to defend him, then?' Bernard Cracker asked.

'Mmm. Going to try to get him bail, soon.'

There was an explosion of snorts from around the table.

Bernard's large Australian brother-in-law, whom everyone except Bernard's sister uneasily avoids, said, predictably, 'Better to put a b*oo*llet in his head.'

'Thanks, Stig, we were waiting for you to say something like that.'

'Don't call him Stig,' Bernard's sister snapped. Since Bernard started calling him Stig we've all pretty much forgotten what his real name is.

'There's no way that you'll get this guy bail.'

'And quite right too.'

'The man is a maniac,' Stig announced mournfully.

'You're a maniac.'

Benkie was looking dogged. 'He can't have bail, there's no way that could be justified. The law can't operate in some sort of vacuum.'

'Like Stig's brain.'

We were at the round table at the Balcony. I caught the barman's eye as he looked up from his corner in the bar; he had been watching television with the sound turned off. The programme was *Sale of the Century*, I recognised the loutish presenter (Steve!) in his brutal green suit and Hush Puppies, his angular assistant (Jude!) fawning over a gleaming appliance.

After a while Una and I went out for some air. We stood on the veranda sharing a cigarette.

'How's it all going?' she said.

'Stuart and I are going to Seabrooke tomorrow morning. The next few days are the only time we'll have free to do it.'

'Doesn't it all give you the creeps sometimes?'

'Oh, no, Stuart's under a lot of pressure, that's all.'

'The crime. I mean the crime.'

'Oh the blood and guts, sort of thing, the death and horror aspect . . . No, I mean it's all an academic exercise. Justice is blind. You know what I mean. It doesn't bother me.'

Una stubbed out the cigarette and held both her hands around her wine glass. She shivered and pulled her jacket around her shoulders. 'Since I had Harry I can't read the crime page any more.'

We stood looking over the dark street. I thought of a bizarre confession I read a couple of days ago. A teenage boy who stabbed his neighbour. He said, 'As I stabbed I wasn't saying anything, but I was howling. Aaaoooww, like a dog.'

Bernard's sister came clicking across the veranda. 'They're arguing in there,' she reported flatly.

Bernard's sister Julie usually fills me with hate and boredom. But the three of us talked for a while in a cosy way and it was pleasant, I started to like her, helped in this by the wine. We talked about shopping, fashions, cookery, we discussed supermarkets, car prices, car crashes. There was a sixteen-car pile-up on the southern motorway last night. Benkie worked on a man's leg all night, and saved it from amputation. 'Life is such a lottery,' I murmured. 'It's a wonder we're not all terrified all the time.'

Julie put an arm around my shoulders. I leaned back, feeling loved, rich, warm. Julie said, 'I don't know about you but I feel in my heart that there's some great Being out there controlling everything in a great scheme of things . . .'

She talked on snugly in this way for several minutes. She gave me a little consoling squeeze. Nudged awake, hate and boredom tiptoed quietly back onto the veranda . . .

Inside they were getting through a bottle of port and Bernard was saying to Stuart, it's all a bit of a game to lawyers, I think, all they care about is the legalities, they don't have a sense of social responsibility, and Stuart was saying it would all be a shambles if lawyers didn't concentrate on the law, and Stig was in favour of hanging.

I headed into the pastel glare of the Ladies and was taken aback as usual by my appearance: it was rough, up close under the bright hot lights, cheeks reddened, eyes befuddled. I joined the line along the mirror, the ladies with their hot eyes, busily shading and painting. We laboured away in the neon silence with our rouges and sponges and pencils not looking, like men at the urinal; you don't look. There is nothing angular in my face, I reflected, in fact it looks like the face of someone a bit short. Short on bone structure. Staring out of the mirror as I worked I looked surprised, wary, unreliable. Then I looked. To the left I saw the expensively scalloped splendour of my neighbour's handbag, the tiered mirrored gilt of its interior, the costly products, the gold-plated compacts. And to my right a country mouse struggled to extract her orange chapstick from a pencil case.

I marched back into the restaurant. Across the table Una was as slender and pale and elegant as the Virgin Mary. She smiled sleepily. Stig began to talk earnestly to Julie about a current film, an epic romp in full period costume, widely tipped to win many Oscars. 'Superb,' Stig breathed, his eyes wandering with the port. 'The mansions, the interiors . . .'

'The lovely horses,' Julie sighed, 'the music . . .'

'What about the dialogue?' I suddenly roused myself from the corner of the table. 'The awful dialogue. The corn of it, the schmaltz, unbearable!'

Shocked, they stared at me. They shook themselves. Suddenly there were gulfs, oceans, canyons between us. Lonely and red-faced I wavered, then stuck to my guns.

'You can't honestly take that bit seriously where he cut off his own foot to escape from the mine shaft and she goes back to the place and finds the foot and . . . ' I chuckled merrily, but in vain. They hated me.

Stig was looking at me coldly and Julie said, 'Well, I thought that was a true expression of the character's feelings, and who are we to knock it?'

'We're the audience,' I said, to Stig.

Una came and sat down. Julie said to me, 'What's wrong with you is that you've got no imagination.'

'You like to spoil other people's enjoyment, do you,' Stig said in a low voice.

'What are you talking about? I'm just offering my opinion, about a crap movie.' (Hanged for a sheep as a lamb.)

Taking Julie's arm Stig got up, pulled her out of her chair and led her out onto the veranda.

'I actually thought it was quite a beautiful film,' Benkie said, frowning.

But I really didn't care any more. I just sat there hating myself. What's wrong with me these days? I sat there until it was time to go home, in shame.

Stuart and I strolled arm in arm out to the car. Reeling around on the kerb, refreshed by the night air, I took a deep breath and said, 'It is *not* my turn to drive.' Silence. Stuart put his elbows on the roof of the fat little Porsche. He opened his mouth as if to start to say, so I have to do it like I have to do everything and you just swan around, but then he just shrugged and shut his mouth again and held out his hand for the keys.

Slowly we wove home in the spluttering car. There wasn't a single other car on the dark streets. Stuart steered the little bronze beetle up the drive. Gently he manoeuvred it into the garage, guided it forwards with confidence, another tap on the pedal and another, one last burst, and dully I heard the crack and the smash as we hit the back wall of the garage.

'Don't forget to turn it off,' I called, opening the door and falling out. Oh, I thought, how drunk we are, how drunk. Stuart swam beside me up the basement stairs. Blundering and fumbling in the warm dark, elbowing and jostling we floated our way to the bedroom. It was so dark. How I love the dark.

In bed Stuart rolled around and heaved the covers about and said something from a long way off and soon we were wrapped up together and still I felt drunk, so drunk that I was swirling and sinking into a mood that was like euphoria or peace, the shadows of the trees outside moved on the walls and I felt as if we had sunk underwater and were drifting downwards through waving branches of underwater weed, and then the weight lifted off me and he was gone, and I sat up in bed eyes shut, head spinning, lost in the dark, until he launched himself at me again in a slow underwater tackle knocking me down, forcing me down, pinning me to the bed. Oh I love you, he said.

Looking out of the bedroom window at the harbour I imagine the sleeping city spread out over the hills, from the squalid sprawl of Mangere and Otara in the south (poor Mangere and Otara, those garbage suburbs), back through the middle-market suburbs, over wealthy Remuera with its mansions (Una at the window with a night-light, singing Harry to sleep), to the prison where Carlos lies dead-still in his grey bunk, through the central city, over to me in the north in my house on the cliff, up the slope to the Roundabout Road, where Leah drinks another coffee and stays up late. Somewhere out there Mrs Fink-Jensen snores in her groaning queen-size, with her ghostly little husband by her side, and Kendrick Stain is slumped on frowzy sheets (not his own!) with a woman of easy virtue or a judge's wife. And where is old Romaniuk tonight? Nobody knows. But wherever he wakes up this morning, like Stain, he won't hang around for long.

In the early morning the wind gets up, and out on the balcony I'm still in the grip of this post-drinking insomnia, sipping tea and watching the yachts tossing around down at the marina. We are to go to Seabrooke today. How unwelcome the daylight will be. Sitting up here (I am practically on the roof) in the warm, black, howling dawn, while Stuart sleeps in the rickety bed and all the wooden planks in the house creak and groan, I could be on a ship sailing away to the Islands, I could be tossing on the warm Pacific Ocean.

A thousand tiny waves churn the surface of the marina. Look, out there in the dark, a lone yacht, heading for open sea.

6. South

Eight a.m., the sky low, heavy and dark, we hit the bridge. A clear run into the middle lane. The commuters jostle for space, all going one way into the city. We don't speak. Beyond the rail, far below, the harbour heaves, a sullen green. Further out in the harbour the sea is paler and choppy, it's windy this morning and warm, and rainy. The clouds are moving and shifting and reshaping and black with rain. The metal struts flash by. The bridge gives off a deep metallic drone.

At the top we are held up, threading our way through a slalom of plastic cones and flashing lights. Spots of rain on the window, behind us the North Shore receding, the far west side of the harbour a dark green blur. All around us the swirling air. Water above and water below. If we don't move faster we'll still be on the bridge when the sky gives way and falls into the sea.

I have the map. We're heading down through the island, through to Tauranga and the town of Seabrooke.

SOUTH the signs say as they flash by, this way to Hamilton,

Taupo, Wellington. Big blond Germans and Swedes with towering backpacks dangling sleeping bags and cooking pots, tiny Japanese on overloaded bikes braving the off-season (they're not just on holiday to lie about on a beach, you know!) lift their faces to the sky and drink it in. The cows in the paddocks are motionless. Seagulls perch along the fence lines. Beyond the paddocks lies the silent bush and beyond the bush, more bush, and beyond that, the sea.

Stuart mutters an apology as we roar through a puddle and the hitchhikers reel back under a wave of road water.

Driving past a lone, luggageless Maori, waving his big brown thumb, wearing gang patch and tattoos, Stuart says, 'He looked like a guy I acted for years ago, aggravated robbery I think, he was a nice guy. He had fourteen brothers and sisters. All but one of the brothers were in jail.'

Stuart drives at twice the speed limit. Watch for cops, he says. He looks elegant in his oversized jacket and jeans. He eats Jaffas. We drive mostly in silence. I have a pile of documents on my lap, all typed with the usual form: This notice of motion is filed by Stuart Rainer Chicane whose address for service is at his offices at 31/119 Biss Street. I notice that Vera has made the usual series of glaring spelling mistakes. I correct. I sigh. I eat a Jaffa, and stare out at the green, wet, melancholy land. Stuart twiddles with the stereo and opens a packet of pineapple lumps with his teeth. At the far end of a small town stands a corrugated-iron bus shelter spraypainted with the mysterious word, 'ballsacks'. By the bowling green opposite, old ladies in white uniforms huddle under a marquee. The green is covered with puddled tarpaulin. No play today.

We pull into a roadside tearoom, called the Roadside Tearoom. The counter is manned by a huge stern woman who shouts orders to someone out the back in a heavy Dutch accent. Stuart starts nudging me and snorting and points out a cardboard sign on the wall that reads STRICTLY NO BREAST-FEEDING.

'How about that?' The Dutch battleaxe glares at him. 'I feel like flopping my *dick* out at her,' he whispers down over the brown wooden tray, the two metal pots of tea and two steak and kidney pies in their crackling cellophane. He squirts the sauce out of the red plastic tomato. 'I dare you darling, go up there and flash her your tits.' He chuckles his way through the piping hot pie, all cheery, what with being on the road and out of the office.

We hit the road again. I try to concentrate on my documents but the power lines and the wire fences loop by so rhythmically that my mind becomes dull and my eyelids droop, and every few seconds the roar of the engine seems to stop and a tiny gap of silence fills my ears, as if the car and time and everything else has just stopped, roar stop roar stop it goes, as the power lines swish by. Stuart Rainer Chicane whose address for service . . . the words of the documents blur on the page.

Stuart, humming beside me, steering the car with one finger, glances over at me with that hard look he gives, both steely and amused. His childhood made him tough, he told me once. His parents were either fighting or didn't speak for days at a time. His mother finally died when he was fifteen and his sister was twelve. He told me about his mother once, on one of the rare occasions when he talked about anything pre-dating the 1980s.

Her name was Miranda Chicane. She had Stuart in Wellington at the beginning of the fifties, a few months before she married his father, Martin Chicane.

Before Stuart was born, he told me, Miranda had lived with her mother, but ten days after the birth she took the baby to the suburban house where Martin Chicane lived and presented him with his son. She moved in. The next night Stuart's father went out on the town to celebrate. During the early hours of the morning he came home with his friends and woke the baby by singing drunken songs in the sun porch. When the sun rose in the morning Miranda found Martin on the lawn, covered in frost and nearly dead with the cold. She had to soak him in a hot bath to bring him back to life.

Stuart's mother was a nervous young woman of eighteen and she found her new husband difficult to handle. He, in turn, was bored with her after a few months. Martin was hyperactive, he wanted action constantly, day and night. He was frenetic and frantic and never sat still. After the baby was born Miranda was tired all the time. She retreated into silence.

'Say something,' Stuart's father would say. 'Say something amusing. What have you been doing all day? Have you got a brain in there at all?'

When she offered him no entertainment he went back to playing with the shop assistants in his grocery store. There was a steady supply of jolly girls, eager to get on with the boss. 'Climb up that ladder,' Stuart's father would say, 'get me that box of screws, stretch girl, stretch, reach for it, hooray!'

Stuart told me that the Chicanes' bungalow was built on reclaimed land. The land had once been a rubbish dump, although by the time Stuart's father had bought it you would never have known. The gardens were green and the hedges were trim and pretty. But one morning when Miranda went to the screaming Stuart's cot she began to scream herself, shouting for help and flapping her hands. A huge rat had crawled up from under the house and into the cot and was attacking the baby. When she beat it away it fell onto the floor and scuttled into a corner of the room where it crouched, thrashing its tail furiously. It was bigger than any rat she had ever seen. She snatched up the baby and ran from the house. The baby's head was torn and cut. Hysterical, she ran to the neighbours' house, and a doctor was called to stitch the baby's head. The doctor sat Stuart's mother down and gave her a sedative, she was so distraught. The neighbour's husband and son were eventually sent across the lawn to kill the rat, but it had gone.

After that incident the residents of Everest Street began to see more rats. Stuart's mother saw them often. Under the houses, in amongst the layers of ancient rubbish, the rats were prowling, fighting, eating and breeding. As their numbers increased they began to come up to the surface more regularly. Stuart's mother never got over the sight of the huge rat gnawing the baby's scalp. She pleaded with her husband to let them sell the house but

Martin ignored her and spent most of his time at the shop. The local council set up an eradication programme about six months after the rat had attacked Stuart. The programme was largely successful, but his mother went on seeing rats. Pregnant again, and lonely and in despair, she was well on the way to going mad.

For a long time she kept everything going, Stuart said. She loved Stuart, but a couple of times she took him to the neighbours and left him there, saying that she didn't think he was safe in the house. Stuart's father told him that she would wake every morning at three o'clock, filled with dread. She heard the night man as he went through the silent suburb, emptying the outside lavatories. Night men were always ex-convicts, killers, lunatics. No one else would take such a job. She could never settle back down onto her pillow until the night man had passed on down the road. She heard rustling on the lawn outside and knew that it was rats.

One morning she got everything ready for a trip into town and was stepping out the door when she was seized with a terrible feeling. She couldn't breathe. Her clothes were too tight. Her hands shook. Her whole body had become useless and floppy. She couldn't do anything except lie on the bed and wait for the feeling to pass. Another day she suddenly felt as if she was growing taller and taller and that her head was a tiny pinhead on top of a huge stick figure. Any minute her head was going to separate from her body.

With all these strange feelings coming over her at odd moments Miranda began to tell her husband that she couldn't really go out. It was safer to stay at home where she could hide her fear and shame. But home was full of rats. At night she was troubled by the fear that sharp objects were going to come up through the bedding and stab her. She lay in a ball, with her arms protecting as much of her torso as possible.

'Look, buck up, woman,' Stuart's father would say. 'What have I married, a fruitcake?'

Yes, thought Miranda, secretly terrified. You have.

She was outwardly a stylish woman with a sense of pride. She had another baby and made it into her thirties before she was found out. During a bad bout of her secret problems Stuart's father finally decided that she needed expert help. She was admitted to a mental institution one cold June morning soon after, and began to die there slowly, of shame.

The further south you go the bumpier are the roads. The plan is that we check into something called the Kiwilands Lodge outside Tauranga, and then venture on from there to Seabrooke. 'We don't want to create any fuss. We just want to have a look, check out the scene, and leave. We'll stick out like a sore thumb in this car, so we'll get hold of a more low-key one. If we roll up in a Porsche the locals'll just automatically think that we're wankers and won't talk to us. It's better if they don't know who we are. I favour hiring a ute actually, and putting some hay bales in the back, what do you say, Stellie old man?' He sings: '"You can't hide your lying eyes" . . . Hey baby, it's like we're on holiday.'

Vrrooom. We tear into the south. I take a turn at the wheel. Stuart map-reads, badly. 'No darling, turn left. Back there. Bloody useless map.'

'Give me some warning . . . Jesus.'

In a narrow road between two high banks a man in a swandri flags us down. 'Watch out for the sheep, mate!' A minute later we are surrounded. We inch through the warm, woolly, panicky sea. We watch the sheepdogs running over the sheeps' backs. Sheep thud against the body of the car, bleating their high, sad cries. Stuart reaches out the window and pats the woolly backs. 'It's greasy stuff,' he says, wiping his hands on his jeans. 'Hello, mate, off to the slaughter?'

When we are almost through, one of the sheep twists its body and falls by the front wheel of the car. Stuart shouts and leans out the window. 'You hit one, you've gone over its leg!' The sheep is flopping around noiselessly on the road by the side of the car.

'I can't have run over it, it's just tripped over . . .'

The others keep on going, stepping over and on it. Stuart starts to open his door but the sheep gets to its feet and starts moving on in a see-sawing hobble. Stuart signals to the farmer following the herd in his tractor. The herd clears around us. The tractor pulls up.

'She hit one. My . . . wife. I think she drove over its *hoof* . . .'

The big farmer stares down at us from his perch. He looks over the sea of sheep, deadpan. 'Can you, ah, describe the one you hit?' He spits into the road and scratches his huge stubbly chin. His big brown face is immobile, only his eyes are full of bloodshot humour. 'Don't worry, mate, if it drops out of the race I'll find it. Always sling it on the barbie.' He starts up the tractor, manoeuvring it round the Porsche. 'You'll need a wheel wash,' he calls, and chugs away.

Stuart winds up the window furiously.

'See that. That *indifference*. They're all *brutalised* in the country, darling. They're all inbreds, you see. Brain damaged. They're immune to animal suffering. It's a different world out here. My God . . .'

Some hours later we find the Kiwilands Lodge. We turn into a steep driveway covered in brown paving tiles. Ferns in bark gardens grow along the edge of the drive, illuminated by fluorescent green lights. It is only afternoon but the clouds are heavy. It is already getting dark. We pull into a large courtyard and point the car towards the main entrance. A green sign says RESSEPTION.

'Re-what? You go in and ask the inbreds at "Resseption" whether they've got us down. I'm staying here.'

He hunches down in the passenger seat. I cross the courtyard. The place is much grander than I expected, with a restaurant and bar, and a set of conference rooms, 'marvellously situated', as the brochure says, on the top of a headland overlooking the sea. It has spas, saunas and an immense white satellite dish on the roof. Varnished wooden signs point the way to the Logan Room, the Pohutukawa Lounge, the Kiwilands Restaurant and Bar.

The office is furnished with plastic ferns and winking green fluorescent lights. I flick through a stack of pamphlets advertising marlin fishing, sea cruises and night fishing.

When I ding the bell a narrow, bearded type in brown sweeps out and greets me cautiously. 'Chicane, yes, you're in Kauri Block, it's very pleasant, clear view of the sea, just the one night?' He taps busily on his keyboard, prominent little teeth sticking out through his beard. Dinky nylon slacks, of the *sans*-a-belt variety. Little grey shoes, with zips. He smiles shyly as he hands over the key. 'You're lucky to get a booking tonight, Ms Chicane. We're ab–solutely full.' Looking like a rat peeping apologetically through a dunny brush he hands over some pamphlets and a map of the area.

'Thanks. It's been a long drive.'

'Enjoy your stay!'

'Hey,' Stuart yells from the car, 'you'll get wet!'

We spend some time trying to find Kauri Block in the heavy rain. Finally we discover that we have to get out of the car and walk to a second entrance around the side of the building. Kauri Block has little patios with ranch sliders looking out over the sea. There are paths with ropes for holding on going down the cliff to the beach below. Far out to sea curtains of rain are moving across the ocean. Closer in the sea is grey-green and choppy. The air smells wet and salty and fresh. Along the path the summer-season deckchairs and umbrellas are sodden and flapping in the wind, and a trellis has collapsed, leaving the winter-brown vine trailing on the flattened grass. A green water-wing hangs from the branch of a swaying pohutukawa. Stuart struggles with the key to Kauri Block 9. At the door a small wooden sign says WELCOME. The door gives and we burst into our unit and close the door.

The walls are made of concrete block, like all motel walls. It's very quiet. The windows are covered with net curtains. Symmetrical beds, cold clean sheets, a spotless empty fridge, little sachets of coffee, a carton of milk in the fridge door. Pamphlets on scuba diving. Kiwilands pens and envelopes. A flimsy little shower made of fake wood, into which Stuart disappears, cursing its minuscule size. I lie on the bed and read about the Down Under Scuba Diving School.

Stuart comes out wrapped in a towel, dances around the room for a while, then flops down on the bed. 'Don't you love motels?'

'I've been thinking about your mother.'

'God, don't be so negative. I've got a good idea. Let's go to a pub.'

'There's one here, the Kiwilands.'

'No, no. Let's go to the dive we saw on the way.'

Mmm.'

The wind splatters rain against the ranch slider and the fridge ticks into another gear. The receptionist suddenly races past the window wearing a brown anorak and carrying an armload of folded deckchairs. Out at sea the rainy light is thickening into darkness. A fishing boat is beating its way home through the choppy bay. Stuart stares out at the dusk, at the blinding rain, the winter sea.

'Jesus it looks melancholy out there. There's nothing as sad as a motel in the off-season. All that high maintenance, lost profit. My uncle Norv had a motel. It killed him in the end.'

'But Stuart. The motel's *full*.'

An hour later Stuart says, 'Darling, we're in a horror movie. Soon clocks are going to start striking thirteen.'

As far as we can tell I have steered the car into a small ditch, which is now filling with water. We are on a narrow road into the town, surrounded by sodden paddocks. A group of cows huddle together in the white path of the headlights. Further down the road the lights of the town are visible through trees and bush.

Stuart thrashes around in the passenger seat.

'Christ I'm hungry, I'm dying for a drink. Did you have to do this, I mean did you really have to . . . Fuck!'

'Well, I'm sorry but it's so *dark*. Anyway you're always banging the car into things.'

'Right OK, let's walk into town, we can't stay here and drown.'

He reaches into the back of the car and picks out a Smith and Caugheys carrier bag. He flings open the car door and puts the bag on his head.

'Oh bugger, fuck, shit . . .' I hear as he slams the car door. Crossing the headlight beams he resembles an elongated Noddy, with his red jacket and the tall blue carrier bag pointing upwards and tilting forward at the top. He tiptoes warily through the cow shit, flapping his arms at the cows. Startled, they move towards him.

'Getton there Jessie!' he calls shrilly. Mooing uneasily the cows surround him.

'Toot the horn!' he shouts and bursts out of the circle, leaping spastically over the mud. At the first parp of the horn the cows turn and shamble off into the dark and Stuart leaps back into the passenger seat.

'I hate the country,' he says. 'I hate all this *nature*.'

We walk single file into town. I wear a tall green bag, decorated with the words 'Pet Heaven'. At a small takeaway bar we dry ourselves off and eat fish and chips, and drink poisonous cups of greasy Nescafé. We sit at the vinyl-topped table in the tired neon light and watch the locals come in to collect their steaming packages of takeaways in oily newsprint. Stuart dries his face and hair with paper napkins. A sign on the door says in thick black felt pen NO GANG PATCHES INSIDE. NO DOGS OR PETS. The man at the counter in his long bush shirt must weigh at least twenty stone. His wife is even larger. They offer us more chips, for free. 'From Auckland, eh? Big place, big place . . .' The main street is empty except for a tiny Maori boy kicking up the rubbish as he wanders along.

'Got twenny cents? Ah seeya later eh!'

We wander along under the shop verandas, looking in the small town shop windows with their fly-blown curtains and dusty advertisements, ten years out of date. Round a corner we find a pub. We dive in, past a large sign that says that those who throw jugs at others will be banned from the pub for two weeks. We find a table by a long fake brick bar.

'What'll y' have Stellie, couple of gins? Jug of port?'

The pub is a huge, low-roofed barn, stretching away into the mists of cigarette smoke. Drinkers lurch out of the mists with their fists full of empty jugs, shouting for refills. We settle in over a couple of flagons, the alcohol settles hotly over the fish and chips, and our clothes steam in the heat.

After a long, quiet period of contented drinking I negotiate the outer reaches of the vast room and find a brown door entitled CHICKS. In the long, narrow room an electric hand-drier is roaring, and a toilet is flushing endlessly in one of the cubicles. When I try to wash my hands the tap seems to be blocked, then suddenly lets out a spray of water, resoaking my shirt. I struggle to turn it off but the top of the tap has lost its grip and is useless and the water runs unchecked in a small fountain over the sink and onto the floor.

Outside in the heat and grime of the bar the music thumps with an endless repetitive beat. The barman lounges behind the bar in his string vest, drinking beer out of a jug. I shout at him over the music that the plumbing is all wrecked and he nods briefly, as if things are just as they should be. He has a blue bird tattooed on the side of his neck and a ragged purple scar, running from the corner of his eye to his neck, cuts the bird neatly in half.

Back at the table Stuart is talking to a thin blond man in a blue suit. He pulls me down into my seat and says, 'Stella, this is Don, he's staying at the Kiwilands.'

The man looks at me in a friendly way and says, 'I hear you're stranded. I'll give you a ride back to the motel.'

'Big of you, Don.' Stuart slaps him on the back. 'Don says he's from Wellington. The old home town.' He goes off to get another round of drinks. The man sits down next to me.

'So,' I say, 'are you on holiday?'

'No.' He sits staring at me while I wait for him to say more. His eyes are pale blue, bloodshot around the edges. He smiles at me and picks his fingernail with a match. He has a strong jaw, long nose, very white teeth. He looks shrewd.

'So do you work at the Kiwilands?'

'No.'

He takes out a packet of cigarettes and offers me one, looking alertly at me.

'Nice weather we're having.'

'No,' he says.

I roll my eyes and he grins.

'Why are you all wet?'

'Well it rained. Then the tap in the toilets malfunctioned and soaked me.'

He leans forward, considering me and says conspiratorially, 'Actually I'm at the Kiwilands for a conference.'

'Oh?'

'A drugs conference.'

'So you're a chemist? Drugs rep?' Struggling to feign interest now, I slouch in my chair, struggling to hear him over the steady blare of seventies disco music. In one corner between the tables, under a cardboard sign saying DANCE FLOOR, a small group sways and falls drunkenly to the music.

'I'm a detective in the drug squad. Wellington CIB.'

'That explains the way you look.'

'What do you mean?'

'The way you stare at me. As if you're filing my description in your memory.'

'Oh yeah? Well. Maybe I am.'

When it's his turn to buy a round Don announces that he's tired of beer, he wants something stronger. He buys whisky for himself and Stuart, vodka lime and soda for me. Now we are all drunk. The music has been turned up and up until the jarring vibration of the bass beat seems loud enough to damage the ears, loud enough to be felt in the bones. Feeling the throbbing in my throat like a new pulse I wonder, could the heart become confused under such a barrage of alien rhythm? Could it get out of step, or stop? Now more people arrive and crowd into the bar, all heading in from the silent countryside (moths to the porch light), eager to cram together, to be intoxicated, blinded, deafened, stimulated half to death.

Stuart leans back in his chair and slaps Don on the shoulder. He shouts, 'Don mate, how come I never ran into you in Wellington? I know all cops, I'm always friends with cops.' He is slurring his words. He looks exhausted. Don's elbow slips off the table and he laughs. 'I was undercover.'

Stuart snorts.

'Deep undercover. Deep deep . . . Beard and everything . . .'

'How long have you been in the drug squad?'

'Ages, mate,' Don shouts, half closing his eyes. 'You get sick of being a member. Always going to the same bars, doing the same things. That's why I came here tonight. All the others are back in the Kiwilands Bar, I needed a change.'

'Did you have to take drugs when you were undercover?' I ask.

'Well that's actually classified.'

'Course he did,' Stuart says. 'They all end up in rehab in the end, don't you, Don.'

'What do you do at a drugs conference?'

'Collaborate, evaluate, assess, compare,' he says with his eyes closed. He opens them. 'We compare notes. It's very useful.'

He sits up straighter, takes off his tie and stuffs it in his pocket. He leans over and says in my ear, 'Anyway. What are youse two doing here?'

'Going to Seabrooke tomorrow on behalf of a client, to look at a scene.'

'There was a shooting in Seabrooke, Lemon, Lemman something . . .'

'That's right. That's the client.'

'Cold-blooded killing, wasn't it? Guy a psycho?'

'No Don, no no no,' Stuart shouts, waving his index finger.

'Just a nice guy, was he, had a bad day.'

'That's it buddy, that's it.'

'Oh yeah,' Don says and raises his glass. 'Yeah cheers.'

Around eleven o'clock Stuart starts to sing quite tunefully, in his drunken baritone. Don stands up and heads for the bar. After a few minutes he stumbles back out of the mist.

'It's closing time, they're going to kick us out. I offered them something to stay open and they said to leave or they'd call the police.'

Stuart roars with laughter, struggling to open his eyes. He stands up and sways and Don catches his arm to stop him falling.

'Oh buddy,' Stuart mutters, holding his head, 'oh I'm pissed, I've had too much, didn't eat anything, that long drive . . .'

He sways again. Don holds him around the shoulders.

We blunder around picking everything up. Stuart is laughing weakly. Suddenly all the lights come on, and the pub is illuminated in harsh neon light. The huge room looks like the aftermath of a battle, smoke swirls over the stained carpet, bottles, cigarette packets and overturned chairs litter the floor, the last of the weary and broken drinkers pick their way slowly through the destruction towards the doors. The scarred barman walks among the tables wearing thick gloves and carrying a large plastic sack. Outside in the carpark there are screams and shouts, engines revving, the sounds of smashing glass.

Swaying and coughing, holding onto Stuart, we lurch out into the warm wet night. My ears are ringing. The rain is falling in a fine mist, the carpark is surrounded by the dripping, rustling bush. Don is telling Stuart to take deep breaths, Stuart breathes obediently, then trips over a judderbar and falls on his knees onto the asphalt. We haul him up and load him into the back seat of Don's car.

'Don't crash,' I say to Don.

'I won't get breathalysed, I'm police.'

'Just flash your badge, do you?'

'S'right.'

'Why can't I have a badge?' Stuart shouts from the back seat. 'Nice get out of jail free. What I need . . .'

'Anyway, I said don't crash, not don't get caught.'

'I've gone fucking *deaf*,' Stuart shouts.

I catch sight of the marooned Porsche lopsided in the ditch as we sweep past on the narrow road. After several wrong turns we find the motel and drive down into the yard. The crickets are clicking loudly in the dark garden, the air is full of the smell of earth and compost. Together we pull Stuart out of the back seat and then Don wraps Stuart's jacket around him and guides him carefully around the buildings to Kauri Block. Stuart, steadier now, mumbles with drunken dignity, 'Fine now, very kind, over-tired . . .' and while I search for the key he sleeps standing upright against the dripping ponga fence.

I open the door and he staggers over to the bed, lies down and is immediately asleep. Don squats down beside the bed, care-fully takes off Stuart's shoes and covers him with the candlewick bedspread. We stand looking down at him. He snores, turns over, a fleck of spit bubbles at the corner of his mouth. 'No,' he mut-ters, 'no me. No me.'

'Whasshesaying?' Don pushes up his sleeves and sits down on the edge of the bed. I notice a light shower of dandruff on the shoulders of his suit.

'I don't know. He's shattered.'

'Well, I've got an idea. Want to go to the Kiwilands Bar? It's still open.' He squints up at me and grins. 'Come on . . .' His eyes are very pale blue in his bony face. He is thin and strong-looking. His hair is coarse, like blond wire. He jumps neatly over the bed and goes to the door. 'Come on.'

We walk on the path around the lit swimming pool. The water is fluorescent green, it looks thick, heavy, poisonous. I sit down on a deckchair in the light rain and he goes into the bar and comes out with two tall glasses decorated with cherries and straws and umbrellas.

'What are *these*?' I take the ridiculous-looking glass.

'Cocktails,' he says cheerfully and we drink them down and he tells me about cannabis plantations in the cornfields and under-cover nights and lonely surveillance out of battered vans on winter days, while the rain speckles the surface of the pool and the water swirls and steams under the ferns, like a witches' brew made of rain and tears and poison.

It must be some hours later when I start to surface. Oh the pain. Oh my head. Oh my heart. I am already weeping way before I am awake. There is a terrible heat behind my eyes. My jaw is aching, my head is shrinking. No, no, go away I croak as I zoom up into consciousness. Also I seem to be tied up. I can't face it, I just can't. My arms are pinned. My legs, when I try an experimental wriggle, just don't move. Oh mother mother, break it to me gently. I've been slaughtered, buggered, fucked and stuffed, I've been thrown over a cliff. I open an eye. I am face to face with – Don. He leans over me. 'Stop *moaning*. You'll wake up the whole motel. No, you're not tied up, you're just *tangled* in the quilt, yes you've just got a headache, that's all, I've got one too . . .'

Businesslike, he frees me from the strangulating duvet.

'You look like you're in a bit of pain. It was the cocktails, remember. The Tropical Night, the Scorpion's Claw, the Scarab. The Wailing Wall.'

'God, the Wailing Wall.'

'We did them all, remember. You started making them up yourself. After the Wailing Walls we had Screaming Meemees, then Bleeding Hearts. What really finished you off was the Mad Cow.'

'Ha aah . . .' It hurts to laugh. 'Don't forget the Corker and the Rabid Dog . . .'

The room is a wreckage in the grey dawn light. There is a double bed strewn with paper cups and clothes. There are suitcases and bags all over the floor, and a laptop computer and printer. Don's blue suits hang in an open wardrobe covered with plastic drycleaning bags.

'I wrapped you in that duvet. You told me you were dying. I had to carry you across the room in it. Lucky you're such a midget. You weigh a ton. I wondered whether to lay you out in the bathroom in case you threw up.'

'Thanks.'

Painfully I climb off the Lazy-Boy armchair in which I have been lying trussed, like an unwilling dental patient. Don is in the kitchenette. He comes out with a cup of tea.

'Here, don't cry. Come outside. Come and look.'

Blindly I stumble after him onto the tiny patio. Don is standing on the short wall looking out towards the sea.

'Look,' he says, 'the world has disappeared.' And so it has.

There is nothing in front of us but fog. The sea has gone. The air is so full of water that it surrounds the patio in a moving, swirling mass.

'The fog came in at five o'clock,' he says. 'I watched it blot out the sunrise.'

I climb up onto the wall. I breathe deeply. It is very quiet; only the seagulls are crying down on the shore. What a funny thing, to be no part of the world any more. What a blind, dizzy thing. The trees are dripping at the edge of the cliff. Don leans his head back and sniffs the air.

'It's weird, isn't it,' he says. We watch the white world, the air moving in front of us, in currents, reshapings, up and down draughts. His wiry hair is frosted with drops of water, his hair stands up on end, his eyes are bloodshot. I sob involuntarily. My head aches, so badly.

'I'll make you some toast. Don't cry. You're just hung over.'

I sit stunned and sighing on the bench in the little kitchen while Don makes some toast and cups of tea. He moves around cheerfully, showing no sign of fatigue. He looks older than he did in the night, he could be in his mid-forties. Outside the window the white air moves and curls, hurries and slows.

He says, 'Y'know I've met Stuart before, he just doesn't remember. That's why I went over to him in the pub. I recognised his face but I couldn't remember who he was. I was thinking he must be with the conference.'

I nod, fighting a wave of nausea.

'I met him a long time ago in Wellington, it was some minor drugs case. I knew about him when he lived there, the police always know all about defence lawyers. Wellington's a small place, everyone knows everyone.'

'He's based in Auckland now.'

'I know. He just suddenly dropped everything and moved up to Auckland. Left a big practice. Split up with his wife.'

'Mia,' I say, resting my head against a cupboard door. My eyes feel hot.

'Mia. They had a daughter. The wife's still in Wellington with the young girl. She and Chicane were a glamorous couple in Wellington, I remember. They were real socialites. But she did him evil, so the gossip went. And those to whom . . . well don't listen to me.'

He peels open a plastic jam container and spreads jam over the toast. He hands me a piece, I take a bite and my throat constricts, the bread sticks like wet cardboard to the roof of my mouth. 'Water,' I croak weakly.

'Here, mate.' He fills me a glass, then cuts the rest of the toast into triangles and piles it on a plate. His hands are quick and neat. He looks even thinner without his suit on, spry.

'I'm divorced myself. I've even got two kids. Daughters. What a cockup. My wife and I couldn't sort it out. We started having an argument in about the late seventies, didn't stop until we called it a day. We tell everyone we're on great terms, you know, the best of friends, no hard feelings, all that bullshit. Actually I still want to get her on a dark night and smash her face in. You look a bit faint, I'll make you a bowl of Cup-a-Soup, look, here it is in the packet.'

Out on the patio on the curly iron chairs we drink Cup-a-Soup and watch the sky swirling around our feet. Just like in the fairy story. The sky has collapsed. The sky has fallen in.

At 6.25 a.m. at the far side of the fluorescent swimming pool the bearded receptionist appears out of the fog. 'Morning,' he says shyly, leaning on his broom, the drops of water clinging to his beard. 'Are you lost?' I mutter good morning at him and slink past towards Kauri Block.

I locate the key and open the door, into the warm silence of the room. Stuart's clothes and shoes are scattered around the floor, all is still. But he is wide awake, sitting up on the bed, wrapped in the quilt. He rears up off the bed with a squawk of twanging bed-springs.

'I woke up and you were *gone*.'

'How are you feeling?' I ask, stepping gingerly into the close-ness of the room. He steps in front of me, poised and waiting.

'Where have you been?'

Carefully stepping around him I start taking off my clothes, looking around for the suitcase, rummaging for the Panadol, for pain relief.

'Where have you fucking *been*?' he shouts, agitated, sweeping the pile of pamphlets off the dressing table.

'I stayed up at the Kiwibar,' I begin to explain, holding my temples, 'with the detective, with Don. It was fun, but I've got this . . . this terrible *headache*. I feel like *death*.'

He bobs around over me, his face contorted and strained. He rubs his hands jerkily over his sweating forehead as I begin to stuff my smoky clothes into the suitcase.

'Where were you *all night*?' he says furiously.

'I fell asleep on the armchair in his room.'

He stares, his face turns whiter, then red, his eyes water and suddenly he is lunging forward over the bed, grabbing my arms and shaking me, his fingers gouging agonisingly into the muscles of my arms, shaking me and shouting, 'I've been waiting and waiting, do you think I'm a fucking idiot? What have you been doing, what-did-you-do?'

'Nothing!' I struggle to get free, my ankle turns and I over-balance and half fall into the suitcase. He pushes me aside, swearing and shouting. I plunge into the lid of the case.

'Nothing happened!' I scream back, falling around on the jumble of shoes and clothes. 'He's just a funny little man, we drank and talked and I slept on a chair . . .'

He turns away trembling, sick around the mouth. The skin around his eyes looks black.

'I trusted you.' He leans against the wall. Suddenly he gives me a bright, twisted little smile. The grey light through the lace curtains makes a pattern of scales on his face. 'A little bitch like you.'

'Oh come on,' I say, flapping around on the floor, struggling to get up.

'Oh yes . . .' he coughs, rasping and blinking, with the weird little smile. 'You keep talking. Say whatever you like. I'll kill you before I trust you again.' He grinds his knuckles into his eyes.

'Oh for God's sake . . .'

He picks the toilet bag up off the bed and throws it hard at my head. I shriek and duck, glass smashes, pill packets rain down, a toothbrush bounces off the mirror. He shouts, I shout back, back and forth we rage and storm while the hangover seeps its poison through my ears and nose and throat and the air tastes of chlorine and the pain behind my eyes glows and pulsates, all neon and lurid, pool-green.

Later, out of steam, he stands at the window staring angrily at the mass of fog hanging over the cliff, the metallic light over the trees. I search dumbly around in the mess on the floor and he sinks down in the cane chair by the door and puts his head in his hands. Painfully, slowly, I clamber over the bed to him and hold out my trembling hand.

'Panadol?' I say. And, 'I didn't do anything.'

He lifts his head and looks up at me blackly, infinitely weary. He reaches over.

'Make it fucking two,' he says.

7. Seabrooke

We have been there, to the scene of the crime. We went in and got out as soon as we could. As soon as we possibly could . . .

The first thing we had to do, Stuart decided, was to get rid of the car. It gives us bad luck anyway, he said. Always crashing itself. We needed to hire something more discreet. But after we found the garageman we didn't bother with Avis or Hertz. Stuart had something else in mind.

Rupapara's Garage stood way out by itself on the narrow South road. After paying for his Jaffas, pie and petrol, Stuart leaned closer to the counter and said – he loved this cloak-and-dagger stuff – 'Buddy, do you see that old car parked out there, that rusty old station wagon out the back? Who does it belong to, can you tell me that?'

And deeply silent and suspicious the garage owner contemplated Stuart (smiling slyly under his black hair, hands in the pockets of his city jeans) and the shining little bronze Porsche parked at the pumps and the long, empty South road beyond the pumps, and sighed eventually and said that it was his, not that it was any business of anyone else's, and who wanted to know?

Stuart took him aside and they walked out around the pumps, the overalled garageman stiff-backed and unfriendly, and Stuart a tall, lean supple figure, leaning into him, clapping him on the back, catching his arm, like a cat on its hind legs about to climb up the trunk of a tree, until the garageman came back with a sheepish smile saying that it was all the same to him, and out the back was a secure lockup where the Porsche could be stored, just for a day or two.

Meanwhile, while they negotiate some more, I've sidled along the tank and am viewing the interior of the station wagon with some concern.

'Course it'll get us there,' Stuart said, swinging us out onto the highway, clipping a BP sign and shearing a hedge, sawing on the wheel and persuading the huge saloon out of the path of the oncoming traffic. 'The steering's a bit loose, that's all. The point is it looks rustic, you know, rural. We'll *blend*.'

The drive was a long one for Stuart, given that it took an act of brute strength and a certain amount of nerve to negotiate the gentlest of corners. After a few turns I opened a can of beer, and after we skidded breathlessly to a halt inches from the steel gird-ers at the beginning of a one-way bridge, I had another. It took us half an hour and many false starts to cross the narrow bridge, and when we got to the other side we parked for a while to rest, and to allow streams of finger-waving motorists to roar past us in indignant clouds of dust. The last motorist wound down his win-dow and threw some sort of large, rotten root vegetable which splattered onto the bonnet of the car.

'Great,' I said thickly from the back seat, 'we're really *blend-ing*.'

After another hour of driving Stuart started to get the hang of it. When a bend was approaching he began to turn the wheel some seconds in advance, to allow the car time to respond. In this way we progressed quite well, until Stuart got hot with his exer-tions and turned the switch to operate the cooling fan inside the car. There was no response except for an angry grinding noise, and then suddenly there was a chugging cough, and the vents released a spray of twigs, leaves, ash and earth which whipped around Stuart's head, blinding him, and causing us, once again, to drive off the road.

The sign on the letter box said in faded scrolly lettering *Welcome Inn – Cyril and Tina-Lee Leonard*. We drove past it towards the general store. The store sign said CIGARETTES GROCERIES EATS. Behind the shop a herd of sheep bleated anxiously. Seabrooke's main street was empty. We parked, the only car in a row of painted parking spaces. The door of the shop was open.

'Well, let's go in and . . .'

'Buy an ice-cream,' I said.

'The main thing to do is get a general idea of the place. The lie of the land. It might help us and it might be no use to us at all. But it has to be done.'

'Right,' I said.

But now that we were here we were reluctant to get out of the car. We felt exposed. In the dental clinic next to the shop the venetian blinds were turned to allow just a slit of a view of the street. The atmosphere was intimate. It was as if we had parked our huge rusting tank in the middle of someone's garden. It didn't matter that this was the main street. It felt like private property. We didn't belong. We couldn't even pretend that we belonged.

Tina-Lee Leonard moved away from the town after her husband was shot. Cyril Leonard was an electrician. He drove his van around the country, he had customers for miles around. After he died none of the lights in his house would switch on. So they said. There was a light on a lamppost outside his house. After he died this light could not be switched off. Tina-Lee and Cyril had been married for four years. After he died she had no reason to stay in the dark, haywire house in Seabrooke. She went to live in Auckland at an undisclosed address.

Stuart gets details like this from one of his friends, a detective from Auckland who was on the team that investigated the shooting. This detective's name at the police station is Kina because his brown hair sticks up like the spikes on a sea egg. He regularly tells Stuart about investigations, and asks for nothing in return. He likes the way Stuart relishes small details, ironies, snippets of gore. They are friends but they have to be careful. When anyone is looking Kina treats Stuart with the customary suspicion and contempt reserved by the police for slippery bastards like him. Kina said that Seabrooke was a strange, intense place. 'You get a funny feeling there,' he said. 'The people are clicky. Very *clicky*.'

The sheep cried their high, sad cries. I opened the door of the car. Stuart's door opened with a long graunching creak, like the sound of the horror movie coffin opening to reveal the awakened ghoul within. He grimaced, trying to shut the door quietly. It squawked. Long plastic strips hung from the doorframe to keep out the flies. Stuart eased the door closed with a final raucous heehaw of the ancient metal. He grimaced again. I sniggered suddenly. Behind the dairy a cow gave a mournful bellow.

We pushed aside the plastic fly strips. 'Gidday,' Stuart announced rurally. A large, redheaded woman with a great jutting chin emerged from the door behind the counter.

'Hoi,' she said shortly. She wore a dark green Crimplene smock. I went to the back of the shop and looked for things we genuinely needed. Some orange juice, some rolls, some Jaffas. Also a large packet of crisps. I felt hollow. The goods looked dusty and I checked sell-by dates. The woman at the counter began to put prices on packets, leaning over the counter with a sticker gun, sweating in her Crimplene smock. Her hands were broad and short, with fat fingers. Her wrists were freckled. She put down the sticker gun and rested her hands on the top of the till while we piled up our supplies.

'Just passing through here?'

We nodded.

'Well,' she said, leaning back, heavy and confident, 'if you don't mind my asking, what are you doing driving Bradley Rupapara's car?'

Back in the station wagon we consumed the crisps in silence. The occasional ute or truck drove past. Behind the dental clinic and far away across the rolling paddocks the south–north highway rose out of the bush and curved away out of sight.

We had some difficulty finding the Lehmans' house. We had a rough map of the area but there were more roads in Seabrooke than you would expect. The land around the town was mostly cleared, with just a few pockets of thick bush in gullies and along the edges of streams. We needed to see how long it took to drive from Cyril Leonard's house to the Lehmans' house, and back again, the time it took Lehman to go for the gun and drive back with it.

The Lehmans' house was out of sight of the road, up a long right-of-way. We drove past it a couple of times before we found it. We could look down on the town from the right-of-way. It wasn't really a town, just one street with a few shops, a takeaway bar, a petrol station and a library which was actually a vacant lot with a small rusty caravan on it, bearing a sign that read LIBRARY. BOOKS. MAGS. CHILDREN'S.

Behind the shops were small wooden houses with big, scruffy fenced-in gardens. Beyond the gardens were paddocks, and the cows leaned over the back fences and stared at the washing blowing on the washing lines.

We decided to leave the car on the road and walk up the right-of-way to the Lehmans' house. The road looked muddy and slippery, as if you'd only make it up there in a four-wheel drive. 'The last thing we want to be doing is getting the bloody thing towed out of a ditch,' Stuart said.

The right-of-way led steeply up a hill. At the top of the hill the land stretched away, flat. A line of pines grew along the dirt road. We walked in silence. Sheep skidded away from the fences as we passed, bleating into the empty air. The road seemed to head into the horizon without any deviation, but as we walked on it dipped and we came to the turn-off behind a grove of pines and a letter box that read 'Lehman' and the roof of the house was visible just below the road.

It was a three-bedroom bungalow, with a return veranda. Around the side of the house we came upon the large scorch mark where a half-hearted attempt had been made to burn it down. We stood on the front veranda. The paddocks stretched away, somewhere in the distance was the sea, and in front of the house was the land where Carlos would have had his plantation, sheltered by the curve of the hill behind, and by the shelter belts he had set out to grow.

'Over to the west is the land owned by Boyderman Leonard. All the land up to the dirt road belongs to Carlos. Down the hill is the creek where Boyderman Leonard frightened Leon. It looks on the map as if the Lehmans' land is almost completely surrounded by the Leonards'. The Leonards own most of the land right down to the sea, but they also own land behind here, behind this house, I mean. The other big landowners are the Garlands and the Seabrookes, but they're over on the other side of the town. Leonard's stock could have been allowed to stray onto this land from all directions.'

Stuart tried the door of the house. It was locked. He said, 'Did I tell you that when Leah tried to put the land on the market she was told by the agent that Boyderman Leonard was interested in buying it? That made her sick. I suppose the bank will get the land in the end.'

He unlocked the door with Leah's key. Leah's parents had come in a truck and taken all the furniture away after Carlos's arrest. They had taken everything, including carpets and wallboard. There was a strong smell of damp and cut wood. The floors were strewn with bits of rubbish and leftovers from the hurried removal.

'Listen. There's no wind. It's really well sheltered. It was a good spot. He knew what he was doing, didn't he. He wasn't just some . . . *no-hoper*.'

In front of the kitchen windows was the vegetable patch. Leah had been standing at this window when she heard the truck coming along the metal road. The engine was roaring. Behind her the baby was bouncing in the harness that Carlos had hung from the kitchen doorframe. Leah took the baby out of her bouncer and went back to the window. The truck door slammed. She called out to Leon who was playing on the floor with his Lego. It was Saturday. The older boy and girl were staying with her parents in Auckland, for the long weekend.

Carlos was coming across the vegetable garden. She watched as he strode through the tomato plants, smashing them into the ground as he went. Kicking out, he knocked down the small wooden trellises and scattered the wooden plant holders. He went around the side of the house. She heard his boots on the veranda.

'Dad's home!' Leon rushed towards the porch. 'Just a minute, just a minute,' she hissed, pulling him back. She felt fear running over her shoulder blades, her heart raced. She held onto Leon by the back of his jersey and waited, hiding behind the kitchen door.

Carlos had seen her as she stood at the window. Their eyes met. Staring her in the face he kicked and smashed about him until most of the plants she had put into that part of the garden were destroyed. His face was contorted, it seemed as if he didn't recognise her. Kicking, his face immobile, he moved towards the house.

'Oh God now what the hell,' she muttered, holding Leon's hand tightly as Carlos thundered over the veranda and wrenched open the front door. The thin wooden wall separated them. He didn't come into the kitchen. Leon whined and twisted in her grip.

'Muuumm, get off!' the boy squeaked and pulled away. He ran into the living room. Leah ran after him, holding the baby. Carlos walked out of the bedroom and slapped Leon to the floor. Without speaking or looking back he walked out of the front door. From the window Leah saw him unlock the shed, take out the shotgun wrapped in its grey cloth, throw the cloth on the ground and disappear around the side of the house. After an indescribable minute during which she crouched on the floor with the children, pinning them down and moaning into their hair in a tiny whimpering drawl, she heard the truck start up, and the engine roar again into the distance.

In a couple of minutes she had gathered up the children's jackets, nappies, her wallet and the carry-cot. She strapped the children, both screaming, into their car seats. She ran back into the house for a blanket. She couldn't really feel what she was doing at all. She wasn't thinking. She snatched the keys off the hook. There was only one road to and from the house. She drove the long straight kilometre at high speed, expecting at every moment that his truck would turn out of the road into town and head towards her, that he would run them off the right-of-way and shoot them as they sat, screaming in their seats. She passed the town road. She didn't slow down and when she hit the highway she speeded up. Oh God Almighty, she whispered under her breath.

She drove on to Tauranga. She didn't think she'd see Carlos ever again.

'Leah knew, as soon as she saw him. Something had gone horribly wrong with him . . .'

I was standing on the veranda taking photos of the boundary fences to the west of the house.

'Yeah yeah . . . Stella, come in here a minute.' Stuart was inside, standing on the edge of a wall nogging, looking through a high louvre window. 'There's someone up there on the road. A man.'

I went in and climbed up beside him. I was looking across the top of the rainwater tank. The driveway curved away up the bank.

'I can't see the road.'

'No, but someone just looked over the top of the letter box up there. I saw a face and a hat. There's someone standing up there looking down.'

I looked away. The sun was moving a thin finger of light across the bare floor. Wood dust drifted down through the yellow air.

'There, *there*.' Stuart gripped my arm, whispering. A man's face appeared above the letter box at the top of the bank, and just as quickly bobbed back out of sight.

'He's taken his hat off.'

We stood on the nogging waiting for him to reappear. The wind blew in the pine trees. Behind us, outside the living-room window, shadows were starting to spread across the low hills. The sea was a darkening smudge of blue, far away. Somewhere, a long way off, a car engine started up.

Stuart said quietly, 'I wanted to see if I could use the loo.'

I looked at him blankly.

'It's in the outhouse,' he explained. 'It's on the site plan. It's where he had the gun stored, actually. But I also, you know, darling, need a crap.' We both sniggered. 'If that's Boyder-man Leonard out there we're likely to be peppered with buckshot.'

'Why don't you just wait,' I said suddenly, not wanting to stay in the house. 'We've taken all the photos we need, we've measured the distances, we've seen the plantation site. Why don't we just go and you can find somewhere in the town to go.'

'In the town. You must be joking, there's nothing there.'

'Well, you can go behind a bush, Christ.'

'Behind a *bush*?' And we were both snorting again, under our breaths. Suddenly we clutched each other and ducked down as the head appeared over the letter box. This time the head peered purposefully from left to right and left again, searching. The head cocked to one side, listening.

'Oh Stuart, let's go.' I didn't like that intent singleminded peering. It reminded me of a bird, a feeding bird.

'Look this is silly,' Stuart said reasonably. 'We're going to have to go past him to get to the road anyway. You wait here, and I'll go around the vegetable garden and into the shed that way. Then we'll go back to the car and head off. OK? I'll come back round and get you when I've finished.'

'Oh no no, I'm not staying in here by myself. I'll come with you.' All I wanted now was to get away from the little wooden house. The shadows on the hills were lengthening to jagged points. The wind had dropped. Evening was not far off.

We walked through the ruined vegetable garden, noting the broken trellises and the smashed flower boxes. Bamboo stakes stood along the edge of the house under the kitchen window, with seed packets skewered to the top of them. Wires were strung overhead, for climbing vines. Underfoot the plants had tangled together in a mass of untended roots and dead vegetables, and weeds were spreading over the brick paths. Stuart glanced briefly round the side of the house and up towards the letter box, before striding towards the lopsided little outhouse. I stood outside the door, listening. All I could hear were the mournful cries of the sheep and the sigh of the air in the grass. The windows of the little house were dark now. I listened for footsteps on the road. The sun was sinking towards the sea. The cistern emptied. Somewhere under the house a pump started up. Stuart pushed open the door.

'OK,' he said, 'got everything?' As we walked towards the drive, Stuart said quietly, 'I could see him through a crack in the wall. I watched him for a couple of minutes. He went along the road and down the bank. He was behind the water pump. He was looking at you.'

The road was empty. We walked close together. Stuart put his arm over my shoulders. We walked at a steady pace, skidding on the loose metal. Now it was getting darker and the last patches of sunlight were disappearing on the hills and the sand dunes in the distance. At the top of the short rise we looked back at the little wooden bungalow. The two front windows were lit up gold and burning by the last of the light. By the time we reached the turn-off to the town it was completely dark, and we walked guided by the silhouette of the fence line.

'OK. This is the end of the right-of-way bit. Just down here past that culvert was the high dirt bank and just after that we'll be nearly there.'

We speeded up, crunching over the heavy gravel. It was cold.

We passed the high bank. We walked on. And further on. Gradually we both became aware without saying anything that something was wrong. It was not possible that we had made a mistake. We came to a halt, clutching one another lightly. The car was gone.

We crept forward mechanically along the edge of the dirt road. 'If only we had a *torch*,' Stuart muttered between oaths. I didn't think a torch was a good idea. If we turned on a light we'd be visible. We would see but we would also be seen. I was still thinking of the silent man at the bungalow. We walked close together, breathing softly. We strained to see ahead in the blackness. 'Jesus Christ!' Stuart hissed, stumbling over something on the road. 'Oh Stuart,' I whispered, 'I don't like this at all.'

A cow mooed, very close. We jumped and grabbed one another.

'*Fuck*,' Stuart said. Straightening up he added, 'Look, pull yourself together. We're not wrong, are we? We're looking in the right place. Right? Are we sure?'

'Oh shut up,' I muttered into my collar. I thought of the windows of the Lehmans' house, blazing with the reflected sunset. The darkening hills, the jagged shadows. How tiny the house was in that landscape. Tiny and empty and burning.

'Should we go back?' Stuart thought aloud. 'Should we retrace? Recheck?'

'The bloody thing's *gone*. We know the way back to town, let's go, let's get moving, I want to go . . .' I wanted to weep. How could it be so dark? Where was the moon?

We walked in the direction of the town, following the fence line. Our footsteps crunched rhythmically on the loose stones. We marched together, in time. Quite near, a car engine suddenly roared. Headlights shone on the road behind us.

'Quick, quick. Get down. Hit the deck!'

'Don't be stupid,' he said, pulling me up by the collar. 'We don't need to hide, we can get a lift, for Christ's sake.' He stood at the edge of the road and waved as the car approached. 'That's it, mate,' he said to the car as it slowed, 'help your fellow man!'

The car stopped ten metres away from us. We waited, swaying on the roadside, for it to move towards us. Stuart opened his mouth and stepped forward, then stopped. We were dazzled by the headlights. The driver sat motionless behind the dark windscreen. 'Stuart . . .' I moaned. This was wrong. This was not right. The driver switched the headlights to high beam. Then he began to press the accelerator without engaging the gears. We began stumbling backwards. The engine revved higher and higher until it sounded as if the car was screaming. Shrieking, I staggered through the roadside ditch towards the fence, and Stuart followed, leaping over the ditch and pushing me over the barbed wire into the paddock. We landed in a heap. The revving stopped. The car began to move forward slowly. At a leisurely pace it rolled past us along the road, rounded a corner and was out of sight. We lay on the wet grass, listening. I wanted to crawl into a tiny hole and hide. How could it be so pitch black?

After a few minutes Stuart was furious. 'Bastards. Bastards. *Fucking bastards!*' His voice was frightened. Anything could happen out here. There were no houses, there were no streets. There was no law. Like thieves, we moved along the fence line, inside the paddock. My eyes were round and marsupial with fright. I probed and probed the darkness. I held onto the back of Stuart's coat. We walked along the edge of the road for another quarter of a mile. Then ahead of us, at the bottom of the hill we saw the lights of the town.

'Come on, we're nearly there. They can't all be deranged inbreds.' He began towing me down the hill, while I wept silently and prayed, and died for a last cigarette.

At one of the first few houses we came to on the road a large blue and white sign towered over the letter box. ROYDEN B.J. SLOACOMBE. COMMUNITY CONSTABLE.

'Here we are Stellie, we're saved.'

We went through the gate. The path led across a small lawn dotted with ornamental garden gnomes and a concrete fawn. A pink concrete pelican guarded a birdbath mounted in the middle of the lawn. Inside the house, behind a large, uncurtained ranch slider, a man was watching television.

Stuart tapped on the glass. The man pointed a remote control at the television. Then he swivelled the armchair around and stared at us. Stuart waved. The man didn't move.

'Community constable? Mr Sloacombe?'

'It's unlocked,' he said finally. 'Come on in.'

We elbowed our way into the warm room and stood in a shambles before Mr Sloacombe's tartan couch.

He was in his fifties, with a broad flat face shaped like a spade. His body was heavy and squat and his arms and hands looked powerfully strong. He wore an old tartan shirt and remained in his armchair without moving at all while we explained that our car had been stolen, that we had been menaced by unidentified persons on the road, that we had no way of getting out of town. The concrete pelican stared in through the ranch slider with one painted eye. Mr Sloacombe traced a pattern on the back of his broad hand with the TV remote. Finally our explanation trailed off and we stood defeated, while Sloacombe's coffin-shaped grandfather clock ticked and whirred electronically.

Then he said, 'We'll use the Rover.'

'What for?' we said together, like anxious children.

'To find the car.'

'But it's gone!' we exclaimed. 'It's stolen, we came back and they'd taken it, and they deliberately stopped in front of us and revved and—'

He held up his hand. He leaned forward in his chair and cleared his throat. 'Look,' he said. 'Sit down.' We sat down obediently. 'The way I see it is this. You thought the car had been stolen. You were lost, you went back to the wrong place, you were mucking around on the edge of the road, you caused concern to a motorist by stepping out in front of him, he warned you off because he didn't know what you were playing at, he drove on, you found your way here.'

We sat in silence on the loud orange couch. The pelican in the circle of light outside the window seemed to shake its head slightly and the grandfather clock tsked to itself.

'Now wait here while I get my keys.' He disappeared into the back of the house.

'Jesus,' Stuart sighed wearily.

'Do you think he's right? I mean, were we in the wrong place? Was the car just sort of, well, I don't know . . .'

Stuart looked around the room hollowly. There were dark circles under his eyes. 'All I know darling is that I'd prefer at this moment to be tucked up in intensive care with a nice magazine.'

Sloacombe came back into the room wearing a swandri and a large pair of furry carpet slippers.

'Right then,' he grunted, 'let's go.' He glanced at Stuart. 'You'd be Chicane,' he said.

'Well, how do you know that, sort of bush telegraph was it?'

Sloacombe said nothing. He smiled nastily. He locked the ranch slider and we followed him around the side of the house to the garage. A heavy green Range Rover was parked on the driveway outside the garage. We got in. Sloacombe got into the driver's seat and reached for his key. Then he stopped and wound down the window. 'That's my phone,' he said. We could hear nothing. 'I'm bound to answer that,' he enunciated lightly.

Stuart rubbed his hands over his face. 'By all means,' he said.

Sloacombe got out and went into the house.

'What is he *doing*?' I hissed. 'I didn't hear any phone. Did you hear a phone?'

'Calm down.' Stuart peered over the back seat into the rear compartment. 'He's got spades and things in the back there, he's probably rounding up a posse of grave diggers. Did you see his carpies? What a wonderfully sturdy old pair of carpie slippers they were. We're about to be slain by the sheriff of Seabrooke and a gang of carpie-wearing vigilantes. God, I love the country . . .'

'Anyway where are we going? It's not as if he knows where they've taken the car.'

The back door slammed. Sloacombe opened the Rover door

and climbed in. 'Move over, girlie,' he said out of the corner of his mouth. He lit a cigarette. 'Now,' he said in his nasty, held-in voice, 'you parked at the end of the right-of-way, correct?'

'Correct,' we said firmly.

'The right-of-way leading to the Lehman land?' Sloacombe said, leering.

'That's right. We were viewing the land for the purpose of conducting Mr Lehman's defence. Now,' Stuart gestured coldly, 'if you please, it's getting very late.'

Sloacombe glared for a moment, his mouth lopsided. He had a tooth missing at the edge of his curling lip.

'By all means,' he said.

Twenty minutes later we had driven around the circumference of the tiny town. Sloacombe drove with heavy precision. He peered ahead to the left and right. We drove through a thick belt of pines, the thick trunks lit up white in the headlights. Possums appeared on the road blinded by the lights, their eyes huge and staring. I could feel Stuart becoming furious beside me.

'Surely we've established that the car is stolen. Whoever has it will be miles away by now. Shouldn't we go back, make out a complaint and arrange some way for us to get to Tauranga?'

Sloacombe said nothing. His swandri smelt of manure. We bounced onto a dirt road.

'Where are we anyway?' Stuart said, irritated beyond politeness. 'This is just bloody ridiculous. Can you please explain to me where you are taking us and for what purpose?'

Sloacombe made an amused sound, 'Oink!' The road was getting steadily rougher, we were bouncing over deep pits and ruts. Sloacombe's heavy thigh pushed against mine. All at once he turned off the road and we were driving fast over a long strip of sloping eroded paddock. The earth under the torn clumps of grass was reddish and loose. Rabbits skidded out of the beam of the headlights. The land dipped again and suddenly we were plunging down a steep bank, so steep that it seemed that the Rover would tip over its nose and roll us over and over into whatever gully lay below. Then the track flattened out and we roared over a concrete culvert.

'For Christ's sake!' Stuart shouted. Sloacombe changed down. We slowed. We stopped. In front of us the town road curved away into the dark. At the edge of the road, neatly parked, was the large, squat, rusting wreck of the station wagon. Sloacombe switched his lights to high beam. Moths whirled and dived around the light.

'Just where you left it.' He turned and smiled, so that the gap in his teeth was revealed, and licked his grey lips. In profile he looked like a dog, the sort that hunts and lunges and snaps.

'No,' I said. 'This isn't right. This is where we came back to. This is exactly where we left the car, and it's exactly where we discovered that it was gone. Someone's *brought it back*.'

'Brought it back!' Sloacombe chuckled horribly, a mirthless sound, staccato, like a blocked sink pipe. 'Brought it back, yuk, yuk, yuk.'

Stuart said nothing.

Sloacombe looked up at the rearview mirror. His reflected eyes glared down at me, no longer laughing. 'Why would anyone bring it back, girlie? Why would anyone take that heap of junk in the first place? I ought to bounce Bradley Rupapara hard for having it on the road. You people have made a mistake. As it's easy to do around here, if you don't know the area, if you don't know your way around.'

'You'd have lived here a long time, I imagine?' Stuart asked suddenly. Sloacombe took his eyes off the mirror.

'All my life,' he said.

'When Lehman had trouble with his trees being trampled, equipment smashed up and stolen he would have come to you?'

Sloacombe reached over and opened Stuart's door. His greasy swandri brushed my face. I smelt oil, old slippers, old male sourness.

'Well, I'm the police around here,' he answered, smiling his dog smile. 'There's no other police for miles.'

We climbed out of the car. Stuart stood hanging onto the

passenger door. 'So how many times did Lehman come to you for help? How many times did you turn him away?'

Sloacombe leaned across and wrenched the door away from Stuart. He pulled it shut. Still leaning over he said through the glass, 'Don't waste any more of my time, cunt.'

He straightened up and started the engine. The Rover roared. Sloacombe gave two jaunty little toots on the horn, as if he'd just wished us a nice day. Slowly he drove off down the road towards the town.

'Shit,' I said, sounding weepier than I intended. All over again it was absolutely moonlessly dark.

But Stuart was already rushing over to the car. He opened the door and found the keys under the driver's mat where he always put his car keys. 'So how did they find those? Well, I suppose they just hot-wired it somehow. I could check if it wasn't so dark. They wouldn't have needed the keys. The nerve, what a bloody nerve . . .'

'So you don't think we made a mistake?'

'I know we didn't. It's dark all right but it's definitely the place we came back to, the high dirt bank . . . the culvert . . . He's driven us off-road to the same place. He's going to pay, that bastard, I'm going to make sure I see him in court explaining just who the hell he thinks he is. What are you doing? Get in. I hope it starts.'

Sitting in the passenger seat I said, 'What if it's booby-trapped?' Stuart hesitated with the keys. We looked at one another. He grinned. 'Nah,' he said. The engine gave an unpromising moan. He turned the key again. The station wagon groaned, hoiked, cleared its throat and chugged into life.

We drove towards the town. We passed Sloacombe's house and rolled down the empty main road. There was no one around. The shop was dark and shut, the long plastic fly strips blowing out from the locked door in the wind. The windows in the houses were lit but all were curtained and blinded. Inside the people of Seabrooke were hidden, with their secrets, their peculiar connections, their complicated private lives.

'How many people live here?' I wondered as we cruised towards the end of the main drag.

'I don't know,' Stuart said, 'but not enough.'

In the last house all the lights were off but a television flickered through a gap in the curtains. In front of the screen shapes might have been moving, faces, heads, shoulders. It was impossible to tell.

Out on the bleak North road the wind began to howl around the car. We drove slowly, because of the steering. We decided to go back to the Kiwilands for the night and then find Bradley Rupapara's garage in the morning. At the beginning of a one-way bridge, under the glare of the bright orange warning light I found marks in the upholstery where someone had stubbed out cigarettes. I scrabbled around looking for signs. Were the marks there before? I didn't think so. A Jaffa packet lay empty on the car floor. We sat close together, scanning the road ahead.

'It's lucky we had all the files and notes with us in the house. Imagine if we'd left them in the car . . .'

We wove our way up the dark, windblown coast. Seabrooke disappeared behind us and we entered thick bush. Stuart struggled with the cornering. He sang under his breath. The road was marked out by white reflector posts. I checked off each post as we swung by. Post by post the ancient heap of a car carried us north, away from the dark.

8. Lawrence

At the ring road junction just before the turn-off to Lawrence workmen were erecting a huge black and white election hoarding. I watched them fitting the panels of the Prime Minister's face together. LET'S GET NEW ZEALAND GROWING, the hoarding said. Our leader beamed down over the clump of nikau palms and feathery ponga ferns growing in the middle of the roundabout. Up close his face was a configuration of black and white dots, his face was made of pixels. The workmen were tying back the palms with wire so that they didn't blow about under his chin, giving him a green beard.

Along the road Stuart was still in the phone box. Trucks roared by, shaking the car. I turned the radio on and fiddled with the dial until I found a station. The voice announced Radio Coromandel and began to play a tearful old dirge by Rod Stewart.

Stuart came picking his way back along the narrow grass verge. 'OK, the Lehmans are home. They don't mind that we're late. It's about forty minutes from here, apparently, down the Lawrence road.'

We drove around the roundabout and turned onto the Lawrence road. A sign said WINDING ROAD, TEN MILES. The narrow road rose steeply through thick bush, up into the Lawrence Hills.

On the radio the mournful song finished and the news came on. The radio crackled with static. 'There's something about Mrs Fink-Jensen,' I said, playing with the dial. I found the station. Two days ago, the radio was announcing over the rasp and fizz of the static, prominent anti-crime campaigner Barbara Fink-Jensen had been arrested. Hauled to the Central Police Station and the District Court and bailed to appear for a defended hearing in three months' time. Only, disappointingly, not on a charge of shoplifting or fraud or aggravated robbery, or even threatening to kill (something she appears to do every week on television). She was charged with importing and possessing offensive weapons, namely Mace canisters, for squirting in the eyes of rapists and muggers, in self-defence. Mrs Fink-Jensen herself was not commenting on the charge, but her wraithlike husband, Norman 'Nong' Fink-Jensen stated importantly that this would be a test case, highlighting the inadequacies in the law relating to private citizens' rights to defend themselves and their families from the rising-tide-of-violence in society today. In a brief comment Kendrick Stain offered his sympathies to Mrs Fink-Jensen and her family. When asked, hypothetically, he replied that he would be happy to represent her himself on her day in court. 'I would devote to her case the care and attention that I devote to all my criminal clients,' he said. I could picture him, grinning at that, shifting from one foot to the other, tweaking the loose threads in his holey, aubergine waistcoat.

The Fink-Jensens were responding to his offer in a restrained manner. Not in a million years. Barbara would rather go to prison for life. We would never stoop so low as to. That appalling man. That criminal.

Nong Fink-Jensen said he had been touched by offers of support and sympathy from the 'wider community out there as a whole'.

Unfortunately his wife could not honour any mail orders for

Mace canisters, since they had all been seized as evidence. Mrs Fink-Jensen was impressed by the courteous treatment she had received from the police and realised that like her, they were the meat in the sandwich at the end of the day.

'Oh that's so funny,' I crowed, trying to turn it up. 'Good on the police for arresting her.'

But Stuart didn't laugh. I glanced over and he was looking sideways with a strange expression. What could I have said? I had thought we were friends again . . . For a moment his mouth contorted into an odd and bitter smile, he eyed me with a kind of rage. His eyes were bright, as if I were a rodent and he was poised, to swoop down . . . He saw my surprise, and turned his head away. He said quietly, to the windscreen, '*Hooray* for police . . .'

The radio said, 'Unconcerned by the delay, the Prime Minister joined the old folk in a rousing rendition of "God Save the Queen".'

Stuart drove on, wearing a strange remote expression.

'What are you thinking about?' I asked.

After a silence he said, 'I've been to Lawrence. It's beautiful. A tiny little settlement. Lovely white sand beaches. One shop. Rolling hills. Pity we won't get a chance to enjoy it.'

It started to rain hard. The road was unpaved and the gravel moved treacherously under the wheels. Small streams ran out of the bush, turning parts of the road into churned-up troughs of mud. It was clear that the road hadn't been properly graded for weeks. 'One thing I've been thinking,' he said in a more normal voice as he struggled to keep the car out of the patches of mud, 'is that by the time I'm finished with this thing I'm going to make the jury want to lock up the Leonards.'

As we drove further up into the hills I gave up fiddling with the radio. It had completely cut out. I looked out at the steep banks of bush, the impenetrable tangle of the trees. I thought about Carlos's parents, the Lehmans. 'I suppose it's natural the Lehmans still want him around, after he's killed someone. But you'd think if your son got into that situation you'd feel *put off* him . . . I mean how do they actually know he's not going to go off his nut again and slay them in their beds?'

Stuart said irritably, 'He's their son. Familiarity breeds contempt. To them he's just boring old Carlos, not the crazed gunman of Seabrooke.'

'But everything's changed. He can never be boring old so-and-so again.'

'It's not necessarily logical but it's why they're not scared of him. Look at the wife, she wants him back. She was frightened of him when he had his big breakout. She's screened that out now. She still loves him.'

The road wound around in a corkscrew, we crossed a bridge across a stream made roaring and swollen by the heavy rain, and then the road levelled out as we reached the hill summit. Through breaks in the bush we could see the grey sea a long way below. The horizon was black with raincloud. We began to descend, gradually at first, then more steeply through a narrow gorge. Stuart was silent and tense, peering ahead through the fogged windscreen. He began to accelerate impatiently at stretches where the road straightened out. The car shuddered unnervingly. I leaned against his shoulder and tried vainly to keep up a conversation. Some small talk. 'Did I tell you Benkie said that the Minister of Justice has AIDS?'

'Yes . . . but he'll be lying. He's a medical bullshit artist. He tells career-destroying anecdotes that aren't even true.'

'That's not true. What are you talking about?'

'It is true. He told one about the Deputy Prime Minister having cirrhosis of the liver, something like that, being brought into hospital. I knew it wasn't true. You know why? Because he'd told the same story months ago, about a *different person*. Exactly the same story, different body.'

'You're making that up.'

'No I'm not.'

'You're just being nasty.'

He looked at me and smiled suddenly, and patted me on the knee.

As we were winding our way down the hills he said, 'Hold the wheel a minute' while he felt around for his diary on the floor under his feet. The rain was drumming on the roof and streaming down the windows. I turned the wheel too quickly on a corner, the angle was difficult. 'Slow down,' I said. 'Eh?' he grunted, and the car began to turn side on to its trajectory, and kept moving forward anyway, sliding towards the bank, and Stuart pulled his way upright in his seat and fought with the steering wheel until the car was back on track.

'You do these things on purpose,' he said. 'You're trying to kill me. You probably don't even realise it. It's subconscious.'

'Trying to kill myself too then, since I'm in the car with you.'

'It's M.A.D. – Mutual Assured Destruction.'

I laughed and he began to look more cheerful. The road began to level out and we drove out of the bush onto a clear area of flat sandy beach. The radio came back on. Out of the static came the voice of Rod Stewart, clear as a siren, wailing.

Dolph Lehman pointed out the scratches on the side of the Porsche. He and his wife were waiting for us on their driveway. They greeted us formally, shaking hands.

'Vot a shame, vot a shame,' Dolph said, running his hands gently along the car's damaged flank. 'My nephew, you know, is a fontostic panel beater. He could fix this in a trice. Man, young woman, come in. We will have coffee.'

Millicent and Dolph Lehman wanted their son to live with them if he were to be granted bail. For them there was no alternative. He must come home. Sitting in their lacy front room filled with china knick-knacks and a wide view of the cold sea, Stuart explained to them that alleged murderers don't get bail very often.

'Nevertheless,' he said, 'even with that in mind, I have a feeling. My colleague and I have absorbed a tremendous amount of detail about the case. We have just been to Seabrooke. We have a proper picture, er, in our minds, as to the forces at work in that town.'

Dolph was tall, with a long face and bulging watery blue eyes. He had abundant hair, thick and straight and combed off his forehead, back into a blond quiff. Millicent was tall and big-boned, in sensible slacks and orthopaedic shoes, thick glasses and a sturdy cardigan. We sat on a tasselled, baubled, velveteen lounger while the brass clocks bonged and twanged and the china figurines smiled mildly down from the crowded shelves. Millicent served coffee out of a china jug. She served in a gentle sing-song, one and one and so and so, and you and you and you. Behind her glasses her eyes were a pale and vulnerable blue. Her eyes apologised for everything, for the whole world.

'He is our son. We have no other children. They can say what they like, but I know he isn't evil. We want to help him. Leah has told us about the people in the town, how they drove him mad.'

'We have had him, you see, since he was eight years old,' Dolph said. 'We couldn't have the family of our own. But he was such a bright boy and a nice kid. He did well at school, at sports. We felt so lucky to have him. You know, some years ago he paid for me and Millicent to go to Fiji for a holiday.'

He was an informal adoption, arranged between the families. Dolph and Millicent weren't related to him, but over a period of about five years they had come to know Carlos's family well. They had gone on holiday up north one year in their caravan. They found a campsite at an unpopulated bay on the KariKari Peninsula. The bay was part of a large piece of land owned by Carlos's extended family, the Ihakas. Carlos had come to live at the bay with his mother's aunt and uncle. The Lehmans got permission to camp on the beach. The family welcomed them and they all became friendly very quickly.

The bay was right at the tip of the peninsula and the access road was blocked off by a private-property sign. No one came through the wooden gate except Carlos's Maori family and, once they had been accepted onto the land, the Lehmans.

Mrs Lehman said, 'When we first met them it was a blazing hot day. Dolph left me in the car and climbed over the gate. How can the whole road be private property? he said. He walked past the marae and the houses and down to the beach. He couldn't find anyone home. I sat in the car dying of heat, embarrassed, wishing we could just go somewhere else and camp. A nice camping ground . . . although the bay was the most beautiful place we'd seen. Then I heard cars coming. It was the Ihakas coming home. Three carloads of them, they had been to a funeral. A tangi. There I was stuck in our car blocking the road and Dolph had the car keys. They all got out. I felt such a fool but to my relief they weren't even annoyed. They parked at the gate and we all walked up to the main house.

'Carlos was there, walking with the other little children. He must have been about three and a half. A really handsome little boy. The children were all marching, carrying toitoi sticks. Carlos had bright green eyes. Even on the first day I saw him I admired him. He was so quick and such a jolly boy and he was friendly too. Early on I loved him, as if he had always been mine. It wasn't like adopting a newborn baby, the thing an hour old and completely unknown. I saw what he was like and I fell in love with him.'

Millicent peered at us through the bottle bottoms of her specs, smiling gently, shrugging her shoulders.

Dolph said, 'Mrs Ihaka and Millicent were both interested in the church. Earl Ihaka and I were interested in fishing. We got on very well. We were living in Auckland then, and in the wintertime they would stay with us. They would bring Carlos and when he got older he used to come and stay by himself. Then Earl got a job in Australia and the Ihakas left Carlos with us while they lived in Adelaide. When they came back, Carlos didn't go back to them, he stayed with us. We sent him to Dilworth School.'

Millicent arranged the coffee jug nervously, with her big hands. She was around six feet tall. She said, 'Leah has always told us everything. She and Carlos were very successful with their fish export business. They had high hopes for Seabrooke. Leah is a very good young woman, we see her often. We have always tried to help them. They told us about their problems with Seabrooke but we couldn't help, of course.'

'Carlos has never been violent,' Dolph said. 'Never with us or

Leah or the children. He has always been strong-willed, but always cheerful and enthusiastic. We went to see him. We asked him. We tried to understand. He couldn't talk about it. He said he couldn't remember. I could see how upset he was getting so we just talked about the children instead.'

'You know Leah saw him with the gun, that she was terrified?'

'Of course, of course, but she's not frightened of him now, she's frightened for him. She loves him. And now he's lost.'

Mrs Lehman stared out the window at the white sky. She said, 'I would just like him to come home. But everything is changed, the family has been blown to bits. When I heard the news I felt as if I would fall onto the floor and die.'

We all looked out the window, stirring our coffee, picturing Mrs Lehman crashing to the floor in the small room, the china shepherdesses and the gilt-edged plates jolted off their stands, lying around her in shards. And Cyril Leonard reeling and spinning in his doorway, the plastic fly strips blowing around him. Leah and the children screaming in the speeding car. It began to pour. Big raindrops smacked on the window. Rain was falling out on the dunes and on the cold sea.

'Oh Dolph,' whispered Mrs Lehman through her great hands, 'why must it be always the rain?'

Mrs Lehman excused herself and went out to bring in her washing. I followed her and offered to help. We loaded the huge cotton towels and bloomers and singlets, all white, into a red and green plastic washing basket. The rain pelted down. 'Thank you,' she said, breathing hard, 'it was nearly dry.'

'Hasn't it been raining all day?'

'No, not down here. Only up on the hills.'

We hurried back inside. Looking at the back of her head I had a memory of my mother long ago, standing at the window with Una and me, peering out at the rain. Phoebe would stare gloomily out at the watery garden, her bristling hair looking just like Millicent's, dampened by the humidity, so that it formed a flat plane across the top of her head. 'Well, girls,' she'd say, 'it's coming down in buckets today. All over the world!'

She always said that; she liked the sound of the words, they sounded melancholy to her. She liked being melancholy. She liked to drift around when it rained, doing nothing in particular.

I dumped the bulging washing basket in the porch. Cold rain ran down the back of my neck, and Mrs Lehman brought me a towel to dry my hair.

She hung the towel on a wooden towel rack. 'Carlos made the clothes horse,' she said. The rack creaked and sagged brokenly as it took the weight of the towel. She straightened it impatiently. 'He was no use at woodwork, not like Dolph. Dolph is quite a craftsman. Carlos is a farmer.'

She went to the sink and said, arranging some cakes on a tray, 'Friends in the church made these scones, they're really nice ladies. They keep sitting me down lately to talk about Carlos. They say I've done my best but it's well known, bad blood will come out. It's real kindness to adopt a child, but it's a terrible risk. They say I have to let him go and get on with my life, let someone else deal with him now. But what do they know about Carlos? I've been his mother for twenty-seven years, I have to let him go? They think he's a cat, to be taken away by the vet.'

Millicent took off her glasses and wiped them on the towel. She screwed up her eyes and rubbed them with her fists and glared out at the rainy sea. 'They talk about his nature, you know. They talk about him as if he isn't *mine*.'

On the long drive back from Lawrence Stuart and I went through more of the evidence against Lehman. I read extracts to him while he drove. The first was by the arresting officer, Royden Sloacombe, Community Constable.

After shooting Leonard, Carlos had walked slowly away. He dropped the gun. He walked along the main road leading through the town and headed towards the intersection with the main highway north. He hadn't got far before Sloacombe drove up behind him in his Rover, jumped out and pointed his own shotgun at Carlos. Sloacombe ordered Carlos to lie down on the roadside. Carlos complied. When the Armed Offenders Squad arrived later Carlos was still lying on the road on his stomach with Sloacombe standing over him.

According to Sloacombe, Carlos had asked whether Leonard was dead. Sloacombe replied that he believed that Leonard was dead and on hearing this Carlos replied, 'Good. Serves the bastard right.' Then he chanted in a deranged fashion, 'I'll kill you all, I'll kill you all.'

('Oh did he? Well we both know how believable Sloacombe is,' Stuart said.)

According to Morven Garland, Lehman's behaviour had been causing concern in the town for some time. Lehman had been running along his fence line shouting at people walking past on the road, and the Garland family had been alarmed by him gesticulating at them and shouting obscenities on two occasions when they were walking past his property on the way to church. The townspeople had gone out of their way to make Lehman and his family welcome, but the Lehmans chose to ignore all social overtures and offers of help, and increasingly the townspeople 'began to avoid Mr and Mrs Lehman because of their strange and aggressive behaviour'.

On the day of the crime Morven Garland had been in the front garden of his house opposite the Leonards' house. He had seen Lehman drive up to the Leonards' house. Lehman had gone inside the house and spent about five minutes in there. When he came out Cyril Leonard came out after him. Leonard said a few words to Lehman and Lehman began to display considerable agitation, shouting and waving his arms and kicking over a letter box. According to Garland, Leonard 'appeared to be trying to calm Lehman down'.

Lehman got into his car and drove off at high speed. Ten minutes later Garland saw Lehman's car 'screech to a halt' outside the Leonards' house. Lehman got out carrying the shotgun. Mr Leonard appeared in the doorway of the house. The two men spoke briefly to one another again. Lehman then raised the gun to his shoulder and fired once at Leonard, hitting him in the head. Leonard fell to the ground and Lehman walked away.

When he judged Lehman was a safe distance from the gun, Garland ran across the road and picked it up. He then ran to Mr Leonard and found that Leonard was dead.

Tracey Garland said in the first of her recorded interviews that the Lehman family had always been rude and antisocial. Lehman's wife had attended the local fair with her children but had behaved so oddly that Tracey Garland had wondered whether Mrs Lehman had been drunk or drugged. On one occasion she had expressed some concerns to Mrs Lehman about the state of health of the Lehmans' younger son. He had seemed to her to be sick and weak and underweight. The child had appeared to be very unwell on several occasions when she had seen him in the town. Mrs Lehman had reacted violently to the suggestion that the child was unwell. She had sworn at Tracey Garland and pushed her roughly aside. Mrs Lehman had then picked up the child and thrown him into the car so that he hit his head on the doorframe.

Tracey Garland said that she and the other townspeople had initially tried to be friendly to the Lehmans, but that their offers of friendship had been met with hostility and increasingly threatening behaviour. People in the town had been concerned that the Lehman children looked neglected.

Tracey Garland had been in the house opposite the Leonards' when she heard the shot. She looked out the window and saw Cyril Leonard lying on the ground. She did not see Lehman walking away . . .

After the Lawrence Hills we drove for another hour reading the statements, until we felt hungry. We pulled over at a motorway service centre and parked on the wide tarmac outside the burger bar. Over the oily rainbows of the drenched asphalt and the emerald green of the swampy paddocks the sky hung low and black. It looked like rain, and rain and rain. We trailed yawning and stretching into the bright hamburger restaurant. In the harsh neon light Stuart's face was dry and chapped. Sitting in the plastic cubicle he picked his nails and stared around at the fat diners, the floor covered in paper packaging, spillages of sauce and milk-shake, the attendants with their greasy skins and acne under their paper hats.

Hunched over our boxed meals we read over the interviews with Boyderman Leonard. Boyderman said that Lehman had consistently strayed over the boundaries into land that was not his. His behaviour was always aggressive and irrational. He believed, mistakenly, that stock had been allowed to stray onto his land by people who wanted to destroy his trees and drive him off the land. Lehman had never spoken to Boyderman Leonard except to shout abuse at him across the boundary fence. Boyderman Leonard had feared that Lehman was going to commit some act of violence in the town, and had voiced these concerns to the Community Constable two weeks before his brother was shot.

Stuart chewed his nails. He said, 'They're all rallying round, aren't they. Portraying him as a nutter. And yet, does it ring entirely true? Not to us, we've been to Seabrooke. We know what it's like down there. But to someone who doesn't know anything about it, wouldn't it sound a bit funny anyway, the way they are all at pains to say that Lehman was crazy, and that they were all terribly nice to him?'

'Well, no . . . Not really. If you didn't know anything about it you'd just think he must be crazy. It all stacks up against him, when you read them all together.'

'It's true, it stacks up. And he did shoot someone in the head at close range. But you can tell, reading these staements, that they're aware of things that they're not going to talk about. They're just a tiny bit on the back foot. Underneath they know that some of them played a part in it all. He did something terrible, but some of them drove him to it. Imagine playing the game they played, destroying a man's livelihood, wrecking his crops and equipment. They're all farmers down there. They're not urban delinquents. They know what it means to cause that sort of damage, it means ruin. And they kept on doing it until one of their own got killed. Now how would that make them all feel?'

I thought back to the detail in the file. 'Cyril Leonard didn't have much to do with the harassment. Lehman was looking for Boyderman Leonard when he went to Cyril's house. He wanted to talk to Boyderman. So Lehman says.'

Stuart was scrabbling around, finding the right pages. 'So certain people in the town have been playing this dangerous game and as a result, boom, little Cyril the electrician, who's no trouble at all and who everyone likes, is killed. Wouldn't that make them feel a little bit guilty themselves? At least, like people who have something to hide? And Carlos, he has nothing to hide. He denies nothing. This is his main advantage.'

'But he's got no one to back him up. No witnesses to say he was harassed. They'll all just say he's lying, or that it was all in his head.'

'He's got Leah.'

'Yeah. Only her.'

Stuart slurped on his milkshake. 'We should think through the law on this. He says he was provoked to such an extent that he lost control of himself at the crucial point. Suddenly he was not a master of his own mind. Cyril wasn't involved in the harassment and vandalism, but he taunted Carlos about his failure to fit in in the town. His failure to get his land producing. The second thing is that when Carlos was provoked by Cyril he didn't attack Cyril outright, he went away and got his gun and then came back and did Cyril in.'

Stuart was getting into his stride, emphasising his points with his milkshake straw. 'It doesn't matter that Cyril didn't participate in the harassment and vandalism. What Cyril did was taunt and jeer at Carlos about his problems. In isolation a bit of teasing and taunting doesn't look much of a provocation but in context it was the final straw. Also Cyril was Boyderman's brother, and Boyderman Leonard was responsible for most of the confrontations and unpleasantness, and, in Carlos's opinion, for most of the damage and thefts. To Carlos, Cyril would have looked as likely to be responsible as his brother.'

Behind the burger counter two of the workers were arguing,

the senior in her paper crown berating the bowed junior in his nylon tam-o'-shanter. She waved a clipboard at him, stabbing her finger into the paper, he glared up at her out of the rash and the raw of his acne. I said, watching them, 'But it would be simpler if he'd picked up a brick and attacked Cyril straight away.'

'Well, he has to show that the state of mind when all control was lost lasted throughout the time he got in his car, drove up the road, got the gun and came back. If there's a period of time between the provocation and the killing it starts to look premeditated. If it's premeditated, well . . .'

I took some notes. 'Get us another fishburger darl,' Stuart said. He looked out from under his eyebrows. There were faint shadows under his eyes. Sitting there in the neon glare he looked cynical, hard, amused, like a criminal, filled with cunning, with criminal know-how. Those blue-grey eyes, how much they took in. How little they missed. He was looking at me looking at him. And yet his eyes were softened by his long lashes, his hair was thick and dark, and his hands were awkward. His hands were touching. I went for the fishburger. When I got back he was studying some affidavits. He laughed out loud. 'Listen to this,' he said. 'Some of the things people say, they're so fucking *green*.'

And then, driving down the motorway towards Auckland, we decided to stop for some wine. 'Get some white,' he said, pushing me out of the car door at a red light. 'I'll park around the corner.'

'Some white,' I muttered, staring along the chilly street. I turned into the Wine Barn, a huge cavernous shop filled with everything, from schnapps to Babycham, low alc to high alc, champagne to Old Pale Gold sherry, all arranged in aisles and specials bins and everything On Sale! Reduced! Two for the price of one! In one corner a promotional person in a gorilla suit handed out free promotional snackettes, in convenient bite-sized packettes.

I trailed down the noisome aisles. The purple carpet and the rustic bargain bins, the defectively blinking neon lights, the swaying oldies with their furtive bottles of sherry filled me with a sense of depression. How harsh everything looked. How ugly. How did I find anything in this huge warehouse? Did they have a white section? I flusteredly enquired. 'Round behind the Beer Grotto,' I was told. 'To the left of the Nibble Nook.'

At the Nibble Nook I purchased a packette of Kashoos. Then a packette of Krisps. The gorilla approached holding his Snackette Sak. I stood before the towering whites shelf. The gorilla whispered behind me, 'Feeling peckish?' The labels swam before me. Blindly I reached for one bottle and another. A small headache started up around the bridge of my nose.

Back at the car Stuart paced, stretching his legs. He waved me over, jogging and snorting and doing star jumps on the spot. We got in and headed out onto the highway. 'Got any cash left?' he said cheerfully. 'Let's get takeaways.'

I pulled his wallet out of his jacket to look for change. We were heading along the highway towards the eastern junction where the width of the road quadruples eventually and the motorway begins. It was starting to get dark. The lights of the city cast a dirty orange glow into the sky ahead. I played with his wallet, noticing that the leather stitching was coming loose. Deep down in an inside flap I found a small photo of a woman with dark wavy hair. 'Who's this?' I asked, knowing who it was.

He glanced over. 'That's me,' he said.

'It's not you. What do you mean?'

He reached over and snatched the picture out of my fingers.

'Me. Mia. My ex-wife,' he snapped. He shoved the picture in his shirt pocket. He drove faster, past a police speed check.

'Careful,' I said nastily, 'you can't just flash them your badge.' He shrugged his shoulders angrily and speeded up.

He reached over quickly and took a look at the bottles of wine I had bought. He looked again, then pushed the bag onto the floor of the car. 'One of these is *Riesling*, Stella,' he said, his voice gone cold. He leaned forward over the steering wheel and began to work himself up. 'Riesling! . . . If there's something to be done you do it wrong deliberately, don't you?' He pushed his wallet into the back pocket of his jeans and began to raise his voice. 'You drift around, you take no fucking notice, you go and buy Riesling, you buy stuff that nobody likes and then it's up to me to fix everything, all your uninterested disorganised attempts at things. How do you think I feel, I work all day and who knows what you're doing. Just going around pleasing yourself, your own little agenda, your little secret life!' He started to choke and cough on his anger.

Slowing to ninety we entered a roundabout, causing a small Toyota to drive up onto a traffic island. Then we got onto the highway and really started to move. Flattened in my seat I watched the scenery shoot by in a rainbow paste, houses and cars and trees blurred into one long tube of colour, telegraph poles flickering, wires looping and merging. Over the scream of the engine Stuart's words were indistinct, they came to me hollowly, the volume distorted, sounding high and then low, like words on a broken cassette, mad noise.

He looked over at me, opening his mouth to say something else, but the car shuddered and then we were all over the road, swerving across the lanes, nearly clipping the side of a truck, bouncing away into the fast lane, sweeping back across the path of our horrified fellow motorists. I saw, in slow motion, as we blazed across the front of a family Volvo, the right arm of each passenger go up simultaneously to cover each screaming face. I watched them go behind me as I went spinning towards death, closed my eyes, waiting, only to feel the car begin to steady, the speed to slacken, and we were back in the slow lane motoring along like a couple of ordinary berks who'd entered the lane in a normal fashion, rather than rocketing in a death-spin out of the truckway. All around us cars began to evade, dropping back or changing lanes. No one was going to put up with that again. No one wanted to be anywhere near us. There was a stunned silence in the car. Stuart wiped his forehead on his sleeve.

'You're completely crazy,' I started to shout as we motored along. After the fright I felt mad suddenly, like a dog going berserk on the end of a chain. 'You're cracked in the head, you're mentally ill.' Gathering momentum I raved, 'You're trying to kill me, you're wrecking my nerves. I do everything for you, you slavedriver, I run around after you and you criticise and complain, half the time you're nasty and cold and all the time you don't tell me anything, you want me to drive you round, you want me to work on your files and you just throw money at me, you don't know how to have a wife or a family, all you know how to do is throw money, you act like everyone's your whore.'

On and on, revving and slowing, veering and weaving, the darkening afternoon streets. Black rage in the screaming car. Writhing, sickening, slavering rage.

And afterwards (as we park, dust ourselves off, straighten our brows), the misery in the tiny internal voice, oh I didn't mean all that, oh how have we gone so wrong, so terribly wrong. Oh can't we start again.

'I'm sorry,' I wanted to say, as we walked, faces averted, towards the open gate.

9. A disgrace

'It's a disgrace.'

'Appalling.'

'Shocking. The people of this country have a right to ask what is going on. Just what is going on?'

'No one will be safe in their beds.'

'Pour yourself one, darling. Pour me another. There's life in the old dog yet.'

We paused for a moment on a bench in Albert Park, coming out of the library after the rain, the concrete around the statues steaming, the lush trees sodden and heavy-green, the flowerbeds lurid under the rain-black sky. The spring wind sent the weather racing, the clouds dumped water and moved on, a heavy shower drenched Queen Street while up the hill the sun brightened the park and a rainbow rode over the Hyatt Hotel. I thought of Millicent Lehman waving us off from her veranda, peering blindly out through the spring rain.

Stuart was murmuring under his breath, with his eyes shut

tight. He opened his eyes, sat up and looked at his watch. Carlos Lehman's bail application was set for 2.30. It was time to go. I gathered up the notes and files and we walked briskly together to the courthouse. Inside the building the echoing foyer was dark and cool, noise floated up into the void of the high ceiling and swirled around and floated down, the low voices, clicking foot-steps, heavy doors slamming, a baby's wail, all distorted and time-delayed, like the cases being heard behind the dark wood doors, here was court, where normal transactions cease. We con-sulted a clerk, who told us that the chambers hearing was to be heard in one of the small upstairs courtrooms, number 101.

Upstairs Stuart took his place at the front of the empty court-room and I slid into a wooden seat at the side of his table. Cecil Dykstra, representing the Crown, walked in briskly with one of his assistants and greeted Stuart in a friendly way, as if he didn't expect to have any problems.

We waited for about ten minutes for the judge to arrive. The application was to be heard in front of Justice Rigby, a tough judge, notorious for favouring the Crown.

Eventually the side door opened and the judge tramped in, a heavy woman with a large grey plait of hair woven around the top of her head. She peered severely around the room, acknowledged everyone and fell to organising the papers in front of her on the desk.

After a while she looked up and made formal noises, inviting everyone to begin. She gave no appearance of hearing a word Stuart said as he stood up and began to outline the basis for the application, and to refer her to the affidavits in support of it. He set out at length, in his formal nasal barrister's twang, the reasons why it would be reasonable to grant Lehman bail. He emphasised his words by gesturing with his left hand, the thick fingers splayed open, the right hand held behind his back. He told her about the family's support for Carlos Lehman, their ability to provide sureties and their willingness to look after and supervise him if he got bail. He referred to the wife and four children. He wove in references to the circumstances of the shooting.

Justice Rigby, slumped above us, appeared almost to be in a trance. She sat shuffling the papers in front of her, patting a hand over her big stack of hair, staring up at the high wooden windows of the courthouse. The sun shone beams of light through the dusty room, the particles of dust were drifting and falling through the yellow air. From somewhere far away, outside or below, voices were suddenly raised in shouts or cheers, as if someone had been acquitted, or convicted. Beside Stuart, Cecil Dykstra doodled on his pad, shaking his head gently.

Stuart came to a stop. The judge looked down at him. There was a pause. She and Stuart sat still for a second or two, considering one another. She went to speak as he was about to add something. 'Go ahead,' she said.

'No please,' he said lightly. 'After you.'

There was another pause, and she smiled thinly. Cecil Dykstra scratched his head and looked boredly over in the direction of the blonde court clerk.

'I'm thinking very carefully about this,' the judge said. Her accent was broadly Kiwi. She was reputed to be formidably clever, and was famous for having five daughters who all looked exactly like her, all Amazons, over-achievers, with great crackling haystacks of ginger hair.

She made some notes. 'I've read the papers and they're reasonably interesting.'

She looked coldly over her spectacles, and said in a casual voice, 'May I say before we go on, that I'm inclined at this point to consider the application with favour.'

Cecil Dykstra looked up in surprise. She turned to him. He got awkwardly to his feet and began to shuffle with his papers. In a slightly disorganised fashion he began to outline the objections of the Crown. Justice Rigby listened to him alertly, taking notes.

After a couple of minutes Cecil Dykstra relaxed and began to get into his stride. The facts clearly showed that Lehman was a danger to public safety. There was a distinct risk of him re-offending. There was the probability that he would flee from justice, especially since he was charged with such a serious offence. It would be impossible to impose enough proper restraints on him if he were to live in Lawrence with his adoptive parents. There were the witnesses in the case to consider: their safety could be compromised. To release Lehman would be an affront to the family of the deceased . . .

Cecil Dykstra ran on, reading from his notes. It was not in the interests of justice that a man charged with such a serious crime should be allowed bail. It was inconceivable, he concluded, that Lehman should not remain in Mount Eden jail until such time as he could be tried.

He finished, taking a deep breath and slamming his notebook shut. Justice Rigby was silent again, stroking her hair. Quietly at his table, Stuart spread out his fingers and looked at his hands. He took a tissue out of his pocket, fumbled with it and carefully wiped the end of his pen.

The judge shuffled her papers. She looked enquiringly at Stuart, raising her eyebrows. He stood up and spoke briefly again. Lehman would not and could not flee. There was no basis for saying that he would intimidate witnesses or commit further crimes. He would return to the bosom of his family. He would never leave the grounds of his parents' house. He was a family man . . .

The judge wrote everything down. Then she laid down her pen and stared curiously at Stuart for a moment. He sat down, his eyes modestly lowered. She cleared her throat. I listened as she began reading the notes she had written, while Stuart looked straight ahead with a bland smile and Cecil Dykstra began to shift uncomfortably in his seat. It was as simple as that: no pre-amble or speech, sitting with her great brown hands folded in front of her, in her harsh old voice, the judge began imposing the conditions of Lehman's bail.

'I knew I was going to get it,' Stuart said, as we trotted down the steps of Constitution Hill, 'because I could tell Rigby wanted to know all about Lehman. I knew she'd read it all carefully. She had the depositions in mind. She was quite open to the idea that

Carlos could commit the crime and yet be no danger to anyone now. Another judge would have worried about causing controversy. But it took her imagination. And Carlos won't do anything wrong while he's out. He'll just live quietly with the family until the trial.'

After the judge had given her decision and swept back through her side door the Crown Solicitor allowed himself a few disgusted oaths and then stalked from the court. He was now looking at the decision with a view to making an appeal.

'Like hell you are,' Stuart said. 'How are you going to tell the judge anything new?'

And now we marched up Parnell Road in a sun shower, the papers and leaves and raindrops blowing madly around us in the spirals of the spring wind.

At 5 p.m. the following afternoon Carlos stood with us at the dusty wooden counter in the long, low prefabricated outbuilding at the gates of the jail. He glanced up into the neutral face of the waiting clerk. Picking up a Biro he signed his name at the bottom of some Xeroxed forms, which were fanned in front of him on the desk. The clock above his head, encased in its protective grille, ticked out his time. Outside, the outside waited, in the long white cloudy afternoon.

The prison officers had made it a point of honour to hide their surprise. Most had affected quiet, affronted disgust. A couple wished him well. He had never caused them any trouble. Now, clutching the large envelope containing his personal effects, he stood goose-pimpled and shivering inside his thin baggy clothes. He hadn't gained weight in jail, instead he had lost an alarming amount. His feet looked like snowshoes at the end of his stick-like legs. He stood passively, waiting for direction.

We had wanted to congratulate him and slap him on the back when we arrived at the jail but we checked ourselves when the jingling warder ushered him into the room. He looked so shell-shocked and strained that we began to talk in low, hushed voices, and when he had signed the forms we gathered up his things and ushered him carefully towards a chair to wait for the final call.

In the carpark Mrs Lehman smoothed the sheepskin car seat cover with her big hands. At her feet were packages of Carlos's clothes, and a large Thermos. They had arrived two hours before. Certain formalities had been performed. Mr Lehman had spoken at length with Stuart and signed a number of forms, and talked to several officials and clerks. Remember, Stuart said to them, this is only step one. He still has to be tried, and sentenced. Enjoy his company while you can . . . Then they were told there was a delay. They went to wait in the car. Nervous, they sat in silence, holding hands. After a while Mr Lehman turned on the radio talkback hour, where callers rang in to discuss current events. They listened for minutes and then turned it off. All over the city people were ringing in. From every suburb, north, south, east and west. It was despicable, they said, that a killer was out. They wanted him back in. Or better yet, dead. He was better off dead.

'Oh good Lord,' breathed Mrs Lehman, twisting her glasses case in her hands. Over Mount Eden the great white cloud banks massed and shifted, darkened and lightened. She stared and stared through the window into the sky until the air danced in a billion particles, rising and falling with her breath, and she thought of all those calls whipping through the electronic air. Filled with venomous voices, shrill suburban complaint, righteous rage, the sky shimmered at her, sinisterly bright. Looking ahead, she saw the gates open and a small uncertain figure emerge. How little and bent he looked as he made his way through the cars under the invisible anger, the enemy sky.

The people were ringing Talkback Radio Quay. Down at the waterfront in his large studio looking out over the Gulf, DJ Maurice Schipt was talking through the afternoon's faxes. Ever since the announcement the previous afternoon that Carlos

Lehman was to be released on bail his radio station had not concerned itself with much else. On days like this Schipt called his station, Talkback Radio Quay, the People's Voice. Schipt wanted the voice to be heard, this was his calling. He liked to think that he pulled no punches. He was fond of saying, 'Here at the Quay, we take no flak we can't give back.' He knew that he infuriated and revolted some people. He knew he was the subject of much vicious satire and the butt of many jokes. It didn't matter. So much the better! He would never stop being heard. And that was thanks to the ratings. No one could argue with the ratings. In greater Auckland, he reminded us, all over the country in fact, he was wildly, sensationally popular.

In his studio now he would be adjusting his toupee, brushing the cake crumbs from his *sans*-a-belt slacks, leaning towards the microphone, curling and uncurling his toes inside his corduroy shoes. Schipt's big topic for the day was crime, crime being a popular topic, particularly with an election near and people being encouraged by both sides to think about crime all the time. (The government is soft on it! The Opposition can't deal with it!) Today Schipt was strongly in favour of capital punishment. He didn't sit on the fence. He put his money where his mouth was.

He began to send out his next message. 'Thank you for your calls and your faxes. Do you know, I've read them all. And boy, do I agree. You people out there, ordinary folk, law-abiding folk, for too long we've put up with this kind of namby-pambying from our courts. Criminals walking amongst us, murderers in our midst. The courts doing nothing to protect us from beasts in our community who go amongst us, threatening the very fabric of our children. And I say this, let's bring back hanging, let's bring back the birch. Let society give back the flak with the birch, with the rope. Let there be a buzz in the square, let the small boy look, mouth agrape, at the fate that will befoul him on the path of violent crime.'

At the director's desk tension would be beginning to mount, the studio boss whispering into Schipt's microphone, 'Good good, but not *kiddies* Mauree, tone it down there, mate.'

With perfect poise, Schipt began to wind it down. 'Remember, people, turn that dial and find the Quay. You're not alone, with 4968 WP.'

Over at the director's desk the guys would all be there saying Jeez, that Mauree, always giving us a heart attack. What a guy. What a guy he was. He sighed audibly into the mike. Soon he would go home and take off his hair. He would have a hot meal, relax, shake off the weariness of the day. Then he would lie there surrounded by the ferns in his steaming, swirling spa pool, with a *Penthouse* or one of his *Come!* or *Eat!* magazines and do all the things he liked to do while looking up women.

And now Carlos is driving away to Lawrence already hearing it, the silence and calm of the beach and the bush, and over to the north, sitting in our deckchairs high above the street on Stuart's top-floor veranda, we have all the hectic blare of media, all going at once.

'Pour yourself another one, darling,' says Stuart, reclining on his *chaise-longue*, looking as louche and smug as it is possible to look.

Vera twiddles with the radio. She says, 'Shouldn't it be . . . didn't he mean . . . "mouth *agape*? . . ."'

She blushes uncertainly. Stuart is watching television through the French doors. The news reader says, 'Carlos Henry Lehman was granted bail following a hearing in judge's chambers in the Auckland High Court yesterday. He is to live far away from Seabrooke, at the home of his parents, in the small settlement of Lawrence, near Coromandel. Strict bail conditions have been imposed, and Mr Lehman may not travel out of Lawrence without the permission of the police. He must report to the local police every day. Meanwhile in Seabrooke, the town where Mr Lehman allegedly shot local electrician Cyril Leonard, residents are shocked and angry at Mr Lehman's release. They say that they fear for their safety and that they will be arming themselves against any further violence or threat to their town . . .'

Released. Sprung. He's going home. In Seabrooke they can't

believe it. Does no one care about them? Stuart takes a few notes and sips on his gin. There's no doubt about it, our Stuart knows what he's doing. He homes in, he convinces, he persuades. He knows what makes us do what we do.

10. The news

The bail drama goes on. Holed up in the house with our gin and tonics, Stuart, Vera and I watch the story unfold on television. Members of the Leonard family appear and express shock that Lehman has been bailed. They request extra police protection for witnesses in the case.

'As if he'd go down there and threaten them,' Stuart snorts. 'Get off the grass.'

Solicitor General appears to say that there can be no appeal of the grant of bail. There is, he says, no right of appeal to the Court of Appeal against the decision of the High Court to grant or refuse bail before the trial. Finally he comments darkly that he thinks there should be a change in the Bail Act.

'That's right,' Stuart says, stirring his gin, 'bolt your stable door.'

News Hour reports that Carlos Lehman drove quietly into the town of Lawrence this evening. People in Lawrence were reluctant to be interviewed, but those who did speak to journalists indicated that they had little objection to Mr Lehman living in their town. The Lehman family were well respected in the area. The people of the town were defensive, and protective of their town. They hurried on their errands, with their heads down. The main complaint in Lawrence was that the place was suddenly full of journalists . . .

On a later news bulletin we watch Guy Nightdown, the maddest of the Opposition MPs, complaining bitterly about the decision. Guy Nightdown is always good for a laugh, with his sideburns, his walkshorts and socks, his short-sleeved shirts. His dubious business connections. He demands that Justice Rigby's decision be revoked by the government. The Minister of Justice explains patiently to a breathless interviewer that the government can't just *revoke* judicial decisions when it doesn't agree with them, it has to *abide* by them.

'Waffle!' retorts Nightdown, banging his fist on the table. 'Cowardice! Bunk! Get off the field!'

Later, answering the phone I hear the familiar drawl. 'Hey. Interesting noos . . .'

Stuart takes the receiver. 'Stain. How are you?' Covering the receiver with his hand he hisses, 'He's round the corner in his car. He wants to come over. Quick, get Voodoo to go down and lock the front door!'

'Voodoo?'

'I mean Vera, get Vera to head him off.'

But Voodoo is down in the office reading *The Mind in Balance* by Phyllis du Fresne. 'Listen to this,' she says. '"The psychopath uses a range of techniques to gain control in relationships. These techniques involve indirect rather than direct attempts to control. The display of *complete lack of feeling* – perhaps a humorous indifference to subjects that normally evoke emotions of horror, fear or disgust . . ."'

Vera swivels around in her chair and puts her feet in pointed shoes up on the desk. Her stocky calves bulge under the crimson stockings. Around her neck she wears a necklace made of large dried beans, and her bun, which sits square on the top of her head, is held together by a small sharpened stick.

'I've read quite a lot, trying to sort Frederick out.' (Frederick, her husband, a tyrannical invalid.)

There is a loud knocking at the window and Stain appears, waving his mobile phone. He taps jauntily on the window pane. Vera and I hesitate. Do we let him in? Pull down the blind? Sighing heavily, Vera waddles over to the window. 'You'd better come around to the door.'

He enters, stamping his long yellow shoes. Behind his thick glasses his eyes are avid and bloodshot. He screws up his long nose and sniffs like a dog. Twitching and shrugging in his shambolic clothes, he exudes an air of gruesome hilarity, as if deep down he is convulsed over the appalled reactions he creates. When I first began living with Stuart, Stain would ring me on some afternoons when he had nothing doing, and breathe obscene messages into the phone which made us both cackle with laughter, until Stuart would come in and start to frown and nag, about idleness and frivolity.

'What a lot of publicity. The beast on bail.' He runs his finger gently along the edge of Vera's in-tray. She glares at him, bored. Baring his big yellow teeth he says, 'I have a file I want to discuss. The Crown's case is a *house*, built . . .' he pauses for effect, 'on *sand*. Sand!' he repeats, peering at us madly, stroking Vera's pencil case.

'Stuart's not here,' Vera says stolidly. 'He went out.'

With a soft laugh he fingers the tip of Vera's cactus plant.

Stuart finally slouches in, having given up hiding out the back of the house. 'Stain,' he says coldly. 'Vera, get us another gin.

'That Nightdown. What a country. I don't know why you wanted to come and live in this country, Stain. Big talent like you, your dress sense.'

'Ah well.' Stain gives a secretive smile. 'Where I grew up was not so nice. This is a clean country. No talent, but no corruption.'

'Why don't people think there but for the grace of God . . .?'

'You'll be sorry if Lehman blows his parents' heads off,' Vera says suddenly.

She smirks. Stuart glares at her. 'He won't. He loves them. They're not going to be torturing him.'

'Hide the shotguns!' says Vera.

'I met Mrs Lehman at the prison,' Stain says. 'They were playing with the electronic doors, taking their time letting her through. She looked a delicate small thing in there, anxious face. You say she has four children? She looks very young.'

Stain looks slyly through his eyelashes, and Stuart, irritated by the thought of Stain approaching Leah, gets up off the window seat and walks restlessly around the room.

'So you talked to her?'

'No, not really, just passed the time of day while she was stuck behind the grille. I wished her the best of luck.'

'Gave her your card . . .'

'No, no.' Stain smiles, closed mouthed, forgiving. 'I gave her nothing but my sympathy.' He fingers the cactus again, gently.

Abruptly, with one of her mock screams, Vera heaves herself to her feet and starts gathering up her shopping bags, magazines, tissue boxes and chocolate wrappers. 'Goodness, the time. Frederick will be *berserk*. He thinks Stuart and I are having an *affair*.' She chuckles and winks while Stuart rolls his eyes behind her back. Big Vera. She slams down the phone, she bangs doors, she trips over the furniture. When the word processor breaks down he restrains her from shaking and whacking it, giving it a good honest thump.

'She looks like a Satanist,' Stuart says, watching her go down the path. 'That caftan . . . Sometimes,' he says, suddenly chilly and morose, 'I feel as if I'm running a *sheltered workshop*.' Vera struggles with the ignition, then revs the engine into a scream and manoeuvres the car forward in a series of jolts and jerks while Stuart watches from the window, rolling his eyes at the hopeless inefficiency of the world. 'Another gin, Stain?' Glaring around the room he adds, 'I'll get it.'

Stain reaches over and pulls my sleeve while Stuart is clinking around in the kitchen.

'Hey, when are you going to come and work for me?'

'Yeah yeah, sure.'

'I got some things on at the moment you'd love. Like Mrs Niedpath. Listen to this.'

Stain lights a cigarette, preparing to go into one of his monologues. 'The police knew she'd been murdered, right, and buried but they didn't have the body. They reckoned her neighbour had murdered her. They knew she was somewhere in the bush. They fixed on a slope and they ploughed over it for weeks using toothbrushes and toothpicks, you know, anything not to disturb the evidence. But after a few weeks they got fed up, they started to go over the ground a bit faster and a bit more careless, until one morning they were totally pissed off, they were sick of it, you know. The guy in the digger who's meant to be clearing the bush, he just takes off and goes roaring up the last bit of slope hell for leather. He's been out there so long with the flies and mosquitoes, he just doesn't give a damn any more. And they all go after him, they all think oh to hell with it, she's not here, and bang, at the top of the slope they strike her: poor Mrs Niedpath, after all, gets dug up and flung a hundred yards in every direction, and they have to spend the next few weeks on their hands and knees trying to pick up all the bits. Oh so funny. I split my side . . .'

Stuart comes back in with the gins, eyeing us coldly. 'What are you two laughing about?'

He glares. 'The kitchen is a mess,' he says to me.

'Oh man,' sighs Stain, wiping his eyes, 'why don't you clean it up then. Brother.'

Una says, 'You did it then.'

'Stuart did it. He was very smooth. He was brilliant.'

'The persuader.'

'Have you been watching the news?'

'I read an interview with Cyril Leonard's wife in the *Women's Daily*. She said that after Cyril was killed she decided to commit suicide. She said she thought to herself, Cyril has done it after all, died that is, and *he's* all right. Then she realised he wasn't all right.'

'Strange the way the mind works.'

'Benkie's at work. I'm on my own for the night.'

'Nice and safe in Remuera.'

'Well, it's a respectable neighbourhood, but that's why burglars come here. They *commute* here every night in their Chrysler Valiants.'

'Where did you read about Mrs Leonard?'

'The *Women's Daily*. Listen, forget about all that, I've got something to tell you.'

She tells me.

'Oh! Congratulations! Well done. Are you pleased?'

'Pleased and sick. I can't really understand why they let Lehman out, actually. Considering what he's supposed to have done.'

'Everybody knows what he's supposed to have done. They don't know what was done to him.'

'Why is that relevant? Nobody attacked him, did they? Nobody threatened him. He can't have been acting in self-defence.'

'Bit by bit they drove him mad. Every day they wrecked something he owned. He wanted to make the place a success and they wouldn't let him. They probably all enjoyed tormenting him. It was destroying his marriage. He began to feel as if they were killing him . . .'

She says impatiently, 'He could have just given up, sold up and walked away. If it was killing him.'

'But people don't do that, do they. They don't just walk away. They can't. That's why they're in trouble.'

She doesn't say anything for a moment. 'I need to go and be sick,' she says quietly.

'Oh it's great news, Una. I'm really pleased.'

I hang up. Another baby. This must be the reason why my sister has turned into a phone addict. She keeps ringing me to tell me about her days. I move around with the phone, listening while doing other things. Her communications are frequent, intense, full of hypersensitive detail. The inscrutable Una, suddenly talking so much. 'Now tell me about your day,' she'll say. Tell me everything . . .

Now all the rooms are dark. In the office Stuart sits on the window seat looking out over the harbour. Down at the marina the spiky masts bristle and sway. The sun is sinking down and on the horizon the islands are black against the silvery sea and the ferries making their way over the water are lit with swinging lights.

And far away in Lawrence, Carlos, lying in the dark on his parents' veranda, hears water running over rocks in the stream and the drip drip drip of the heavy ferns and the sound of the sea that has no waves only movement, only heavy water moving and sand shifting in the swell, and the stillness and calm and space all around him, hearing it.

11. Heat

Now the weather is really getting warm.

Waking in the morning in the top-floor bedroom, I feel the heat from the sun already spreading over the iron roof. The room is full of hot yellow light. Rolling slowly over, squinting in the glare from the edge of the curtain I see that Stuart has already gone. He gets up at dawn these days, to get everything done. Tomorrow we are going to Lawrence, to talk to Carlos Lehman. Outside, the neighbour's boy shouts from the next-door garden, a sharp command, 'Mum, Mum!' The buzz buzz of his mother's reply comes back over the noise of the radio and the dog barking. From far away I can hear the drone of cars commuting over the viaduct, queuing already to enter the city, the drivers in their sunglasses, hunched over their mobile phones. The clock says seven o'clock.

Outside in the front garden a tui warbles through its mad repertoire. The sky is perfect ceramic blue. I lean shakily out of the window, stretching, feeling the hot sun on my face, taking deep breaths, squinting up at the brash blue sky. It feels good to be alive . . . Behind the hedge, the neighbour and her son are arguing amiably. On the driveway a cat rolls in the dust.

'"Onward Christian soldiers",' I sing quaveringly under my breath as I make my way slowly towards the shower.

What a night I had, last night.

Yesterday evening we were in the office late, trying to print out some documents. Suddenly the machines seemed to shut down completely. The printer piped up with a persistent, infuriating electronic beep and the word processor screen died. Vera and I fiddled about and became more and more frustrated, and soon our exchanges were full of knives. The sun sank lower and the sky was streaked with pink, and Stuart sat wearily on the window seat and went through the manual trying to decipher the unreadable diagrams.

While I struggled with the printer Vera began to remind me of the dumb baby of some gang, running along behind, determined to lob her brick, falling over, boo-hooing, getting up, running home. Confused, irritable and ineffectual, she frowned in her purple caftan, fists clenched. Unable to decide what to do next, she suddenly gave in to a blaze of malice.

'Stella has damaged one of the components,' she said smoothly to Stuart. 'It doesn't break down for nothing.'

'I haven't broken it. You're the one who's always hitting it.'

'I do not,' she said indignantly, staring into the middle distance.

'You pull it around and karate-chop it, no wonder it's packed up.'

Vera went into an angry spasm, appealing around the room for witnesses. 'Well, there's no need to be so confrontational and . . . and . . .'

I went to get Odd-Jobs Wayne, who was drifting around the garden in the evening light, poking the plants with a trowel. He wore a ragged shirt with a tear in the back of it, as if someone had tried to rip it off. There was a long purple scratch on his cheek. He looked at me through the greasy strands of his fringe and came stiffly across the lawn. I watched him. Sometimes he wanders through the garden as if he is a moon walker, an underwater man, a flake whirling through the heavy liquid in a toy snowstorm. Whatever he puts into his veins, it holds and anchors and steadies him, so that he carries himself with a slow, swinging, heavy grace. Other days – and they must be Wayne's bad days, his going-without days – he is raw and irritated as he chops and slashes the hedges and trees, and he walks as if crushing insects underfoot. He approached, scratching his reddened neck and frowning and shaking the mud from his boots. 'Yeah what?' he asked, squinting down at me out of the dead green pools of his neutral eyes.

In the office Wayne and Stuart shifted the printer and the Xerox, got down under the desk and fiddled about with the tangle of wires while I read to them pointlessly out of the manual. Finally Stuart straightened up and said it would have to be fixed tomorrow, because he had to go out.

'Where are you going?' I sat back.

'Alita Kulay's,' he said.

'What for?'

'Her speeding and Breathalyser thing.'

'Oh that,' I said. Alita Kulay, her fleet of sports cars. Her love of fine wines and champagne. Before driving.

There was a silence. Wayne played with a piece of wire, and Vera swivelled around in her chair and gave me a look of baleful triumph.

I ate alone in the silent kitchen. I could hear the dog roaming fitfully about on the veranda outside. While I was still eating I began to read a file of documents I had found on the desk in the office. I read a while, stopped, then went back to them again. I went through a couple of statements. The statements set the scene: a woman in her kitchen in the suburbs, cooking the evening meal. She had a cask of wine on the bench. Her husband had not come home, and she started to drink the wine as she cooked. The children were there, waiting to eat. The meal was ready, the husband still didn't show. She was angry with him for not turning up and she drank more. When she finally heard him coming up the drive she ran around locking all the doors. He went around the house, trying the doors, shouting at her to let him in, but she wouldn't. He found a window open and started to climb in. Furious and drunk, she attacked him as he levered his way in. She threatened him with a kitchen knife and in the struggle it penetrated his chest about an inch. He died halfway in the window, slumped over the kitchen sink, while the three children looked on . . .

I stopped eating. The food tasted terrible. I scraped it into the rubbish, and went upstairs. I stood at the window, hoping that Una would ring.

She rang at 10.45, going on about being sick. 'I can't stand it, the heat, this nausea,' she was saying.

'It's making me weak, I tell you. I smell coffee or garlic and I suddenly get faint. The smell of coffee makes me sick.'

She told me how she got up in the morning and vomited the cracker she ate at 4 a.m. then the crust she nibbled at 5, then just strings and strings of hot yellow bile until Harry came running in and was frightened thinking she was dying and she had to explain to him why she was being sick all over the floor.

'Why do they call it morning sickness? I feel worse now, in the evening, so tired. And so hot, I'm burning up. I'm sorry to be so boring. Are you still there? I saw Stuart today, did he tell you? On Parnell Road. It's funny the way he leans over one, have you noticed? He looked nice, actually. He had on a beautiful suit.'

'He buys his suits in Italy,' I said, trying to open the upstairs window with one hand.

'In Italy, mmm.'

Outside the owl had begun to hoot. Its voice sounded higher, madder.

'What's the time?'

'About eleven.'

I manoeuvred the window lever and pushed the window as wide open as I could. Sitting on the sill, I leaned out until I could see as much of the garden as possible. The wide stretch of lawn was orange under the security light.

'Where's Stuart?' she asked.

'I'm expecting him to come home any minute. Any second, actually. The security light's just gone on.'

'Well, I'll leave you to it then.'

Stuart had gone out without the car. He was going to get a taxi home, to avoid being breathalysed. I hung up the phone. The garden was still, in the warm windless night air. The orange light remained on, the bushes and pot plants were black silhouettes. Long black shadows slanted across the grass. There was no sound of cars on the road. From the darkness at the far end of the garden the owl hooted again. I opened the window wide and stared hard into that inky black grove along the back fence. Five minutes ago, listening to Una, staring absently into the darkness I had seen, or thought I saw, the shadows rearrange themselves and form a new shape, which might or might not have then begun to move slowly along the fence line in the direction of the back door.

I listened to my own breathing. Had the security light just gone on, or had it been on the whole time I was speaking to Una? It could be set to go on whenever anything moved inside the boundary. Or it could be switched over to being permanently on. I couldn't remember seeing it go on. I couldn't remember exactly what I had seen in the shadows by the back fence.

Listening to Una as she filled me in on her last twenty-four hours (such a familiar pastime) seemed to screen out external perception. Naturally, by habit, I would picture Una as she talked to me down the wire. I would see the expressions on her face. Her clothes. Her bedroom. All else would fade. But not quite all. Struggling with the window I had become more and more monosyllabic until she thought I was bored. Now, with Una gone, my head cleared. Something had moved, something much bigger than a cat.

The hairs on my arms were beginning to prickle. Cold and poisonous fear began to seep over my shoulders and concentrate itself in my upper arms. How I hate being alone in the house! I am prone to imagining the worst. Like most Auckland houses, Stuart's wooden mansion is not secure. Spacious, open plan, glassed and terraced, the house and its grounds are a cinch for potential marauders. The living area and the vast deck outside are spotlit from every angle. Anything you do can be seen from outside. There is no burglar alarm. In fact Stuart has no inkling of proper personal security. Other criminal lawyers live in fortresses. Alarmed, cross-beamed, armed and wired, they keep a safe distance between themselves and their clients. There are always dissatisfied and vengeful clients, as well as infatuated clients (that old nuisance, erotomania), and clients who want to rob back their fee. But Stuart carelessly combines visible afflu-ence with an open-door approach. His door is always unlocked. He has never been burgled, possibly because he owns a noisy hound and possibly because burglars can't believe security could be so lax, and fear a *trap*.

Upstairs, at the open window, I winced and squinted into the darkness. I could see nothing. The striped garden was still. Nothing moved over the orange grass, through the black shadows of the quill-shaped conifers, which slanted across the ground like a row of sharp teeth.

And then, as the fear gripped my shoulders and held me by the arms, I heard unmistakably the sound of the back door-handle being slowly manipulated and the gentle scrape as the door was pushed open. How clearly the sound travels in the silent open-plan house! This was not Stuart clattering in the door after a few cold ones. This was somebody creeping and furtive. Somebody standing now with the door open peering into the cave of Stuart's large, tiled kitchen, while directly above I sat on the floor wildly palpitating, frozen.

The intruder was making his way slowly across the dance-floor-sized kitchen. Weeping mutely I heard the squeak and squelch of rubber track sole connecting with and peeling off the tiles. Silence again. He was at the foot of the stairs. He paused while I prayed that he would head into the office at the front of the house and busy himself with carrying off the word processor or prising open the petty cash. But no, he was heading for the bedroom, there, he was on the second step.

Without thinking I was up and springing, flying noiselessly into the small *en suite* bathroom. Climbing up on the lavatory seat I worked desperately on the stiff window catch. Outside the warm night was black and starry, and labouring at the window I prayed, let me out, let me out of the house, let me get outside. Why are people afraid of being outside at night in the warm dark? *Houses* are the real places of terror, where there's no open ground, no high ground, no way out, there again, he'd reached the fourth step.

With my praying and weeping and labouring, the window gave and in a second I was out on the roof. I pushed the window shut. The roof was solid tiled stuff, it didn't graunch and creak the way corrugated iron would. I was able to scrabble silently over the roof of the bedroom and crouch down behind the chimney, and rest my face against the cool orange brick and breathe the gentle night air. Clawing in my panic at the window, I had nevertheless managed to leave no trace of my escape.

I didn't take my eyes off the bathroom window. But the window remained shut. He must have reached the bedroom. Shivering, I imagined him sniffing at the bedclothes.

Out in the open air I couldn't hear anything but the rustle of the silvery leaves and the distant cars vibrating the harbour bridge and the owl hooting and squawking in a far-off garden. It occurred to me that the mobile phone would have been useful. It was probably in the office . . .

A crash, as of breaking glass, and coming distinctly from the bathroom, sent me fluttering and panicking again into the deep shadows at the base of the chimney. But nothing moved. He must have knocked over some bottle of perfume or aftershave, I concluded, gnawing on my knuckles.

I craned over at the street: it was deserted. The suburb slept, oblivious to my plight. No nosy neighbours peered out through twitching curtains. Minutes passed. A car cruised along the street at a steady pace. I waved hopelessly as it droned out of sight. Below me the visitor made no more sound. I considered screaming for help. But all the neighbours were octogenarian, it seemed to me. By the time they had roused and defogged themselves my unwelcome guest would have located me and skewered me (with one thing or another) to the chimney brick. Better to wait. Let him do his thing. Let him get it out of his system and leave.

More time passed. I discovered that my position allowed me to see the front drive, the only access route into the property. I would see him leave if he went out that way, or if he tried to go across the lawn and get over the back fence.

As time went by and there was no more sound, a new and unpleasant possibility occurred to me. Perhaps he was *waiting*. Waiting for us to come home, or waiting for me to come out of hiding. Perhaps he knew I was in the house. He could have been watching me. In fact, if I saw him move at the end of the garden in the shadows by the fence, he must have seen me. These thoughts made me shrink down against the chimney. If he knew I was in the house then he wasn't just an ordinary burglar, honestly bent on theft. A normal burglar, the unperverted kind, waits until the coast is clear. Another thing was beginning to exercise my mind at this point. Where was the dog? Why had he not let fly with his usual joyful roar? Was he dead on the back veranda?

I leaned out as far as I dared, to scan the garden. It seemed I had been out on the roof for at least an hour. Perhaps, though, only twenty minutes. Time drags, in such situations as this one, I knew. The stars shone down benignly.

I began to wonder whether I could climb off the roof. Next door old Mrs Corbunion turned on her bedroom light and crossed the strip of light between her curtains, sending me into a frenzy of silent and futile waving and mouthing from my lonely rooftop. I felt like a shipwrecked sailor, waving to the ocean liner as it glides past, my shouts muffled by the fog. Old Corbunion sailed back to bed with her glass of water and I sank down to crouch on the boards of my marooned skyraft, mouth dry with bitter fear and fatigue. I lay down on my stomach to watch, but nothing happened. Somewhere inside the house the lurker lurked, his business unfinished.

At the end of the street, in the bend, before the road turns to head to the main road into the city, a large pile of plump rubbish bags, filled with a mixture of household rubbish and builders' debris from the construction site of new apartments, had been increasing in size and ripeness for a number of days. Now, as I stared over the top of the pile and prayed for the sight of Stuart's taxi rounding the bend, I caught sight of a busy little four-legged figure slipping in and out of the shadows at the base of the mound, a creature darting, pausing, sniffing and rootling, disappearing then reappearing with a flash of kicking hind legs and a spray of garbage, a skip and a twirl and a jaunty cock of the leg: Howard, happy in his doggy work.

The dog! The *worthless* dog. Below me I could hear nothing. As I watched, Howard worked his way anticlockwise around the base of the mountain. He disappeared. For minutes and minutes he busied himself out of sight. I stared up into the sequined sky. Out there under the black blackness of the neutral universe and the spangly stars and the moon and the Milky Way I began to get an unreal feeling. Steadily steadily burned the stars. I watched a satellite move between two points on the skymap, east to west, making its way quite briskly between the jostling stars. Then I heard the click-click of Howard's paws as he trotted along the pavement towards the house. All at once I was not calm. Fear returned.

I knelt. Howard tritt-trotted over the veranda. He stopped by his water bowl. I listened to the slow, regular slop slop slop of his big tongue as he drank. He stepped down onto the lawn and rolled in the grass. He sat down on his heavy haunches and gave himself a good, snuffly working over, with grunts and snorts and little snappings of teeth. He shook himself. Then I heard his contented sneezes as he strolled to the dog door, swung it open, and entered the kitchen through the back door, as the intruder had done, an hour or two before.

And then again, silence. A bank of cloud, gathering to the west, was beginning to obscure the stars. A slight, chill breeze blew over the roof. A wavering finger of cloud drifted slowly over the middle of the crescent moon, cutting it in two, and in the garden the shadows lost their hardness. The owl gave a curious hoot containing a question mark and a farewell as it swooped over the low roof of Mrs Corbunion's kitchen. And suddenly from inside the house a slamming door and an explosion of hysterical barking sent me leaping to my feet and dancing on aching toes to the edge of the roof.

There was a crash and another crash and Howard gave a roar of canine rage from somewhere between the landing and the upstairs bedroom, and a door slammed and Howard's barks rose to shrieks, and then there were footsteps running through the house and across the kitchen and onto the veranda, and, craning over the guttering, I saw the back of a head with streaky brown and blond hair and a back in a black anorak and legs in blue denims as the marauder ran for the boundary, leaping over the rose trellis and tearing along the pavement towards the rubbish mountain and the twinkling top light of Stuart's taxi as it trundled around the corner and into the street.

And so a minute later Stuart came upon us barricaded in a corner of the veranda, Howard wild-eyed, with shreds of spit hanging from his foamy teeth and I, hissing and gesticulating into the mobile phone a stream of instructions and explanations and expletives while the emergency operator took it in his stride and traced my call electronically, being unable to decipher who I was or what I was saying, or in what language it was that I spoke.

Now, in the luminous new morning, Una on the phone again. What a night it was, last night.

'What a night!'

'Can you imagine . . .'

'God . . . Just after you finished talking to me . . .'

'It seems a blur.'

'And they didn't catch him!'

'No, they had dogs, but he slipped through the net.'

'What if he comes back?'

'Yeah, thanks . . . I know.'

And at the end of the conversation she says, 'You'll have to come over and see me. It's strange, but I've started to feel better, just in the last hour or so. It's the first morning I haven't been doubled up and heaving.'

'A prowler?' Benkie shouts from somewhere in the background. 'They need a proper burglar alarm.'

Una says that since Benkie is off work she is going to lie in the garden and throw up into the flowerbeds, she wonders whether it will make compost. I can hear Benkie in their kitchen, talking to Harry, calling out to Una, rattling the plates. She hangs up the phone.

Now over there the curvaceous Una will be walking out between the grapevines and setting herself up on cushions under the lemon tree, stretching out on the warm grass and staring up through the lacy twigs and the feathery leaves at the pale blue of the shimmering sky, and when Benkie comes out with a book and a cup of tea and Harry dressed in his sandals and sunhat, Una will prop herself up on one elbow and wave them on their way feeling grateful and warm, and oddly and sickly happy.

And what if he comes back? What if he does? Una said to me on the phone, 'He *won't*. Everything will be all right. Everything's *fine*.' She sounded happy. The prowler was a distant story to her. She was lying out there with her books, in the walled garden, in the sun.

Stuart says jokily, 'I don't think this is anything to do with the phone calls we've been getting, or the hate mail, or any of that Lehman stuff. It was just a *rapist*, darling, don't worry. Howard saw him off. We'll start locking the doors. There's no point going off to Una's, there's too much to do.'

Stuart nips about, watering plants, polishing ornaments, murmuring into his pocket dictaphone.

Later in the day I load up the car for our trip to see Carlos Lehman tomorrow, with maps, luggage, Jaffas, and all our other long-distance necessities. Howard roams the veranda pumped up with adrenalin and pride. I underestimated the mouldy canine, I admit. At least he barks.

But nothing in the house has been disturbed. There were no open drawers or rifled files or open cupboards, no evidence for the big sweaty cops who milled around the house jangling their equipment and taking notes with thick clumsy fingers. I sat palely in an armchair staring at them as they looked under tables and shone torches into the back hedge. They rebuked Stuart mildly about the lax security arrangements and checked in over the radio with the dog team who had picked up a trail but lost it out on the marina, where the fingers of concrete stretch out into the black water and make a maze of paths and the creaking boats sway under the whispering rigging and a man could hide easily and never be seen or heard.

I liked those big gingery cops with their great wedges of ham and wrist and hairy elbow, muscles bursting under their nylon slacks, bushy moustaches on podgy faces. I sat silently in my armchair and watched as they went about their wholesome business while Stuart moved around them like an elegant hawk, older, taller, and unmistakably keener.

To a freckly detective I supplied a statement describing the incident. After writing it out, the detective, Ham McCourtie, to my intense embarrassment, read my account back to me! I curled my toes inside my shoes as I listened to the sloppy, inarticulate rushings and ramblings of my statement, its exclamation marks and wows and gees and goshes. It was all full of 'freaking out' and 'couldn't believe' and 'at that point', and on it went unbearably while I cringed and died.

Detective McCourtie, noticing my face growing grimmer at every line, stopped kindly and asked whether I was reliving the experience, he murmured things about shock and called for someone to mix me hot sweet tea. Then while I sipped and mopped he ploughed on, reading the thing to the end. 'I was really really relieved,' Ham read, 'to see Stuart coming up the path. I really had been freaking out, at that point.'

'OK?' rumbled Ham. 'Good with that?'

Of course I wanted to shout no! and snatch it from him and attack it with a bottle of Typowhite, but I sank back in my chair and nodded unhappily.

It was only after the police left and we went to bed that I relived anything, as my grey cells recycled and reworked the last six hours. In my sleep I rode the ghost train at the Easter Show, through pitch dark and hard glare and grinning faces and screaming skeletons and dark and light and dark and light, I was the bewildered body jerking along in my little ghost car, mouthing and blinking in the light, shrieking at the spectres, squinting into the dark, shunting and jolting until my bones were shaking and my teeth were rattling and all my nerves were screaming, and screaming I woke the house.

All our nerves are shot. Vera can hardly stand it. She's the one who has to open the mail. Ever since Carlos Lehman was granted bail, nasty letters have been arriving.

'We're taking the heat,' Stuart says.

On the grey table in the office Vera makes a pile of the daily mail. Ordinary to the left, hate mail to the right. The hate mail is filed away after inspection in a bundle which Stuart intends to send to the police.

One evening Ken Stain and Stuart drank a couple of bottles of wine and lined the exhibits up along the hallway floor. Most are letters, but there are some interesting items, including a plastic Playmobile barrister with a noose around its neck, which Stain found hilarious, and a number of envelopes containing plastic dog turds.

'It must be coming from the same people,' Stain said. 'All those letters with biblical quotations.'

'You'd think people would have forgotten about Lehman by now. At least no one's bothering him. He's just lying low. I think he'll make it to the trial all right. We're going to see him . . .'

'Is he with the wife?'

'No, she visits. She's living in Auckland. He lives with his parents.'

Stain wore a pair of macramé trousers and a short-sleeved shirt, for the heat. Holding up a letter he read, '"The place for scum is at the bottom of the harbour. Why don't you walk to Rangitoto Island. Wearing your concrete shoes. *You* scumbag fuck let filth run our city. You and your crones. Your time will soon be run . . ."'

'That's one of the saner ones.'

'Goodness.'

'Me and my crones.'

'Crones? Cronies?'

'My crones, Stellie and old Voodoo.'

Stain read out some more. He fell about laughing on the hall-way floor in his obscene trousers.

'I can't believe you're a barrister, mate,' Stuart said, twirling his wine glass between his two hands. 'Look at you. Not even my saddest, most deranged client would wear those strides. I can see your jocks through the back of them. You're just a disgrace. And what you wear to work is not much better. I hope no one knows you keep coming around and plaguing me in the evenings.'

Stain poured some more wine. They drank in matey silence.

'Not like you,' said Stain eventually. 'With your Moss suits.'

'Boss. *Boss* suits. I take pride in my presentation. I can't believe people in this country, getting about in their flip-flops.'

'I have always been puzzled by walkshorts and long socks,' Stain opined from the floor.

'I'm puzzled by your whole wardrobe, buddy.'

'Boss suits.'

'Yeah. Actually there are a few puzzling things about the New Zealand rig. Old ladies with purple hair. Jandals. Walkshorts. Long socks and sandals. What about Island girls wearing bathing suits with shorts over the top.'

'That's modesty.'

'Anyway. The police won't do much about these letters, I can tell. They don't care if we get hate mail. Saves them doing it themselves.'

'Do you ever wonder about police surveillance?'

'Of us? No. I sometimes wonder whether they might tap the phone, just to give themselves an inside look. It wouldn't be all that much use to them, would it?'

Stain held up a grubby piece of A4 paper.

'"There is a cancer in the heart of society, it must be CUT OUT. Jails like HOLIDAY CAMPS. Bastards making money out of MISERY. Hang them. Castrate them. Flog them. CUT OFF THEIR HANDS."'

As he was leaving Stain said, 'I must talk to you about my new client. He's the North Shore chap, supposed to have got into an elderly woman's house and raped and murdered her. I'm afraid the forensic report's somewhat grim. It appears that she was stabbed in the vagina.'

Stain peered through his thick glasses, rubbing his hands up and down the front of his jacket. Tiny insects whirled around the light.

'Sorry, Stella, if that makes you cringe.'

Stain took off his glasses and wiped an insect off them. He squinted into the light, holding up the spectacles, teeth bared. Putting them back on he smiled and shook hands and tramped off down the wooden stairs.

'Don't worry about Stella,' Stuart called after him. 'She's got a forensic mind.'

Stain sat in his car on the street with the door open, rolling a cigarette. The interior light was on. He looked up at the veranda and mouthed something through the glass, something exaggerated, with his big mouth and his big square teeth. He sat mouthing and laughing in the yellow carlight, then sucked in smoke and let it trickle out so it swirled around his bobbing head, then reached across and pulled the car door shut and the light went out and he was gone.

12. Carlos

Before we set off for Lawrence I rang Phoebe. 'Where did you say you were going?' she said.

'To talk to this client. He can't go anywhere so we have to go and see him.'

'Good-oh.'

'So how are you both?'

'Well, I'm never better, dear. I've discovered drinking yeast. It's a marvellous pick-me-up. You drink it and feel sick for a few minutes, then you feel marvellous.'

'And how is Jacques?'

'Oh, he's well. Never better. He's building us a sauna in the old garage. It's going to have Scandinavian wood panelling and a special burner. If we were in the northern hemisphere we'd come out after saunaing and roll in the snow and beat each other with twigs. Marvellous. Jacques says it will be finished by the end of summer. Sealing it properly is the trick. He's been spending days down there.'

'Well, I'd better go.'

'So things are going well with your criminal?'

'He's fine I suppose . . . We've had a few hitches.'

'All right dear, so long as he's well. I'll send you both some yeast, and a recipe. Oh and another yoghurt bug if you'd like it, and an instruction book this time, about how not to let it get out of hand. Good-oh. See you soon.'

'Yeah. Soon.'

Stuart played loud music on the way to Lawrence. He sang tunelessly, drumming his fingers on the steering wheel. The pylons flashed by. It was hot and the heat reflected up off the black road, making the air shimmer.

We had got up early. The sun came into the bedroom at six o'clock in the morning, filling the room with slanting yellow light and heating it up so that we pushed the covers off and lay grumbling in the linen. He pushed his face into the back of my head. 'Come on,' he whispered, 'come on.'

I turned over. 'Just a minute,' I murmured, still sleeping. He pushed his long nose into my face, holding my arms with his hands, not holding me tight, or squeezing or hugging, but holding me so that I couldn't move. He held me in that grip and kissed me and whispered at me and there was something in his hold that I thought of as fury, contained. He is a big man and solid, but he can seem as light as a bird. He pushed his face up against mine with his keen, amused eyes, the elegant nose, the small mouth. I struggled to wake myself up. He got up and was going through his chest of drawers, bustling about. It was hot. Another day in our lives. I felt I was made of lead as I swung my legs over the side of the bed.

'Hurry up,' he said in his energetic way, leaning against the chest of drawers. His long bare back from neck to hips was solid and strong. His legs were long and slim and his thighs were hard with muscle, you almost felt as if you could tap on them, as if they were made of wood. He leaned over me in the yellowy light, I looked into his face with its shadows and angles, the shrewd mouth, the clever tongue, the faint dark circles under the hard, hurt penetrating eyes.

'I can't get up,' I said, lying there. 'Come back to bed.'

'Come on,' he said, rolling up the blind. 'You shower, I'll shave.'

Over the radio came the forecast. Dry. Hot. Burn time: ten minutes. Forest fire danger: high.

In the harbour the black rainclouds gathered far out over the islands and the sun shone on the marina and the shore, and the hot wind churned the water into a desolate stretch of turquoise and white, mile after mile to the silver horizon, a million tiny choppy waves.

Carlos was waiting alone at the Lehmans' house when we arrived at three in the afternoon. The Lehmans had driven to Auckland to shop and to see Leah and the children. Carlos opened the door wearing a khaki bush shirt and army trousers. In the kitchen he fumbled about politely making tea and offering muffins shyly and wiping teaspoons for us on a frilly Dutch tea towel. He was sunburnt and well. He had put on weight. Now he looked at Stuart in a way less hunted than before, less haunted and spooked and bewildered. Now when he made conversation and poured tea it was with a kind of hopelessness, and shame.

'I've lost everything. The family are all here but I won't be here much longer. I'll come out of jail an old man if I ever come out at all. I've lost the kids for ever. I feel as if I'm already dead. It's all my fault, the whole family is wrecked for ever . . .'

He flicked the tea towel over his shoulder. His forearms were sunburnt and covered in white scars. A small frilly sign above his head said GOD IS LOVE.

Stuart said, 'Any milk, mate?'

Carlos hunted in the fridge for the milk, which turned out to be in a jug fashioned in the shape of a large Dutch clog.

'Cheers,' Stuart said, taking the jug and pouring milk out of a hole in its pointy toe. He put it down. We sat looking at it. Carlos grinned suddenly. 'Sugar?' he said. The sugar bowl was a merry gnome with jolly red cheeks. The sugar poured out of a hole in his merry hat.

'Nice gnome.'

Carlos gave a big broad grin. He looked very Maori suddenly, and handsome. He sighed. 'Shall we get on with it then?' he said.

We spent the afternoon sitting on the Lehmans' back veranda looking out over the lupins and the marram grass and the silvery sand dunes rolling down to the sea. 'We're close to the beach but Dolph dug down really deep to set the foundations. He thinks this place will never move.'

Stuart set out files and notes. He said, 'I want you to give evidence at the trial. Normally I avoid getting people up there but I think you'd do well. You've got a good manner about you. Your wife will have to get up there too. You've got to explain what was going on. It's madness otherwise, what happened. It's incomprehensible.'

'It's madness anyway.'

'You've got to help yourself, for the sake of your dependants if for nothing else. Think of it that way. Now, can you tell me all about it all over again, from the very beginning . . .?'

Later Stuart said, 'What about the police? There's the record of all the complaints you made.'

'I made complaints to the Community Constable, B.J. Sloacombe. He didn't seem to do anything. Then he threatened to charge *me* with things. Boyderman Leonard told Sloacombe that I damaged his electric fence. B.J. Sloacombe heavied me about that. He came over to the house and tried to tell me not to create problems in the town. I didn't expect anything else from him, since he's Boyderman Leonard's cousin.'

'Oh really? His cousin . . .'

'They're all related up there. They stick together, like a tribe.' Carlos slapped his hand against the arm of the deckchair and scratched his forearm violently. Angrily he repeated, 'They're a tribe, they stick together . . .'

He was beginning to take the skin off his arm and didn't seem to notice. Glancing over at Stuart he stopped talking abruptly and stared emptily away over the dunes, resting the raw arm on the balcony rail.

A long way out at sea the great, sad curtains of rain swept over the water. The bay was sheltered and the sea was a flat silver under the afternoon cloud, and along the horizon line the islands were faint pale grey shapes in the delicate light. The sky was covered in a thin layer of white mist. The air was hot.

Stuart asked questions about the gun and Carlos started to laugh in a strange way as he talked, the laugh rising almost to a giggle. His face and neck broke out in drops of sweat. When he moved a faint smell came off him, of sweat and heat and something else, a sweetish sickly tobacco smell, like pipe smoke or cannabis. He ran his tongue over dry lips and stared blankly out over the beach, drumming his fingers on the wooden rail. When Stuart tried more direct questions Carlos drummed harder and his mouth turned down, distorted, as if he was trying to talk but couldn't get out any words. He said, 'I won't be able to talk about it in court. I can't. I'll do something crazy, I'll lose control. I might even laugh.' He began to laugh again, scratching the reddened arm.

Stuart stood up and gathered up the cups, and directed me to make more coffee. When I came out with the tray Carlos looked calmer and Stuart was picking up his files.

'We'll have to work on all of this, buddy,' he said to Carlos, and Carlos looked depressed. Stuart eyed him sharply, sizing him up.

Carlos said desperately, 'I'm sorry, eh. I appreciate what you're doing . . .' He trailed off, looking humiliated, and Stuart relaxed the hawkish look and seized Carlos by the arm, patting him on the back. 'Don't you worry. Everything will be *fine*.'

Then Stuart was all briskness and bossy charm. After making some more notes he went to look for his mobile phone, leaving us to wait on the veranda.

Carlos tried to smile. His mouth was twisted, the smile turned into a leer. His nose and cheeks were red. He looked down at his forearms and then rolled his sleeve down over the rashy skin, glancing at me from under his heavy fringe. He tried to grin again and I stared back numbly. His grin died and he looked away. 'What a mess,' he said.

Stuart came out onto the veranda. He eyed us in a calculating way. 'I have to make some pretty uninteresting calls. I suggest that you two go for a walk along the beach. Have a chat. Let yourselves unwind.'

I started up out of my chair to protest, make an excuse, anything, rather than walk out alone with Carlos on the empty beach.

'Shouldn't we start the drive back?' I said weakly, and Stuart spoke to me with a lilt in his voice that seemed saccharine, threatening.

'Get some fresh air, Stella. Carlos will show you the beach.'

Carlos jumped up awkwardly and walked across to the steps with a hobbling gait, complaining that his legs had gone to sleep. At the bottom of the steps was a metal grille on which was piled a mound of fish heads. Flies buzzed over them, droning hungrily, swarming in the fishy stench. Carlos apologised, explaining that he had been cleaning the fish in the morning and hadn't had time to get rid of the heads before we arrived. From the veranda Stuart looked down at me with a smile that suggested the licking of his chops.

We stepped out onto the warm sand. It was low tide. At the north end of the beach the black rocks were glistening, uncovered by the receding sea. Piles of seaweed lay along the waterline. Beyond the bay the great expanse of sea lay flat and grey in the hot, bright cloudy light. Behind me I heard the electronic beeping of Stuart's phone, and smelt the raw tang of the decomposing fish heads.

Carlos limped along beside me playing with a stick. Slowly we trudged together through the dry sand, over the hot dunes and through the scratchy lupins, through the small clouds of tiny flying insects which flew into our mouths making us gag and spit, and down onto the hard wet sand at the water's edge. It was late afternoon. We walked along the shoreline towards the dark north rocks. The beach was deserted.

Thinking over the conversation on the veranda with Carlos I was tense and confused, and a hundred thoughts crowded together in my head. I was jumpy. Climbing over a tree branch on the beach Carlos turned and gave me the same crooked smile from under his fringe. He picked up a dead starfish, its red, coral-like arms dried hard and brittle, and he handed it to me, pointing out its spines and its dead octagonal mouth. Behind us in the distance Stuart paced along the grass strip outside the Lehmans' house, phone in one hand, gesturing with the other hand, stopping occasionally to stare up into the dark impenetrable bush on the Lawrence Hills.

I didn't want to reach the north rocks. I suggested that we sit down on a patch of dry sand at the edge of the water. Carlos took off his sandshoes. Miserably looking over his shoulder I saw that Stuart had disappeared from the front of the Lehmans' house. I listened hard but could hear nothing except the sound of the gulls and the wind in the marram grass.

Carlos said, 'You remind me of Leah.'

Again I smelt the strange heavy tobacco scent as he lifted his arms above his head. He stretched, and let his arms fall again.

'I don't know if I can do without this . . .' He pointed out at the sea, moving his finger along the horizon, across the hazy islands, the tiny black cloudbursts, shifting curtains of distant rain.

'Years and years not going outside. Not seeing Leah. That's what will kill me. Leah's just a part of myself.'

'Does she come to see you often?'

'Yeah as often as she can. Not at first, she was too freaked out. But she's stuck by me . . .' He made a face and smiled wickedly. 'Corny, eh.'

He stood up and rolled his baggy army trousers up to his knees. He said that there were thousands of pipis and other shellfish out there at low tide, waving his arm slowly over the water, pipis and maybe even toheroas that would be good for dinner, steamed open in water and flavoured with a bit of lemon. Further out, if you had scuba gear you could get scallops. There was a big scallop bed near the rock in the middle of the bay. He had been told recently he shouldn't dive with a tank, because he was asthmatic. The GP had told him that his lungs could explode, literally, if he was far underwater and became unable to exhale. Behind us, near the edge of the rocks, the flax leaves grew up out of the bank like shiny green swords. He said, 'The first time I saw you was in Mount Eden. You were looking in through the grille. It was strange. Your face looked so fragile.'

I turned away from the flax spears. I realised how big and broad he was, how powerful his arms and chest were. He came closer, stabbing his stick into the damp sand. Quickly I looked up the empty beach towards the house. Stuart was still out of sight. The sun was getting lower. Shivering, I blurted out, 'Let's go back, it's getting late,' and stood up to go, angry and afraid that we were there at all on the lonely beach in the middle of nowhere. He stepped between me and the distant house, blocking my way and coming up close, so that I could see the top of his bare chest under his shirt. My heart began to beat fast. Tears started up in my eyes. I stepped backwards with my fists clenched. Around me the jagged teeth of the flax bushes, the dark rocks and the sea blurred into tears. Cornered, angry, afraid, I squinted up at him. He was silent. I wiped my eyes on my sleeve.

He was peering at me looking concerned. He said, 'What's wrong?' His expression was kindly, brotherly, even slightly amused. Furious, I began to weep in earnest, gagging and snivelling into my sleeve.

'Why are you crying?' he asked, bending down.

'My nerves are shot,' I whispered.

'Ah,' he said, straightening up, 'I know what you mean.'

When I'd dried up I said, 'That's not very professional of me.'

'I won't tell,' he said.

He waded out into the water to look for pipis. He rolled his trousers right up to his thighs and did a little dance. I watched for a while, then took off my shoes and followed him.

The water rose to knee deep as I waded out, then didn't get any deeper. Further out Carlos was only up to the tops of his calves. I caught up with him and we bent over, feeling for shell-fish in the sand. The evening sun was hot on my back despite the thin high cover of cloud. Carlos struck a cluster of pipis and called me over. We trampled the sand with our feet, working down to the shells with our toes. Carlos pushed the wet sandy shellfish into his pockets, then as we found more and more he took off his shirt and made a bag out of it, tying it around his middle. We worked fast. Under the sand the pipis were trying to move out of range.

'They're huge,' I said.

'You should see the scallops. You can have a feast here. There's a guy called Witi Riggs who brings them to Dolph in a sack. The scallops are bigger than your hand.'

I wondered why the water was so shallow so far out and he said you could walk a long way out at dead low tide, right out to the mouth of the bay where it would get deep suddenly when you reached the sand bar. He waded on towards the bar, leaving me digging. The air was warm and the water was as warm as a bath. As the sun got lower the light became golden and the sea was silver, and Carlos called out, 'You look as if you're walking on the water.'

I took a deep breath and stood up straight. Bending my head backwards I stared up into the sky and watched the seagulls turning and diving in the empty air, and then I kicked up a shower of spray and trotted through the water to where he was standing.

'Let's go all the way to the bar,' I said. I thought of walking along the bar to the headland, over the top of the shining sea. 'It looks like mercury,' I said.

I started to wade away but he called me back. He said it was dangerous. The bar was treacherous, there were holes where it got deep suddenly and we could easily drown. He said we should turn back. I waded back to where he was waiting. Overhead the sky was high and tinged with orange, there was no sound except the swish and sigh of the sea and the mournful cries of the wheel-ing gulls. On the beach a freshwater stream running out of the dunes was struck by the light and looked like a lava flow curling and trickling its way down the sand to merge with the burning sea.

We started to wade back to the shore. I caught sight of Stuart. He was pacing again on the grass strip in front of the Lehmans' house. Then he began to walk through the dunes along the path leading to the shore. He was a small black figure against the white sand, hurrying towards us as we made our way in to the beach. We walked slowly.

Carlos talked about his natural mother, whom he had never really tried to find. She was thought to have moved to Australia. He had been thinking lately that he would like to find her, but he could never go looking for her now, because it would be a terrible thing for her to find out what he had done. He had always thought that he would go looking for her one day when the time seemed right. Now that he felt he couldn't contact her, he wished that he could.

I said there was no real reason why he couldn't try to look her up, but he said never, he never would now. He would be too ashamed.

Stuart was waiting for us when we waded out of the water. We walked up the beach scratching our legs, itchy from the salt water. Stuart was holding my shoes and he threw them at me, glaring.

'What have you been doing? I said go for a walk along the beach, not wade out into the *ocean*.'

Carlos looked sideways at me then knelt on the sand and took the shellfish out of his pockets, wrapping them up in his shirt. I waited for him to offer explanations and apologies but he ignored Stuart. Over the beach the high cloud was no longer orange but the silvery grey of fish scales, and the light was fading out at sea.

'You were right out there, *look*!' Stuart pointed. 'What were you doing?' he asked again sounding less indignant, more tentative, staring at Carlos.

Way out at the mouth of the bay we could see the sand bar, beginning with a line of choppy waves and a rippling strip of current going against the waves, and the darker, deeper water of the open sea beyond. The horizon was a dark bank of blue-green cloud and the distant islands began to disappear. The delicate orange and pink and silver had completely drained away and shadows began to move over the surface of the sea.

'It's going to rain tonight,' Carlos said, getting up off the sand and slinging the shellfish over his shoulder. He said to Stuart, 'We've collected a load of pipis. I'll be the only one home tonight, do you want to stay for a feed? I've got the fish too.'

But Stuart shook his head, collecting himself, saying in his singsong sociable way, 'Just another cup of coffee will do, mate, and we'll be on our way, we'll be back soon to talk some more, as you know.'

He took Carlos by the arm and walked him up the beach, slapping him on the back, leaning into him, pushing the shirt full of shellfish away from the shoulder of his crisp linen suit.

The low cloud had rolled in closer to shore and it was dark where we had stood out in the water and darker now on the dunes where I lagged behind, scratching my salty legs and thinking how it would be to walk out onto the sand bar, single file along the strip of sand, on one side the shallow water of the bay lapping knee deep and on the other the heave and swell and slam and pull of the open ocean stretching for ever out of sight into the evening, and on the shore in the dark the lights in the wooden houses, fading, flickering and disappearing, snuffed.

'But actually,' he said, stuffing pipis into an orange stockpot in the Lehmans' kitchen, 'it wouldn't be like that. The bar is not so defined. It's not like a path that you can walk along, ah no. I told you before, if you tried to do that you'd be swept away. They would never find you. You'd be lost.'

He filled the pot with water then drained it, then filled it again and left it to stand so that the pipis would spit out their sand.

'All for me,' he said in a comic Maori accent. He was cheerful, boiling the kettle and fetching the cups and the milk in the clog and the sugar in the portly little gnome with its leer and its hectic flush. Each teaspoon was decorated with a windmill and tulip pattern. Every surface in the kitchen was filled with tiny gewgaws and knick-knacks, ships in bottles, crocheted elfin scenes, framed portraits and little pottery shepherd folk. Carlos moved gracefully around the kitsch interior, deftly covering up the coffee pot with a tea cosy knitted in the shape of a pineapple.

Out on the veranda he had lit a kerosene lantern and hung it from the roof where it swung in the wind giving off kerosene stink and a trickle of oily black smoke. He poured me a cup of coffee and then added milk and a teaspoon of sugar and stirred it, smiling down at me.

'One teaspoon or two?' he asked. 'I can never remember.'

I took the cup, feeling cold suddenly. 'It's none.'

Stuart watched in the reflection of the window. He leaned forward, patting his knees, smiling a little.

'Carlos . . .' he began, but Carlos was talking to me. 'You've got to help me eat the pipis. Since we got so many. I'll show you my secret way of cooking them, you'll love it. I'll show you a recipe . . .' He jumped up and opened a drawer under the kitchen sink.

'Carlos,' Stuart said again, sweetly. Carlos went on looking through the drawer. Stuart coughed delicately. 'Stella has prepared a number of questions which relate to the moment when you shot Mr Leonard. They relate to your state of mind at the time of the shooting. Difficult as it is, I wonder if we could embark on that area now, since we're here, and there's so much ground to cover?'

Out the window the lantern hissed and flickered. One of Millicent's clocks went off with a bing-bong and a tinkle while a circle of gambolling lambs rotated around its face. Carlos went still and looked down. All the expression went out of his eyes.

'There's nothing to tell,' he said, flat voiced, staring out of the neutral holes in his face.

'Don't you remember anything?'

'I remember *rage*, when Cyril started taking the mickey out of me. I remember him laughing over everything that had happened. He said I'd never make it. He said that everyone pissed themselves laughing when I walked past. He said I couldn't take care of my kids. I remember driving away from his house. I wasn't myself any more, driving along. I lost myself. I remember the flash of the shot hitting his head. I'd come back. The thing blew his head apart. I realised I'd come back and killed him. Then all I wanted to do was walk away. I didn't have a state of mind. It wasn't me. It was me but a different me, is how it feels. It was a separate part of me shot him, and now that part's gone. It's finished and only I'm left.'

He smiled briefly and stared out from under his fringe, black eyed. Then he got up and began to drain the pipis of the sandy water, heaving the heavy stockpot onto the kitchen bench. Still agile and smooth in the way he moved he set the pot on the stove, flicked on the element, filled the kettle, shifted a breadboard. He padded around the kitchen gracefully, like a big, fit, heavy animal, smoothly avoiding the china elves and brass egg timers, the crowding figurines.

Carlos sat down at the table and put his chin in his hands. He said sadly, 'I don't think Cyril Leonard ever touched anything on my property. It was all Boyderman Leonard. I didn't realise it then but I know now he wanted my land. I kept trying to show him where the boundaries were and prove to him that I owned all the land up to the creek, but I realise now that he knew where the boundaries were. He just wanted to get rid of me. He's a drunk and a violent bastard. He threatened my kids. But Cyril didn't care about anything except being an electrician. He never really did anything to me. He wasn't anything. And he was small, a tiny guy . . .'

Carlos looked away at the kerosene lantern spluttering and smoking and swinging in the evening breeze. 'You know how tall he was? *Five foot six*. I'm six foot three. I never knew exactly how tall I was until I was arrested. He was five foot six and I blew his fucking head off. I could have killed him with my bare hands.'

Carlos laughed and smacked his fist into the other hand. The pipis in the pot began to boil over and fill the kitchen with a delicious salty stench. Stuart's phone rang in his pocket. He answered. 'I know,' he said, 'mmm-hmm, yuh, I know.' He wandered to the window, murmuring.

I took a mouthful of sweet coffee. On the table was a photograph of Leah with her fine features and skinny shoulders. She wore a blue sundress and carried a brown baby on each hip. She had an eager face and curly brown hair, and one of the babies looked like Carlos and one looked like her.

Stuart switched off his phone and started picking up the files. 'The difficulty is,' he said, 'that we haven't got anyone independent to back up your claims of harassment. The police never took you seriously, the townspeople will all deny any harm was done to you. Leah will back you up, but was there anyone else? Any friend who saw what was going on?'

Carlos sat slumped at the table. Friends, in Seabrooke? He spread out his hands.

'No?'

'No.'

We got ready to leave. Carlos jumped up and stood around looking anxious, trying to persuade us to stay. 'You can smell the pipis,' he said, 'how can you resist?' But it was late and the drive was long, and we had to cross the hills on the metal road in the dark which would take a long time to start with. As we walked to the car Carlos thanked Stuart again and Stuart slapped him on the back. 'Go and enjoy your pipis, buddy,' he said.

In the car Stuart opened a pack of chewing gum with his teeth. 'What do you reckon, darling?' he drawled, one hand on the wheel. 'Is he going to see this thing through?'

'What do you mean?'

'There's no fifteen-minute suicide watch out here in the bush is what I mean. I wonder if he could go at any time. You don't think much, do you? What did you think you were doing, wading out to sea with him? He blew someone's head off, after all, did you think about that?'

The bush lit up in the headlights was dense and alien as we crawled up the Lawrence Hills. The road was loose metal and there were no street lights or houses. Possums started out of the dark, froze in the headlights and careered away again into the shadows. Staring out at the pitiless bush a feeling came over me. As if the world was closing in. As if there would be nothing left soon except fear.

'You said,' I began steadily, 'that I had to go for a walk with him. You knew I didn't want to but you made me. Now you're trying to tell me it wasn't safe. Now you talk about him blowing someone's head off. You knew I didn't want to go with him, what are you trying to do?'

I was starting to shout and he held up his hand and laughed angrily. 'Keep calm,' he said. 'What are you, some kind of fruit-cake?'

'And now you say he might kill himself, but you talk about it as if it's a joke that he's alone, that he could kill himself any time. You don't even care.'

'What are you talking about? Of course I care. What do you think we've been working on for the last few months? I'm going to save his *life*.'

Stuart laughed again and looked at me hard, chewing his gum, one hand on the wheel, and then suddenly he stopped the car, reached over and opened my door. He tried to take hold of my arms and I slapped him away, and for a couple of seconds we struggled in the darkness until he found my wrists and held them.

'Calm down,' he said, 'or I'll kick you out of the car. You can go back to Carlos. You like him? You want to walk out to sea with him? Then get out of the car. Go on, *get out*.'

He opened the door and started to push me out onto the road. All around the dark bush was alive with rustling animal sounds. We struggled in silence. In terror I had an iron grip, he could not push me out. He gave up and I slammed the door. He sat back, panting. He started up the car and drove. We were breathing hard as we passed the hill summit and began to coast down the other side. I hunched in my seat shivering with terror and rage, counting off the miles, thinking of Carlos alone at the window of the Lehmans' house watching us drive away, all the days and days of desolation in his empty eyes.

Later at a twenty-four-hour gas station on the open road weakness overtook me and I sobbed and wept, sitting in the detritus of the journey, the takeaway packets, the dead Jaffa packets, the ruined interior of the car. Stuart stood in the sterile white light of the service station shop paying for petrol and as I watched he turned away from the counter, pocketed his change, took out a handkerchief clumsily and blew his nose. Then he trudged out to the car and got in swearing dejectedly, leaned over and put his arms around me, talking into my neck, mumbling and weeping into my hair. I lose everyone, he said. Nobody knows me like you do. Don't leave me. Don't leave. You're my world. Only you.

We took a motel for the night, somewhere near the end of the motorway. Stuart sat up in bed in his woollen jersey, hair on end, dark shadows under his eyes. He wanted me close, he wrapped his arms around me. He went into a deep sleep while I lay awake in the dark, hour after hour until dawn, watching and waiting. Beside me he sighed and whimpered and made childish sounds, scratched his rumpled hair, rubbed his crumpled forehead, while I sat motionless, watching the early shafts of yellow light creeping towards his sleeping face.

13. Provocation

Out in the harbour the yachts speed across the choppy water, the hot pink and burnt orange and yellow sails fill with hot wind, the hard light strikes the water, the sun burns down on the sunburnt, zinc-coated, sunglassed crews, the wind burns, the light is too bright, all are squinting and peering and shading their eyes against the white glare and the fierce wind and in the high, high sky not a cloud can be seen.

Under the veranda the dog lurks, seeking the deepest shade.

At the flat on the Roundabout Road Leah Levine watches the children running through a sprinkler on the lawn, the four of them screaming and gasping and falling through the spray while behind them in the house a fly screen bangs loose in the breeze and on the lawn the light makes a rainbow on the sheen of water drifting in a fine spray mist through the bright air. Bang says the screen, and the hinge wire squeaks as it flaps in the hot wind. Squeak bang. Sometimes the sky can be so blue, Leah thinks, that it is on the verge of being black. Closing her eyes she watches the photo negative of little bodies dancing and falling against the red sunrise of her lids. A fly drones around her head, darting and buzzing and spiralling down, the sheets on the line billow and flap like white flags and the fly lands, the hinge wire squeaks, the children dive and scream. Bang says the screen, smacking on the window on the sunny white wall. Squeak/squeak. Bang.

On the Lehmans' deck Carlos fills plastic containers with seashells for Millicent's garden: mussels, pipis, toheroa and scallops to cover her paths and line her borders. He has already raked over and expanded her vegetable garden, adding more plants and windbreaks and a proper little watering system with tiny jets which come up out of the ground. Such a green thumb, Millicent says, beaming through her heavy specs. The beach is dotted with groups of sunbathers lying inert on their beach towels and down at the water the swimmers splash and call as they wade out into the high tide, flapping their arms and screaming as the water chills their sensitive bits, and Carlos stops sorting shells to watch two girls fighting in the water to push each other under. They look like two Maori girls with strong brown arms and flying black hair and he thinks of his cousins long ago fighting with him in the sand around Whatuwhiwhi Beach and of his cousin May Rangi running home screaming because she had accidentally bloodied his nose and he had lain on the sand and pretended to be dead. He continues sorting shells but thinking of May Rangi, the tiny girl in her flowery tank top and shorts and the long ago upside-down view of the marram grass waving and the shiny backs of her brown legs as she raced away from him up the dune, bellowing so loudly that the adults came looking and told them off lazily – Hey you kids, behave! – and he finishes sorting the shells, puts lids on the boxes and puts them away, then sits sadly in the shade watching the beach while the sunbathers lie open-mouthed, scarlet and motionless in the coloured pools of their towels.

It is exactly noon. Hunched over the keys in Vera's creaking chair in the empty office the assistant sets out the relevant research, the cases, the texts, the highlighted notes, the subject being the specific defence of provocation, the questions as follows: what is provocation? What constitutes it? When can a person be said to have been truly provoked?

In the early morning (Saturday), Stuart packed a small sports bag and left the house to go sailing in a yacht owned by his friend Alita Kulay, that yacht now tacking its way up the channel loaded with crates of champagne to be discharged with the party at Rangitoto or Kawau or some other sheltered island for a swimming picnic on the sparkling beach. The assistant, left behind in the silent house, wanders gratefully from room to room – how quiet it is, how peaceful – before settling at the word processor over the chaos of the ongoing notes.

Provocation (I read) the basic definition: Defence to a charge of murder entitling the accused to be convicted of manslaughter. Reading on: The burden of proof is on the prosecution, this meaning that once evidence is raised supporting a finding that the accused was provoked, the onus is on the prosecution to prove beyond reasonable doubt that the case is not one where there was provocation.

Show me that there was provocation, says the judge, and I will pass the question to the jury in something like the following form:

Was the accused actually provoked so as to lose his self-control?

And, would the reasonable man have done so?

To break it down further, what is a 'reasonable man'? For the purposes of the question a reasonable man is a person having the power of self-control of an ordinary person, but otherwise having the characteristics of the accused.

What does the jury base its answer on? The evidence. What happened? When? Who did what to whom?

Words alone can constitute provocation. Provocation need not be something done by the dead person to the accused. It may be something done by a third person in some way connected with the victim.

Highlighted, emboldened, underlined, the words appear in grainy orange on Vera's greasy screen while above the fan on the ceiling rotates slowly, barely moving the heavy air. Out in the Gulf the yachts are skimming into the spray, nearly horizontal; here in the office in the sepia light behind the ricepaper blinds the papers barely stir. Out in the Gulf Stuart is winching and hauling as the yacht zigzags its way up the channel, leaning over the water to balance the boat, singing out as they turn about, efficiently skippered by Alita Kulay. Outside Howard clicks over the veranda towards his bowl. Vera's cactus plant glows a surreal pink in the brown light. Somewhere far away there is a sound which could be an owl. There must be a sudden and temporary loss of self-control.

Sudden temporary loss. Coming over the accused quickly and departing reasonably quickly. Losing it, doing your nut. Losing your cool. There must be no element of planning, no whiff of premeditation. There must be no retribution.

Where there is an interval or time gap between the provocation and the killing the question of provocation can still be put to the jury. It will be a question of fact in the particular circumstances whether the time gap is sufficient to negate the requirements of suddenness and spontaneity.

The cases. There are many, useful ones. One which says that the defence is available where the last piece of provocation closest to the time of the killing is relatively minor, but is also the last straw that causes the accused to snap. Even though the last provocation would not on its own have made the accused lose his cool, the defence can succeed when the provocation is viewed in the light of what has gone on in the past.

What about the 'characteristics' of the accused? Was the provocation sufficient to deprive a person having the power of self-control of an ordinary person, but otherwise having the 'characteristics of the accused', of the power of self-control?

According to the cases, 'characteristics' do not necessarily have to be permanent characteristics, like a limp or a big nose.

'Characteristics' can be all factors that would affect the gravity of the provocation when applied to the person to whom it is addressed. 'Characteristics' can be the accused's circumstances at the time, what's going on, as well as what he is, who he is.

What went down? Who did what to whom? It's subjective: did the provocation actually deprive you of self-control, inducing you to commit homicide? It's objective: would the reasonable man (with your characteristics) have done the same?

There's quite a body of law on the subject. Quite a body count.

There is a certain rhythm that can be achieved in this kind of straightforward research. Find the right notes, ascertain their value and relevance, if necessary copy them down. While typing on the word processor screen it is possible to divide the mind, one part copies, the other part wanders. As with driving, one can wander mentally far away from the task in hand and come back to find that one has held the road reasonably well. Things are as they should be, largely. This only applies to automatic tasks: copying, driving. In Vera's case it is different. No matter how much she squints and concentrates, sighs and labours over the machine she can only achieve a stab at spelling, a bash at grammar, a vague gesture towards getting it right. (She cannot be fired, because she is the only one who enjoys bathing the dog.) 'Sea above,' I read in her notes. 'Blackstones' Crimminel Practise.'

It can be words. It can be a small thing that makes the last straw. It can be done by a third person. It can have happened some reasonable time before. It can reduce your conviction. It can give you another shot.

Copying case citations now I wander away, remembering. Long ago I crossed the street and saw Stuart standing on the veranda by the front door, arms outstretched to wave me on in, hurry up he called, I've made you something nice, and I sat on a deckchair watching the sea while he bustled about and shone and beamed, and served me lunch and asked me to stay for ever. You'll never leave me now. I'll send a car for your things. The sun shone and shone, like today.

Last night it was hot and pitch black in the bedroom, the air was close and the wind blowing through the open window was hot and smelt of smoke as if bush fires were burning on the islands out at sea. We rolled and tossed and fought in the sheets, pushing each other for space. My head ached. Sleeping on and off I dreamed, a taxi had come for me, the driver made small talk and drove steadily enough, but each turn he took was wrong. He was cordial, apologised, made U-turns, consulted a map.

We drove onto a road which went in a spiral downwards, like the rampway going into an underground carpark. Down and down we drove, round and round, I expecting the road to level out and open up. Then we stopped and it was clear that we were at a dead end deep underground and the driver was turning to me with a look of intent that sent me scrambling out of the car and trotting upwards, trying not to panic, calling in a level voice, as if to pretend that I hadn't realised he had brought me there deliberately would make it all right, hello, is anybody there, we're lost. Can anybody help?

Then in the dream as I jogged upwards I heard him break into a run after me in the tunnel. I jerked awake, my whole body aching, poisoned with adrenalin, made more afraid by the fact that I wasn't altogether awake, I felt I could slip back down into the pit of sleep and face the terror again.

In the bathroom I switched on the light and forced every part of myself awake. In his sleep Stuart clawed at the shroud of his sheets. Under the bed the dog breathed in ragged pants. The wooden house squeaked and shifted in the wind. I walked through the silent rooms, checking the locks.

I must see more of Una.

Wednesday morning this week Detective Ham McCourtie phoned. I wandered out into the humid garden with the mobile phone and sat down under the lemon tree.

'How are you, Stella? Recovered?'

'Yes. Yes thank you, Detective.'

'Well, Stella, we have been looking into your prowler, as you know. I can tell you now that the print team found two handprints, one lifted from the dog door and one from the window on the west side of the kitchen.'

'Oh. Were they significant, Detective McCourtie?'

'Call me Ham.'

'Ham.'

'They were no use to us. The hands were gloved. We have to disregard them, so to speak.'

'So you have no idea who the prowler was?'

'At the end of the day, correct. We're still at square one. Just keeping you abreast, as such.'

'No other leads . . .'

'At this juncture, none. You've updated security, I would hope?'

'We've got an alarm with infrared beams that criss-cross the floor. Also we've started locking the doors.'

'It's a start. I will liaise, if any more develops.'

'Thanks.'

'Another thing. There's something you might like to know.'

'Yes?'

'Regarding Shaylene Marks. We're not proceeding with her case this week.'

'Which one?'

'The prosecution against her father. Poppy Marks is in a coma. He was found in his garage in a terrible mess. Beaten up.'

'Oh. I'll tell Stuart . . . Badly beaten up?'

'To a pulp. Smithereens. Hardly anything of him left.'

'Oh . . . thanks.'

'All part of the service, so to speak.'

'Ham?'

'Yo?'

'Are you . . . married?'

'Correct.'

'Oh.'

'Why do you ask?'

'Oh nothing. I don't know. Do you think life is getting more dangerous?'

'Keep that alarm on. Locks down at intersections. Keep hedges near windows sensibly trimmed.'

'Well, thanks, Ham.'

'For sure.'

'Goodbye, Ham.'

'No problem. In any event. No problem at all.'

'Stink bum stink bum bum bum,' sings Harry.

'It's the age,' Una sighed, too hot and languid to be amused. 'All the words he can manage are obscene or lavatorial.'

Una served lunch on the picnic table in her garden on Wednesday afternoon. 'I'm glad you've come,' she said. 'Why do I see so little of you at the moment? Doesn't the bastard let you out? I'm feeling so slow I need people to come around. You especially. Look at me – I'm starting to look a bit rounder.'

Sitting back I looked her over. Really the Una-form was not much changed, apart from being fractionally bigger at the front and slightly heavier in the thighs. Perhaps the face too was rounder, heavier in the jowls. She was suntanned and happy.

'You look great.'

'I'm so relieved to have stopped throwing up, driving the porcelain bus, as Benkie would say. Now I eat a lot and sleep all the time. I go to bed at about seven o'clock.'

Behind us Harry sang softly from his hiding place between the grapevines, his little voice droning sweetly above the clack and scratch of the cicadas and the shrieks of the small birds fighting on the hot iron roof of the garden shed. The dog lay still in the shade of the whau tree, his gaze fixed on Una as she lay languidly back against the trellis eating a pitta bread and murmuring in her new slow voice, 'You should have got an alarm ages ago. You're often alone in the house. I've started getting Benkie's mother to come over when Benkie goes away. If I try not to argue with her she's good company.'

I told her about Detective McCourtie. The gloved hand.

'God. It's all very creepy.'

She frowned, squinting at me in the bright light. 'Things

seem a bit unusual at your place at the moment. Can I . . .?'

'Oh no,' I said, 'everything's fine.'

The flies droned in the still air in the lee of the shed and the dry-stone wall. In the walled garden next door the neighbours' sheets rippled slackly on the line, like empty sails in the warm pocket of the sheltered air.

Now the digital clock says 1.15 and drowsiness begins to overtake me, weariness with the heat, the bleached light in the empty office, the rhythmic grunt of the ceiling fan. With effort I wade through Ibram's case (1981) 74 Cr. App. R 154, in which the provocation consisted of 'gross bullying and terrorism', and the last instance of provocation took place seven days before the accused's premeditated fatal attack. Here the accused was unsuccessful with his defence:

> Formulation of the desire for revenge means that the person has had time to think, to reflect, and that would negate a sudden temporary loss of self-control which is the essence of provocation.

I read on, propping open my eyes, Ahluwalia's case [1992] 4 All ER 889, Lord Taylor CJ:

> In some cases the interval between the provocation and the defendant's reaction might wholly undermine the defence of provocation. However that depends entirely on the facts of the individual case and is not a principle of law.

I work through the pile of Xeroxed cases, the embittered husbands, embattled wives, domestic nightmares, neighbourhood wars, the mundane and the weird.

Provocation does not have to be an illegal or wrongful act. Even a crying baby can constitute provocation, for the purposes of the defence.

In the garden at Una's on Wednesday I outlined the provocation defence in a general way to Benkie, who was on a free shift and due to take Harry to the beach. I threw in a few cases as examples.

Before they left for the beach Harry burst out from between the vines and clambered onto Una's lap, smothering her with hugs. Then he trotted happily up the path holding Benkie's hand, sending back over his shoulder a couple of waves and blown kisses and inarticulate shouts of farewell.

'He's such a sweetie,' Una said, sighing richly, while I looked away over the vines to the distant hillside of Mount St John's where a recent landslide had ripped the grass and topsoil away leaving a long, dirty, reddish scar across the undulating green of the fertile slope.

'What about this one,' I said to Una. 'In one case the defendant, having been provoked, head-butted then strangled the deceased, then, panicking, put live wires in her mouth, electrocuting her.'

Then I said, 'Oh sorry, I'm sorry, we won't talk about this stuff any more.' I poured her an apple juice and handed her a tissue.

'People like you keep forgetting that I'm pregnant,' she said.

Carlos Lehman killed a small man whom he knew only slightly, after a verbal exchange of ordinary insults. He didn't even kill him outright, but went away and got his gun. A victim who appeared largely blameless, a killing which appeared essentially random.

Yet clearly and intentionally the brother of the deceased was ruining Lehman, and others in the town were also involved. In a population that small is anyone really a lone individual acting alone? Everyone knows everything, the who did what and why, to whom. Cyril knew, and thought it was a joke. Provocation may be something done by a third person in some way connected with the deceased.

And those insults, 'failure', 'loser', 'headcase', struck at Lehman's vulnerable core. He was all those things. He had become those things because of the townspeople, the Leonards, the Garlands and the Seabrookes.

Records show that Lehman, before giving up on the police, reported fourteen significant thefts of plants and equipment, five incidents of vandalism, and made several complaints about fences being cut and stock being allowed to stray onto his land, destroying all his newly planted trees. By the time he shot Leonard most of the capital from his previous business had been eaten up. He would soon have been unable to maintain repayments on the land and equipment. He was facing foreclosure and possible bankruptcy. His marriage, which had always been solid, was turning into a desperate, miserable mess, and for the first time in his life he was a failure. He was eaten up with shame.

'Loser,' Cyril said, tiny eyes wet with malice. 'Fucking dropout. Moron.' So Lehman lost himself and went far away, driving back to the house in a red mist, hearing only the mad thumping of his heartbeat, the blood throbbing in his head. No memory of seeing Leah and the children, no recollection of their terrified crying as he pushed them aside, no proper memory of anything but the red haze, the beast in his chest, the beast in his arms in his head in his stomach driving him on down the dirt road, the screaming metal in the burning engine, screech of brakes, cloud of dust, the roar and kick of the gun, the small man thrown back, spinning with it, the stunned silence as he died face down on the grey stones. Then the lightness walking away. The lightness of having lost everything, and everything gone, for good.

The wind rattles the rose trellis, the fan revolves with a creak and a clunk, the slumbering dog sprawled under a deckchair groans nasally and sighs, and from the garden I hear a new sound of energetic digging, heavy boots on hard turf, the tinny jangle of a radio and the clearing of a throat. Out there in the heat Wayne is sweating over a huge pile of rich black earth which he is transporting by the spadeful onto an unsown flowerbed.

He stops, straightens up, digs the spade into the pungent pile of earth, and takes an envelope of tobacco from his pocket. He rolls a small cigarette, sticks it in his mouth, lights it and spits on his hands, ready to return to work. But he begins to gaze at his hands instead, holding them up to the light, viewing the spit on his palm from all possible angles. For a minute he is motionless, fascinated, completely absorbed.

I must pick up the pace. Time is getting on. Provocation must be things done or said. Mere circumstances, however provoking, do not constitute a defence to murder. Flood, fire, act of God do not excuse a resulting killing. If, on finding that your house has been struck by lightning you lose control and kill your neighbour, you will not have a defence. You may not embark on a killing spree just because your life has turned into a nightmare. That would be random. That would be murder.

Struck by a thought I lean out the office window.
   'Wayne,' I call, 'hello, Wayne . . . I've just thought of something. Do you know Poppy Marks?'
   'Who?' He looks up scowling, wiping his hands through his curly hair, scratching the sunburn on the back of his brutal neck.
   'Poppy Marks.'
   'Yeah. I know Shay's father.'
   'Didn't you live with Shaylene Marks?'
   'Years ago. Why?'
   'Oh, nothing.'
   'Yeah . . . I been hearing from the old pervert . . . Always on at me for maintenance for Shaylene's daughter.'
   'Oh?'
   'She's always reckoned her kid was mine. I haven't got any money. I never wanted a kid.'
   'Well anyway . . . Hot out there?'
   'Yeah. Serious.'

There is something about little K'Tel Marks which reminds me of Wayne. Her pale skinny face, freckles on her nose, freckles on her shoulders sticking out of the too-tight too-small grubby sundress she always wears, narrow little eyes. A sidling, wheedling, crafty girl, too small for her age. Her green eyes are slanting, suspicious, watchful. She has curly hair. Streaky brown, streaky blonde.

On Wednesday Una drove me home. 'It's too hot to walk and we can keep talking,' she said. We passed Romaniuk heading down Remuera Road. He had on a new hard hat, shiny blue instead of the usual yellow. He carried a large stick.

People know Romaniuk's name because he goes into the City Council building to read the maps. He spreads the survey and town planning maps and the ordinary street maps on the floor of one of the map rooms and studies them for hours. This is the only thing he is seen to do besides walking. He leaves his wallet at the desk in the map room for security. It contains nothing, no photos or cards or money, only a library card and some sort of ID from the office where he collects his benefit. As he reads the maps Romaniuk is heard to talk to himself in a steady monologue. So far no one has figured out what language it is that he speaks. Out on the road he walks fast, not looking around. Once he has set himself on a course he doesn't like to be interrupted and if you step into his way inadvertently he will jerk his head up and stare into your face as if he has been brought out of a trance, then clutch his stick with an angry and frightened look and hurry around you on his way.

'What do you think he's doing when he looks at the maps?' Una said. 'Is he planning the next route or working out where he's been?'

'Someone should attach a tracer to him and find out exactly where he goes. Would it be random or would there be a pattern? What would it look like?'

'A spiral. A star. A web.'

'If you followed him he would sense it. He would know.'

'He never looks anywhere but straight ahead.'

Romaniuk crossed at the lights against the flow of the crowd,

adjusting direction jerkily at each obstacle, forever scurrying forward as purposeful as an ant, running on, like time, running out.

In Lawrence Carlos lives on, on his borrowed time. He knows *his*
time is running out. There won't be an out for him, at the end of
it all. Even if his defence stands up, he'll be convicted of
manslaughter. With manslaughter what he gets is up to the judge:
three years, five years, eight years. And if the defence is unsuccessful and the case is proved it's murder, and the sentence is
compulsory. Life.

So he lives on in the house by the beach, watching the time
pass, watching it run by. Out in the Gulf the fishing boats sail
across the painted islands and in the hot light of the long afternoons the sea light flickers iron silver iron as the clouds cross the
sun and the islands hang in their watery colours, separated from
the sea by the dancing strip of the silver mirage. A red tractor
crosses the green of the distant ridge and every morning a woman
swims overarm in the shallows, with each downstroke she lays her
hand gently, palm first then fingers onto the surface of the water
as if smoothing the wrinkles from a slippery sheet. Sleek, heavy,
seal-like in the heavy water, she turns and breathes audibly with
closed eyes, the wide mouth rubbery under the rubber cap, she
leaves no wake. Some nights Carlos wakes at 3 a.m. filled with
dread, looks at the clock and sighs: still three hours until dawn,
luxury!

And in the township of Seabrooke all enquiries have drawn a
blank. There isn't a single person willing to back Carlos up. This
harassment, they say, it's all make-believe. This *provocation* he
talks of, it's all in his head. It's all just something in his head.

Some time after midnight when I've long abandoned my research
Stuart comes reeling up the front steps.

Undressing, staggering around in the bedroom, he says, 'The
big thing about Alita Kulay is that she's an *heirloom*.'

'A *what*?'

'An heirloom. Her parents are loaded. Swimming in money.

She can do whatever she likes, whenever she likes. You should see her yacht, it's sensational, huge, interiorly designed. She owns it with her brother, his name's Sodom, or something like that, he's gay. They've got a couple of houses, one's over in St Mary's Bay, a real manse it is. It used to be quite shackledown apparently, but they've spent five years doing it up. Rooms quilted in thick brocade, colours rising to a crescendo of splendour and Alita's legs striding amidst the pageantry, oh they're beautiful and long, longer than your toothpicks, darling. She's four feet taller than you, she's a *willow*. She's a dream, all thin and floaty with those slitty eyes, all *narrow* with *bean counting*.'

With a sick rush of jealousy, I say lamely, 'Glad you had a nice time. Lush.'

'I'm not *drunk*. I'm hungry.'

'It's one o'clock in the morning. Phone for a curry.'

'You've missed me.'

'No I haven't. What have you been doing?'

'Didn't you miss me? You're my family. You're my life.'

'You're delirious.'

'I don't care that you're poor, darling, and a dwarf.'

'You don't tell me anything, you're probably fucking everybody.'

'You're my light in the window on a dark night.'

'What a lush.'

'You've missed me. You would always miss me. If you ever left me you would miss me all the time.'

You will miss me for ever.

In bed he smelt of burnt flesh, alcohol, garlic and salt, like an overdone roast. He tossed and turned, moaning about roomspin. At 3 a.m. he woke and groaned for water.

'Don't leave me, darling,' he croaked, 'not with this headache. Don't leave a dying man.'

He clung to me, drily sobbing. 'Ah fuck,' he said, 'I'm getting old.'

At 4 a.m. he crashed to the floor of the bathroom. 'Never drink cocktails,' he muttered weepily, clutching my shoulders as

I dragged him back to bed, applied (relenting) a cold flannel to his forehead, gave him water, gave him paracetamol, turned out the light.

'Tomorrow is . . .' he said, and slept, clutching my hand.

Last week Carlos rang Leah. She said he told her this: One night, soon after he had been bailed, in the house at Lawrence Beach, he lay on his bed until well after midnight watching a rerun of an old TV programme, and afterwards he came close to an idea of what he had done.

The TV flickered in the darkened room, the TV story moved to its climax, a car chase, a chase on foot, a fist fight in a warehouse, SWAT teams converging, a helicopter, a lovers' scene in a restaurant with palms, tropical cocktails, tables by a luminous pool. He turned off the set. It was quiet in the room. He saw a mental picture of blood. Worse than blood, torn skin. A battered head with pieces of skull broken and protruding. He curled himself into a ball. He felt that he was gasping. A feeling came over him of pure horror, terror, evil. It was as if a door had opened and he had seen everything which had been hidden. He felt what it was to look at a corpse and he was shaken loose from everything that held him together, he was adrift, overwhelmed with horror.

And then he heard Millicent coming along the hallway, shuffling heavily in her furry slippers. She put her large curly head around the door, peered into the room, whispered in a stage whisper, held out a mug of tea, shuffled to his bed and sat down beside him. She was crying. Don't shut us out, she said, sobbing into her big hands. Don't torture us with silence. We are suffering so, Dolph and I. Help us to understand.

She sat hunched in her dressing gown, so loved and familiar, so irritating, and comforting her he was anchored again and in despair because she had brought him back from understanding. She had prevented him from seeing what he needed to see. He never came close to that feeling again.

His worst pain was his lack of pain. He knew what he ought to feel and he knew that he could not feel it. He was maddened, distressed, beyond distress. He said, 'I'm like a paraplegic watching someone cut off my legs.' It was this grotesque numbness that made him wish he was dead.

Leah listened to him, helpless and desolate. Later she rang him back. She was angry. 'That was your pain you were talking about,' she said. 'What about the Leonards' pain? What about them?'

'It's the same thing,' he said.

He could tell her nothing more.

14. Leah Levine

According to the television we have had the hottest February and March since recording of temperatures began. The news is full of speculation about changing world weather patterns, global warming. I watched a scientist last night giving a worst case scenario, of tsunamis, crops ruined, the inexorable rise of the sea. But now it's April and the weather is on the turn. There are three weeks to go until Carlos's trial. It's going to be the Lehmans versus the whole of Seabrooke, two against two hundred.

Looking for witnesses or any useful information, Stuart hired a private investigator, a retired insurance assessor called Wallace Noble who was based in Tauranga. Wallace Noble promised to look around in Tauranga and Seabrooke and see whether he could find anything useful. On his second day in Seabrooke Noble's briefcase was stolen from his car and his tyres were let down. Then he came down with a catastrophic stomach illness, some bug, according to his graphic accounts, of the degree of severity of dysentery or cholera, and he had to spend a night in Tauranga Hospital being rehydrated. Reporting faintly on the phone from his bed he wondered whether someone in Seabrooke had sold him some rotten food.

He finally admitted defeat after a week, submitting a modest bill – no doubt he felt he had suffered enough. According to his report, as expected, no one in the area had anything good to say about the Lehmans. The Lehmans had never made any friends in the town. Everyone thought Carlos Lehman and his wife were purely evil, they deserved to be locked up, they deserved to be strung up.

So it's up to the two of them to put their side to the court. They were lonely in Seabrooke and they're sure lonely now. With all of the town lining up to give evidence, I have a terrible feeling no one is going to believe a word they say.

On Tuesday Noble's full notes came in the mail. Stuart and I went through them together out on the deck under the greenish sky, in the evening light, trying to find something useful in the jumbled pages. '"Sheila Dick, farmer",' I read, '"Len Spindleshank, farmer, Ineke Rover, psycho and aromatherapist, Clayton Ballseck, war hero" . . . *war hero?* . . . these are all the ones who would actually talk to him. Most people said no comment . . . "Stee Flarps, owner of mobile fish shop, possibly sold me rotten pie. Uriah McClinchie, Bing Grogan," blah blah blah. Stee Flarps mentions a woman living with Boyderman Leonard's family around the time of the shooting and then says he doesn't know who she was. Won't say anything else.'

'He was feeling shifty about the poisoned pie.'

'There's no record of any extra woman at the Leonards'.'

Stuart stretched out on his deckchair and sipped delicately from his beer bottle.

'Stee Flarps later in conversation denies mentioning woman.'

'I have to go to Hamilton this week,' Stuart said, considering.

'So we could go back and have a last look.'

'I could go to Tauranga on the way back from Hamilton. Although there's probably no point. You'll have to look after the shop. Get Leah over, see if she has any ideas about anything. We've got nothing to lose now.'

I hesitated, looking down at my hands. 'The thing is, I don't like being here on my own . . . the nights . . .'

'It won't be *long*. And Wayne will protect you.'

Stuart left for Hamilton the next day. I spent the first day at his desk going through a pile of files while Vera sighed over her keyboard in the next room and the dog clicked back and forth over the veranda outside, barking occasionally into the still air. The light has changed. The sky is clear and bright, sounds are muted in the thin air, and in the early mornings there is a late-summer chill, hint of ice in the high blue sky, in the mornings the sunlight is golden on the city, on the mirror buildings and on the tops of the hills, but in the shadows and valleys, in the canyon of Queen Street and the flat green suburbs under Mount Eden the air is cold. I stare up into the blue. This blue is the beginning of the dark. The air is dry.

The dog, like me, is restless. He roams over the garden as if there is something important there that he has lost.

At this time of the year the light sharpens perception. In the late afternoon I drove across the bridge and parked, and walked through the city, into Victoria Street, up Bowen Avenue and over the hill, down into the flatland of Stanley Street, up onto the bright slopes of the Domain, looked over the harbour and out to Rangitoto Island, saw the horizon beyond the yachts a silver line, heard the seagulls shriek as they dived over the War Memorial and heard the wind screaming in the strings of the kites flying in loose formation against the dark of the brilliant blue, under the cold eye of the sun.

On my long walks I sometimes feel regret, nostalgia, a faint nausea. It is the time of year. All tastes and smells are infinitely enhanced. I roam over the terrain whenever I can get away from the house.

The day after Stuart left I rang Leah. She answered the phone after a lot of rings and agreed to come over. I was sitting in the office when she knocked on the front door. She had May in the pushchair, the other children were at school. I walked here, she explained. Really your house was not all that far away. She had felt restless, in need of exercise. May needed fresh air. She was shy and embarrassed, half wishing she could just go back down to the street and carry on walking.

I put aside the files and ushered her in. I made her coffee and we fed the baby bread and cheese. May wore pink sparkly plastic sandals. She was beautiful, with curly hair and dark, wide-spaced eyes. Leah said she was fifteen months old, walking but not yet talking.

After a while Leah said she was glad to have come, lately she couldn't stay in the flat during the day, it was too cramped and she didn't know what to do with herself. She had never been unemployed before. She was a solo parent now, and she hadn't managed yet to get herself a job. She said that she spent a lot of time out, with May in the pushchair, walking, trying to figure out what she would do in the future.

I dragged out the file and we went over the witness question, but it didn't take very long, she and Carlos had no friends or sympathisers in Seabrooke, of that she was sure, and she said that the only people who knew what went on in Seabrooke were the Garlands, the Leonards and the Seabrookes, and they all stuck together in everything they did.

'What about a woman living with the Leonards at the time of Cyril's death? Someone who's no longer around?'

Leah shrugged and looked vague. She didn't know. She stayed for an hour and then left, taking a bottle of water and a piece of cheese for May. For some reason, I found myself urging her to come over again.

The following day I looked out for her but she didn't come. The next time she turned up it was mid-afternoon. I heard May calling in the street and I raced out to let them in. I offered Leah a beer. May trotted around the house inspecting the ornaments and eventually breaking a vase.

Leah said she was going to walk back, picking up the other children on the way, feed the kids, and then after they'd gone to bed she would eat pasta and tomato in front of the television along with a glass of wine, then smoke a cigarette or two before going to bed. She said, things like that, the pasta, the wine, two cigarettes, I look forward to them *intensely*. I enjoy them intensely. I earn them by going for a long walk, organising the children. The hard work and then the pleasure. She said, 'I am learning to live alone.'

I hunted around for something for May. I wanted to do something for her, and I offered to cook her some oven chips. I cooked a whole packet of chips but she wouldn't eat any. She wanted cheese. As they set off along the street Leah turned the pushchair around and the tiny figure waved her fistful of Cheddar.

Before she left I told her she should come over whenever she wanted if she felt like a stop on her walking circuit. I felt awkward saying it, but I wanted her to, I really did. She looked at me with her lopsided smile, her expression wry and amused. I looked away, embarrassed, and put my hand on the silky top of May's hot little head. 'Bring May, of course,' I said, clearing my throat, 'she must need a walk every day,' and Leah smiled then and said that May would trash the flat if she didn't get her walk. So they came again the next day and stayed longer.

I tried out changing May's nappy, although not a shitty one. It was a disposable, bulging with its contained load of liquid, the urine mysteriously sliding about inside while the outside of the nappy remained dry to the touch.

Never having brought myself to change Harry's nappies (I would gag and retch from the doorway while Una patiently swabbed and scraped), I found that there's really nothing to it, nothing to the non-shitty ones anyway. May eyed me suspiciously from behind her hands. While I cleaned her off, applied zinc cream, fastened the sticky tapes on her new nappy, I admired her smooth skin and her muscular little brown legs. Set on her feet again she trots away automatically. Her hand movements are graceful, like those of an Indonesian dancer. She is so small and pretty I feel as if I love her.

To my surprise I look forward to seeing them. Normally I hate visitors, and if I am required to make small talk during the day I have to fight the urge to pace the floor like a caged animal. The thought of sitting down 'for a chat' fills me with rebellion and claustrophobia, I want to fling open the door and run away, out into the air! I am particularly bad at talking to other women, apart from Una. Women throw me, they make me awkward. I don't know what's going on with them when I talk to them. I feel no line of communication. I don't understand women or know many of them. As a child I always played with boys, and with Una. Nothing has changed. But every day now I look out for Leah and May trundling together slowly along the street, roaming through the afternoon, May toddling sometimes, riding sometimes, Leah with her sharp face, May with her gap-toothed smile, her nose screwed up and scornful, tiny legs in big flowery shorts.

It's not a call. It's a pit stop *en route*. For the sake of the child. Come in, I say, thinking up things to give them. I wonder about offering them money, as we sit together on the couch stuffed with banknotes, as May unearths trinkets and baubles from the flowerpots. But that would seem wrong. I want to be friends.

When they left I went over in my mind the things Leah had told me. Yesterday she told me what it's like to have children: it's a *mind fuck*, you can't get anything *done*, but still sometimes you feel like having more of them. Some part of you goes on wanting to be even more thoroughly fucked.

She told me things about Carlos and the past. They used to export crayfish to Japan. The fish are worth most when they arrive in Japan alive, to be sold alive. For export the fish are chilled down into a barely alive state of suspended animation, to minimise stress during the journey. When they arrive they are warmed up and revived for the buyers. On one occasion the carrier airline let the temperature *en route* get too low and this killed all the fish. Carlos had to threaten to sue in order to get compensation for the loss of profit, since the fish were worth so much less dead. Eventually the airline settled out of court. Carlos had got a big city firm to act for him and had spent a great deal of time trying to telephone the elusive solicitor acting, but being fobbed off instead onto some bored and frivolous junior. They made jokes to each other about dead fish. Finally he received an extortionate bill, which included a huge fee for advice given over the phone.

Leah said, 'Carlos is usually sharp with money, though. I was always surprised about how much we made. And the airline paid us a lot in the end. We sent Millicent and Dolph on a trip to Fiji with some of it.'

'Do a dance,' I said to May. I can't get tired of watching her. She danced across the room in her plastic shoes, stamping and twirling, crashing into the couch. Behind the couch in a cardboard box were the fragments of a number of Stuart's ornaments and knick-knacks, awaiting furtive disposal.

The dog watched May through the glass. He is banned from the house. He could take her tiny hand off with one snap, and since his fight with the prowler, Howard has changed. He seems to have put on weight, and become fiercer and more serious. Where he would once have slobbered and licked and whimpered he is now poised and silent. He used to lie in the sun on the veranda, on his back; now he sits neatly on the steps, upright, watching.

Leah told me about her domestic disasters. I listened intently. She must regard me as a bit of a friend by now, because she's told me all sorts of details, about her life now and her life long ago. Sometimes now in the flat on the Roundabout Road the boys refuse to go to school, sometimes May dirties her nappy just as they are leaving the house and it goes all over the nappy and all over her clothes and they're late again and it's a nightmare, sometimes Leon gets wheezy in the night and is too tired to go to school and throws tantrums, or the boys have a fight while the phone is ringing, the shit is being trodden into the carpet, May is eating soap or baby cream or trying to open the fridge and no one can find their shoes or their jerseys or any clean clothes at all and every day an appliance breaks down and a bill arrives and the ringing phone turns out to be Carlos, small and faint on the crackling line, asking an empty question, something out of date, did you try defrosting the fridge first before calling the repairman, did Leon get to the doctor all right . . .? I've been thinking all night about the fridge, I'm sure I know the thing to do . . . But she snaps at him, heaving the baby up under one arm, holding the phone between her shoulder and her chin, wiping up bits of dribble and snot, no, the fridge is fine, it's the washing machine, OK? the washing machine, leaked all over the floor and wet the carpet, everything stinking of mould.

The washing machine! Carlos staring out at the cold beach, the brassy sea. The washing machine, how could that go wrong too, and how could the fridge be fixed already, when he'd thought about the problem off and on all night, wondering about the best thing to do. How strange that they go on living over there, in the gaps between phone calls, that they go on living without me. Without me, he repeats in his head, and hangs up, numb.

'Life moves fast when you have kids,' Leah said. 'I mean in the sense that you can never go slow, you're always running, like a waiter in a restaurant full of mad diners screaming. When there's only one of you you have to move even faster.'

Leah has a special travelling kit full of baby things. It opens out into a changing mat. It has pockets for all the gear, the nappies and swabs, the lotions and creams, the spares and socks and snacks. All of it is very spruce and clean. I notice that May has on a new outfit each time they come, all spit and snot left behind.

Leah talked on, sipping her beer. She said, 'I fought with my parents about everything. I went to a private school. My parents wanted me to be a nurse, then marry a doctor and settle down. They didn't like Carlos, he wasn't suitable at all. When I was at university I went wild, they thought – I spent all my time going to nightclubs. I lived in a flat with the staff of the Megadrome club. They partied all night and slept all day. My father was beside himself, he thinks it's decadent to stay up after midnight. But those friends drove me mad after a while anyway. They were so idle, so inane. One day I was sitting around at that flat and I thought, what am I doing here? It's all wrong. It's a kind of depression. So I moved, and finished my degree. But Carlos wasn't at university, he never went. He was working, would you believe, at McDonald's.'

We discussed dogs. Leah wants to buy one because her flat is not secure. I nearly told her about the prowler and then stopped myself. She says you feel more vulnerable when you have children. As soon as you have a baby the world seems a more hostile place.

At nights, with Stuart away, I have been setting the new alarm. It can be programmed to go off if anyone walks through the living areas of the house. The bedroom and bathroom remain unwired so that I can move around. Howard sleeps under the bed. I am wired up, cross-beamed (mobile phone under the pillow), snug. At night I lie awake staring at the line of light under the door. Stuart and I bought the alarm system from a security firm owned by a terrifying Afrikaner called Klimpt. It took Wayne a whole day to wire it up.

Leah listens to the things I say, but not closely, she looks away. She is preoccupied with getting on. I want the kids to swap schools, she says, they have too far to go each day. She says, I used to ask Carlos's opinion on things like this, but now it's not possible.

'You can visit, talk to him on the phone.'

'He's not here. It's not easy to give him the picture. It's not the same . . .'

Beside us on the floor, May worked her way through some cheese on toast, pulling long strings of cheese off the toast and dangling them into her mouth. With her hair tied back off her face she looks a lot like Carlos.

Leah is also preoccupied with the past, as if she is going over it for clues. She no longer checks whether I am interested, she can see that I like listening to her.

'Did you fall out with your parents?' she said.

'No.'

'You were a good girl, then?'

'Sometimes I was bad. But my parents didn't notice. They

didn't mind.' I dragged up a memory, parents' evening at school, the gesticulating teacher, Phoebe nodding politely as she gazed out the window at the moon over the playing field. Or Jacques in his tennis outfit being berated at the school gate, weighing his wooden racket in his hands, smiling mildly at whichever vicious old bag had cornered him, 'Yes indeed, did she *really*, thank you for letting me *know*, Miss O'Frump.' I remember well the battle-axes and dragons at my single-sex grammar school, their floral frocks and orthopaedic shoes, their relentless disapproving drabness.

Leah thought aloud about Carlos and I listened, thinking how unlike Stuart's other clients she seemed. She has something to say about everything. I wonder, before I got to know her did I talk to her in tones that were faintly pompous and patronising? I cringe at the possibility. I remember when we were first introduced, her lopsided smile, the ironic light in her eye.

Yesterday she said, 'When I was young I used to be a bit hysterical, a masochist, malicious, a bit of a liar. I had no dignity. Nothing was sacred, I would have giggled at a funeral, whatever. I was all over the place.'

She said she admired Carlos. He was honest. He had honour. He had a sense of occasion. He was fair. She wanted to be like him, she wanted to imitate him and become better, smoother. She felt that he would show her how to have more self-respect. He used to pick her up when he'd finished work at McDonald's at two o'clock in the morning. He would double her to his flat on his trail bike, the machine spluttering and groaning under their combined weight. He made her laugh a lot, he made all sorts of silly jokes. When she first stayed with him she asked to borrow his toothbrush and he said very nicely, of course, although he did use it to clean the inside of his bum. It seemed hilarious to her at the time, it was the polite way he said it. They slept on his single bed together and he was an insomniac, still is. She would go to sleep and whenever she woke up at any time of night he'd be awake, reading or smoking. He used to beat everyone at chess, although he said his parents had had his IQ tested and according to the results it should have been a struggle for him to walk. He always made her laugh and then made her feel stupid for laughing. He used to say, look at what you're doing, it's like watching a bloody one-year-old, and he used to tell her off for being slobbish. He'd say, don't flick your ash there, and his shoes were always clean. After a while she bought some shoe polish, and stopped missing the ashtray.

She said, 'He looks like a Maori but his eyes are very green, have you noticed? My mother used to call him "my son-in-law the kitchen hand". My mother used to think of him as a bumpkin. Now of course she calls him a maniac.'

May and the dog eyeballed one another through the glass. May pushed her nose up against one side of the window, the dog squashed his snout up against the other side. May screamed and laughed. She banged on the glass. The dog sneezed, turned away and walked to the edge of the veranda. He coughed and shook himself, and snarled softly as he stared over the garden in a troubled way, but there was no one around except Leah and May and Wayne, down at the fence, uprooting a dead tree stump with a regular chop chop of his heavy machete.

Leah left in time to pick up the other children. I think about her routine. I turn over in my mind the things she says. She is ordering her life, she is working to make it liveable. She is learning to live alone.

That night I rang Stuart, wondering what he was getting up to in his southern motel room. I was connected to his room. There was a pause, there was breathing. The phone was fumbled with, then there was a crash as if it had fallen from the bedside table onto the floor.

'Mmmf,' he mumbled, and made other sounds. 'In bed. Mmmpf, gmmpf. Late. Mmmm.'

I kept him talking, listening for background noise. He had talked to Wallace Noble again, was going to meet him in Tauranga on the way home. There was nothing to report. 'I've set the alarm,' I remarked, hearing a high-pitched snort from his end of the line.

'Woof,' he said. 'Pppfm. Alarm. Yoops.' Suddenly he gave a little squawk.

'For Christ's sake!' I shouted, losing control. 'Is someone with you? What's she doing, going over you with a feather?'

'Mwerk,' he said, and the line went dead.

The nights. They creep up on me, descend on me, they sap all my strength. And they go on so *long*. The night-time lockup becomes a ritual. Each window to be checked twice. French doors inspected, bolts secured. The dog sent out for a last piss, then imprisoned for the night. The bedroom warm and dark, and at the end of the bed the lurid square of light beaming me CNN, the warm smiles, the cheery suits, the news readers not only anonymous of feature (uniform noses, perfect chins), but anonymous of race/creed/nationality; Piotr Cheung and Mervyn Harare could be of any ethnic origin you could think up, any one or a mixture of many, and they shine out of the dark all through the night telling me everything and nothing, all that detail, all that on-the-spot live-action minute-by-minute stream, of being there first, telling it first, telling it for the sake of telling. Being there in the night, live all night. Never going dead. The hours pass and the strip of light under the door stays half an inch wide and in the end the morning comes, another golden day under the cold sun. This morning I dreamed that I was weeping without knowing why. I moved through the morning feeling wounded somehow. Oh get above it, I mutter. You've only been alone a few days. A few days? Oh man it feels like a year.

The next day Leah stayed away and I stood out on the street watching for her, worrying, wondering what was going on. Eventually I closed up the house and went out looking for her, walking along Helms Road, across the motorway towards Outland Road, Fall Road, the Roundabout Road, on and on until I lost my way and sat blankly down at a bus stop on a wooden bench by a dry-stone wall in the autumn sun, and there by the side of the street with its rows of wooden houses stretching away into the suburb I could see no one, not a person in sight: the houses were all deserted, the streets were wide open under the terrible blue of the empty sky. I felt I could go on walking towards the Waitakere Ranges rising on the horizon across the water, on until I reached Piha or KareKare or Whatipu, walk over the black sand to the winter sea, lie down on the sand, stare up into the black of the blue and let the tide wash over me and the surf crash around me, feel the rip sucking me in, the waves lifting me up and smashing me down, the whirling sand, the boiling waves – carried up, dumped down, lifted again, carried away, from the empty streets, the empty world, the yawning gap of the sky.

But squinting into the fridge at the grocery store I saw (on some street, Long Avenue? Point Grenadier?) that I could not decipher the sell-by dates on the packaged meals, and opted for pasta and a ready-seasoned jar of tomato sauce, and, adding Parmesan cheese and a bottle of wine, felt steadier now and set off for home.

I sat up late in the silent kitchen, warming myself with glasses of wine. What is madness? The endless detail of kitchen objects, where to look, what to start with, to wash or not to wash, to reorder or to let it all go to hell. Madness is fear of everyday things, an inability to look at knives, fear of the light under the door, fear of windows. Fear of the sight of the back seat of the car when you glance behind while driving alone through the dark streets to the empty house with the silent rooms, the creaking floor. It all starts with loneliness. Too long alone.

I rang Phoebe at 9 p.m. 'I'm glad you rang,' chirped the old bird, 'because tonight there will be an eclipse of the moon. Watch out for it. For some time the sky will be *complete-ly*, moonlessly black.' She hung up, I stared at the face, the dumb dial of the phone.

I will show you fear in a blender, a knife rack, in a drawer full of spoons.

The phone rang late at night. The voice on the end growling, dangerous and low, 'Hey, sexy, hey, babe, wanna wangle my dangle, wanna drool on my tool?'

Or some such drivel. 'Fuck off,' I said, 'I'm not in the mood.'

'When the cat's away,' Stain whispered coyly.

'Yeah yeah.'

'Anyway I hear things.'

'I'm sure you do.'

'Your man, is he as lonely as you?'

'Bugger off.'

'I had a win today, heartless.'

'Not Pirelli?'

'No no. Mrs Niedpath. I have liberated her neighbour. Not guilty of murder, it took the jury ten hours. Not enough evidence to convict. Not enough *body* in the case.'

He emitted a burp of mirth. 'So what do you say, I come over, bring some drinks, some drugs, ha ha, yawp, whoop, I have the hiccups, baby. I fear I may be drunk. Don't think, say yes.'

'What things do you hear?'

'Let me in. I'm right outside, I'll tell you all.'

'You're not outside, I'm looking now.'

'I'm near, I'm driving off the bridge.'

'Well, close your eyes and accelerate. If you know something tell me now. Tell me or I'll ring the cops. Drunk driver on bridge. Drunk *lawyer* on bridge.'

'I'm coming to you, speeding to your door. I'll tell you all, about my wife, my life . . .'

'You haven't got a wife.'

'No, darling, I haven't. Only a life.'

'Stain, I'm hanging up.'

Leah doesn't answer her phone. Where can she be? I'm really starting to fret.

Stuart rang. I sat up in my chair, knocking over the wine. For several seconds I played it cool. Oh it's you, uh huh. Me? You know, busy days . . . Twenty minutes later I heard him say, have you finished *now*?

'It's just . . .' I sobbed, 'I'm just . . .'

'Darling I can't sit here all night listening to you crack up. You're what? I can't hear you. Blow your nose. You're a wreck. Pass the tonic?'

'What?'

'Nothing. Are you there now, are you sane? I'm relying on you, darling. Remember that. I've got a list, some things to do. Can we be professional. Scratch my back?'

'What?'

'I've got some depositions here I'm going to fax back. I want you to go over them with a fine toothcomb. There, higher, ah. I'm going to fax them tomorrow morning before we start.'

'It's a fine-tooth comb.'

'What?'

'It's a fine-tooth comb, you stupid . . . not a fine toothcomb. You stupid . . .'

'Darling, you're delirious.'

A door slammed. He lowered his voice and changed his tone. 'Are you missing me? Are you sad to be all alone? When the trial is over we'll go away, somewhere tropical to soothe our stresses away. How hard we work in our little lives, for so little reward. Are you taking care of my Howie? Does he miss his dad? Hmm?' He gave a rich little chuckle of love. 'I think about you and How all the time, my little family, waiting to see me home . . . from the wars. Hmm?'

'It's just . . . I've spent a lot of time by myself . . . At night . . . At least Ken Stain has come over a few times, filled in a few moments.'

A pause, the crackle and sigh of the long-distance line.

'What?'

'I said Kendrick Stain's been over.'

'When?'

'A couple of evenings.'

'To do what?'

'Just for a visit, you know how he does.'

'When you're alone?'

'Yes.'

'You let him in?'

'Well yes, why not?'

'You let him in when you're alone.'

'Yeah . . .'

'You invited him over. You *welcomed him in*.'

'Yes. No. He just came over.'

He laughed. 'Just like that. Just like *that*.'

'Yes like that. What's wrong with that? Wait, don't hang up, please don't go.'

'Stella, I will phone you tomorrow with further instructions.'

Cold anger in the level voice, the deathly click of the phone. Don't go, I whispered into the void. Oh the pain of that click. How completely I came to grief at the end of it all, face down on the crackling couch under the watching windows, in the jagged shadows of the silent room.

And then she rang. *Just like that*.

In the background the children babbled and squeaked. I fought my way out of the cushions, speechless.

'Hello?' Leah said softly, over the sound of a pot lid banging, the giggling kids. 'Hello?'

'It's you. It's you. Where have you been?'

'I've been here. Just here. Oh and I took the kids to stay with a cousin of mine for a couple of nights, not far out of town. Nothing special.'

'I wondered . . . Well, how are things?'

'Oh fine, just the same. I'm cooking actually, we got back late. I'm just ringing because I've lost something of May's, a prescription. I thought I might have left it with you?'

What's it like, your kitchen? I wanted to ask. Small and cluttered, full of children, full of the steam off the pasta pot boiling on the stove, little kids bickering, the radio on. Lying on my couch stuffed with cash in the shadow of the looming antiques I took another swig of wine and asked, what are you cooking? She told me. I got up and scanned the room for the prescription, which was not there.

'The children are well, they had a nice time. Do you have a cold? It's the time of year. I'm going to put them to bed in a minute, they're so tired. I didn't think we'd be so late . . .'

She talked on like Una, the phone stuck under her chin. Women in the kitchen with their cooking and their phones, all that life going on in the lighted room, never a minute to themselves. She drained the pot, she doled out for the kids. Their chairs squeaked on the linoleum floor, they fought over who got the Spiderman plate and who got Winnie the Pooh.

While I listened the baby threw carrot on the floor and one boy shouted at the other you kicked me you shit face and Leah told me that they had been to some hot pools where a sign said do not put your head under the water and Leon had gone and dived in and she hoped he wouldn't catch something terrible like meningitis, since he was always catching things.

'I can't find the prescription,' I said, 'but I'm still looking. Let me check the office. And the children, can they swim?'

I found something belonging to May stuck down behind the cushions of the couch. A crimson headband, stretchy. Oh I didn't know I'd lost that, Leah said. I told her I had been looking at some depositions. Royden Sloacombe, Boyderman Leonard, Morven Garland. Those bastards, she said while stacking the plates, I bet they're enjoying themselves. Someone had offered to give her a pedigree puppy, a good dog that she could train. You get a good guard dog young so it can get used to the kids. If you get the right animal it will protect you faithfully, whenever you're alone. A good dog will live for a long time, ten years, twelve, maybe fourteen years. Life.

Listening to Leah I became aware of a tapping on the window and levered myself up off the couch to look. It was black out there in the chilly night. Following the noise into the kitchen I shrieked at the face pressed up against the window but it was only Wayne, holding up the keys to the garden shed, and smiling.

I unlocked the glass door and he stepped into the room. I reached over to take the keys. He dangled them out of my reach, still smiling. His smile grew wider. He swung the keys in his fingers. Eyeing him impatiently, I felt around for the phone and found it under the table.

'Are you there?' I said to Leah. 'I got such a fright but it was only Wayne, Stuart's gardener. He was peering in the window. Yeah I dropped the phone.'

I took the keys out of Wayne's hand. He stopped smiling.

'I didn't realise you were on the phone,' he said unpleasantly. We faced each other across the table. I glared at him.

He took an apple out of the fruit bowl and bit into it hard, with a loud gnashing sound. Chomp. We glowered at one another.

'Have another one. Take them all.' I pushed the bowl towards him. On the other end Leah said, 'What?'

'Nothing. I'm just saying goodbye to Wayne. Goodbye, Wayne.'

He smiled nastily. 'OK,' he said.

At the door he turned and winked. 'Nighty-night,' he said, before I slammed the door in his face.

Leah said, 'I'd better go and do the children.' I said goodnight and hung up. I stood listening at the door. I knew Wayne hadn't gone down the steps, he was there on the other side of the door. There was no noise. I waited without moving. Then he said quietly, inches from my ear, 'Bitch.'

'Hey, fuck off!' I shouted, banging on the door, and heard him clatter down the steps. I watched him walk casually off along the street.

At the corner a car tooted and he waved. The beaten-up brown Hillman Hunter wove its way along the road and I heard loud reggae music from the smoke-filled interior. Stain executed a neat park, opened the door and fell out.

Oh that Stain, no one can believe he's a barrister; that is, no one who gets a proper look at him after hours. During the day, in the foyer of the High Court, with his robe covering his scorch marks and stains and his high collar done up under his chin, he has a gaunt kind of grace and authority. He stalks through the hushed halls with the robe billowing out behind him. His face is battle-scarred and ravaged, his expression is remote and amused.

At the courthouse I sometimes feel the force of Stain's presence when I'm doing an errand there. He sweeps in looking like a big crow. There is a restlessness and power in him that disturbs everyone. Those waiting shift uneasily in their seats, children start to fight, babies begin to wail. Stain will go further, say more, dare the unthinkable. Look at him now, reeling around at the garden gate. He lives dangerously. He gets away with murder, that's what they say about him, one of these days he'll come unstuck. People like him, they always go too far.

'Hello!' he called from the bottom of the steps. 'I know you're in there. Come out and show yourself, the night is young . . .'

But I couldn't be bothered, and as he sang and warbled at the front door I felt my way upstairs in the dark, took off my clothes and got into bed with Kieran Yep and Flip Spiceland, lay in the glow of the television while down below on the wooden steps the big crow flapped and grumbled and sang for one hour and then another and drove the evil spirits away with the melody of his croaks and groans.

I thought about Leah. There was a story I liked that Leah told me as we sat on the veranda looking out over the Gulf. When she was a child she lived next door to an old woman who had come to New Zealand from Czechoslovakia after the Second World War. The children would sneak into the old woman's garden and steal plums from her plum tree. After they had eaten a lot of plums they would start to throw the fruit onto the old woman's corrugated-iron roof. The plums would hit the iron roof with a crash and roll down into the guttering. After the bombardment had carried on for a while the old woman would come running out of her back door with a broom and chase them out of the garden. If she cornered Leah, which she sometimes managed to do, she would brandish the broom, rolling her eyes with rage and shout in her heavy Czech accent, 'Vas it you? Did you throw these missiles?'

And when Leah shouted, 'No! It wasn't me!' the old lady

would seize Leah by the shoulders and roll her eyes even more fiercely and say, 'It is the *lies*, Leah. Not the plums vich kill me, but the *lies*. The *fiendish* lies . . .'

And Leah rolled her eyes and did for me the old woman's voice, the harsh foreign whisper.

'It is the *lies*, Leah. The fiendish, terrible, endless. It is the *lies.*'

I slept but something began to bother me, something was *there* in the disorganised corners of my mind. I shifted and turned and tried to find a more comfortable plane, but an aching in my legs – all this walking – brought me nearly out of sleep and then I began to dream. I dreamed I could hear a noise, *there* and there it was again, a scraping or a filing, as of nails on dusty wood or glass, it was dry, urgent, scrabbling. For a moment I lay suspended, detached, dreaming of small animals, woodpiles, the wind blowing in a pile of kindling, the sighing of the wind in dead grass. I turned and sighed, and dreamed in a sudden flash of a man's pale hand, dark hair on the back of the bony fingers, the fingers waggling, spider-like, waving hi, and with that I was rigid and awake, full of the horrible image of the blind hairy wriggling thing. And *there* was the scrabbling sound again, coming from the bricked yard outside. I felt the adrenalin poison, the ache of the chemical fight-or-flight boosters building up, building up as I lay frozen on my side, thinking clearly, with sudden certainty, *Wayne*. It was Wayne that night, waiting for me, creeping through the house while I . . . *Christ*. And now I was off the bed, creeping low across the bedroom floor. Did he wait for Poppy Marks too, hide in his garage and beat him half to death? I reached the wall, my nose against the carpet. Why? Because he thought Poppy was a pervert? Because Poppy wanted money from him? Or just because Poppy was there, because he was there and *all alone* . . .

Of course it was you, I thought, snaking myself up the wall and over the window sill and then I fixed on something down there, straight away. It was small, hesitant-purposeful. It was backing and filling and tugging and pulling its heavy burden, working,

working, and now there were two of them, two busy furry backs, they seemed to come together, confer, separate and come together with the dry scrabbling and pattering of little claws on dusty brick. They were a healthy size, for possums, and they were absorbed down there in their work. Quickly and deftly they worked the entire package of stale bread out of the rubbish bin and hauled it in its winking plastic wrap across the bricks, down the steps and away into the dark, humid jungle at the end of the garden. I watched them go, listening to the friendly pitter-pat of their busy paws. I cheered them on, I wished them bon appetit, *Jesus*. I sank back onto the bed feeling tearful, hollow, exhausted.

But soon I propped myself up on an elbow and thought about Wayne. Was I right? Should I ring the police? I reached for the phone. But what would I say? I was woken by possums. Instinct tells me that I have your man. I knew what they would say. Are you currently under threat from the possums? If not, ring in the morning (you fruitcake, you nut). I would have to talk to Stuart in the morning. I thought about it for several seconds more before deciding to double-check everything: alarm, doors, windows, phone. I prowled nervously round my small electronic perimeter. Everything seemed to be secure. I lay back down but couldn't sleep. I couldn't relax. It was being woken like that, for a start, then an empty stomach of course, always makes the mind race (and the kitchen electronically cordoned off). And then there was the fact of how incredibly *frightened* I was. I curled myself into a ball and still felt exposed; I felt as if swords might come up through the bed and run me through.

A long time went by. I looked at the clock. A long time had gone by and it was only five minutes later. I wanted something to eat. I wanted a glass of wine. But then I'd have to turn off the alarm and then who knew what would happen in the black cave of the kitchen while I was ferreting around in the fridge. *Wayne*. Where was he now? I struggled with my hunger for another impossibly long time, before deciding to watch some CNN. I turned it on then turned it off again. I couldn't watch because I needed to be listening. This is what people mean when they say 'unnaturally alert'. I was *unnaturally alert*. I lay there like that while a lot of dark, dead time went by.

'It's the lies, Leah,' I whispered miserably, curling myself into a tighter ball, and then another idea came to me and set me thinking more. 'The lies,' the old Czech woman said to Leah long ago. Leah and lies, now ran the train of my thought, Leah and childhood, Leah and old women, Leah and children, and there was a memory, a scene Leah described in the office one day to Stuart and me and Phyllis du Fresne. Leah at the Seabrooke school gate with Leon beside her, the little son with his broiling, rashy face. Looking at Leon, Mrs Seabrooke says to her friend, 'Why can't they look after the child's skin, it's a *scandal*.'

And Mrs Seabrooke's friend, who looks on and says nothing, the friend is *Boyderman Leonard's sister*.

I thought about it, staring at the strip of light under the door. This could be the woman mentioned by Stee Flarps, this woman who was living at the Leonards' at the time of the shooting, who never said anything and who has now disappeared. No one else in the town has ever mentioned that Boyderman and Cyril had a sister. There are no statements from a sister . . .

It was late but I couldn't wait. I felt under the pillow for the phone. She was awake, to my surprise.

'What are you doing up so late?'

Her voice was dry, ironic, far away. 'Same to you,' she said, and I thought I heard the clink of a glass.

'Listen,' I said, 'long ago, Mrs Seabrooke gave you grief about your Leon, about his face. You were at the school gate, Leon was sick, Mrs Seabrooke turned to her friend and she said . . .'

'It's a scandal . . .'

'It's a scandal, about his face.'

'So?' Leah said, and sounded as if she was turning away.

'I'm sorry, it's late. But Leah, wait. Who was Mrs Seabrooke's friend?'

She sighed impatiently, an empty sound. 'She was the Leonards' sister, Boyderman and Cyril's.'

'How did you know that?'

'Everyone knew, I just knew. Besides, the Leonards were all practically identical. She was the same build as them. I wouldn't be surprised if they wore each other's clothes.'

'Where does she live? With the Leonards?'

'I don't know. She didn't have a house in Seabrooke. She came and went. Her name was . . . her name was . . . I can't remember.'

'Well she's never said anything to anyone. People can't just disappear. I . . .'

And she sighed again, the phone shifted in her grip. 'Are you alone?' I asked, hanging on, hanging on.

'What do you think?'

'So am I . . . It's a drag, isn't it?'

'It's something to work on,' she said, suddenly brisk, and wished me goodnight and hung up the phone.

15. Pearl-Rae

I began ringing Stuart's number early the next morning, but his mobile phone was switched off. *Please try again later*, the electronic lady advised. I ate some cereal, sitting at the table, looking out at the chemical blue of the morning sea. The autumn sun on its low trajectory sent bright shafts angling into the room, early morning yellowlight, like light through the window of a plane. The high April sky hung above, in its absolutist blue. Against it on the deck out there the dog looked as black as a piece of coal. I scooped sodden Weet-bix out of the pottery dish, feeling two-dimensional in all that bright light, like a playing card. These long nights, they turn me into paper. Keep me away from water and flame. I tried Stuart's line again. *Try again, try again*, the robot woman replied.

No longer *unnaturally alert*, I became frustrated, *frustrated*. Ten o'clock came, half-past ten, still there was no reply. He had checked out of his motel, he was on the road I supposed, somewhere down there in the land of kiwi fruit and salad. Finally at eleven or so, I heard his gruff reply, and resisting the temptation to berate him, denounce him, hang up on him, I told him quickly about the sister, this missing Leonard, who was no longer around.

'Where are you?' I asked.

'I'm at Wallace Noble's. Near the port. What sky, what a morning, it's startling.'

'Should we look for this woman?'

'Of course. I'll tell Wallace now.'

'When are you coming home?'

'Tonight.'

Oh thank Christ, I thought, and I said, 'Stuart. Listen. There's something much more important. The prowler. I know who it was. It was *Wayne*.'

'The what?'

'The prowler. Here. In the house, that night.'

'Oh?' Coldly polite, tapping his fingers on the phone.

'It was Wayne. *Wayne*.'

'My Wayne.'

'I'm sure of it. I'm sure. What're we going to do? Shall I call the police?'

There was a silence.

'You're full of fears, aren't you, Stella?'

I hesitated, surprised. 'Well yes, if someone breaks into the house . . .'

'Darling. No one *broke* in.'

'Crept in, what's the difference?'

'There's a difference, Stella.'

'Look, shall I call the police now? Or wait until you get back?'

'Darling, why're you telling me this? You want to have my client arrested. On what grounds, darling. On what basis?'

'Yes, because it was *him*. Who came into the house . . .'

'He works for me, darling. He's always around the house. He's allowed to be around the house.'

'Not at night. Look . . . this is crazy. I *know* it was him.'

He gave a tiny delicate cough. Of patience. Forbearance.

'Well, if it was only him, Stella, what have you got to worry about?'

'Stuart!'

He said in a blaze of irritation, 'Wayne's come a long way, Stella. He's achieved. Do you want to bring him down, on a hunch? What are you going to say? That someone who works for me came into the house. And did what? If you're afraid of the dark, Stella, why don't you lock the doors? My advice? Don't let fear rule you. Negativity drags others down. Remember that. Goodbye, Stella.'

'Stuart . . . !' He switched off the phone. I slammed down the receiver, furious. I paced up and down. I snatched up the phone book and looked up the number for Central Police Station. I dialled, the operator answered. I hesitated. 'Auckland Central Pleece?' she said again. But was I right? That terrible night, in the house, cowering up on the roof. Or was Stuart right? And what did right mean? He didn't even say he thought it wasn't Wayne. He said it didn't matter if it was. *Did* it matter if it was? I pressed my fingers to my aching head. It's always the same. Always when I'm sure of things he confuses me, he throws me off balance. What seemed concrete suddenly turns into sand. He turns crime into no crime at all – it's what he does, after all. Every day. Imagine if Wayne was arrested. Charged. Even with evidence, what was the crime? Was I being neurotic? Loneliness. Fears in the night. Pointing the finger at Wayne. It was harder to tell now, in the yellowy warmth of the bright room, whether Wayne was a plausible suspect at all. What a difference the daylight makes. Perhaps in the night, in the stew of loneliness and fear, perhaps I got carried away, let my imagination run riot?

Abruptly the operator hung up. I put down the phone and sat down heavily in the swivel chair. If I did ring and Wayne was brought in to the police station, who would he call? He'd ring Stuart. He'd ring here, and I would answer the phone. It was impossible, hopeless. At least if Stuart didn't come home I had another course of action planned. I couldn't stand another night, no. I'd scrape up some cash and check into the Hyatt Hotel.

Then the phone was ringing. I snatched up the receiver. But it was only Vera, telling me that she had the *flow*.

'The *what*?'

'The flow, I'm not coming in. I'm all bunged up.'

'Jesus.'

'I caught it from Frederick, no doubt. He's always coming down . . .'

'Oh the *flu*. Sorry. See you tomorrow then? *Bye*.'

So alone again, I manned the phones. Alone again. Hardly anyone rang and no one came around and I sat uneasily by the window in the creaking swivel chair, turning it over and over in my mind. I would ring the police. Forget about Stuart. But what would I say? I felt so unsure. If I was wrong . . . I could imagine Stuart's ferocious disapproval, his bitter scorn. The ground is always shifting under my feet these days. Am I going mad? I don't know what's going on around here any more.

He turned up around six, gunning the engine up the drive, slamming on the brakes and levering himself out of the car. He greeted the dog and its welcoming hysterics and strode up the path to the back door. 'Hey,' he called, 'would you believe!' I hurried out of the office to hear what he had to say.

They had found out who the Leonards' sister was, and pretty soon after that they'd found where she was living. Old Wallace Noble had become efficient, once he had something positive to look for. He had got importantly onto the phone and rung his sources, whoever they were, in government departments, public records, the local police. He discovered that she was born after Boyderman and before Cyril, and that she had lived in Seabrooke through her childhood and some of her adult life.

Her phone number was even listed in the directory. They hesitated, wondering whether to ring her or whether to wait and call on her unannounced. 'Don't ring her,' Wallace the old sleuth urged in melodramatic tones. 'She'll flee the jurisdiction.'

'She'll *what*?' Stuart, already tiring of the corpulent old Trojan, pushed him gently out of the way. He rang the number. She was home. He explained who he was, what he was ringing about. She was cagey and reluctant, even aggressive, took a lot of time to understand what he wanted. But eventually, after many near hangings up and much persuasion on Stuart's part while Wallace lurked in the background growling and shaking his head, she allowed herself to be reeled in and grudgingly agreed to meet. She was divorced with two children and lived in South Auckland. Her name was Pearl-Rae, would you believe. Pearl-Rae de Gruchy.

Stuart was agitated now, restless, striding about, unpacking his bag. 'We'll meet her tomorrow and see whether she's got any-thing to say, probably nothing – *don't touch that!*' He snatched his wallet away from me.

'What's wrong?'

'Nothing. Jesus, just give me . . . give me some privacy.'

'I was just putting it on the table.'

'OK.'

'OK, OK.' But now I felt raw, stung. I turned away and went upstairs. I stopped. I made a decision and came back down. Stuart was sitting at the table. I faced him across the table and said with difficulty, 'I don't want Wayne working around here any more.'

Stuart stopped what he was doing. He threw his pen down on the table and looked at me coldly. He opened his mouth to say something.

I said, 'I'm going to call the police if he comes around. And then I'll leave.' I watched his face. He struggled angrily. He gave in.

'OK then. Excellent. I'll tell him tomorrow. I'll let him know he hasn't got a job any more. Because you've got a funny feeling. He can walk the streets. OK?'

'Good.' I choked on the word. He turned away. I fled upstairs.

When I came back down later he was reading a letter. He looked up, folded it carefully and slid it into his pocket. I stood over him, hopelessly, willing myself to say nothing. I would bide my time, I would be strong . . . 'Can I just ask, on the subject of meeting people, who was in your motel room when I rang you all those nights? Who was it I could hear tinkling around in the background?'

Immediately he got up and began to pace, emphasising with his left hand. 'Can we be professional. Suspicion is a terrible thing. If you force me to I'll tell you. There was no one in my room, ever. Satisfied? Feel good now? Quite frankly I'm tired of this . . . this third degree. Night after night, these suspicious accusations. Why? Why are people like me positive and people like you negative? I am a doer! I achieve! You, you suspect and complain and pull me down . . .'

He continued. I stood at the window. The sun was going down over the harbour out there, big shadows crowding out the last of the light. Can we be professional, he says. What have we come to? What have we become? In the kitchen I unloaded the dishwasher, making no sound. I stacked the cups with precision, the plates slid into place without a click or a clank. There was a smell of woodsmoke. Above the house in the thin autumn air the seagulls screamed and cried. This heaviness I feel lately, this dread. Is this what it feels like to be bereaved?

Mrs de Gruchy's street ran narrowly along the top of the map and came to a dead end at the edge of the southern motorway. A low-rent street, full of ragged kids with their ears ringing and their brains full of lead playing under the humming webs of cable stretched between the huge electricity pylons looming over the prefabricated houses. Dead cars on the lawns, tricycles on the driveways, the odd kid over the years getting through the iron barricades and onto the motorway to be rescued famously from the median strip (how he made it they'll never know) or bowled by one car then another and another until there's not much kid left just the awful mess and the poor mother coming back from the shop with the carton of Winfield Red and the bottles of DB to find that the little shit's got out the window again and the cops are pulling up outside. The streets you see as you fly down the motorway south, the dead backyards in the dead afternoons.

Stuart sat in the passenger seat, the map on his knees.

'Pearl-Rae used to go back to the family patch in Seabrooke every few weeks. But this is where she lives. I got the impression she's got no respect for the brother. She said she doesn't go back to Seabrooke any more. I don't blame her. All those staring inbreds down there, they give you the creeps. All of them hanging about looking like Picassos, you know, eyes on one side of their faces, upside-down mouths. Hang on, I'm lost . . .'

He riffled through the pages of the map.

'I missed you when I was down there. Then you attack me like you always do. Why do you attack me when I'm your greatest fan? I'll tell you something, the looks you give me, sometimes you dent my confidence. There's something about you, you can be so dark, and me your greatest fan . . . We're all doing our best, darling, in our fragile lives, struggling forward . . . hmm? . . . strutting and fretting till all hours, on life's stage . . . oh here we are, Tomo Street.'

'And?'

'Quick with the Jaffas, darling. Turn left then right. And hand me one of those. Look! A pineapple lump!'

We turned into Pearl-Rae's road. Her section was the last in the row, a small square house painted green like a dental clinic. A garden gate stood ridiculously by itself, without a fence. In the rockery a gnome fished at the edge of a pink birdbath, and a frog crouched beneath a concrete bridge.

'More gnomery,' Stuart whispered as the doorbell donged out the first few notes of 'Frère Jacques'. '*Dormez-vous, dormez-vous?* Come on, you old boiler, open the door. Ah, Pearl-Rae, my dear. And how are *you*?'

'The house used to be a dental clinic,' said Pearl-Rae grimly. 'My husband Pidgy had it towed here and done up. Saves you on building costs.'

'Pidgy?' Stuart had his pen in his mouth, sorting through his notes.

'Short for Pigeon. Pidge. Sometimes they called him Pid. They all knew him around here. Piddles de Gruchy, never a dull moment. I never had a duller moment than when he left me in the middle of winter, me in the clinic with the two kids, not even a carbonette in the house, the children living on porridge.'

'All right all right.' Stuart was exasperated.

'Would you be wanting a cup of coffee, Mr Chicane?'

She made us a cup of coffee and drew Stuart down beside her on a brown candlewick-covered couch. She was thickset and dour with a heavy face. Her tiny eyes were set deep in the dark rubbery flesh. She talked for a long time, in a flat voice, about her husband, who had run away to live with his girlfriend in Bondi, leaving her to look after their two sons, Jared and Masport.

'His new girlfriend, Trellis, she's Australian. She's a professional shoplifter.' Pearl-Rae was triumphant with disgust.

'She steals to order. They're rolling in money. Videos, TVs, anything not nailed down.'

'Trellis?'

'I'm always poor. I've been really down and out, feeding the boys on scraps. But I've always been honest, more or less. I've told my boys they'd better turn out straight. Anyway I was going to talk to you about boy.'

'A boy?'

'My brother. Boy. That bastard. When we were young, the things he put me through. Always peeping and peering, undressing me with his eyes.'

Pearl-Rae and Stuart shuddered simultaneously at the thought.

'He was bad then. Always drinking. Now he drinks even more, hits the children, bashes up Nerolene.'

'His wife?'

'His second wife. The first one left him. Gordon was her name.'

'*Gordon?*'

'Gordon was a beautiful person, we all loved her. One day she vanished. We never saw her again. We searched, of course. We got in touch with the police, through B.J. Sloacombe. But she was just gone. She was probably right to hide herself away. Boy would have killed her just for leaving him. After Gordon left, Boy went right downhill. Nerolene has a terrible time these days.

'I've always put up with Boy because he's family. But I can't put up with the things he's been doing. His thieving. Especially being here in the clinic with nothing, knowing what Pidge and Trellis are up to over in Australia, rolling around in their dirty money. It makes me sick, I'm surrounded by thieves.'

Stuart leaned forward eagerly. 'Boy is a thief? Can you be . . .?'

'I'd been spending time down at home before it all happened. I'd had to move down there because I was completely broke. I was trying to rent out this house and I had to stay with Boy and Nerolene on and off for months. I had no choice.

'Boy was shocking. He would drink and beat the dogs. Once he killed one of the farm dogs with a hosepipe. Can you imagine how long that took? He just tied it to a stake and beat it and beat it until it died. Nerolene used to cry all day sometimes. She carried her bible with her all the time. She was afraid that Boy would kill her. Whenever she got a chance she would read her bible. Nerolene is deeply religious. I thought she should leave Boy, but she wouldn't. She's feared him so long she can't get away. The only people she trusted were me and Cyril. She trusted Cyril because Boy always bullied Cyril and so Cyril understood how Nerolene felt. When she heard that Cyril was dead I think she just gave up hope.'

Stuart and I scribbled furiously in our notebooks, nodding our heads.

'All through last year and the one before Boy would go out late at night, often on his horse. Every morning there would be something new in the house that he had brought home in the night. Tools, seeds, batteries, nails. Coils of wire, rope, pesticide. Paint, firewood, building wood. Bags of cement. Even children's toys. They all came from the same place. The Lehmans'. Boy wouldn't steal from anyone else in Seabrooke. Practically everyone else is family or close friends. They would've come round to the house and seen the stuff. So it all had to come from the Lehmans.'

Stuart glanced at me sideways and raised his eyebrow. Watching him, Mrs de Gruchy set her mouth in a grim line. She

paused and he looked quickly back at her; she lowered her voice
and carried on.

'B.J. Sloacombe would come over and say that that coon
Lehman had reported another theft. He and Boy would laugh
about it together as if it was a joke. Once I saw Boy give B.J.
some tools that I knew didn't belong to him. Nerolene and I
were disgusted. Nerolene said that she hoped the Lord would
punish Boy for what he was doing. But she would never confront
him herself. I would meet Mrs Lehman at the shop and I
couldn't look her in the eye. When I heard that Lehman was
complaining about vandalism and trees being destroyed I knew it
was Boy. Nerolene and I talked about it together and we knew
something terrible was going to come out of it. I came back up
here. I had a very bad feeling.

'Then Nerolene rang me. She was close to a nervous collapse
because she thought God was going to punish them all. She was
going mad really because she was afraid of Boy all the time. I
don't actually believe in all that religious stuff and I tried to stop
Nerolene praying all the time and hanging onto her bible. It
scared the kids.

'When I got back down to Seabrooke she wanted to have a
seance to call up her father to help her. She'd flipped her lid, I
told her. Get a grip, I said. I told her to come back down to my
house with me but she didn't dare, of course. She said she
thought Boy had been looking into the bathroom and watching
the girls getting dressed. I knew all about that one. The maniac.

'One morning, Sunday, we went to church with the Garlands.
Nerolene made me go, she wanted to get me praying although I
wasn't much interested. We walked past the Lehmans' land and
the man was out at his boundary fence. He started shouting about
his fencing, about someone cutting his fence so that the stock
would get in and trample down his trees. He was in a rage. Boy
and Morven Garland were laughing. Boy shouted out something
to him, like you've really cracked up now you useless bastard.
Then Boy got aggressive and said that Lehman had better shut
up or Boy would go over there and wrap his fencing around his

neck, or something like that. Morven and Boy were laughing about it all through church.

'I think Morven and Boy wanted to get rid of Lehman and buy his land. When he bought it they had been wanting to buy it together but they couldn't afford it. Boy still wants to buy the land. I suppose he will one of these days.'

'How did you know that Boy and Morven cut Lehman's fence?'

'I heard them talking about it. They let the stock in so that the Lehmans' plantation would be trampled. They wrecked all his young plants. I heard them arguing about it because Morven was worried that Lehman would start shooting at the stock. Boy reckoned he wouldn't dare, he'd just keep moaning to the police. Morven said he'd seen Lehman point his shotgun at some of the Garlands' cows. Boy told him not to worry about it, it wasn't a big deal after all. Just a few plants and a bit of fencing.

'Nerolene complained to Cyril about all of this but he wasn't about to interfere. He was afraid of Boy because he was younger and had always been smaller. He acted as if he thought it was a great joke that Boy was playing, but if he had disapproved he wouldn't have dared say anyway. He told Nerolene once that when they were young Boy tried to drown him. Cyril needed a kick in the backside sometimes, some of the things he'd say. He even told Nerolene that Boy must have done something terrible to Gordon to make her go away. Cyril said he found a woman's shirt under a concrete slab down at the dog kennels a few months after Gordon disappeared. He was just working Nerolene into a state for the fun of it. That was his speciality, winding people up. He could work and work on you and make you angrier and angrier, and then he'd laugh. And he was always dreaming up stupid things.'

Stuart stopped writing. 'What did you do after Cyril was shot?'

'I told Boy I was getting away from the family altogether. I'm going to move to the South Island. I have a friend who can get me a job in a hotel in Twizel. I don't intend to tell the family where my boys and I are. They can all go hang as far as I'm concerned.

Even Nerolene, she's as silly as a chook, spending all her time reading the bloody Bible while her daughters go to the pack.'

Mrs de Gruchy took out a packet of Internationals and extracted one of the long cigarettes. Stuart took the lighter out of her hand and lit it for her, murmuring soft encouragements. I saw I had written about fifteen pages of notes.

'What about Nerolene, would she make a comment about all of this?'

'No way. She's made all her little no-comment statements. That's the end of it with her. All these weak people, all running scared. Boy doesn't scare me. I told him he was a bloody thief, that he started all the trouble. He doesn't answer when I give him what for, he just sneers and giggles like a schoolboy even though he's a great powerful lump. He's scared of me. He wants me well out of the way. I don't know what he's told everyone about me down there, but they don't talk to me now and I don't talk to them. They're all hopeless as far as I'm concerned. Cyril was a good sort of bloke but he was all over the place, always dancing about playing silly buggers. If you told him to put his hand in the fire he would. He never knew how to look after himself.'

She leaned back against the couch. Stuart stretched his long legs out so that his feet reached the green Lazy-Boy on the opposite wall. He finished another page.

'You've never made any statements to the police?'

'No, I was in Auckland when it happened. No one wanted to talk to me. None of them would ever have talked about me. Boy probably told them not to.'

Stuart put on a solemn face. He put down his notes, and leaning towards her he said, in a voice both soft and supportive, 'Mrs de Gruchy I realise that this is a difficult time but I see that you are strong . . . What we need to know now is whether you could bring yourself to relate some of this detail to the court. If we can get it down to essentials, there's no need to get you too involved. You could provide the court with some very helpful background. I think I can say that these days the modern courtroom is not the intimidating place it once was, why—'

'Stand up in court, in front of everyone, in front of Boy and all the families? Everyone from Seabrooke hearing everything I'm saying?'

'Yes . . . I'm afraid . . . It would involve . . .'

'Not a problem,' she said flatly.

'Oh . . . really?'

'No problem at all.'

Leaning back against the pink wallpaper, under the framed portraits of the family Picassos, Pearl-Rae folded her massive arms over her chest and smiled a cruel smile.

Waving goodbye, hanging onto the flapping bundles of our notes, we hurried out of Pearl-Rae's gate and down the shabby street. At the end of the road the edge of the motorway was fenced by a metal and concrete barricade fifteen feet high, the graffiti splattered and spiderwebbed across it, the American-style gang tags sprayed on by wannabe urban warriors living at the edge of suburbia, at the far edge of the world. Trying to be Gangsta and Mobsta and Ice Cool and T with the open sky overhead, the tide coming in over the mangrove swamp at the edge of the motorway, the cold wind rippling the water as it creeps over the estuary mud, filling the crab holes, turning over the tiny shells, the inlet turning to silver as the water moves in towards the bridge and the scratched and peeling dinghies are lifted and turned to lie side by side at the end of their ropes, bobbing and tugging in the green swirl of the channel. Gangsta and Mobsta and T at work with their spraycans dreaming of city heat while the seagulls look down with cold eyes and scream and the hills cast their long shadows and the wind blows in the weeds growing over the old cans and the bottles and the paint, splattered and congealed on the grey stones. Stuart kicked an old can high into the air. 'She's good isn't she? She's fucking *great*.' He stared intently out over the mangroves. 'I could see into the bedroom. Did you notice? There were old wires, bits of instruments, clinical things coming out of the wall. *Disgusting*.'

'Disgusting but perfect.'

'Boyderman, Cyril, Pearl-Rae. Wow. What a family. I hope Pearl-Rae doesn't disappear before the trial. I do *not* want to be traipsing around the country looking for her. We need her. We'll have to treat her well.'

He put his arm around my shoulder. 'We need a holiday after this, somewhere tropical, a lonely island stocked with treats. Some place where you and I can hide away . . .'

'Somewhere *sunkissed*?'

'What, yes . . . I'd like to go somewhere where Howie could run free as the wind and you, darling, you could . . .'

'Run free? Play poker?'

'Where you could be . . . *naked*. Naked as . . .'

'Naked as?'

'The wind.'

Naked as the wind. *Mais oui.*

We drove to the Balcony.

'She had on those carpet slippers, did you notice? Why do they all wear *carpies*? Or jandals.'

'She's tough, like Boy.'

'She's tougher than Boy. Those eyes, like black marbles. Do you want wine? A bottle of wine?'

'Why does she want to get involved?'

'Ancient hates. Revenge. Who cares? A sense of right and wrong.'

Intimate connections. Private lives. Pearl-Rae's carpies were green and lined with sheep's wool. Zips ran from the bottom inside to the top of the fur-lined inside ankle. She wore brown stretch pants and a heavy green cardigan. Her hair was wiry brown and tightly woven, growing like a helmet over her solid brows. Strong jaw, powerful hands. Those arms, thick with muscle. She was short, like a weightlifter.

Sitting beside her on the couch Stuart was in a fever of note-taking. He leaned away from her while he scribbled and she watched him. Her eyes travelled up and down his long person and back to his face. Her eyes lingered on his shoes, his colourful tie. As he looked up she was ready for him, 'Another cup of *coffee*, Mr Chicane?' as if coffee were a weakness or a sin, or a sedative. By her feet a small heater glowed, red lights through fake coals. Stuart wrote fast and awkwardly, turning his wrist away from him, the handwriting sloping backwards as if he should be writing right to left. Over his wrists the cuffs of his white shirt were spotlessly clean. His silk tie was an elegant mix of turquoise and green. He hummed and rubbed his cramped hand; reaching in his pocket he fumbled for a handkerchief. Mrs de Gruchy stirred the coffee with a grimy spoon.

'Boy's problems started early,' she said. 'He was deprived of oxygen at birth. He lay at the end of the bed turning blue. My mother had fainted with loss of blood. Her cervix was torn, they had to give her ether. The doctor brought Boy back from the brink of death. Born dead, my mother used to say, and now look at him. Well, indeed. But she was so proud.'

Blenching, Stuart carried on with his notes. There were violet shadows under his eyes, the exhausted skin. He glanced over at me. Pearl-Rae kept up her scrutiny, her eyes on his face.

'Mother never knew that Boy was a drunk. Mother died of dementia. At the end she screamed and screamed for four days. She spat and spat until she couldn't spit any more. She swore at us all with swear words we'd never heard her use, at all of us except Boy. She never said one word against him and then she died. She thought he was an angel. Compared to Boy the rest of us were just clods of earth to her. And all the time, the things he used to do . . .'

'So, Mrs de Gruchy, it would be safe to say . . .' Stuart said suddenly, cutting her off. 'It would be safe to say . . . oh . . . never *mind*.' He waved his notes. 'It's all in here.'

Pearl-Rae stared into her plastic fire. The red lights revolved inside the peeling coals. On the low couch Stuart was forced to sit with his legs sideways, the writing pad on his knees. He was narrow-shouldered, awkward, too long for the room.

At the end she couldn't stop talking, about death and madness, long lives on the empty land, at the far end of the world. Stuart leaned back on the couch with his eyes half closed. She'd given him everything he wanted to know and now he just sat there, absorbing it, letting her go on without him. Outside the gnome fished in the cold afternoon light and the long shadows grew black at the edge of the estuary where the mangroves swayed in the water now filling the silvery bay.

At the Balcony Stuart said, 'Let's not go home, let's eat here. What do you want?'

'Oysters.'

'Are you sure? They serve them on a huge knob of ice. Don't you want something hearty? Some sort of soup or a stew? I'm starving. I want something heavy and rich, something hot. Where is the waitress? Here she is. Give me the soup, the chowder, darling, and then the *boeuf*, yeah the *boeuf*. Give me the berf. *Merci*. You know we've got some ammunition now. Pearl-Rae's the secret weapon.' He hurried on, checking his lists. 'There isn't much time until Lehman's trial and we've got other things to deal with too. St John the pyromaniac, and that business with the tomahawk, O'Kelly. The only other urgent thing is Lovely Josling, she's the threatening to kill. I'm going to have some red meat. I'm probably anaemic, all this vegetarian shit we keep eating, all these salads. Have a steak, put some *colour* in your cheeks. We'll have to tell the Lehmans about this woman, as soon as we can.' Across the table, tucking into his *boeuf*, he gave me an unreliable smile under the shining fringe of his hair.

The restaurant was filling up and the bar was noisy and crowded with money and success people, the perfumed and the tanned. No hint here of sagging wooden prefabs, dead cars on scrubby lawns, kids with sores running under washing lines strung between the trees. I thought suddenly of my Mount Eden bungalow, my student self in bed on cold Sundays, the rain and the smell of the dust burning on the element of the old metal heater, the sadness of the squalid kitchen in the green-brown afternoon. They can kill you, houses. I do not want to go back.

Stuart sipped his wine happily and cast his eyes over the table.

He picked up a knife. 'Look at the cutlery in this place, it's like pitchforks. Why does it have to be so big?' He fussed, caring as usual about things it would not occur to me to notice, in the same way that he likes to pick fights about the table before guests arrive, staring silently, erupting suddenly. 'Why put it all on a bare plate?' he might say, smacking the food down on the table with all the petulant force he can summon up. 'You're making it look like forensic exhibits, why can't you put it all on lettuce leaves or something? Make it look nice. See!'

And with much fury and tsking he arranges something that is indeed beautiful while I stand back silently, one part of me admiring his display, the other measuring the distance between my hand and a piece of the table arrangement: in one movement I could send a hotplate, a dish or a heavy vase smashing into the back of his argumentative neck!

'Excuse me,' he was calling to the waitress, 'can we have another bottle and can I have a different fork, one not so much the size of a *rake*,' and the waitress backing off looking uncomprehending but smiling showed that she liked him, the demanding guy, all over you with his smiles and his wants, his beautiful hair.

'Did you miss me?' he asked me suddenly, catching hold of my hand, drunk and uncaring, shining with charm. The jagged smile, the glittering eyes, face lit from within. I felt my eyes prickling. *Yes, oh yes. I missed you. I love you. Don't go away again* . . . But I looked away, saying nothing. Playing it cool.

Beside Pearl-Rae this afternoon he was exhausted and delicate and almost feminine, with his long limbs, the bright tie done up at the neck of his crisp cotton shirt. Now he was restored, pumped up with wine and food, shouting over the noise in the crowded room, flushed, wild-haired, not giving a fuck. Different again from his morning self, at the kitchen table for example in the weekend, the weight of him, in jeans, heavy black shoes and big blue jersey, his feet square on the floor as he leans over the newspaper, silent, closed-mouthed, the thick square fingers drumming occasionally, monosyllabic, calm, a fifteen-stone man. Solid. Always milder in the weekend before the week with its pressures moulds his face into a tougher shape.

The flushed and flying waitress brought out some cutlery for him, a tiny cocktail prodder and a miniature knife; giggling, she set them down.

'Much better!' he shouted at her. 'Much more elegant. I don't like to feel I'm levering it all in with a *crowbar*, do you? More wine? Why not!'

He leaned forward. 'All this detail about Boy . . . Remember that Cyril provoked Lehman too. Cyril *taunted* Lehman. According to the Lehmans Cyril teased Lehman quite a few times about what a loser he was, how he'd never make it.' Stuart waved his tiny fork thoughtfully. 'Things like this are so delicate. We can't have people thinking Cyril was just an innocent, that it was all Boy's fault. Cyril was a *tormentor*.'

He swigged his wine merrily. 'What you need is a dastardly victim, a handsome accused and a story to pluck the harp strings of the jury.'

'Heart strings.'

'Argue with me all night, baby. We're nearer now to what we need. The ideal scenario. We'll have to get Lehman really spruced up for court, in a suit and a good tie. He's reasonably handsome, wouldn't you say?'

'Very handsome.'

'Very? Well . . . good. You've got funny taste, darling. Anyway he needs all the help he can get.'

He doodled on his napkin, drawing a diagram of the scene.

'Morven Garland across the road from Cyril's house. Mrs Leonard in the house. Boyderman Leonard driving a tractor over the back paddocks. Tracey Garland across the road with Garland. Mrs Leonard hiding in the back of the house and then running for it out the back and hiding in the cow sheds across the paddocks. There wasn't anybody else around. No disputes about identification . . .'

'Mrs Leonard would have thought she was going to be shot.

Would you do what she did, run away, or would you feel you had to go out and help your spouse?'

'Every man for himself in that situation. What else could she do? She wouldn't have had time to think about it anyway.'

'Someone told me Mrs Leonard said she'd found herself thinking she wasn't afraid of death because Cyril had dared to die and he was all right. Then she realised he wasn't all right.'

'The things we find ourselves thinking. The things we say.'

I realised I still hadn't read Mrs Leonard's account in the *Women's Daily*. I thought of the women I knew. Do they read that sort of thing? Leah, Pearl-Rae. The women left behind.

'Hello, baby.' Stain slid into the seat beside me.

'Why do you talk like that?' Stuart said, stabbing the air with his little forklet. 'You're just a huge ridiculous fraud, mate. Carrying on like you're Bob Marley.'

Stain tipped his drink back. 'You've been away.' He winked across the table. 'Leaving your darling alone.'

Stuart scowled at him. 'Didn't take you long to move in. Drinking all my alcohol. You owe me a lot of gin.'

'Did you have fon down south?'

'Fon? No I didn't have any fon. No fun either.'

I looked around the yellow room, listening to the chatter and the talk, and I couldn't shake off the image of Pearl-Rae's house, the peeling walls, the stained cups, the squat, swarthy woman crouched over her heater, staring bitterly into the revolving coals. I saw Stuart's friend Alita Kulay glide out of the smokebanks of the bar and sit down at a table with two men. Costly and beautiful in shimmering green, she ran her hand through her fiery hair and looked casually over the room. Beside me he turned and stared. He got up abruptly, excused himself and went to her table, put his hand on her shoulder and sat down. They began to have a long discussion, their heads close together, while her friends looked on and I struggled with the effort of not looking over, and was awkward and exposed, the room was full of eyes and I smiled and laughed painfully while Stain rambled on.

Now Bernard Cracker, magnificent in a mauve suit, fought his way through the crowd to the table. 'Hello darling,' he said, kissing me on the cheek. His girlfriend tottered over and stood doubtfully at the table. 'This is Leanne,' Bernard said, pushing her forward brutally. 'Not Leanne, but Lee-ahne. You've got to pronounce it right or she sulks. She's much classier than me. She's making me change my name, as it happens, to B'nahd. Lee-ahne bought me this outfit for my birthday. Like it?'

'Sensational.'

Leanne turned her clownlike face to whisper in my ear, 'Such a prick sometimes thinks he's funny.' Her face was beautiful and empty, all clean symmetrical curves and lines, making me think of Jacques' sauna, the blond wood walls, curly wood shavings, the sweet-smelling room with nothing in it but the idea of getting naked, getting steamed, rolling round in the snow in the wordless landscape, naturally.

Stuart came back with a tray of drinks and Stain whispered to him, nudging and winking, 'How goes fair Alita?'

Bernard was trying to wave people over. 'Get over here, stop mucking about, Stuart's here without his dog! I loathe your dog, Stu.'

'Yeah, yeah.' Stuart gave him a bored look and turned back to Stain. 'She wants to buy a hotel.'

'She's a tough little woman.'

'She's going to spend too much. She needs to set the offer lower.'

'Have you told her?'

'To go down? All the time, mate . . .'

'What are you talking about?' I leaned across the dead-eyed Leanne.

'Alita Kulay.'

The heirloom. Yeah, her. All along.

Steady on with the wine, I thought. I sat up straighter, getting a grip. I was getting that throbbing feeling, time was derailed, we galloped through half an hour and dawdled through a minute.

No more for me, I said to Stain, and knocked back a couple more, until Leanne took me by the arm and dragged me outside where we stood smoking under the weeping willows, side by side, dry eyed. Eventually Leanne said, 'The thing about Bernard is that he makes me come every time. But is he supportive out of bed? No way. Our relationship is not holistic, you know?'

'So it's a kind of Oneness you're seeking, Lee-ahne, a spiritual meeting, a sense of bonding together in the quest for spiritual growth?'

'I want a joint credit card.'

'Ah.'

At 2 a.m. only Cracker and I remained at the table. Alita Kulay, he snorted drunkenly, she's so stacked, should call her Alita Each. Then he leaned against my shoulder and talked about television, horse racing, male cosmetics. Stain had roved out into the night in his usual restless, prowling way, looking for something to keep him amused until morning. Leanne had been packed off in a taxi at midnight after reeling around the room denouncing Bernard (poser! fraud! tiny dick!). Grandly ignoring her (everyone *knew* it was huge), he presented her with ten bucks for the fare home. Alita Kulay had left with a small entourage an hour before and Stuart sat hunched over a bottle of cognac at a table full of lawyers across the room. He looked over at me and beckoned, trying to wave me over. 'Hey,' he called, 'people want to meet you.' The group at the table looked expectantly, I glanced over briefly, gave a frigid wave and then ignored him, paying him back for Alita Kulay.

Bernard took my hand. 'Why is life so disappointing?' he mused, nuzzling my palm. 'I search for more, more. I thought I might buy a helicopter, what do you think?'

All around the room the diners were slumped, flagging, peering at one another through the smoke, and the wind outside blew the tiny lights strung in the trees and the first drops of rain began to fall on the wooden deck. 'Time to move on,' Bernard sighed, inspecting my fingernails in a desultory way. 'You're beautifully unmanicured, darling. Your hands are like a tramp's. I love it, so natural. Filthy little fingernails. Do you ever wash?'

'No. Never. I don't believe in it.'

'Mmm. Disgusting.' He yawned.

Stuart came to the table and sat while I practised ignoring him, the ignoring (a new idea) gathering momentum and pace until he was left staring silently at the back of my head, and he left the table again without a word.

At three o'clock the bar closed and the restaurant was emptying out, and Stuart was coming back across the room. He staggered slightly and Bernard stood up and took him by the arm. 'I'm off, darling,' he said.

Stuart shook him off coldly. 'We're going,' he said, staring at me angrily. 'Go and get in the car.'

I walked out to the car, waving goodbye to Bernard who stood hanging over the edge of the balcony shouting goodnight. He blew me a kiss. The fine rain drifted down without making a sound, the tiny drops blowing crazily around the street light, more mist than rain, the air just full of water. Stuart marched out to the car and unlocked it, and we drove slowly through the drenched streets, past the dripping verandas and the empty strip-lit shops. Above the bridge the pale wafer moon floated and sank in the cloudy soup of the sky.

In the house I floated up the stairs in the warm dark, pleased to be home, looking forward to closing down, crashing into bed. He turned on the light. I blinked in the glare.

'Turn it off,' I said.

'You think you're clever, don't you,' he said and punched me in the face. There was an explosion of light inside my head. I opened my eyes and he was coming for more, shouting now about *Cracker* and *flirting* and having an *affair* in front of everyone, did I think he was *blind* and smack came another explosion and another and another and did I think he was a fool, did I think I could make a fool of him in front of other people, was that what I thought?

You're going to kill me, I thought, and was certain of it. I was crawling away from him towards the stairs. He was down on the floor too, overbalanced, crawling after me, clawing at my feet. I turned onto my back and tried to kick him in the face but all that connected was my sharp heel which snapped his head back and carved a neat red furrow vertically through his left eyebrow. Immediately the blood flowed.

Head wounds are showstoppers, aren't they, the way you have a small cut and the blood just pours out. I thought I was making a comment along those lines as he knelt in front of me looking at the blood on his hands, disbelieving. I seemed to have gone deaf. There was a bright silver hole in the middle of my vision.

We both stood up. His suit was covered in blood. I walked into the bathroom and he followed me, we stood together in front of the mirror. Swaying, we stared back at ourselves.

I felt no connection with the people on the other side of the mirror. Something terrible had happened to them. One was punch drunk, the other covered in thin streams of blood, pawing now at the tissues, trying to wipe the blood out of his eye. Trembling and shivering, the man in the mirror dabbed and dabbed at the blood while I leaned against the door of the shower just watching, not doing anything, and he fumbled and wiped and tried to stop it and couldn't and eventually screwed his eyes shut and clung to me shaking with horror and distress while I stood wordlessly, open-mouthed, staring at us both.

The basin was full of blood. There was a spray of blood on the wall already beginning to darken and harden. The floor was blotched and slippery. Something was very wrong with my face. It was too big. It was the wrong colour.

I took his hands off my shoulders and walked slowly out of the bathroom seeing everything double, the double double bed, the double wardrobe looming. Stuart followed me out of the bathroom, staggering over to the cupboard as I let myself down onto the bed. He came and sat down beside me, pressing a handkerchief to his forehead. We sat for a long time, leaning against one another, then he got up and went to one of his drawers.

'Look,' he whispered, bringing out a heavy book, 'let's look at these.'

Through the tunnel of my vision I focused down. Our photograph album. The beach. Picnics. Sailing. The two of us leaning together, smiling, waving.

'Look,' he pointed, 'see this one and this one here. That beautiful day, remember. Remember, darling?'

I looked while he turned the pages of the album slowly: all the things we'd done. I tried to say something but I didn't know what to say. I felt I was looking down the wrong end of a telescope. The tiny bright pictures, far away.

'Help me,' he said, his voice full of tears, 'I'm getting blood on them.' He pressed the handkerchief harder with his shaking hands. I turned the pages for him.

A long way away he and I walked hand in hand through the pinewoods on Kawau Island and sunbathed on the deck of our rented yacht. Smiling we ate lunch on our deckchairs on a sunny afternoon when he said you'll never leave me now. Don't ever leave. He posed at the door of the lakeside house where we stayed for a week just lying around making love and reading old magazines. The skiing holiday, trip to Sydney. Adelaide, forty-two degrees, Stuart in shorts and a straw hat, face baked red by the sun.

Pain was beginning to heat the sides of my head and I lay back against the headboard, feeling the strange new shape of my face. He lay down beside me.

Then we slept and slept, or we blacked out. Down we went, into the black crack of the night. Time passed and the weak moon sailed low over the house and the cold dawn light began creeping in over the twisted wreck of the bed. A sharp wind started to blow, clearing away the cloud, and the cruel morning arrived, full-blown brutal day. A tui sang on the branch outside, bright and severe, ringing its bell.

We woke to find the sky fiercely blue, the sun coldly blazing and the wreckage of one another in the hard light of the ruined room.

16. The wind

We lay there in the full glare of morning light. There we were, there was the pillow-case, streaked and stained. We looked, wincing, and closed our eyes again. We lay blindly in the warmth, and a strange languidness came over me, I remembered being at the train station as a child on a beautiful morning, wanting to lie down on the train tracks. It was beautiful, the sun was shining. A curious feeling, surrender, euphoria, I would lie down under the brilliant sky and nothing would matter. Time would stand still. Time would not bring the train.

'Don't be stupid,' said little Una all those years ago, hands on her narrow little hips. 'Jwanna *die*?'

Hours went by. The suburb slept. I woke to find him gone. He was cleaning the *en suite* bathroom. He emerged wearing his blue robe, his face completely unmarked. The red furrow I had ploughed into his head, origin of so much gore, was clean and uninflamed, and largely hidden by his eyebrow. He climbed back into bed.

'We'll be all right,' he said. We dozed, wrapped up together. I felt a deep, sickly peace. In this mood I whispered to him, 'Someone read my tarot cards once. They came up Cruelty, Luxury and Death.'

'The Death card, it just means change.' Then he said again, 'We'll be all right.'

He pulled the covers over our heads, whispering, 'We'll make ourselves all right. We'll stick together. We'll stick around home, not go out. We'll help one another, then we can face the world again. It's a cold world out there. We'll face it together.'

I lay in bed and drifted, remembering. Long ago little Una wore long white socks and T-bar shoes and tossed the fragrant gum nuts high into the air so that they fell and bounced off the planks and the gravel and the shiny steel track. Watch this, she said, and threw her maths textbook under the train. Screaming with laughter, hugging herself as bits of the book exploded out through the train wheels. That morning she told me a new word: motherfucker. The rudest word, she said, is cunt. Motherfucker is the next rudest. It's from America. As we walked beside the track the tattered bits of maths book carried far ahead by the train began to blow back towards us. We waded together through the pages, heads bent against the summer wind.

I stayed in bed all day. In the afternoon Stuart got up and made sandwiches and we ate them in bed. Later I watched CNN. From far and wide they brought me the news. Top of the hour, top of the pops. Apparently we are having elections in this country; one day I must find out about it. Remind me to watch the news.

In the evening Stuart finally got through to Leah on the telephone and told her the news about Pearl-Rae de Gruchy. He arranged that we'd meet with her and Carlos in Lawrence, at the end of the week. 'A ray of hope, my dear, yes. From quarters unexpected . . .' He sat in bed with the phone, pale and dark-eyed, forking up some leftover chow mein with his clumsy hand. He murmured and sighed, rubbed his forehead, talked of opportunities, all the help we can get, no trouble, darl, *no troub*, he trusted the kiddies were well? He handed over the phone, looking surprised. 'She wants to talk to you.'

I took the phone. She said she would walk a different circuit now that Stuart was home. She didn't want to get in the way. Everything was fine, she thought she might start to take May swimming at the local baths. She was so glad about this witness, this Pearl-Rae. She was excited, she must hang up and tell Carlos. She was so worried about him. She thought he was more depressed. He had rung her twice in the middle of the night and talked strangely. She would tell him as soon as she could get him on the phone. 'I don't know where we'd be without Stuart,' she said. 'He's been so brilliant. We'd be dead without him. Tell him he's a life-saver.'

She had to go, May was crying about something. '*Tell him*,' she said, and put down the phone.

That May, in her sparkly shoes. Does she say anything yet? A word or two? I thought I would go for a long walk soon, down the park hill, across the barren strip between the Roundabout Road and the road to the bridge. Past the pools. How often it is when I am walking and walking, that I am looking for someone. It seems a long time since I've seen them, Leah walking, May in her pushchair, wheeling together through the afternoon.

Stuart took the phone out of my hand and rang for a curry. Make it hot this time, he said. Burn me up.

We sent out for takeaways every night, and went over notes and cases. During the day I stayed at. My head began to shrink to its former size. This didn't help with my other problem: the shiner. Without a doubt my left eye was frankly and monstrously black. Foundation – green and then white – covered it up but left me looking all wrong, still. An east westie. Looking like this I wanted to stay at home. Besides I was sick, sick in my soul. I didn't feel like getting any exercise. I started reading a novel Una had given me one day, but as usual something put me off. I couldn't focus anyway, there was too much of my eye in the way. All day I lay down, staring out the window at the windy street, the wind tearing the leaves off the trees, blowing hair and skirts and papers around, driving everyone insane. Safer to be in here than blowing about out there, going mad. And Stuart stayed around, the whole time. After work he came upstairs with trays of snacks. Then we spent a lot of time having sex. Seemed like every second hour we spent together something was up. There was something wrong about all this, I found myself thinking. Something was wrong somewhere, or broken. Late at night I puzzled over it a couple of times but lost the thread. Late at night Flip Spiceland gave the weather forecast for the entire globe.

I broke my record for watching CNN. I watched it all night while he slept. In the evening I watched the lights of the ferries moving across the dark harbour. Under the harbour bridge the water was whipped into whitecaps and lit up orange in the electric lights and around the container port the black water boiled and foamed. The cars on the bridge crawled slowly in their lanes, buffeted by the treacherous gusts whipping across the water, the cold blasts roaring out of the thin air, out of the universe. On the screen Flip Spiceland's pointer moved across the Tasman Sea and hovered over us for a moment, 'There may be electrical activity,' he said softly. Out there in the dark the globe was turning, electronically his picture changed. The strong winds caused delays, pile-ups, swervings and nose-to-tails. Down at the marina the rigging screamed. I wasn't going out in it. I wasn't going out there but stayed out of sight, all week. In the eye.

I dreamed I was walking along the street to Stuart's house, battling against the tearing wind. Papers blew spinning towards me, flying leaves stuck to my coat. I reached the gate, turned in, climbed the steps and stopped. The house was gone.

Before me was nothing but an empty section with no building on it and nothing growing except thick silvery grass stretching away to the top of the slope and then the empty sky and silence and far away the sight of the long shadows moving over the sea and over the silence the seagulls calling and the swish of the wind blowing over the grey-green hill. Everything gone, vanished, swallowed up and only the rippling grass and the pale sky above, stone-washed and neutral.

Then after the silence terrifying noise! Terrible clanging and shrieking and barking of large dog! I woke to find that the burglar alarm had gone off and the dog had raced down the stairs and Stuart was swearing his way around the dark bedroom trying to find his trousers. A long half-hour ensued in which we went around the house and found no break-in and no sign of anything untoward and an immense security guard turned up in a maroon uniform bearing the insignia of Klimpt Lightning Response Ltd. He inspected the property and then motored off in a tiny little car.

'Look at that,' Stuart said wearily, watching him drive off in his Fiat Uno. 'Like an elephant in a pedal car. Maybe his car gets bigger inside, like the Tardis.'

All the boards of the wooden house squeaked and creaked in the wind. The sky was lightening as we got back into bed, and in the harbour the boats were moving as the tide began to turn. Everyone sleeps just before dawn, in the graveyard hour of deepest silence. Stuart snored, I dreamed again. Images came and went, fragmented, the pictures flickered as if on a TV screen. Out there the dawn was coming, electronically the pictures changed.

By the end of the week I looked quite normal, if you didn't look too close. We were to meet Carlos in Lawrence in the afternoon. Leah was going to come over to the house in the morning. She said she would follow us to Lawrence in her car, so we could make stops together and talk on the way.

Experimentally that morning I walked into the office where Voodoo was laboriously consulting her battered dictionary. She looked up. 'Resind?' she asked tentatively. 'Re-sind? Ressind?'

'Rescind,' I said.

'Oh . . . thenks.'

'Where's Stuart?'

'He's gone to the benk. Then he's got some appointment, he didn't tell me what it was.'

'Oh.'

'By the way, you look different.'

'Oh . . .?'

'You've had a perm, haven't you?'

'A *perm*?. . . Oh yeah. Yeah, Vera, I have.'

'Can't get past my sharp eyes!'

'No, Vera. No flies on *you*!'

Stuart came back, finished his morning's work and we loaded up the car. Soon after that Leah arrived with May and we set off on the road to Lawrence. Driving slowly so that Leah could keep up, we got to the Lawrence turn-off at three in the afternoon. In the bush the car slid around on the loose metal and I sat gripping the seatbelt. We were high on the Lawrence Hills, just starting the descent towards the beach. Far below the sea was blown into whitecaps and the sky was clear after the storm. The beach was scattered with debris, the sand dunes no longer smooth and dry but chopped, washed, banked into canyons and cliffs, the streams full of rain were deeper and wider, running over their short banks, making flat spillings of silver on the dark surface of the sand. Along the shoreline the kelp lay in tangles, whorls, balls of wet hair spat out of the mouth of the sea. Above the blowing landscape of the dunes, over the grey chaos of sea junk, steaming weed and scattered stones, the sky hung fierce and pale in its blue rinse. The light was metallic and bright. We weren't talking in the crawling car, there was only the noise of the engine and the crunch of the tyres on the shifting stones.

Leah drove behind us in her bashed-up blue Ford Cortina. She told me before we left that the car has a powerful engine but the body is falling apart. She showed me the damage. Rust has eaten jagged holes in the bonnet and the doors. She has to be careful: accelerate too quickly and she'd be all over the road. The car has no weight, no ballast. May sat in the back in a child seat, wearing a pink woollen jersey. She accepted an apple from me before we left, eyeing me inscrutably from behind her fringe. That May . . . She wore red shoes, with racing stripes. Sporty socks. When I looked behind, Leah's face was a blur through the windscreen, appearing in the shade, disappearing behind the glare of the sun on the glass. Beside me Stuart drummed his fingers on the wheel.

I hummed and sighed. Sometimes the sky can be so blue . . . Sometimes the sky is so blue that dark things, a brown dog, trees on the horizon, long shadows on the green hills, all these things under the blue look black. It's an autumn blue, the beginning of the dark, the light antiseptic, the air so thin. I've read that there is an *ozone hole* in our sky up there, a patch with no ozone, a nozone. I read that in major cities, in London say, there's too much ozone, they're choking on it, under the soiled quilt of the shit-filled sky. Here in the *nozone* on a cloudless day nothing comes between you and the sun, between you and the light and the sky. The sun will kill you (beware changing moles, dark lesions on the skin), but what clarity, what light! Down on the beach a man threw sticks for a leaping dog, hurling the wood high over the water as the dog smashed its way out into the driving waves, surging out, carried back, the stick clamped in its shaggy jaws. Behind them the cold sand wind whipped over the dunes, combing and parting the silvery grass.

Leah tooted her horn and we stopped. She got out. 'May feels sick.' May's face was pale and sweaty behind the glass. She held one limp hand palm up over her forehead. Small, eloquently tragic in her little armchair, her jaunty shoes dangling and discouraged. 'You go on,' said Leah in practised tones. We moved off, hearing the little girl begin to wail. Further down on the flat the trees drooped over low and heavy and the air was cool and dark where the stream ran along the side of the road. Little May . . . Anxious face, perspiration on her nose. She was going to throw up, I could tell. I remember being carsick as a child. The weather was giving me a faintly sick feeling now too. I used to think it was nostalgia or regret, this autumn nausea. Or perhaps just sensory overload, too much light, too much air, long distances, sharp mornings, golden light on the buildings, cold wind through suburban streets. The blackness of things under the blue. Stuart hummed beside me, tense at the wheel. We drove out of the shade of the bush and onto the stretch of the road lined with toitoi, and the fluffy white spears along the verge blew in formation in the wind, marching single file against the sun.

We stopped and waited for Leah at the end of the Lehmans' drive. Before she arrived Carlos came out of the kitchen door, jumping neatly over the step railing and onto the grass. His khaki trousers were bagged around his waist and rolled up to the knee as if he had been out wading again in the silver stretch of the bay. He had old sandshoes on and wore no shirt. His chest and shoulders were lean and muscular and burnt dark by the sun. We watched from the car as he came across the lawn, walking in a slightly sideways gait, rolling one of his shoulders as if he had cramp. Stuart sat staring through the windscreen as Carlos ducked under the washing line and approached the car. He leaned over Stuart's door and opened it, shaking Stuart's hand and pulling him out of the car at the same time, and as I clambered out he was smiling tensely, still shaking Stuart's hand and saying, 'Where is she?'

Stuart explained that May was carsick and that they'd be along in a minute. Carlos nodded distractedly at me and then led the way up the path. His trousers hung low on his hips, the broad back was tanned and scarred, the back of his neck was ringed with faint white marks of dried salt water and his hair was stiff with salt and sand. Behind Carlos, Stuart stared his sharp stare, the sharp-eyed bird behind the shades, thin-shouldered, eyeing, measuring. Over the neat little house, the clipped lawn and the olive-green septic tank the sky stretched in its thin wash, high blue, and Mrs Lehman's underwear danced on the clothesline as we bent underneath it, Stuart in his suit and Carlos in his sea-weedy khakis and barnacled shoes, the ungovernable trousers flapping in the sharp wind that sent Mrs Lehman's sheets spinning wildly around the wire. He was unshowered, unshaven, only washed and dried by the sea, the tidemarks of salt patterning his back, shirtless under the washing, walking sideways and skittish in his bleached and matted and rotting shoes. No shirt . . . Had he forgotten we were coming? Perhaps he was trying to forget.

Silently, stiffly buttoned in double breast and double cuff, Stuart followed Carlos through the back door and into the sunny kitchen that was familiar now with its wooden shelves and bright curtains, trinkets and knick-knacks and Dutch figurines.

Carlos sat us down and then reached into an airing cupboard, yanked out an old anorak and pulled it over his head. Having made this sartorial adjustment he set about making coffee with Mrs Lehman's gnome mugs and Bambi spoons. His eyes were bloodshot and the skin under his eyes was reddened and burnt by the sun and the wind. He smelt of engine oil and of the sea. He handed round the coffee, sat down, rolled a cigarette, lit it, inhaled, blew the smoke in a thin stream across the kitchen and said, 'What's she *doing*?'

'Leah won't be long.' Stuart hung his jacket on the chair back and took files out of his bag, coolly arranging his papers and pens. Carlos bit his thumbnail and glanced over at me, smiling suddenly under the thatch of his sea-wrecked hair. Strong jaw, white teeth, sunburnt skin and now the grin turning his face piratical, anarchic, as he sat across the table in his sea-junk clothes, snorting smoke out of his nostrils and running his thick fingers over his face. His grin dropped and he gave me a piercing look. Outside Leah called out to May and we heard the little girl's voice and the sound of her plastic sandals stamping on the concrete path. Carlos jumped up and let Leah in; she came in pushing May ahead of her. May appeared and glared around the room, balefully pale and shrinking as Carlos embraced Leah then leaned down to pick her up. 'May. May Rangi Lehman,' he said happily, stretching out his arms to her. But the little girl immediately went still like a small animal, then let out a scream and began to kick and fight and twist away from him, struggling to catch onto Leah's legs. Fighting, with her little brown legs wildly thrashing she landed a kick hard in Carlos's chest.

'Jesus,' he gasped and sat back on the floor, winded. His eyes watered. May retreated behind a chair and Stuart got up quickly and pulled Carlos off the floor. 'They go off you quick but they relearn you quick,' Stuart said briskly, picking up Carlos's chair and pushing him into it.

'Who?' I asked.

'Kids,' Stuart said to Carlos, ignoring me. 'She'll get used to you again.'

'How do you know?' Carlos rubbed his elbow, glancing at Leah. His face was hot and miserable. There was silence. I looked at Leah but to my surprise she said nothing, she seemed not to have noticed, sitting at the table and playing with her keys, staring out at the shifting dunes and the metallic sea.

Recovering himself Carlos got up and made coffee for Leah and explained that the Lehmans had gone out for the afternoon so that they wouldn't be in the way. Then Stuart began to sort through his pages and we sat down to the business in hand, running through the statement of Mrs de Gruchy line by line, and Carlos forgot about May as soon as Stuart started to read aloud. He sat thumping the table and exclaiming along the way, breaking in and interrupting every few minutes. 'It's better than you told me on the phone,' he said. 'It's what really happened.' He became excited, rolling one cigarette after another, getting up and pacing up and down, appealing to Leah at points, asking her to remember dates and times while she sat awkwardly, glancing out of the window, answering in monosyllables. He strode across the kitchen and stood at the sink, lean and brown and restless, blowing out clouds of smoke, scratching his salty hair. He flung the kitchen window open to let out the smoke and when the papers began to blow into a whirlwind he apologised distractedly and slammed the window shut, shaking the kitchen wall and knocking a china windmill off the sill. He began to question Leah about particular incidents, like the day of the picnic when Boyderman Leonard frightened Leon with a dead eel and when Leah replied listlessly, with difficulty, he began to prompt her, rubbing his hands over his face in exasperation when she couldn't remember and didn't reply. May remained behind Leah's chair, crouched down, forgotten.

'What about the bulls, what month did the bulls come in?' Carlos was asking and asking again. 'It all turns into a blur, doesn't it? I can't remember . . .'

'Actually, I've got all the dates written down,' Stuart interrupted, waving a page, but Carlos was standing over Leah now scratching his head, dropping ash on the floor, agitated, restless while she sat playing with her keys and beginning to look angry and hounded. 'I don't know,' she said to his endless pacing and questioning, sitting back finally and staring him in the face. 'Look in the *notes*.'

He looked up, angry and surprised. 'You've got to help me. I need your help.'

'You've got it,' she said, standing up, slamming her keys onto the table in front of her. Behind her May let out a squeak. Carlos said more quietly, controlling himself, explaining as if to a child, 'We've got a chance now. With this Pearl woman . . . I . . .'

'I know, I know!' Leah shouted. 'I'm helping, I've never stopped helping.' She threw her hands up and turned away angrily. She looked haggard and dark-eyed. A blowfly buzzed across the window, braining itself in its efforts to get through the glass. Over the house the seagulls screamed harshly. The wind whistled in the joinery, tugging at the iron roof. Carlos stared at her, scratching his salty arm. Outside the whirlwinds of sand reared up and went spinning over the dunes, toppled down and gathered themselves up again, sand racing over sand, the afternoon light fading now, cold chrome at the rim of the blazing sky. Carlos walked quickly to the window and threw it open again. The cold air roared in and we dived for the flapping storm of papers, tipping over cups in our haste, pinning the riot of pages down and weighting them, trapping the flapping bundles back in their heavy files. 'For God's sake!' Leah shouted, grabbing pages out of the air with one hand and reaching over with the other to force the window shut. She fought it closed, slammed it, fastened the latch and sat down. The china figures, the mild shepherdesses and syrupy fawns rocked gently in the sudden calm. A pompous porcelain owl looked down from the wall in disapproving surprise. Down behind her chair May Rangi Lehman made a small sound, of amusement or fear, it was difficult to tell. Her father stood back at the sink now, wild and dishevelled in his crackling clothes, still staring at Leah, his expression angry, despairing, infinitely hurt. She said, and her voice shook, 'I'm just tired. It goes on and on . . . the long drive. I'm sorry.'

'You,' he said with difficulty, forcing out the words. 'You don't care any more.' He looked at her bitterly.

She twisted in her seat, 'I do,' she said. 'If you knew how much . . .'

'I don't blame you,' he said coldly, folding his arms. 'I don't care either half the time. Look at me. Can you imagine me going back?' He stood while we looked. Wild-haired, red-eyed, sunburnt, like a piece of flotsam himself, scoured and pickled, washed and bleached by the sea. 'Look at me,' he said again, spreading the tattered flares of his khaki strides and this time he gave a weird, bleak smile. There was a small scuffling from the floor. May crawled out from behind her chair and stood mildly scrutinising her father. Hands on his hips he looked sadly down at her as she approached. He bent down stiffly and picked her up and she sniffed his hair and made a face. 'Fishy,' she said.

'See that.' Stuart, who was watching closely leaned over and whispered in a stage whisper to Leah, 'They don't forget.'

After order had been restored and Carlos had sat down, although flatly now, with a hard, ironic air, as if his earlier enthusiasm had been pointless or a joke, with May on his lap and with Leah at his side, after we had gone through his evidence and Leah's and Pearl-Rae's and countless other details and issues to be brought up and related at the trial, after Stuart had talked of first impressions and appearances, displays of family unity, the importance of speaking slowly, keeping calm and addressing answers to the judge, after we had covered as much as possible and packed up the files and were standing at the door saying goodbye, Carlos turned to me and pointed out at the choppy grey sweep of the bay. 'Remember we walked out there?'

I nodded. 'There's holes out there now, it's all chopped and ripped. Things washed up.' He glanced briefly down at me.

'Well be careful,' I said but he was looking away, up at the Lawrence Hills. Stuart was down the drive putting luggage into the car. 'See you soon,' I said, picking up my bag, and hung about for a moment wanting to say something more. He looked back and his expression was intent and strange.

'Go on, then,' he said abruptly, dismissing me, and I turned and stumbled off with the heavy bag under the washing and down the drive and when I looked back from the car as Stuart revved and hauled on the wheel in the narrow drive the kitchen door was closing and the washing danced in the empty yard, the white sheets like curtains hoisted up into the autumn air, rolled up and then unfurled, tugged down again by the salty wind and shut.

Vera was still in the office when we got back, working through a long list of mundane letters and documents. Stuart threw his bag down on the floor of the office and pushed the dog away. His hair was wild, messed up by the wind outside. He was distracted.

'Do you think I should have a junior in this trial?' he said suddenly, chewing his nails.

'Why?' I was unloading files onto the desk.

'Well, I don't really want one but it's a lot of work, and maybe I should get someone in.'

'It's a bit late now. And you've got me to help you.'

'But if I get someone to appear with me I could have you stay here and look after the office, and the junior could do the running around for me at the Hamilton High Court.'

I couldn't believe what he was saying. I jumped up, feeling a tight pain at the back of my throat.

'But you said you wanted me to come! I have to come, I'm not going to miss it now, after all we've done. I'm part of it now, I'm going to help . . .'

'I do want you to come, I want you to but I'm being practical. I always want you to come along and help me with all my in-town stuff. But if I'm going to be out of town I need someone to stay and help me in Auckland. You know it's difficult being a sole practitioner. I can't just let the place fall apart while I'm away . . .'

'But I have to see Lehman's thing to the end. I'm not going to hang around here doing nothing to help, with all the prowlers and nutters, and nothing but the dog for company.'

'All right. OK. Look, I'm just thinking aloud,' he said tensely. 'You have no idea, the pressures on me. You just have no idea. Everybody wanting different things.'

Vera was watching, a small smile on her face. He left the room. I followed. He said, 'I'm just being practical, that's all. I have to keep everything together, everybody on at me for different things.'

'What are you talking about. Who's on at you?'

'Ah damn you!' he shouted suddenly. 'Worrying about yourself all the time. Think about the Lehmans, they're the most important thing at the moment. Think about the Lehmans' *kids*. They need their father! Do you understand that? They're what I have to worry about at the moment . . . *fuck*.' He was red in the face with tension and anger.

He stood at the kitchen window staring at me. I moved towards him and he held up his hand. 'Get away,' he said.

I got away, out into the streets. I'll be at the trial, I thought. He couldn't be serious. I wasn't going to give it up now. I felt rage mounting, driving me on through the streets. The wind had died down as if the cyclone was blowing itself out and running was easy over the pavements littered with bits of stripped leaves and branches and twigs, the gardens battered by the gales, hedges sagging, small trees snapped. I walked staring at the tiny brown pavement stones, the pavements split by the roots of the gnarled pohutakawas growing at the edges of the grass verges. Clouds had rolled in as we drove into Auckland, suddenly the sky was black with rain, now the air was warmer and full of water and the sun somewhere behind the raincloud cast a weird evening light over the streets. In the gardens the wet vegetation glowed in the rainy light. Purple sheet lightning flashed out at sea.

Across the water I could see Rangitoto Island with its black rocks and dark bush slopes, the crater already misted with the rain coming in from out in the Gulf, sweeping in over the choppy sea. All around was the steamy scent of earth, wet foliage and the

sea and then, at the top of the Seaview Road, the rain came pelt-
ing down and in a few minutes my clothes were heavy with water
and the water streamed down my back and legs and into my shoes
as I ran back home through the drowning streets.

Vodoo was finally packing up for the day. She said, 'Can you
tell Stuart a person rang from the bank about a transfer of money.
I wasn't sure what he was talking about. Ooh you're soaked, what
strange weather, changing all the time . . . Tell him I've just
bathed the dog too.'

'Why do you do it?' I asked.

'What?'

'Bath the dog.'

'Because Stuart likes me to.'

'You're his secretary, not his maid.'

'I try to be professional. And Howie is a *lovely* dog.'

He was out on the deck upstairs in his deckchair. Rain
drummed on the overhanging roof and streamed onto the
veranda rail. Currents shifted in the harbour below, the water was
choppy and green. He was talking into his mobile phone. 'I
know,' he was saying, 'oh look I know that yeah, I know. As soon
as I can. I'm not far away.'

I stood over him, he looked up.

'Gotta go,' he said quickly and switched off the phone. 'God,
look at you, you're soaked.' He got up clumsily.

'Why do you do it?'

'What?'

'Talk on the phone to mysterious people, hang up when I
come into the room?'

'I hang up because I want to talk to you. I get tense, you muck
around, there's so much to do.'

'Who were you talking to?'

'Why does it matter?'

'Why won't you tell me?'

'Why should I?'

'I want to be there at the trial.'

'OK. Fine. Get changed, you're sodden.' He put his hands on

my shoulders. 'The feel of you, you're icy. You're freezing cold. Come inside, get a towel. Don't be negative all the time.'

'Who were you talking to?'

'Don't hassle me . . . Vera will be gone soon, then I have to go out.'

'Where are you going?'

'I'm just going out.'

'Why don't you tell me? Why don't you tell me? *Why don't you tell me who you call?*'

There was a large black and white photo of Stuart on the table which I took of him not long ago. I picked up the photo, screwing it up and tearing it, and clawed the black and white face into a hundred shiny strips.

17. Sunday

He's gone. Gone all night. Left me in the empty house.

Out in the streets I walk briskly but the feeling in my head gets worse and worse. Pressure in my brain, heat behind my eyes. Nothing is certain any more, nothing is sure. Only the cold streets and the endless sky, and the strange lurching in my head. There are so many places I can walk to. And there's nowhere I want to go.

'Where have you *been*?' Una threw open the door, holding the phone under her chin while Harry on the floor adding wooden blocks to make a farmyard stacked one block too many and shrieked with rage as the wall caved in. 'Use more blocks,' Una commanded. 'Reinforce it.' Distractedly she handed him half a banana. Pushing the banana away he turned to eye me suspiciously, one tiny finger up his tiny nose. 'You bum,' he said to me quietly, without much interest.

'I rang you this week and got no answer, what is going on?'

'We unplugged the phone. We were working.'

'What's wrong with you, mumps?'

'Hay fever.'

'Your eyes, you look like one of those people, one eye goes east one goes west.'

'Yeah right, you never know where to look.'

She sat at the table, stacked, one boy on her knee and one baby on board, the three of them on the wooden kitchen chair and the yellow room filled with wintry light, steam from the kettle misting the window and the radio on. Benkie's dog snored on the floor at her feet. Harry ate toast and Marmite and sticks of cheese, wiped his hands on his kiddie jeans and leaned against her and the bump, his sibling-to-be.

'When did Harry first start to talk?' I asked weakly, for something to say.

'I don't know, it's very gradual, just words at first. Some time around one, one and a half.'

But May never says anything at all. She runs and walks and dances in her plastic shoes, gives a scornful look from behind her hands. Keeps her words to herself.

Fixing me with a severe look, Una talked about her childcare manuals; she had been reading up, she had been feeling enthusiastic and keen. I sat awkwardly listening. I told her what Leah said about toddlers, only half joking: Show no fear. They will attack.

She snorted, got up suddenly tipping Harry off, and Harry sauntered over to the dog and lay down against the hairy, panting flank, the dog opening one eye and closing it again with a faint kicking of the hind leg, the phantom itch.

'Watch out for the fleas,' I whispered. The little-boy hands twisted the doggy hair, the little-boy face had gone blind, the little head rising and falling on the twitching rug.

Una stood at the sink looking down at me, frowning, running a jewelled hand through her hair. Those rings of hers. I looked away, feeling sting and desolation in the cold autumn day, the roaring wind, the wind blowing the wet plastic on the greenhouse below, everything harsh and full of white noise while I sat in her kitchen red-eyed, shiftless, fraudulent and dusty, and she eyed me sternly, smoothing her hair.

I spread my hands on the tablecloth. There was a bad feeling in the air. The wind, it makes you mad. My nails were garish against the cloth. Dark red.

'When does the trial start?' she was asking and asking again (hands on her rounded hips).

'In two weeks,' I said.

'So you'll be in Hamilton for a while. How long is it going to last?'

'Probably a couple of weeks. I'll be there.'

Finishing at the sink, Una picked up her boy and laid him on the couch singing to him a song Phoebe used to sing long ago. There's a shining gold on the sandy shore and the deep blue of the sea . . .

'It's colder today.' She talked on while arranging her kitchen, organising her things. What did she say to me once? I don't feel trapped being at home. I feel free.

I stared at my shoes. The colour of them. Oxblood. Same as the colour of my fingernails, my eyes, my glow-in-the-dark nose: red. The colour of blood, and shame.

There was a bad feeling in the air. The wind, it howls in your ears, it deafens you, makes you blind. 'Una,' I said, but then I couldn't tell her.

'What is it?' she said, sitting down at the table beside me. 'What's going on?'

But we heard Benkie's car turn into the drive. Little Harry snored lightly on his back on the couch, with one hand he twisted a strand of his shining hair. The car door slammed, footsteps crunched on the gravel outside. The key turned in the lock, the kettle boiled and clicked off as he shouted as usual, 'Hey Una I'm back!' and the dog lay contentedly with one eye open watching the steam snaking and curling up the yellow wall.

'Hey!' he said happily, bursting in. 'Wife and kids!'

'What is it really?' Una asked, but I couldn't say.

How I screamed at him, how I yelled and railed! The pieces of photo flew out of my hands. Stuart said nothing, his face was an expressionless mask. Quickly he took his bag from the wardrobe and his wallet from the side table. He walked down the stairs and out the back door. The car door slammed, the engine revved, the rain came down harder, it smacked on the panes. The wheels screeched as he made the hard turn at the end of the drive. He drove away.

All evening I waited for him, until it was late. Far into the night I waited. At around 4 a.m. on Saturday morning something occurred to me and I searched the house. There was no sign of life. The dog door was locked. He had taken the dog with him too. Before the dawn the dark grey sky was still full of rain. In my armchair in the front office I sat and waited until the light began to colour the clouds out at sea. I watched the road, I listened for the car. He would be home any minute. Any minute he would drive into the road.

But he has been gone all weekend. The rain is still falling, the sky is still dark. I can't tell Una, I don't know what to say.

In the bedroom upstairs, scattered all around, lie the black and white shreds of his face.

Very late on Friday night Carlos rang Leah. The wind howled around her windows, a draught came through the crack under the door.

'I can't do it,' he said.

'Can't do what?'

'I can't give evidence at the trial.'

'Yes you can,' she said to him, struggling to wake up. 'You can go through it calmly. It's natural that you're nervous. I have to give evidence too, remember. I'll be terrified,' she told him. 'You have to do it for all our sakes. Listen to Stuart, he's the only one who can get us out of this mess. We need you, the kids and I,' she said. 'We can't do without you.'

'You'll be all right,' he said desperately, and hung up the phone.

Now, on Sunday on the way back from Una's I rode the bus over the Harbour Bridge. Far below the coloured yachts zigzagged up the crowded channel. I bounced along on the back seat as we roared up the middle lane. Stuart will be there when I get home, I told myself. He will be waiting for me. He will tell me where he has been.

I thought of Leah. Yesterday morning, Saturday, I pounced on the ringing phone. Leah said, 'Stella, hi, is Stuart there?'

'He's . . . he's playing golf,' I said, dredging this implausibility up out of nowhere.

'*Golf?*' She was instantly disbelieving.

'I know,' I said desperately, 'isn't that naff? But what can you do?'

I lay back in the armchair with the phone, turning a letter-opener in my hands. She told me about Carlos, how he had called her late on Friday night. She said Millicent and Dolph were worried. Carlos wasn't eating properly, he was hardly eating any-thing at all, he sat all day on the veranda watching the sea. She said he complained of migraines, the doctor came. He couldn't sleep, the doctor gave him pills, he said he wouldn't take them. He would hardly talk to the doctor, but lay on his deckchair star-ing at the rough sea. The doctor tried to advise him but Carlos moved his finger along the horizon line and talked vaguely about the dolphins he had seen swimming in the waves at high tide. He refused to keep track of the conversation. 'I'm so worried,' Leah said. 'He told me last night he can't give evidence at the trial. He can't talk about what he did. I am going to see him as soon as I can. I am going to try to get down there tomorrow. Please tell Stuart about this when he gets home from *golf*.'

The bus roared down the north side of the bridge. He will be there when I get home, I thought. As we bumped along the off ramp I sang under my breath, an old song. I got home and searched the house. No one had been here. In the kitchen the fridge whirred and ticked. The wooden boards creaked under my feet. Heavy rain fell outside.

Back in the office I sat in the armchair and tried to ring Una but her line was engaged. I put the phone on the arm of the chair.

How green the lawn was, under the thundery sky. The lawn was like a swamp. A blackbird hopped over the grass and the window blurred into tears. The blinding rain fell on the lawn, on the harbour, on the wintry sea. Look at it, out there! Raining all over the world. The green garden, turned into a grave. I had a strange feeling, heavy, sodden, weighed down with dread, as if I was already submerged.

The phone rang. I jumped on it. 'Get him on the phone,' Leah said. 'Get him.'

'What's wrong?'

'Just *get* him.'

'What's happened, can I help?'

'Can you help, no, you . . . get your *boss* on the phone.'

'He's not here, please . . . Please tell me what's going on.'

She sounded angry, panicking, crying into the phone. 'He's gone,' she said. 'Carlos is gone.'

I grappled with the receiver. 'What do you mean gone? Gone? Dead gone?'

'No, gone, vanished, gone bush. I don't know where he is . . .' She took a despairing breath. 'Fuck . . .' she whispered.

No one could find him. He hadn't reported at the police station. He'd breached the terms of his bail. The police weren't going to wait around for him to turn up, they were already starting a search for him in the bush and on the roads . . .

I listened to Leah, trying to think out what to do. I didn't know where Stuart was. I would have to find him. I told her I would find him, as soon as I could. I thought of the police, the Armed Offenders Squad, those trigger-happy iron men, all togged up and someone to kill. Surrounding him in the bush, the sudden movement, the missed command. The riddled corpse dragged down out of the sullen hills.

'Why can't you get hold of Stuart?' Leah shouted at me suddenly. 'Can't you do something useful, what are you doing there, just swanning around?' Her voice cracked with frustration. 'I'm sorry,' she whispered hoarsely down the crackling line. She ran on, telling me what had happened.

She had arrived in Lawrence in the morning and Dolph and Millicent had hurried out of the house. They were distraught. 'He's gone,' Millicent said. 'He's been gone since last night. We've been up all night waiting, he has not come back. He was strange last night, he walked out along the beach late in the evening. Then he came back. He tried to ring you but he couldn't get through. He tried and tried. He said goodnight to us, but so oddly. I was worried later and looked in his room. He was gone. Dolph and Witi Riggs went out, they've been looking all night and this morning. Witi and his brother have gone up the tracks in the hills . . .'

'Oh my God,' Leah said to them.

'We've been trying to ring you since early this morning. There was no answer. We couldn't understand . . .'

'The kids and I went to stay over . . . with my cousins. I wasn't there. None of us was home.'

They sat in the kitchen, waiting. Carlos was due to report to the police station in an hour.

'We should ring the police,' Dolph said heavily. He rested his head on his arms on the kitchen table.

'You can't!' Leah screamed. 'What would they do to him?'

'They would find him . . .'

'And then what? They'll shoot him. They'll kill him!'

'He will come back, if we just wait,' Millicent said desperately, 'I know he will.'

The time for Dolph to drive Carlos to the police station came and went. They sat at the kitchen table. Millicent began to cry.

An hour later Witi Riggs came back with his brother and cousin. They came in and sat down at the kitchen table. They had looked all morning and found nothing, no trace or clue.

Two hours after Carlos was supposed to report in, the police constable from Lawrence drove into the Lehmans' drive. He came to the front door and rapped. Dolph went to the door. 'What's up?' said the cop, pleasantly enough. 'He sick?'

Dolph stood, despairing, holding up his hands. 'We can't . . .
he's not . . .'

After talking to Dolph the constable went back to his car, an
ominous look on his face. They watched him talk into his radio.
Then he drove away. Not long after, droning loudly over the
Lawrence Hills, the first of the helicopters arrived.

'Directory, Bev speaking, which number please.'

'Kulay, Alita, somewhere in Ponsonby.'

'Actually that number is ex-directory, caller.'

'But this is an emergency.'

'Sorry, caller, I can't give out an ex-directory number.'

'Just give me the fucking number, *Bev*.'

'Don't you swear at me!' Tsking indignantly she terminated
my call.

I scrabbled through the address books, found a number and
dialled. No answer. I tried again, drumming my fingers impatiently. There was no reply. I put the phone on speaker and
leaned back in the armchair, listening to the buzzing of the empty
line.

I became aware of a faint noise somewhere at the front of the
house. I hung up the phone and listened. Someone was knocking
lightly on the front door. I hurried to the side window. I knew
who it was. I knew. There was a battered white car parked out in
the road and when I peered out at the front porch I could see an
arm in tattered denim, jigging up and down as he stood waiting
at the front door. Wayne. He tapped louder. I moved silently
back into the office.

I dialled, no answer again. Feverishly I scrabbled through the
address books again. Nothing. I dialled again.

'Hello,' the voice finally answered, and I heard the thump
thump of loud reggae music.

'Stain, I've been ringing and ringing.'

'What's wrong?'

'Turn your bloody Bob Marley off.'

He turned it down.

'What've you been doing? I called and called.'

'In the bath, darling. What you want?'

'I want you to tell me where she lives.'

'Who?'

'I know Stuart's with her, I know that you know. You know all about it. I can tell.'

He sighed. 'It's none of my business, darling.'

He hung up. In a frenzy I rang again. He answered after a long time.

'Tell me,' I hissed, 'or I'll come over there and kill you.'

There was a long silence. 'Ah sweetheart,' he said finally, 'you're right. It's Winter Street. Ponsonby. Number three hundred and sixty-four.'

You're right. You're right. I sat back and raggedly exhaled. But I heard the light knocking again, light fingers tapping, this time at the back door. Then, as I hurriedly scrawled Alita Kulay's address on the yellow pad I saw Wayne cross the lawn outside the window. Looking furtively to the left and right he went to the garden shed, disappeared inside and then emerged a second later carrying a long wooden ladder. Under his denim jacket he wore a holey black anorak, the hood covering his streaks of brown and blond hair.

I ducked away from the window, out of sight. Wayne crossed the lawn with the ladder and carried it quickly around the side of the house. I moved across to the west side of the house and watched out of the side window. Still looking all around, he set the ladder up against the wall of the house, climbed up to the eaves and took a screwdriver from inside his jacket. Working quickly and efficiently with the screwdriver he began to take the main core of the burglar alarm apart.

I flew back into the office and started to dismantle the window seat. Then I moved onto the filing cabinet and the cushions on the office chairs. After taking these apart thoroughly I counted up. Yes, roughly six hundred dollars. Enough for a cab.

I crept quickly through to the kitchen and eased open the back door, walked across the back patio and edged around the side of

the house. He was still up the ladder, working steadily. The outer
cover of the burglar alarm lay on the ground at the foot of the
ladder.

I worked my way along the wall to the bottom of the ladder.
His face was raw and rashy, he panted and talked under his
breath. He laughed wonkily to himself and dropped a screw on
my head. He was working now with a wrench, panting with the
effort and I hesitated, trying to work out the best way, but no, I
thought coldly, steadily, with contained madness, don't hang
back, move before he looks down! and without thinking any more
I seized hold of the lower rungs of the ladder and heaved and
pulled and pushed and shoved until the whole thing tipped and
he shouted loudly with fright and scrabbled and clawed at the
wall before falling off sideways into the boundary hedge while
bits of burglar alarm rained down around me and there was a
crash from Mrs Corbunion's kitchen, as if she had seen him fall
down and dropped a plate with the shock.

'I was *right*!' I shouted, dancing around, beside myself now.
'You *prowler*, you *fuck*. I've called the police!' My voice rose to a
shriek.

A pause. I panted. He lay inert. But no, he was not dead!
Suddenly he began to thrash violently around inside the hedge.
With his legs in the air he was fighting his way out of the under-
growth. Scratched and bleeding he forced his way down out of
the thick bushes and struggled furiously to his feet, tearing
branches and twigs and dead leaves off his clothes. He started to
advance towards me, sneering as I brandished one of the patio
bricks. 'I've rung the *police*,' I shouted again. He tripped over a
clump of weeds and fell onto his knees. From her kitchen window
Mrs Corbunion peered out at me, her hand over her mouth.
Wayne got up again. He put out his hands, his face was contorted now with pain and bewilderment and rage. I tried to shout
and felt myself squawk again in panic, half a shriek and half a terrible laugh. 'I was right,' I said again, and I thought of Alita
Kulay. I lifted up the patio brick and threw it as hard as I could,
aiming to brain him, aiming to smash in his skull. But it hit his

forearm with a dull crack and he staggered backwards. Mrs Corbunion shrieked and ducked down. He got up again, reeled towards me and collapsed again on his side in the weeds. Then, without looking at him I ran around the side of the house and got out of there, into the streets.

Now I was hurrying, over the gravelly pavements, through the watery world of the garden streets. The gutters streamed with rainwater, the grass verges had turned to mud and the trees dripped and drooped in the heavy air. The sky was grey-green, almost black over the sea, and the air was thick with moisture. I walked fast, gasping in the humid air.

At the shops there were no taxis. I paced at the taxi rank, waving in vain at the cabs that cruised past. At last a bashed-up saloon drew up at the kerb. 'Winter Street, Ponsonby,' I said, falling into the back seat. 'Number three hundred and sixty-four.'

We drove sedately over the bridge.

'Can't you drive faster?'

'No.'

'Drive bloody faster!'

'No!'

'Why *not*?'

'I get ticket!'

'Bloody step on it!'

'No!'

Arguing thus we trundled through the sodden streets. I sat hunched on the back seat, poisoned with tension, wringing my hands, grinding my teeth. The cars queued endlessly in the rain, wipers uniformly swishing. Inside the cab a smelly heater roared, blowing bad air and ash around the vinyl interior. Finally, we covered the last stretch of Ponsonby Road, turned the corner into Winter Street and drove all the way down to the end. 'Here you are. Free-six-four. Twelve dollar.'

I threw the money at him and waited until the cab droned away, then stood in the rainy street in front of number three hundred and sixty-four.

It wasn't a wooden house like most of the buildings in the street but a large, expensive modern block of flats painted in fashionable pink and marine, each flat a series of interconnecting box-like levels with tinted windows, patio, roof terrace and satellite dish.

I went through the gate and opened the glass door. There was a white foyer filled with giant maidenhair ferns in pots, and a neat row of white letter boxes, and her name on the fourth box along, A. K. Kulay, three sixty-four bar four. A small brass plaque requested *No circulars or junk mail please*.

I squeezed my hands into fists. I'll give you circulars! I'll give you junk! I bounded up the stairs to number four, a light blue door guarded by two more bushy maidenhairs in wrought-iron holders, but as I raised my hand to ring the bell a high male voice behind me said, 'Alita's in Sydney, she went last week. I'm her neighbour upstairs. Can I help?'

I turned on him. A tall young man in a linen suit, pleasant looking, with blond hair. But he drew back in alarm at the sight of my face. I stared at him, breathing hard. Discreetly he gathered up his bulging shopping bags and hurried on up the stairs.

I rang the bell. The corridor was quiet. The fern fronds waved gently in the draught. Upstairs the neighbour closed his door. Stuart opened the door and stood in front of me wearing a blue and white towel around his waist. In his hand he held a plate and on the plate was a chewed pile of jammy crusts.

'Oh Jesus,' he said, jumped back and dropped the plate, put up his hands, tried to push me back and slam the door but now I was in, racing past him into the hallway, into a black and chrome kitchen where Howard stood by a glass-fronted fridge, through a couple of empty rooms and halls and into a marine living room where the windows looked over a garden and a deep turquoise swimming pool and an elegant dark-haired woman in a Japanese robe was getting up out of her chair with her hands up as if to stop me as I came towards her and Stuart came shouting at me from behind and a door opened and a little girl with brown arms and long dark hair ran into the middle of the room and shouted and shouted until Stuart stopped and I stopped shouting and looked at her, the tiny yelling girl with her flying hair. She was a pretty, skinny sharp-faced girl, about ten years old, running to hide behind the woman who had jumped up in alarm but who was watching me now and looking at Stuart in a way that was knowing and alert, and strangely detached. The woman said something quietly to Stuart, one eyebrow raised, and looked me carefully up and down.

This dizziness, lightness, the floor seemed to sway. I tried to say something but no sound came out. The girl peeped out from behind her mother's legs. I turned from one to the other, turned back to Stuart, trying to say something.

But there they were, the three of them together and the smell of toast and coffee and somewhere in the kitchen a radio on, clothes and suitcases strewn around the room, shopping bags, the remains of takeaways, a child's videotape. All the things they'd done. All the things they would do. The dog wandered in and lay down on the floor.

'He's gone missing,' I whispered finally. 'Carlos is gone,' and I stood there explaining, mechanically. Stuart went quickly out of the room, I could hear him start to talk on the phone. The room seemed too bright, everything was blurred. I peered again at the little girl. She had come out from behind her mother and was inspecting me curiously, with exaggerated, ironic, childish concern. I turned away from her, I couldn't look at her any more. Big raindrops smacked against the panes, the fat drops rolled slowly down the glass. A seagull landed on the balcony rail outside. The woman came over and stood coolly and quietly at my side. Her delicate robe shimmered, turquoise like the pool.

'Can I call you a cab?' Mia said.

This. This is what it feels like to be bereaved.

18. End

You can picture Carlos in the night, walking along the beach under the cold moon, making his way along the miles of flat sand, the glitter of the sea catching the moonlight at his right and to his left the dark mass of the Lawrence Hills. Along alone under the moon, over the dunes, over the marram grass, through the lupins, through the streams that run trickling down the beach to the sea, the sand cool and the water icy on his feet, the night wind fresh on his face. Along alone under the moon and unafraid, of the shadows of the rocks and the blades of the flax growing out of the cliff like swords, and the black ridge of the hills in front of him as he leaves the water's edge and crosses the beach to begin climbing the tracks through the tangled trees, up into the distant parts of the densest bush, veering off the track to look back at the beach and the settlement far below, a few tiny house lights, fading, flickering, lost to sight.

Which way did he walk? They found no trace. They mapped the possible route of his climb up into the hills, far off the tracks, where he thought no hunters or trampers would be likely to find him, where his body could lie undisturbed until it turned to leather and bone and finally to earth and the bush would grow over him, and leave no trace.

You can picture him leaving Lawrence in a boat. Out at high tide, over the sand bar, through the rocks and the treacherous channels and up the coast, meeting a yacht, or landing up the country and driving to Auckland, buying a passport, taking a plane to Australia or further, America even.

You can picture him walking out to sea.

In the days after Carlos disappeared, all of us imagined and speculated while the police and eventually the army combed the area, and the helicopters droned over the bush and the boats went over the harbours and bays, roads were blocked and cars were stopped and everyone had a theory about where he'd turn up. He'd be dead in the bush with a shotgun in his mouth (guns had gone missing since he'd disappeared). He would be hanging from a tree far up in the hills. He had taken sleeping pills, he had walked out to the sand bar and into the sea. He was in a remote farmhouse, with hostages, there would be a long bloody siege. Ever hopeful, the press camped in Lawrence as the police scoured the country, day after day.

It was said that some people in the area were leaving food out for him in case he passed through in the night.

A few days after he disappeared the police tried to trace Carlos's natural mother in Australia, and were unable to find any evidence that she had lived there. When they looked further they couldn't find her anywhere in the world.

Detectives question Leah every day, and follow her wherever she goes. It will be a long time before they leave the Lehmans alone. Witi Riggs is suspected of knowing something, but they always suspect Witi Riggs of something, with his criminal record and all. They questioned every person in the town of Lawrence, but no one had anything to tell.

In Lawrence, Millicent sits and waits, going through her boxes of shells, the pipis and toheroas, scallops and mussels he sorted into sections for her garden paths. The flowerbeds are set in neat rows, sprinkler jets spray the borders, the brisk wind blows in the tiny white flowers. The new trees he planted are coming up well.

Leah stays at home with her children in the flat at the Roundabout Road. She is making no comment about her husband to anyone who asks. She tells the children she thinks Carlos will never come back, it's better that way than to let them hope. Let them get over it, they have to get on, working their way up out of it all. They will take each week as it comes.

When May is older Leah will find work, and buy a house.

I watched the news of the search on a large TV in a motel room near the edge of the motorway outside Hamilton where the bus stopped and I got out and the wide road stretched ahead both sides bristling with neon motel signs advertising heated spa and satellite dish and sauna and free car-clean. I went into the one with the biggest dish, they advertised CNN, and when news of the search for Carlos wasn't on I could flip to Flip Spiceland as he wandered the globe.

So much time has gone by now. It looks as if the manhunt is being scaled down. The army has been sent away, the roadblocks have been dismantled. I do not think Carlos will ever be found. Already he has passed into history. Everyone knows the story of Carlos Henry Lehman. Everyone has a theory, on where he'll turn up.

It will be a little harder to get bail around here these days.

In Winter Street as I went down the stairs the little girl said, 'Daddy, who was that?'

'A client, darling,' he said. 'We won't let her in again.'

Late at night in the motel the television blurs. I lie back in the white glow of its light. The wind screams against the window outside, all the objects in the room are black.

I wanted what Una has. I wanted some of that. I went looking and found a life I hadn't earned.

I turn out of the motel forecourt, the wide road stretches ahead. There is four hundred dollars in my pocket, the bus stop is not far away. I straighten my clothes, smooth my dishevelled hair, walk on under the glittering signs. I haven't stopped looking, *I haven't stopped*. But there's no need to hurry now. First things first.

I am learning to live alone.